D0884379

ACID LULLABY

ED O'CONNOR

Constable • London

First published in Great Britain 2003
by Constable, an imprint of Constable & Robinson Ltd
3 The Lanchesters, 162 Fulham Palace Road
London W6 9ER
www.constablerobinson.com

ISBN 1-84119-615-0

Printed and bound in Great Britain

A CIP Catalogue record for this book is available from
the British Library

For Jude, with love

Contents

'Better by far you should forget and smile
Than that you should remember and be sad'

Christina Rossetti, *Remember* (1862)

The Churning of the Ocean

1

January 1980, East London

Ignoring the pain was impossible. Ignorance made it worse.
Perhaps it could be scoured away.

She handed over fifty pence and walked to the back of the
bus. The vehicle hissed and lurched into motion as she fell
into a seat. Alison's feet were cold. She had waited at the bus
stop for forty-five minutes. Her shoes had succumbed to
January rainwater and her socks were soaking wet.

The bus lumbered south down Walthamstow High Street,
stopping every minute or so to collect small groups of football
fans. Many kept their claret and blue woollen scarves tucked
beneath the collars of their jackets. Walthamstow was a
Tottenham heartland. Travelling West Ham fans had to be
discreet, especially on Derby Day.

Alison studied every face carefully.

She hadn't done the journey before but she was smart and
prepared. She knew the football ground lay to the south east
and that it was located just off the Romford Road. The bus
timetables had given her the rest of the information she
needed. When the incognito West Ham fans changed buses at
Leyton and revealed their colours, she followed them.

An hour later Alison stood outside Upton Park. She could
smell fried onions and horseshit. There were bursts of singing
from groups of fans as they approached the ground and
bustled anonymously past her. The chant floated along
Disraeli Road:

'. . . *forever blowing bubbles, pretty bubbles in the air,*'

Alison sat on a low stone wall that shielded a row of shops
opposite the main entrance to the football stadium.

So many people.

She had never seen such a crowd. There was a fish and chip

shop directly behind her belching out acrid fumes of vinegar and cooking fat. She felt sick. She hadn't been eating. Not since Vince had started on her again. The bruises on her back still stung.

'. . . *they fly so high, up in the sky,*'

She studied the faces carefully. Hard, East-End faces with eyes that hunted with cold intelligence. A huge brown police horse clopped past her. It had a long scar on its hindquarters. Unhappy times.

'. . . *then like my dreams they fade and die,*'

A cloud of conversation rolled over her as a pub emptied its contents onto the pavement. Two men sloshed past. She could smell beer. One had a dark piss stain on the front of his jeans. Alison scoured their expressions for a hint of familiarity.

'Wotchu facking looking at?' one snarled back at her.

Alison looked away.

'Saucy little cow.'

They brushed past. One hacked a green streak of mucus from his throat and spat it on to the tarmac opposite her. Alison withdrew the photo from the back pocket of her jeans. It was an old Polaroid that smelt of chemicals. She was just a baby. The man holding her could have changed in twelve years. Still, the basic features would be the same. Just as they were on the claret and blue football shirt he was wearing.

So many faces. Bodies bumping into each other, flowing in different directions. Singing and chanting.

Alison, watching in growing frustration, began to see the impossibility of the task she had set herself. She decided to move around, to join the flow of blood as it pumped towards the heart; the dark bulk of the stadium. She slipped into a stream of people and questioned some of the less frightening faces.

'Mister, do you know Gary Dexter?' Alison asked.

'Oo?' said the shape in the black leather jacket.

'Gary Dexter. He works in Dagenham.'

'Not for long if the Tories have their way.'

'Oo's she want?' said another voice.

'Gary Dexter.'

4

'I know a Gary Barker.'

'Ee's that prick from Gant's Hill.'

'Wouldn't call the man a prick.'

'Ee's Arsenal isn't he?'

'Fair point.'

Alison broke away. It was 2.45. The game started at three. She grimaced in pain as someone clattered into her back and cursed her for being an obstruction. Her ribcage ached: the pain had kept her awake all night. The bruising was much worse this time. Vincent had kicked her. He'd never done that before. Her mum had just stood and watched. And sobbed.

Stupid useless dirty bitch.

Suddenly, the pressure of bodies increased against her. There was shouting all around her. The crowd surged as a fight broke out. A volley of beer bottles sailed over her head and exploded against the concrete in front of her.

Tottenham fans amongst West Ham. Forcing their way into the main stand. Swearing, shouting, people falling, people scrambling to get away.

Alison was lifted off the ground then thrown to the floor. Boots scuffled and kicked around her. She dropped her photo as she tried to cover her head with her hands. She stretched an arm into the crowd to retrieve it then recoiled in pain as someone trod on her wrist. She screamed in pain. Broken glass punctured her skin through the thin fabric of her anorak. Furious voices ricocheted around her.

'Piss off, you yid wankers!'

'Fuck off back to your stinking ghettos!'

More fists. A man fell to the ground in front of her. His mouth was awash with blood and one of his ears was half torn away. Alison closed her eyes as a boot smashed into his face spraying her with blood.

Suddenly, she felt strong hands on her shoulders. A police-woman dragged her out of the crowd, pulling her roughly from the chaos. With an effort, she hauled Alison up onto the bonnet of a nearby police squad car.

'You okay, sweetheart?'

Alison was shaking, afraid to look the woman in the eye.

5

'Did they kick you? Are you bleeding?'

Alison shook her head.

' I lost my photo,' she said quietly.

The WPC glanced over her shoulder as the fight tumbled toward the entrance to the main stand: an avalanche of petty grievances.

'Do you feel dizzy or sick?' she asked checking Alison's head for damage.

'I don't think so.'

'Are you with anyone? Did you come here with your dad?'

'The photo was of my dad.'

Two male police officers joined them.

'Your head's cut, Wrighty,' grunted one of them.

'I'm okay.'

'We've got to move,' came the unenthusiastic reply.

Sally Wright lifted Alison Dexter's head so she could look her in the eye.

'I've gotta go, sweetheart. You sure you're okay?'

'I'm okay.'

'How old are you?'

'Fourteen.'

'That's too young to be down here on your own.' WPC Wright became aware of blood trickling from the cut to her temple. She dabbed it away with the sleeve of her tunic.

'I was looking for my dad. I know he likes West Ham.'

'Stay out of the way. Keep your head down,' Sally Wright advised as she moved away. 'Wait by the car.'

Alison watched her leave from the bonnet of the panda car, amazed as the WPC ran directly towards the maelstrom of brawling men ahead of her.

Alison Dexter felt ashamed and pathetic. She felt weak: a burden to herself and others. She was alone in a concrete universe. No one was coming to save her.

That night, Alison sat on her bed and listened to her mother and stepdad arguing in the adjacent room. At 9.30 she retrieved the steak knife she had taken from the kitchen drawer and secreted in her pillowcase. She removed the Mickey Mouse watch that Vince had bought her for Christmas.

6

She placed the blade against the pale skin on the topside of her wrist. Slowly but firmly, as the screams grew in intensity next door, Alison Dexter cut herself for the first time.

2

Summer 2001, Canary Wharf

The clock was ticking.

Crouch could only take so much. Every man has a breaking point and Crouch wasn't an idiot. He had done his best to be a generous spirit: play the part of the best-friend lover he had read about in Liz's magazines. It hadn't worked. Nothing had worked. Slowly but inexorably she was sliding away from him and he wanted to know why.

He was prepared to be reasonable. He could take the mind-numbing tedium of his job in Eurobond settlements at Fogle & Moore. He could take the quiet disdain of Liz's loud-mouthed friends on the trading floor. He could accept the steady disentanglement of their sex lives and the recent unexpected revelation of Liz's self-esteem issues. But he wasn't prepared to be screwed around and he was starting to smell betrayal.

In six weeks it would be their anniversary. A whole year since he'd pulled Liz in the drunken haze of a bank offsite. The entire bond department had visited Sandown Park for an evening of racing and champagne. It hadn't been pretty. Fogle & Moore's bond traders were legendary in the market for excessive alcoholic consumption. Each of the currency desks had nominated a patsy for the Vomit Olympics: a pint of neat Vodka then a pint of lager in a head-to-head time trial. Sterling had beaten Euros in the final. The losing traders paid a grand each to the winners. Settlements hadn't been invited to take part – they didn't really count.

Liz Koplinsky had worn a pretty floral dress. In the carnage of the drinking competition it had fluttered like a flower on wasteland. Crouch remembered it fondly. He'd chanced his arm. She was out of his league but he was battle hardened. Like one of those children's toys that you knock back but can't knock over. Nothing ventured and all that.

She had been watching the drinking competition. Pieter Richter, the head of Euro Sales, was being carried to the toilets with sick smeared down the front of his Boss suit. There was much laughter and piss-taking. Liz was on the periphery and this gave him an opportunity. He caught her eye.

'You not joining in?'

She smiled a bright white smile. 'God no! I start spinning on coffee.'

'Cawfee?'

'You ripping the shit out of my accent, bud?'

'No. I like it. New York, right?'

'Right.'

'Whereabouts?'

'It's a big city on the other side of the Atlantic, in a land we call America.'

Her jab connected sharply with his ego. Still, in for a penny. 'I mean whereabouts in New York?'

'I know what you meant. I'm just shitting you. I'm from Queens. It's a dumb accent.'

Crouch was starting to relax. 'It's a great accent. I lived in New York for a while.'

'Really? With the company?'

'A training programme.'

'The Kramer Course?'

'That's right. I did the operations module.'

'Okay. I did the trading module two years ago.'

Crouch knew all about that. Liz Koplinsky was already a minor legend on the trading floor. A working class girl from Queens who had joined Fogle & Moore as a secretary then worked her way on to the Corporate Bond Trading programme.

'Listen,' she had touched his arm and for a second he smelt

8

champagne on her breath, 'I don't know nothing about horses. You wanna help me win some money?'

He remembered feeling an almighty surge of relief. 'Love to.'

Over the next two hours they'd lost about three hundred quid and drunk a lot of Bollinger. Liz hadn't mocked his nasal estuary Essex accent. Most English girls disliked his voice. Liz said it was funny. She had laughed when he called her 'geezer' or 'Doris'. Encouraged, he had tried to teach her cockney rhyming slang.

'We call a pub a "boozer" right? Boozer rhymes with battlecruiser.'

'Beddlecwoozer.'

'That sounds cute! Say it again!'

'Beddlecwoozer.'

'Cruiser!'

'Cwoozer! Whadda fuck! I'm not Eliza-fawkin-Doolittle.'

'Concentrate! We're going for a Mickey down the battle-cruiser then sinking a Ruby Murray.'

'A mickey down da 'cwoozer den sinking a Wooby Muwwie.'

'Pukka!'

'Lawbbly jawbbly.' She was laughing.

'Koplinsky,' Crouch smiled as he shook his head in mock disapproval, 'you are a heartbreaker.'

She'd looked him straight in the eye; fixed him in those big black pupils and exploded his heart: 'Cwouchie. We should hang out more.'

And they had. Eight months of drunken hilarity and vigorous sex. Crouch had become a lost soul. He'd never been in love – the concept had always made him nauseous. But he could feel himself slipping, gradually losing control, like he was falling asleep at the wheel of his life. Then, just as he had given in to loving her, the sex had stopped.

Not immediately. It had evaporated slowly and miserably. Now, six weeks away from the anniversary of their first night together, Crouch considered some stark statistics. Three months since they had last slept together. Three weeks since she'd kissed him unprompted. She'd stopped inviting him round to her flat and hidden behind a wall of excuses built on exhaustion and overwork.

It was a weak argument. Crouch spent endless hours reconciling trades on Fogle & Moore's computer systems. Hard work had always made him want sex more not less. Still, he had reasoned, Liz worked in the front office. Front office shit was always heavier. Traders worked under a different set of pressures: clients gave them shit, Max Fallon and Danny Planck screamed abuse and instructions from their offices, the market could churn and twist their trading books into the red in an instant. He'd decided to cut her more slack.

Their relationship came to centre on emails and SMS messages as Liz started to stay later and later at the office each night. Crouch always finished work by six. He was old-fashioned like that: you work hard all day but at six o'clock you stop. Let the investment bankers and lawyers jerk off in their offices until after midnight. It wasn't his style and on thirty-five grand a year it simply wasn't worth the effort.

Still, he had begun to find excuses to stay late. He found himself inventing work simply to stay longer in the office waiting for Liz to finish. He wanted to get an angle on what was happening. He knew she was freezing him out but he couldn't understand why. A few weeks previously they had been talking about moving in together – she had even given him a key to her flat in Wapping – and now this.

A key to her flat in Wapping.

Now she was stonewalling him. Girls back at his school in Romford had called it the 'mushroom'. When they had been upset about something they'd let their hair fall in front of their faces to hide their emotions. Whenever he tried to confront Liz about the unfortunate state of their relationship, she mushroomed him. She'd mumbled her exhaustion through a veil of chestnut-coloured hair. When he'd asked her over the phone about the evaporation of their sex life she'd claimed to have 'issues with herself'.

Whaddafuck?

Crouch was frustrated and furious. He had fallen back into

the bad habits of his early twenties: drink, nightclubs, drugs. He had started snorting coke after two years of abstinence and had even cracked a couple of Es. His old school friend Chris Aldridge – Aldo – had sorted it for him. Aldo was kind of 'in the trade'. Crouch didn't ask too many questions. Aldo didn't like talking about his business interests but he was happy to give out advice with his pills. That week at a busy Holborn bar he had made his opinions on Liz Koplinsky clear.

'Chuck it. She's obviously porking someone else.'

The thought made Crouch feel sick. 'She's not like that.'

'Bloody hell, Simon! What happened to you? They are all like that. So are you. So am I. It happens all the bloody time.'

'She's at the office all the bloody time. That's the problem. Besides, she says she's got some self-esteem shit going on.'

'That's what they all say, mate.' Aldo expelled cigarette smoke and then followed the dispersing fog with his eyes. 'Take my word for it. She's getting sausage somewhere else. If she's got a self-esteem problem it's because she feels guilty about enjoying herself.'

The words unnerved Crouch: there was something horridly plausible about them.

'Why not tell me, then? At least have the courtesy to tell me to piss off. I hate all this messing around. I'm too old for games.'

Aldo grinned a yellow toothy grin. 'You're thirty-two, mate. Games are all you've got left.'

Crouch nursed his pint sullenly tracing the lines of gas bubbles that rose magically from its depths. Aldo watched him closely and relented slightly.

'You like this girl, right?'

'Of course.'

'You want to find out what's going on?'

'Welcome to the conversation, Aldo!' Crouch snapped sarcastically.

'Then don't be a victim. Take the initiative.' He dabbed cigarette ash in to a round black ashtray.

'I'm not with you.'

'If she's not going to tell you what's going on, then you have to find out.'

'Okay.'

Aldo glugged a bitter mouthful of whisky. 'Consider this,' he leaned forward as if he was about to impart one of the great secrets of the universe, 'what do women do when they've got a secret?'

'I have no idea.'

'Think about it.'

'You've lost me, Aldo.'

'They tell it to their mates. She does have mates, I take it?'

'Of course. But they aren't going to tell me anything. Most of them look through me like I'm a bleeding window pane.'

Aldo shook his head. 'Crouchie, you ain't using your imagination. Look mate, I hate to see you hurt. I'm proud of you. You're the only one of us that's actually done something useful with his life. You've got a proper job, a flat, qualifications. Don't get dragged down by some bird.'

'What are you suggesting Aldo?'

'Bug her.'

'I'm sorry?'

'You can get voice-activated Dictaphones. Very handy they are too. Next time you're at her flat, stick one in a fucking pot plant near to her phone. Then the next time she's having a bleedin' heart with one of her mates you'll have the whole thing on tape.' Aldo sat back in triumph. 'Banged to rights.'

'You are having a laugh?'

'It's up to you. Be a victim or take control. Same again?'

Crouch watched Aldo as he collected their glasses and sauntered up to the bar. He couldn't do that to Liz. It was preposterous and unfair. She didn't deserve that.

Or did she? Crouch considered the issue. He had a right to know. If she wasn't prepared to tell him the truth didn't he have the right to root it out for himself? He persuaded himself that if she was screwing him over then she had surrendered her right to privacy. Suddenly, Crouch found himself clear of the moral quagmire and wandering in the cold light of logistics. It would be difficult but not impossible.

And he had a key to her flat in Wapping.

3

Max Fallon's office at Fogle & Moore overlooked West India Docks. He could see the crawling dinosaurs of the Docklands Light Railway and beyond them the East End shit heap that soiled his horizons. It was always a reminder. A reminder of what he was working to avoid. A reminder that he had a responsibility to the little people that worked for him: the responsibility to make the right calls. Still, he was finding it hard to focus. His mind was on the coming evening's festivities, not on the conference call he was supposedly chairing.

'My concern,' squawked a disembodied voice from the spidery speakerphone, 'is the quality of investors that you have lined up for our bond issue.'

The voice belonged to Andrew Pippen, Junior Treasurer at Fulton Steel; a jumped-up accountant. Pippen had a good line in crumpled, charcoal coloured suits and ropey red ties. Fallon loathed him. He loathed the ordinariness of the people he had to be polite to. *Chippy treasurers with their crappy red-brick degrees: sullen twats imprisoned in cheap shoes and small provincial minds.*

'You see,' Pippen continued nasally, 'Fulton Steel is a traditional blue chip. We want our bonds placed with traditional "buy and hold" investors. Pension funds and the like.'

Fallon groaned and looked across at Danny Planck, the Head of European Bond Trading. Planck shook his shaved head and made a delicate 'wanker' motion with his wrist. Fallon nodded and released the mute button on the speakerphone. Liz Koplinsky smiled as he winked at her.

'Andrew, we understand your concerns.' Fallon's eye crawled up and down Liz's legs, lingering at her crotch. *Be*

13

Commanding. 'Let's be frank. The facts are these. First, Fulton Steel is a debut issuer. You have no track record. Second, the investors you refer to are respectable European financial institutions. Thirdly, you need money quickly.'

'I see your point, Max, and I realize it is in your interest to bring this deal to market quickly.'

Max was irritated. It was a cheap shot and it stung. 'Andrew, we want a successful deal. Our interest and your interest are one and the same.'

'But all these Italian brokerage firms . . .' paper rustled at the other end of the phone as Pippen read through the underwriting list. 'Forgive my ignorance, but won't they just dump the bonds at the first opportunity?'

Fallon pressed mute on the speakerphone and turned to Planck. 'Danny, this is a dog shit credit in a dog shit market, right?'

'That is being generous,' Planck replied.

'So frankly, he's lucky to have a deal at all?'

'Maxy, it's a marketing miracle that we've pre-sold any of this crap.'

Fallon nodded, justified in his anger. 'Talk to him then. Sell him some technical bollocks. He's doing my head in.'

Fallon sat back in his seat and put his feet up on the desk. He wanted Liz to see he was wearing Gucci loafers. He tried not to think about what he was going to do to her later. The thought of Liz chewing on his cock was clouding his judgement. *Focus on the little people.*

Danny Planck thought for a second before turning to Liz. 'You handle this one, hotshot. Feminine touch required.' He released the mute on the phone.

Liz Koplinsky leaned forward slightly. Fallon studied the flowery white lace of her bra as it pressed against her blouse.

'Andrew. It's Liz.'

Fallon admired Planck's thinking. He could almost hear Pippen's trousers tightening. The little prick had been drooling over Liz at the pitch for the deal two months previously. Frankly, he couldn't blame him.

'Oh. Hello there, Liz!'

'For a new borrower first impressions count. If these brokerage firms sell your deal quickly, that ain't necessarily so bad. Quality buyers will snap up their bonds. Take this example. Let's say that you're a big soccer fan and you can never get tickets to see your team. The match is sold out. After a while you're gonna lose interest. But what if some agency offers you tickets at a premium? You get to see your team. The price of the tickets keeps going up. It's supply and demand. Without supply, demand will eventually die out, right?'

'I see what you mean,' Pippen observed quietly.

'You put shit on your roses and they grow better, right?'

Pippen laughed an electronic laugh. Fallon could just see him in his miserable little office in Derby rubbing the end of his useless prick through the pockets of his crackly suit and making his fingers smell. 'I don't know if my board of directors will be persuaded by the scarce football ticket analogy. Most of them support Stoke City.'

'They should be persuaded,' said Fallon, 'it's a compelling argument.'

Pippen cleared his throat. 'Well, thank you, guys. That was helpful. I'll call you back tomorrow with a decision.'

Fallon turned the phone off. 'We got him.'

'Hook, line and fucking sinker. Nice one, Liz.' Plank patted her on the head as he stood up.

'You gotta keep it simple, right?' Liz gathered her papers, and looked Fallon directly in the eye as she left the office. 'See you later, Max.'

Fallon watched her leave.

'You are a disgrace,' said Planck, watching Fallon's hungry grey eyes moving up Liz's legs.

'What?'

'You're old enough to be her father!'

'Wicked uncle maybe.'

'You seeing her tonight?'

'Dinner at the Palais and then she's gonna earn her Christmas bonus the hard way.'

'Pack your Viagra then.'

15

'I'm thirty-eight, you cheeky bastard.'

'Better take two packets.'

Planck watched through the glass walls of Fallon's office as Liz returned to her desk on the far side of the trading floor. 'I thought she was boffing some oik in Settlements.'

'Well, she obviously fancies some pedigree sausage.'

'Sloppy, Settlement seconds.'

Fallon grinned. 'I'll suffer that indignity.' He sat down and began to read through some brochures he'd received from an estate agent in Cambridgeshire. He was tired of London. Finally, he had the money to start thinking about moving out for good.

His digital wristwatch beeped. It was 5p.m.

Two hours and counting.

4

Five minutes later, Liz Koplinsky's burglar alarm started beeping automatically as Crouch entered her apartment. He walked quickly to the control panel in the hallway and entered Liz's code. The noise stopped abruptly. It was an easy pin number to remember: '212' was the dialling code for Manhattan and the '3' denoted 3rd Avenue. Liz's first apartment in New York had been in Manhattan on 92nd and 3rd. 2123. Easy.

He looked around the apartment he knew so well and suddenly felt like a criminal. It was as if his very presence soiled the place. He walked into the lounge area and sat for a second on Liz's low white leather sofa. The apartment had a wide view of the Thames grumbling by two storeys below. The river was a mixed blessing. He loved the sight of it but the sounds had driven him demented. The thumping disco boats had often kept him awake half the night, the honking barges disturbing him at five in the morning.

To the left of the main window Liz had installed a giant fish tank. It was shaped like a huge letter 'H': two hexagonal pillars connected by a horizontal glass tube. It was filled with a galaxy of exotic fish. There was even a frustrated looking crab scratching at the foot of one of the pillars, attracted by the bubbling air filters. Liz had told him that the suppliers had to winch the tank into her apartment, over her balcony. It had cost her thousands. He felt like pissing in it.

After a moment, Crouch stood and began to root through the paperwork on Liz's desk. Mostly credit card bills and air mail from the US. Crouch studied these in closer detail, imagining some stateside sweetheart. However, the letters offered nothing of interest. He replaced them and turned his attention to the phone.

He picked up her handset and dialled 1471. A recorded voice spoke to him flatly.

'You were called yesterday at 11.36p.m. The caller withheld their number.'

Who would call her after eleven-thirty at night? No one from the bank. They knew she had to be up at six in the morning. Someone else then? From outside the bank?

Disappointed, Crouch turned his attention to the answer phone. The red display showed the numeral '1'. He hesitated. If he played the message he would have to delete it. He decided to take the chance.

'Hello. This is Janet from Seamless Dry Cleaning. Miss Koplinsky's suits are ready for collection.'

Shit.

He deleted the message and removed the Dictaphone from his pocket. It had cost him forty pounds and had a voice activated capability. Crouch looked directly above the desk. There was a shelf; a high bookshelf, cluttered with fantasy novels. Liz liked all that goblin and dwarf bullshit. He reached up and rested the Dictaphone on top of the books before taking a step back.

'I am Simon Crouch,' he announced to the empty room. 'I am falling apart.'

17

He reached up and pulled down the Dictaphone. The LCD display was flashing 'STDBY'. He pressed play.

'. . . am Simon Crouch. I am falling apart.'

It sounded worse when it was repeated back at him.

5

At 6p.m. Max Fallon took the lift to the basement of Fogle & Moore Investments and walked into the company gym. He changed quickly into his new Hilfiger gym clothes and crossed into the workout area. He paused briefly to watch an aerobics class as he stretched his hamstrings. He marvelled for a second at the line of sweaty secretaries wearing knickers outside their tights: jigging to the left and reaching to the right.

Fantastic.

It put him in the mood.

The gym was always busy in the early evening and most of the machines were busy. Max found himself a treadmill and started his usual programme. He began to jog and found his eyes wandering across the view through the full length windows: across the redundant dock that was now only a giant water feature, past the ancient cranes that stood forlornly like skeletons in a museum, towards the hulking concrete minimalism of Cabot Square.

The sun threw rosy washes of evening light over docklands. It reminded him for a brief moment of his childhood in India. Of the lonely nights spent hammering a football against the wall of the Foreign Office residential compound or of reading books while his father attended embassy functions. The sun had seemed so close then that it had frightened him. He had imagined the earth being sucked into its giant yellow mouth. He smiled.

Kids' stuff.

He knew he couldn't touch the English sun. Although – he mused – he could probably buy it.

Twenty minutes later Max was in the shower and he took time over himself. He was especially thorough in the places where he hoped Liz Koplinsky's attention might linger in a few hours' time. He still jutted and rippled in the right places. His skin had still retained the olive sheen that his tropical childhood had earned. Viagra would not be necessary. Danny Planck was a cheeky bastard.

He spent some time in front of the mirror. He shaved for the third time that day, thrilling at the smoothness of his skin. When he brushed his face against Liz's Koplinsky's inner thigh later there would be no friction. She would think she was writhing on the tongue of a ghost, or a God. He applied Clinique skin balm. He didn't want Liz fixating on any unpleasant dry flakes of skin during dinner. Finally he applied a sliver of styling mousse to hold his brown hair back from his face and accentuate the brutal jawline that he knew was his finest feature.

Fragrant and empowered, Max Fallon returned briefly to his office on the bond trading floor to stow his gym bag. A baggy-eyed blonde night secretary shouted across the floor that his cab had arrived. Fallon gave her a quick 'thumbs-up' and grabbed a book from his desk to enliven the cab ride to the West End. It would take his mind off Liz until he met her at 7.30. It was a dog-eared copy of a book called *Gods and Myths*.

The Palais was an old favourite: a bright and airy Anglo-French restaurant that overlooked Covent Garden. It was much loved by the West End media mob: advertising executives and TV producers. Its small entrance lobby opened out spectacularly onto a huge glass-domed atrium.

'Cool place,' said Liz Koplinsky, handing her coat to a waitress.

'Best in town,' Fallon replied. He couldn't take his eyes off Liz's bare shoulders. Her black strapless dress was working a spell on him. Liz's skin appeared totally smooth – no rogue moles or blemishes. He wanted to bite her, feel her melt on his tongue like white chocolate, slide over her perfectly smooth body. They were led to their table immediately. Fallon noticed that Liz liked to brush her hand against the leaves of pot plants and the petals of cut flowers as she walked past. She was a sensual girl. He liked that.

'So does this count as fraternizing?' Liz asked as she settled in her chair and a waiter placed a napkin on her lap.

'Socializing,' said Max with a smirk.

'What's the difference?'

'You've still got your clothes on.'

Liz's face softened slightly as she repressed a smile. 'Oh that! It's a New York thing. We don't eat out naked.'

Max switched the subject. He didn't want to labour the point. 'So how did the little girl from the ghetto become a big shot bond trader?'

Liz feigned annoyance. 'Hey, buddy! I didn't come from any ghetto.'

'Queens?'

'It's a very respectable neighbourhood. My father worked at the airport.'

'Carrying baggage?'

'He's an engineer, smart-ass. And he didn't care too much for limeys, either.'

'Limeys!' Max laughed at the tired expression. 'Is this nineteen forty-two?'

Liz bridled slightly. 'Well, don't you have a nickname for us?'

'Yeah,' Max paused for effect. 'Fuckwits.'

'Asshole.'

'I'm kidding. New York's okay,' Fallon said. 'The people are friendlier than Londoners, that's for sure. Central Park beats the shit out of any of London's parks.'

'Central Park is Valhalla if you're a jogger,' Liz conceded. 'I prefer Hampstead Heath, though. I go up there on Sunday mornings. Kids fly their kites on the top of Parliament Hill. Beautiful.'

'Whatever rings your bell,' Fallon sniffed.

'So do you live near here? In the centre of town.'

Max shook his head. 'I've got a place in Chelsea. I'm buying a gaff out in the countryside.'

'Sweet. An olde English cottage?'

'Something like that. I've got this dream of renovating an old manor house. You know, doing the English country gentleman thing. Bring up kids in the countryside. I wouldn't bring up my dinner in London now.' He looked at her, half-embarassed. 'It's silly, really.'

'I don't think so,' said Liz. 'Where have you been looking?'

'How good's your geography?'

'Try me.'

'East Cambridgeshire.'

'You got me.'

'I'm from Cambridge originally. My father still lives up there. There's some great old places on the Suffolk border.'

'That's a long drive.'

'Not in a Porsche.'

'In this country any drive's a long drive. I thought you had a jeep.'

'I've got a Land Cruiser and a Porsche 911.' He noticed her necklace. 'Why are you wearing that Egyptian thing?'

'It's an ankh.' She held it up for him to look at. Inevitably, his eyes wandered down.

'I know what it is. Why are you wearing it?'

'It's a life symbol.'

'Sweet.

'What about you? What's with the book?'

Max looked down at *Gods and Myths*. He smiled. Liz noticed he had very white teeth. 'That's an old friend.'

'How come?'

'I lived in India when I was a kid. My father worked at the British Embassy in Delhi. I used to get so bored on my own. Sometimes I stole books from the library at the English School. This was one of the best ones: Hindu myths, gods and demons and shit. I love all that stuff. It's silly but when I was eight my mum entered me in some school fancy-dress competition as a Hindu god. I've always had a passing interest since then.'

'Why were you on your own?'

Fallon's expression clouded briefly. 'My mum died soon after we moved there. There was a car accident.'

21

'I'm sorry.'

'Don't be. It wasn't your fault,' Fallon replied crisply. 'Unless you were driving a motorbike through the northern suburbs of Delhi in November 1971.'

'Did you win?' Liz ignored his weak attempt at humour.

'Win what?'

'The fancy-dress competition.'

'Of course.'

Liz held up the old book in her hands and flicked through. She winced at some of the pictures. 'Man. This would give me nightmares.'

'Assuming you get to sleep tonight.'

She ignored the flirtation. 'So you're a closet intellectual?'

'Hardly.'

'What did you read at College?'

'Philosophy.'

'No shit?'

'Yes shit. You say "shit" too much, by the way.'

'Bullshit.'

'Actually, I read Philosophy for two years then I changed to Theology.'

'Why, for Christ's sake?'

'That's a bad joke if you meant it. To be honest, I found philosophy boring. Theology was more to do with belief systems and religious mythology: much juicier.'

'I'd never have guessed you were into all that stuff.'

'I'm full of surprises. There's a mythology exhibition at The British Museum this week as it happens. I'm going on Saturday. You should come.' Max waved at the wine waiter who pulled a notebook from his pocket and drifted over.

'I got better things to do on a Saturday than hang out in some stinking museum, bud.'

'Stinking?'

'Good evening,' the waiter smiled at them.

'Champagne,' Max said without looking at him. 'Not the house muck. Something decent.'

'Of course, Monsieur.'

'And you can ditch the accent. I'm not a tourist.'

22

The waiter froze, bit his tongue and walked away. Liz was horrified.

'Max, you are so rude.'

'He's about as French as my nuts.' Max studied her closely for a second, his eyes moving over her. 'I've got a question for you now.'

'Shoot.'

'What's this I hear about you shagging some monkey from Settlements? Slouch or Couch or something.'

'Crouch. That's nothing. Just a kink I gotta iron out.' Liz felt a sudden sting of guilt. She tried to dab the wound away.

'Someone like you doesn't need any dead wood.'

'He's a nice guy but it's never going to work out. He's kind of possessive.'

'Ditch the bitch, I say. There are winners and losers. Blokes like that live in a cheap, spivvy little world. Cheap beer. Cheap clothes. A suffocating mortgage. Motorway nightclubs. Match of the Day. You don't want that. Don't demean yourself.'

Liz shook her head slowly. 'You're just an incurable romantic, aren't you?'

Two champagne glasses appeared before them on the table. Max tasted the wine, gold and sparkling.

'Spot on!' He gestured at the waiter to continue pouring. 'Seriously bloody spot on.'

The bubbles nibbled at his tongue. He felt empowered. Liz sipped her champagne and he noticed the soft smear of lipstick she left on the lip of the glass. It was going to be a long and fruitful evening.

6

The following morning Simon Crouch got into work early. He was at his desk at 7a.m. He hoped to have a chat with Liz before the market opened and she immersed herself in trades, emails and excuses. He walked across the lift lobby from

Settlements onto the hallowed ground of the trading floor. Most of the traders and bond salesmen were already at their desks. Some glugged coffee from expensive cardboard containers, others enjoyed the tits on page three and a few stared intently at their trading screens hunting out the titbit of information that might give them an edge.

Eventually he arrived at the eurodollar trading desk in the centre of the floor. It was distinctive for three reasons: first, it had a line of US flags stretching across the tops of the computer monitors as if they denoted forces on a battlefield diorama. Secondly, a large rubber Yoda dangled above the desk in a noose. The toy had a piece of cardboard sellotaped across its belly that said: 'May the Bourse be with you.' Thirdly, Danny Planck, head of trading, was already booming instructions at his beleaguered foot soldiers.

'The word today is Gas, boys and girls. We are expecting a billion spondoolies to hit the market from Arizona Natural Resources. Now as you know, this is a skittish market. It's jumping about like a kangaroo in a carwash. The extra supply won't help.'

Planck picked up the baseball bat he kept by his desk and waved it around for emphasis. Crouch hung back. He had seen Planck smash up computer screens with his bat.

'Look for simple switches into quality credits. Don't bugger around. Use my tip list. Dangle your balls in the fire at your own peril.' Planck looked around and picked up the bacon roll from his desk. 'Now which one of you piss ants has taken my ketchup?'

Planck spotted Crouch hovering nervously at his elbow.

'What do you want, Crouchie? My trading sheets messed up again?'

'Is Liz around?' Crouch found his Essex accent grew more pronounced on the trading floor, like a boxer using his jab. 'I need to check a couple of trades.'

'Course you do!' Planck winked at him. 'Nice shoes by the way. Oi Adrian! Clock Crouchie's didgeries.'

A curly-haired trader looked up briefly from his glowing Bloomberg Screen and winced.

'Plastic fantastic,' he said with a yawn.

Planck grinned hideously. 'Yeah! Disposable shoes. They are shocking, Crouchie. A man's shoes say a lot. You're squeaking like a fucking hamster.'

'Is Liz around?' Crouch was used to taking flak from the Gucci-shod traders but today it burned inside him, like he'd drunk a pint of wasps.

'She's gonna be late,' Adrian said flatly. 'She was on the lash last night.'

'Thanks.' Crouch walked away, the bile rising inside him. Liz had been out on the piss half the night. *So much for being exhausted.* He ignored Danny Planck's derisive shouts from behind him.

'Eak-eak-eak-eak!'

As he left the floor and crossed back across the lobby that separated Settlements from Trading, he walked right into Liz Koplinsky. She was emerging from a lift clutching a huge Starbuck's Coffee. She had shower-wet hair scraped back over her head. It made her eyes shine brighter, despite the bags beneath them.

'Hey you,' she said wearily; an emotion flickered across her face. Crouch tried to decipher it: panic turned into guilt?

'I called you last night.'

'I heard the phone. I was tired. I had an early night.'

The lies were becoming more obvious. Her eyes darting sideways as she spoke. He would remember that.

'When can I see you?' he asked simply.

She felt a rush of pity. The simple imploring tone of his question upset her.

'Listen, I'll call you later. Big day on the desk today.' She dragged her eyes from the floor with an effort. 'I gotta go.'

Crouch felt the frustration fermenting in his stomach as he watched her leave. He had seen enough. He knew it was over.

Now, he had to know why.

Around the corner, Liz arrived at the Eurodollar desk to a chorus of jeers and 'look-at-the-state-of-that's!' She slumped into her chair and hung onto her coffee for warmth and support.

25

'Good night, then?' Adrian asked without looking up from his screens.

Liz nodded. 'The best.'

'Some loser was looking for you.'

Liz felt another spasm of guilt. She had treated Simon poorly. She had wanted to call it off but had hoped he would get the message by implication. Through the broken glass window of a hangover Liz saw she at least owed him the respect of breaking up properly. She decided to send him an email.

7

The black cab roared up from the gloom of the Limehouse Link Tunnel onto the highway. Crouch sat in the back, cold sweating with anxiety. The cab turned left at Tobacco Dock. The driver looked over his shoulder and opened the connecting window.

'Left here, mate?'

'Yeah,' Crouch replied, 'then down Wapping High Street. It's opposite the tube station. Raleigh Wharf.'

'Gotcha.'

They arrived two minutes later. Crouch told the cab to wait for him. He hurried into the building as the cabbie opened a plastic thermos flask of coffee.

Crouch unlocked Liz's apartment. '2-1-2-3' silenced the alarm system.

The flat was humid and smelt of shower-gel. He was nervous and quickly retrieved the Dictaphone from the book-shelf. He was back outside within a minute.

Back in the cab, Crouch took a deep breath and pressed play on the Dictaphone. Nothing happened. The batteries had died. The taxi rumbled back towards Canary Wharf, bouncing along the ancient cobbles of Wapping High Street. Crouch held the muted machine tightly in his hand.

Max Fallon drifted into his office at 8a.m. Wearily, he turned on his computer and noticed he had twenty-six emails. Three were from Liz. He groaned and necked half a bottle of Evian. She had been a disconcertingly good ride but he hoped that she wasn't a bunny boiler. A barnacle bird at the office was the last thing that he needed. He would trawl through the messages later. For the moment, he would concentrate on fighting dehydration.

Simon Crouch bought two calculator batteries from the shop next to the canteen at Fogle & Moore and hurried down to his office. He closed the door behind him and fumbled the new batteries into the dictaphone. After a deep breath he pressed 'play'. A light flashed on and through the electrical crackle of the playback he could hear snatches of Liz's voice.

'. . . Fogle & Moore . . . giving me a frigging pay rise . . . working my ass off twenty-four-seven.'

There was a mumbling in the background. Someone else was in the room but Crouch couldn't determine who. He frowned as he tried to decipher the answer and cursed the Dictaphone's inadequate condenser mic. Liz's voice broke through the crackle again. She sounded drunk.

'. . . I do work weekends . . . some weekends . . . why are you being such an asshole . . .'

He could hear Liz laughing. There was a crash of breaking glass. Drunk Liz dropping stuff – he'd seen her do it before.

Footsteps. Footsteps on Liz's stripped wooden floor. Expensive footsteps, getting louder. A man's voice.

'. . . are all assholes. Didn't your mother tell you that?'

Fury engulfed Simon Crouch. Fury that she had lied to him. Fury that he had lost control of events. Terror at what was coming. He could hear a rustling sound. Like the crumbling of a paper bag.

'Shit. There's wine down the front of your dress.'

Liz's reply was muffled and indistinct. The man's voice again.

'Why don't you just take it off?'

Crouch stopped the playback and was suddenly sick into his waste basket. He wiped the acid bile from his mouth.

There it was. Cold and brutal. She was screwing him around. His heart was racing. His blood boiled behind his eyes. For a second, he thought about throwing the Dictaphone away. And yet morbid fascination drew him on. He tried for a moment to catch his breath. He removed his tie, its cheapness now stained with vomit. He pressed play.

Liz's voice: 'Whaddya think?'

Man: '. . . king fantasic.'

Liz: 'You planning on doing anything about it?'

Man. He sounded drunk too. 'What about your boyfriend . . . Mr Sad-Act from Settlements.'

Liz: '. . . over. He's nobody. Now are we gonna fuck or are you gonna talk shit all night?'

Crouch sat back in his chair. It would have been better to walk in on them and catch them in the act: better to have fixed a single frozen horror in his mind. Then he could have turned the image into a jigsaw and picked away at it over time. Now, his imagination was painting dozens of terrible pictures.

He was infuriated by his own idiocy. He was the biggest dickhead on the planet. He had cut her so much slack, believed all her self-esteem bullshit, tolerated the evaporation of their sex life. Aldo had been right all along. She was a piece of garbage. Crouch smashed his hand against the plastic desk. How could he have been so utterly fucking stupid?

The playback continued. Grunting through the distortion.

Man: 'You like this?'

Liz: 'Fuck yes . . . Fuck yes . . .'

Man: '. . . knew you were a dirty bitch . . .'

Liz: 'Ugh . . . Ugh . . . Fuck me . . . Fuck me . . .'

Fawk me. Fawk me. Crouch found that her accent suddenly revolted him. As if he was eating sludge raked up from the bottom of the East River.

Man: 'Where do you want it?'

Liz. Breathless. 'Anywhere Max, anywhere you fucking want . . .'

You fawking want. Max. Anywhere you fawking want. Max. Max.

28

The noises went on. Grunting, screams, rustling. Like killing a pig. Eventually, the tape ran out and in the sudden silence of his office, Crouch cried for the first time in ten years. Every time he closed his eyes he saw Max Fallon, the market's quintessential tosser, screwing his girlfriend. The image sickened and excited him. He found his own desolate arousal even more enraging. It took two hours for his despair to harden into fury.

At 10.30 he read an email from Liz saying she needed space.

At 11.00 he called Aldo.

8

Friday afternoon was usually a dead loss. The market indices always behaved erratically after lunchtime as hundreds of traders sloshed back to their desks with half a gallon of lager inside them. It was a sunny day too. The bars around Canary Wharf were already spilling people onto the dockside walk-ways. At 4.30p.m., Fallon gave up and decided to join them. He pulled on his navy blue suit jacket and announced his departure to the trading floor over the intercom: 'I'm off to the pub. I suggest you wankers join me.'

Insulted but unshackled, the weary traders gave up trying to make sense of the muddled Friday market and headed for the door.

Simon Crouch stood at the far end of the trading floor. His eyes still stung. His guts were still twisted in agony. He saw Fallon striding from his office with Danny Planck jogging to keep up with him. Planck asked Fallon a question and slapped him on the back when he heard the answer. Crouch knew they were talking about Liz. It sickened him. She would be another filthy fairy story that fed the cult of Fallon. He would be the nameless sad act from Settlements that got shat on whenever the story was recycled.

He was not prepared to accept that. Aldo had agreed to meet him at six o'clock. Aldo had a plan. Fallon had something bad coming.

The majority of the 3rd Floor bond jocks soon joined Fallon and Planck in Corney & Barrow. Time slipped by. Fallon was feeling generous and bought three pitchers of lager which were greedily, ungratefully received. He ordered a Japanese premium beer for himself. It came in a frosted glass; ice cold. It was a nice touch. Fallon enjoyed bestowing his largesse on the little people. They thought it made him one of them. He knew it was about control.

Tall and imperious Pieter Richter drifted over and floated at Fallon's side. He was ambitious and aggressive: the youngest director in Sales & Trading.

'So come on, man!' Richter boomed, Harvard Business School hadn't quite ironed out his German accent, 'did you stiff her?'

Fallon was enjoying the attention.

'What kind of question's that?' Fallon wore a grin that spoke a thousand words.

'You stiffed her.' Richter turned to Planck. 'Can you believe this lucky son of a bitch?'

Planck solemnly nodded his agreement. 'It's a disgrace. Nice, innocent girl like that.'

Fallon almost choked on his beer. 'Do me a favour! Innocent? She half ripped my flesh off.'

'Show us, man,' Richter demanded.

At the far end of the bar Simon Crouch bought a pint of Heineken for himself and a Vodka Mule for Aldo. He watched the laughing traders. Fallon's voice, pure mockney, rose above them.

'Piss off!' Fallon shouted. 'Just 'cause you don't get any.'

'This is bullshit, man,' Richter teased. 'You didn't fuck nobody.'

Planck grinned. 'You won't say that when you see your bonus.'

Fallon hated being taunted. He was a God. He would provide a revelation for the unbelievers.

'All right, then.' He slipped off his jacket and lifted up the back of his shirt. 'What about that, then?'

Even Crouch could see the angry red nail marks scratched along Fallon's hairless back. He recognized them. Six months ago he had worn them himself, proudly like a medal. He swallowed the acid that suddenly spurted into the back of his throat. Aldo grabbed him by the arm and pulled him out of the bar. The shrieks of the traders tumbled out of the door after them.

There was a small standing area outside the bar that over-looked the dock. Aldo dragged Crouch over and pushed him into the wall. His friend was ready to explode. Tears brimmed in Crouch's red eyes.

'That prick.' He spat the words into Aldo's face. Aldo could taste the beer. 'I'm going to rip his head off.'

Aldo pushed Crouch back into the wall. 'Don't be stupid. We talked about this. You want to get even, then get smart.' Aldo reached into his right jacket pocket and with-drew a tightly folded square of tin foil. Crouch's body began to relax and he watched his friend discreetly unwrap the silver paper.

'What's that?' said Crouch, brushing the tears of fury from his eyes.

Aldo held up the unwrapped parcel so Crouch could see it. 'This, mate, is revenge.'

On the tin foil lay three white pills.

They heard shouting from inside the bar. Crouch could make out Planck's voice rising above the mayhem. He looked back through the doorway.

'Jesus, Maxy, you were supposed to screw her not murder her!' Planck was spluttering lager over the gathering.

'What can I say?' Fallon replied loudly. 'She was out of control. I've got a gift.'

'This calls for a celebration!' Pieter Richter sloshed a shot of vodka into the nearest trader's glasses. 'To Max's prick. For refusing to die quietly.'

There was a wave of laughter. Max was loving it; the adoration of the little people. The control.

31

Outside, Simon Crouch tried to control his emotions and took the tin foil sheet from Aldo.

'What's your idea, then?' His voice was cracking.

Aldo shot a quick look around him.

'We fix the wanker. Spike his drink. Scramble his brain.'

'You're kidding?'

'Am I smiling?'

Crouch picked up one of the pills and rolled it between his thumb and forefinger.

'What are they then?'

Aldo smiled. 'They are what you might call experimental. We call 'em "Lobotomies". Active ingredient is a close relative of an old friend: lysergic acid diethylamide.'

Crouch was dismissive. 'You want to give this prick an acid trip?' He handed the pills back to Aldo. 'Waste of time. I want to kick his head in. Not send him to dreamland for a couple of hours.'

'This is not ordinary acid. Your average street dose of LSD contains between twenty and eighty micrograms right? These little beauties,' he held the three pills reverentially in the palm of his right hand, 'contain two hundred micrograms each. And I am reliably informed that there are one or two other chemical jack-in-the-boxes in there too. These are not recreational, Crouchie. These are strictly for basket cases. Even I wouldn't take these. In fact, I suggest we both wash our hands once we've got shot of them. You want to mess this guy up. This will give him a permanent headache.'

Crouch was uncertain. It wasn't what he had planned. He had wanted to beat the stupid smirk off Fallon's face; to feel the wanker's jawbone snap at the end of his clenched fist. Perhaps there was still a way.

'Will they kill him?' he asked after a moment's thought.

'Doubtful. But he won't be writing any piano concertos. He may have trouble tying his own shoelaces. Spike his drink. Isolate him and then when he's losing the plot we'll give him a working over. I know a place.'

32

'Let me do it.' Crouch took the pills from Aldo and returned to the pub.

The traders were awash: bobbing happily on a frothing sea of lager. The bar was claustrophobic with their noise. Max was feeling the pace and placed his half-drunk Guinness back on the bar. Richter was the first to pounce: 'Brits are such pussies!' he roared.

'What are you on about now?' Planck growled at him.

'You can't take your drink, man.' Richter gestured at Fallon's guilty glass. 'It's common knowledge.'

'Oh, and you Americans can? Don't make me laugh.' Planck snorted derisively.

'I'm half German and half Japanese, man.' Richter sneered in triumph.

'And what a fucking combination that is!' Planck shot back.

Richter ignored the insult and turned to Fallon. 'When are we launching this Fulton Steel deal?'

Fallon was suddenly alert through the haze; like fog lights cutting through mist. 'Wednesday. Assuming we get Board approval.'

Richter sniffed. 'Man, that is a candidate for Pig of the Year. I can smell the bacon already.' He topped up Fallon's glass with vodka.

'It'll work if you Cappuchino Warriors make an effort to sell the stuff,' Planck boomed.

'Listen, I'm all over this.' Richter took a swig of vodka. 'My clients are primed, man.'

Planck was unimpressed. 'You couldn't sell a hand-job in a prison, mate.'

Crouch was standing close by. He held the three pills in his left hand. He waited and watched Fallon's brimming Guinness.

'Hold up!' Fallon shouted, trying to focus on his mobile phone. 'She's only sent me a message!'

'Bunny boiler, man.'

Fallon squinted at the LCD display. 'Back home. Waiting.'

'Bullshit!'

33

'I'm serious.' He leaned forward and Richter and Plank huddled around him, straining their eyes to read the display. 'I'll tell you something else.' Fallon produced a small, transparent plastic bag from his jacket pocket. It contained a small amount of white powder. 'I snorted a couple of measures of charlie off her tits before we got going. Saved a little bit for her tonight.'

Crouch stepped up behind them, brushed past Fallon's back and dropped the three pills into his Guinness. Without stopping or looking back, he walked into the gent's toilets and washed his hands under the cold tap. His heart was pounding. It had taken willpower. He had wanted to crash his fist into the back of Fallon's head as he had walked past. For an awful moment he wondered if the drink had suddenly changed colour or whether it was frothing over the lip of the glass. Had anyone seen him? He hesitated and studied the gaunt lines of his face in the mirror, uncertain how to proceed.

Back in the bar, Fallon was triumphant.

'Told you, boys! She's gagging for it.'

'Jammy git.' Planck was genuinely jealous. 'I've got a beautiful wife and two beautiful kids but I've got to admit, I'd love to give her one.'

'I'll pop round later for another couple of lengths.' Max steadied himself against the bar as exhaustion made the room wobble.

'State you're in you won't be able to get your Y-fronts off.'

'What are you talking about?' Fallon replied in mock indignation. 'I'm just warming up.' He reached back and picked up his Guinness from the bar. 'Tell you what though. My tongue feels like sandpaper.' He gulped hungrily at the black liquid: two quick swallows. He gasped. 'Christ, Richter, how much vodka did you put in that?'

Richter shrugged. 'A drop, man. Brits are pussies.'

Fallon shuddered. 'Tastes like petrol.' He downed the remainder of his drink and winced as it seared the back of his throat.

Simon Crouch edged past them, noting Fallon's empty glass. Planck noticed him.

'All right, Crouchie?' he said.

Crouch said nothing and headed for another corner of the bustling pub.

9

Liz Kopinsky sat in her Wapping apartment. She had just stepped from the shower and had decided not to bother getting dressed. Instead she wore her favourite blue bathrobe and curled up in its luxuriant folds on her sofa to watch her fish tank. The last vestiges of her hangover had abated. She had even chosen to risk a glass of cold Beaujolais from her fridge.

She checked her mobile at 9.15 and again at 9.30. Max had not replied. She knew he was probably drunk and was unlikely to call. If he hadn't gone to bed already. The previous night had been wild. She had been surprised by his ferocity and by her own energy. He had been an animal tearing at her clothes. She had let him shave her pubic hair too. It had driven him crazy. Perhaps he had worn himself out.

Liz put her glass down on her coffee table and lay back on the sofa. She watched her favourite fish drifting across the giant tank. It was a Broad Tail Moor called Frankie. Frankie was jet black with a high dorsal fin and long, flowing tail. His eyes bulged out of his head. He scared the smaller fish. Frankie was funny.

Liz drifted to sleep.

10

Max Fallon had an uneasy sense that all was not right. He felt dry. His throat was sore. The noise of the room seemed to wash strangely over him.

'I need a Perrier.'

A face is close to his. Richter.

'You gotta go bang that chick, man.'

'Igottabanger.' The words all washed together. Max knew he had drunk too much. He could hear people talking about him. Whispering. He was anxious. He had to go.

Fallon fell out of the front entrance to Corney & Barrow, stumbling down the stone stairway. He headed for the familiar lights of Fogle & Moore. His head was spinning and he was starting to feel panicky.

The voice in his head:

> Under the milky ocean, under the milky ocean
> Something is not quite right.

His heart was racing and his head sloshed as if it was full of water. Someone whispered in his ear. He span around. There was no one there. He stopped. Suddenly disorientated as the world moved around him. He had no control. He was in the eye of the storm. Clouds tumbled around him. He was sitting on the spindle of the kaleidoscope.

The voice in his head:

> Under the milky ocean, under the milky ocean
> Something is not quite right.

He tried to focus on the source of the sound but there was nobody there. He was frightened, dimly aware that something terrible was happening.

The voice hissed:

> Under the milky ocean, under the milky ocean
> Something is not quite right.

The voice was getting louder. He knew people were following him: that two hundred and sixteen eyes were tracking his movements.

*'Fifty-four Gods and fifty-four Demons. Shaking the
mountain and churning the ocean.*
*Fifty-four Gods and fifty-four Demons. Shaking the
mountain and churning the ocean.'*

He leaned against a metal rail by the edge of West India Dock.
He was in West India. Where the fuck was that? He knew
India and this wasn't it. This was something else. Something
altogether fucking else. He looked at the water. It wasn't
milky. It was fixed, brown. Rippled like frozen chocolate. It
was like mud, frozen mud. Unreal, fucking unreal.

*'Fifty-four Gods and fifty-four Demons. Shaking the
mountain and churning the ocean.*
*Fifty-four Gods and fifty-four Demons. Shaking the
mountain and churning the ocean.'*

The whispering was louder. It was right behind him. As if it
was coming from the back of his head.
'Who the fuck is that?' he shouted. The wind rushed at his
ears. It felt like he was falling from a plane and for a second
he was: flailing in panic as the ground rushed at him. It hit
him hard in the face. He was eating concrete. He tasted blood
in his mouth. His eyes rolled up in their sockets until he was
staring into the back of his own head. He forced them back
downwards.
Concentrate. Concentrate.
He dragged himself to his feet using the rail. He couldn't
steady himself. The kaleidoscope was still whirling. The
buildings rolling around him like giant, bright white sails of
silk billowing in the wind. The mountain was rumbling,
breaking in pieces, falling into the ocean.
'Under the milky ocean!'
The voices were snarling at him.
*'Under the milky ocean
Something is not quite right.'*
'Fuck off!' Fallon screamed at nobody.
'Fuck *off*!' nobody screamed back at him.

37

Suddenly there were teeth in front of him. Just teeth. He knew they were there: two rows of yellow teeth.

'All right, mate?' said the teeth.

The teeth were talking to him. *Teeth that could talk.* Max tried to remember how to think. *If the teeth could talk they must hide a tongue. But why didn't the tongue fall out from the back of the teeth?*

'Feeling a bit peaky, Max?' the teeth smiled. *Max knew that teeth can't smile. There had to be muscles. There had to be a face.*

'Don't fucking bite me.' Max was scared. *The teeth had intelligence. The teeth were trying to trick him.*

'I just want to help.'

The teeth were lying. The teeth were going to eat him.

He could smell the drool of their excitement. Max sunk to his knees and waited to be consumed.

Simon Crouch leaned over and admired his handiwork. He was impressed. Aldo hadn't been exaggerating. Fallon's brains would be scrambled egg after this. But he hadn't even started on him yet. It was going to be a long night. With an effort, he hauled Max to his feet.

'Come on, Maxy. Be a brave boy.'

Fallon felt himself rising. The teeth had arms. The teeth were pulling him up to the maw. The arms had muscles. Muscles need blood. Blood needs a heart. A heart needs a brain. A brain needs a person. The teeth were connected to a person. The teeth were a person. Relief flooded through him.

'*Fifty-four Gods and fifty-four Demons. Shaking the mountain and churning the ocean.
Fifty-four Gods and fifty-four Demons. Shaking the mountain and churning the ocean.*'

'Please stop saying that,' Max said to the teeth, 'I don't know what it means.'

'I didn't say anything, dickhead,' said Crouch.

'The mountain is falling into the ocean,' Max burbled, 'that's why the water is all brown.'

Crouch dragged Fallon up to Cabot Square. Fallon hung against him; a dead weight.

'You've got big teeth,' Fallon giggled.

'Shut up, you arsehole.' Crouch could see Aldo driving his car up from the Canary Wharf Car Park. The lights picked them out.

'I was born under the ocean,' said Fallon. 'My mummy made me a god.'

'For Christ's sake,' Crouch muttered.

Aldo pulled up in front of them. Crouch opened the back door and Fallon clambered in.

'This is a dirty fucking cab,' said Fallon.

Crouch jumped in and Aldo accelerated away.

'How is he?' asked Aldo.

'All over the place.'

'After what we put in his drink I'm surprised he's with us at all.'

Max was all over the place. He was in India kicking a football against a wall; he was in West India Docks wherever-the-fuck-that-was eating concrete while the mountain fell into the water, he was swimming underwater, he was having a shit.

> *'Fifty-four Gods and fifty-four Demons. Shaking the mountain and churning the ocean.*
> *Fifty-four Gods and fifty-four Demons. Shaking the mountain and churning the ocean.'*

Max could feel his book pressing into his ribcage. He began to understand what the voices were saying.

The security guard waved them through the Canary Wharf checkpoint and Aldo turned left onto the highway. Crouch started to relax.

'Where are we going?' he asked Aldo.

'Back of Brick Lane,' came the reply. 'I know a place.'

Crouch turned to Max. 'Hear that, arsehole? We are going to kick your head in.'

The teeth were laughing at him. Fallon joined in as the car roared towards the East End. He couldn't stop laughing.

It was hilarious. He was swimming in the milky ocean and he knew he was immortal. God swam up to him. God had his face.

It was hilarious.

The journey took less than ten minutes. Aldo parked in an alley adjacent to Brick Lane. There were people drifting past nearby but none paid them any attention. Crouch dragged Fallon from the car and, with Aldo's assistance, hauled him giggling into the darkness. At the end of the alley was a yard surrounded on three sides by crumbling black walls.

'What is this place?' Crouch asked.

'Used to be a match factory until the Nazis dropped a bomb on it. Nobody ever bothered to rebuild it,' Aldo replied.

The two men released their grip on Fallon and stepped back as he slumped to the floor. Fallon was oblivious to their conversation. He was climbing out of the sea, crawling up the side of the muddy mountain. Demons fluttered across his field of vision like butterflies. He swatted and snatched at them; laughing as they fell through his clumsy fingers. A story was playing in his head: a repeating loop that he couldn't break. At the top of the mountain he lay back and listened to the thunder, flinching as the lightning struck at his body. Then, suddenly, Max Fallon saw the image of his dead mother.

Aldo and Crouch went to work on Fallon with their feet and fists. They soon became extremely frustrated by their failure to make him scream. Max felt numb. He tried to touch the beautiful image before him. His mother's soft eyes were filling with tears, her face glowing with pride.

'You made me so happy,' she said, 'so terribly happy.'

She placed a tall hat on his head: it was covered with brightly coloured jewels.

'Hello mummy,' he said.

'Do you remember who you are?' she replied. 'Do you remember the beautiful little boy who made mummy so proud?'

Fallon was confused. Images rushed at him: pictures flashing past him down the motorway of his barely conscious mind.

'I don't remember,' he said.

She reached her arms around him and buckled a silver belt of moonlight glitter around his waist.

'Do you remember now?'

Fallon wanted to cry. 'I remember,' he heard himself say, 'you made me into a god.'

'You beat everyone. You looked so beautiful. You made me so very proud.'

'Then why did you leave me?' Max asked angrily. 'You fell into the river and never came back. I climbed out of the water. Why couldn't you?'

'You were a little god. I was so proud.'

'You're making me sad.'

'I want to dream now, Max. Sing me to sleep so I can dream.'

Fallon felt himself sliding away from her; tumbling down the mountainside, grasping vainly at rocks and plants to slow his descent. He fell through the clouds and saw the glittering sprawl of London racing up towards him.

He opened his eyes and stared into the black hearts of his attackers.

11

Ten hours later, Max Fallon awoke with a terrified start in his shower. He was naked apart from a single sock. He had no immediate sense of where he was. The floor of his shower was stained with his blood except to Max it appeared golden not red. He tried to focus through the lights that flashed across his eyes. It was as if he was having a migraine, areas of his field of vision were swamped in bright, spiralling lights. Max began to feel the pains in his arms and legs. He began to focus on the cuts and bruises that leaked his golden essence into the shower.

After an hour he stood and, feeling more attuned with his

surroundings, took an agonizing shower to wash the mess from his skin. He could only remember fragments of his experience the previous night: sticks flashing around him, smacking into him, faces he half-recognized contorted into terrible demons, itching insects crawling under his skin. He had been swimming at the bottom of a tranquil white ocean and then, as he climbed the mountain, a voice had told him he was a god.

He climbed from the shower and studied himself in the bathroom mirror. His face seemed unfamiliar to him. He had the contours and structure of a man and yet he felt curiously inhuman. He wasn't even sure if his limbs were attached properly, they seemed to be floating away from him: he had to keep pulling them back.

You sailed in a ship with golden sails under the milky ocean.

Max was confused. The voice sounded like his but he knew he hadn't spoken.

You sailed in a ship with golden sails and saw the face of God.

The voice was right. He had seen the face of God. God had Max Fallon's face. He tried to structure his thoughts. Maybe there was another possibility.

After what we put in your drink I'm surprised you're with us at all.

That voice wasn't his, he whirled around almost losing his balance. 'Who the fuck said that?'

This is a dirty fucking cab, I'm surprised you're with us at all.

Max staggered out into his hallway. He knew there was someone in his flat. He could hear them talking.

They had put something in his drink: something that had turned him into a god.

He squinted at the unfamiliar shapes of his flat and began to laugh. He could hear everybody. Everybody in the world was having a conversation and some of the things they said were really funny. He stumbled into his living room and listened to mankind chatter in his head.

Max heard them debating what kind of god he would be.

42

What was His name? He knew that God had a name but he couldn't remember it.

What kind of god couldn't remember his own name?

At Cambridge he had studied philosophy. Surely he could find an answer.

Socrates told Meno that knowledge is stored memory. Five multiplied by five makes twenty-five. But how can someone recognize that twenty-five is the correct answer unless they already know? Max possessed the knowledge that he was a god. But how could he recognize that god unless he already knew its identity?

Unless the answer already lay in his memory?

12

On Monday morning Max, dressed in jeans and a jumper, walked outside. He had forgotten to put on his shoes and the ground felt very cold. He waved down a cab and gave the driver an address. He found it difficult to speak: impossible to articulate the strange and beautiful sentences that were forming and reforming inside his head. They were the pieces of a jigsaw: splinters of memory and knowledge that were slowly coming together through waves of pain.

Max found the journey through West London peculiar. He felt as if he was seeing everything in negative. The streets and faces seemed drained of colour and expression as if frozen in the white light of an explosion: an expressionless, colourless city. It was a grey wasteland of mobile phones and wandering dogs, crumpled suits and loose change, cheese sandwiches and tube tickets. It bored him and he began to fall asleep dreaming of a temple to befit his new divinity.

The taxi jerked to a halt outside the British Museum thirty minutes later. The connecting window slid back. 'That'll be seventeen fifty please mate,' the cabbie barked over his shoulder.

Max's eyes struggled to focus on his new location. 'Where are we?'

'British Museum. Russell Square. That's what it said on your bit of paper.'

This is a dirty fucking cab, I'm surprised you're with us at all.

'What did you say?' The cabbie turned in anger.

'I didn't say anything,' said Max, looking around for the source of the voice himself. 'Here's some money,' he handed over a note. 'Keep the change.'

'This is a pony, mate!' called the cabbie as Fallon stepped outside.

Max tried to filter his confusion. He steadied himself on the pavement and looked up at the huge white bulk of the British Museum as the cab pulled away behind him. He couldn't see any ponies.

Negotiating the steps up the main atrium was trickier than he had expected. Once inside the vast glass, domed space he found himself at an information desk. There was a middle-aged woman smiling at him.

'You look lost,' she volunteered, looking with interest at his bare feet.

Max nodded. 'You can help me. I am looking for Mister God.'

'Excuse me?'

'Mister God Expedition,' he said suddenly finding his own words confusing, before he remembered the impenetrability of the divine language he had absorbed.

'Oh!' the woman exclaimed. 'The Gods and Myths Exhibition. I'm sorry I misheard you.' She handed him a free programme and pointed across the Atrium, 'It's on the Upper Floor. Take the lift. Go through Roman Britain and follow the signs.'

It took Max half an hour to find the exhibition. He had a vague sense of what he was looking for: a fragment from his childhood, a story his mother had told him in India. He needed to fill in the blanks but the specifics eluded him. He found himself staring at fragments of clay pots and strangely

44

patterned coins in glass cabinets; at carved animal figures and bronze statues. None of them made any sense to him: they were disjointed, like the wreckage of an explosion scattered through time. Coins from Mesopotamia, figurines from Egypt, jewels and sword handles hauled up from the ancient earth and deposited, absurdly, in the London Borough of Camden.

A tour party drifted past him. He decided to drift with them. The obese and breathless male tour guide was talking in an abrasive American accent that cut across Max's whispering mind like a flamethrower.

'The last set of artefacts relate to ancient Hindu religious writings and myths.' He gestured the group to join him around a large display cabinet. Max pushed himself to the front of the group. 'The British plundered a number of Hindu religious sites in India and Kashmir during the nineteenth and early twentieth centuries. These illegal excavations revealed a number of extraordinary artefacts relating to the religious practises of the Vedic Civilizations. The museum has chosen the artefacts that you see in the cabinet as illustrations of scenes from the Rig-Veda. This was an epic Sanskrit writing produced two thousand years before the birth of Christ.'

Max stared into the cabinet. His attention was focused on a small wooden carving about seven inches high. He had seen it before: a photograph in one of his parents' books. It was a carved depiction of the Hindu deity Soma. The name was familiar to him. Suddenly he remembered a children's costume show that had taken place at the English School in Delhi some thirty years previously. Each of the expatriate children had come dressed as a figure from Hindu mythology. His friend Josh Gould had been Indra; little Kathy Desborough had been an implausible Shiva. Max's mother had dressed him up as Soma, the god of plants and the moon. He had worn a tall hat bedecked with plastic jewels, a white billowing tunic and a plastic belt made silvery with glitter. He had carried a beautiful heavy-headed red flower. He had won the competition. His costume was the best. Max suddenly recalled the dream of his mother, standing on top of the mountain with pride swimming in her eyes.

Stunned, he watched as the lights in his eyes whirled around the face of the wooden icon. His face. He tried to read the typed card that had been placed next to the carving;

'Soma the Hindu plant god is described in over 120 verses of the Rig Veda. It was believed that the other Gods obtained immortality by ingesting the essence of Soma. The Rig Veda describes the mixing of Soma juice with milk and curd to produce the elixir of immortality.'

Now, Max remembered the legend of the Soma. The strange deity whose existence was indistinguishable from the liquid that fed the God's immortality. The Soma created at the churning of the ocean. He had drunk the Soma. He had seen the face of God in his dream.

His face.

He remembered a car plunging into black water: thick muddy water like chocolate milk gagging in his throat. He heard the silent scream of his birth.

Knowledge flowed from memory. He finally recognized the knowledge he had always ignorantly possessed. It had been unlocked. Now he remembered.

13

Max Fallon did not return to Fogle & Moore until the Wednesday after his confrontation with Crouch and Aldo. His mind had cleared sufficiently for him to understand the urgency of the phone calls he had received from the office: the growing sense of irritation that underpinned the voices on the other end of the line.

He did not feel confident enough to drive: he had still not yet mastered the lights behind his eyes and so had risked the

Underground. Delays on the Jubilee Line meant Max had been forced to change to the Docklands Light Railway. The agonizingly slow progress of the train as it crawled out of Limehouse towards Canary Wharf had encouraged Max to close his eyes. When he opened them again he was in Island Gardens at the southern tip of the Isle of Dogs with Canary Wharf Tower blinking behind him.

Max was relieved to find a taxi outside Island Gardens and eventually arrived at Fogle & Moore shortly after nine. He found the lifts difficult to understand. He rode the crowded lift up and down the hollow spine of the building until he remembered the location of the bond-trading floor. He recognized his office at the far end of the trading pit and walked steadily but uncertainly towards it. Danny Planck caught up with him quickly.

'Welcome back, Maxy, feeling better?'

Max looked at him, curious and only half-understanding. 'Migraine,' he said.

'It's all gone tits up this week. Market is saturated. That prick Pippen at Fulton Steel is having a baby about his deal. He wants to launch, I think it's a bad idea. There's four jumbo deals in the market already today. We need to postpone but he's got to hear it from you.'

Max nodded. 'I need a drink,' he looked around at the blurred room, 'someone get me a fucking grapefruit,' he frowned, 'grapefruit juice.'

They entered his office and Max fell into his seat.

Planck seemed anxious. 'So why don't I get Liz and we'll call this tosser straight away and put the deal back.'

'Sounds good,' Max agreed. He looked out of his window. There was something sitting on the window ledge. It was like a bird but seemed to be carved of stone. It had the face of a gargoyle. It turned its head to look at him. Max blinked and it had gone. Confused, he stood and stared out at the distant brown swirl of east London trying to see where it had gone. In a new corner of his mind he realized why the demons were following him.

'Hey you!' said Liz as she re-entered the room with Planck,

'you feeling better? I've been worried. I called you about fifty times.'

Max recognized her. He could still feel her sweating underneath him. Still smell her perfume on his bed sheets. This was Liz. He liked Liz. 'Migraines,' he said forcing a smile, 'bad week.'

Planck leaned over the star-shaped speakerphone and called Andrew Pippen's number. It immediately connected and rang twice.

'Treasury,' snapped the voice at the other end.

'Andrew, it's Danny Planck here with Liz Koplinsky from Fogle & Moore.'

'Right. About time.'

'I've got Max Fallon with me.'

Pippen's voice lost a little of its edge. 'Good. Are you feeling better, Max?'

Max started as he realized a small bottle of grapefruit juice had appeared at his elbow. He unscrewed it and took a greedy gulp.

'Spiffing, Andrew. I understand you are concerned about your deal.'

Pippen spoke with a new urgency. 'Indeed. In your absence I have been receiving confusing messages from your staff about the viability of Fulton Steel's bond issue.'

'Oh dear,' said Max sagely. He imagined ripping Pippen's head off. He would secure it with rope and dangle it above his desk.

Planck took over, sensing Fallon was not on top of his game, 'Andrew, the message has been consistent and it has been clear. We think you are a viable credit but the timing is bad.'

Pippen was beginning to sound angry. 'I want to launch today. Otherwise I'll offer the deal to Deutsche Bank.'

Max had heard enough. The blood from Pippen's ragged neck was splattering on his blotter. 'Andrew, you appreciate straight talking and I respect that. Here's what we're going to do. We are going to launch this baby today.'

Planck was shaking his head and desperately making gestures at Fallon to stop.

'This morning, in fact,' Max continued. 'We will buy back unsold bonds and make the market liquid. We'll launch in twenty minutes.' Fallon pressed the cancel button on the phone.

'Max, what are you doing?' Planck was horrified. 'You've committed us to a deal that can't work!'

'Don't be such a faggot,' Max snarled. 'It's my responsibility. Get on with it.'

'Your responsibility,' Planck reiterated, pointing at him. 'I hope you heard that, Liz.'

'I am a director. I get paid to take responsibility,' Max proclaimed. 'There are leaders and followers. There are gods and mortals. I've been carrying you for too long. Go and earn your bonus for once.'

Danny Planck stormed out of the office in disgust. Liz looked in shock at Fallon. 'Maxy, maybe you should be at home. You don't look well.'

'Something's happened.' He frowned trying to remember the strange floating faces, the voices, the pain. 'That guy you dated.'

'Crouch?'

'Him.' Max could see Crouch in his mind's eye, standing over him, saying something.

'What about him?'

Max suddenly lost his train of thought. For a split second he saw Liz Koplinsky on her back giving birth to his baby. She was screaming. Screaming.

'Max?'

He was back in his office. Liz stood in front of him. Fallon rubbed his eyes.

'Just leave me alone.'

The Fulton Steel Euro bond issue was launched at 11a.m. that morning. The price collapsed in the aftermarket. Fogle & Moore Investments lost approximately half a million pounds in twenty minutes trying to support the issue. And it kept getting worse.

As the mess unfolded on the financial news screens, and tumult grew on the trading floor, Danny Planck picked up his

49

phone and called Richard Moore, the company's Chief Executive.

In the midst of the chaos, its chief architect disappeared.

In a different part of the building, Simon Crouch handed in his resignation to Susan Joyce, the head of personnel.

'I must say, Simon,' she commented, 'this is rather unexpected.'

'It's a two-month notice period,' he said, 'I'm happy to work it all.'

'That probably won't be necessary. Perhaps you could stay until you've done a handover.'

'Whatever.' He couldn't believe he was leaving: five years of grief, commuting and stress up the spout because of some girl.

'Can I ask you why you are leaving?' asked Joyce who was overheating slightly in her pink woollen suit. 'You always seemed to be Fogle & Moore through and through. Your assessments have all been exemplary.'

Crouch wondered whether he should be honest: whether he should tell Joyce that he had got himself stupidly involved with a woman at work, that she had shat all over him, that he had dropped acid into Max Fallon's drink then kicked the incapacitated wanker into a bloody mess.

'Personal reasons,' he said simply, 'no reflection on the company. I've had some happy times here.'

'Do you have another job lined up?' Joyce was discreetly making notes. Crouch knew the score – her next question would be 'And how much are they paying?' Personnel always liked to be on the money.

'No, I don't. I'm going to take a break for a few months. Maybe travel. I've been doing this job since college and I reckon I owe myself a breather. I'm thinking of going to Thailand. You know, see some temples. Sit on the beach. Take stock of things.'

'Very brave of you,' Joyce observed, closing her file. 'It's hard, isn't it. The pressures we all work under now. Sometimes, the courageous thing to do is to say "enough is enough".'

Max Fallon returned to the office at ten the following morning. After the launch of the Fulton Steel issue, he had returned to the British Museum and assimilated as much information as he could about the Soma legend. He had purchased a couple of relevant books in the museum shop and then walked down to Charing Cross Road where he eventually bought a copy of the Rig-Veda. He spent the evening in his Chelsea apartment trying to understand the strange text and relate it to his experiences. The whispering had kept him awake.

When he eventually arrived on the trading floor, Richard Moore was waiting in his office. Moore was immaculately attired in a navy pinstripe and scarlet tie. His neat white hair exaggerated the hard lines of his face. As Max entered the room, he realized he had forgotten to shave.

'What's going on, Max?' he asked. Moore didn't mince words.

'Sorry I'm a bit late, Richard. Bloody migraines.'

Moore looked surprised. He knew the trading floor was a rough environment but he did not expect his senior managers to swear at him. However, he had more important issues to discuss.

'What happened yesterday, Max? Fulton Steel was a disaster. A first year graduate wouldn't have made the mistakes that you did. We lost best part of a million quid by the close of trade.'

'Ouch,' Max giggled.

'I don't find it funny. That money is coming out of the bonus pool. We all have to pay for it.' Moore studied Max's dishevelled appearance. 'Look at the state of yourself, man! You haven't shaved, your suit jacket doesn't even match your trousers.'

'I'll wear whatever I like. It's my trading floor.' He leaned towards Moore conspiratorially. 'Promise you won't say anything. but I am becoming a god. I swear. Even my dick is getting bigger.'

Moore had seen enough. Danny Planck's assessment had been correct. 'Max, I want you to listen to me very carefully.

51

You are going to come upstairs with me to personnel. I have a strong suspicion that you have been taking drugs. That is not permissible on a trading floor as you will know from your contract of employment. Personnel will organize for you to take a drug test in the company medical room: a blood test and a urine sample. Do you understand what I am saying to you?'

Max nodded. 'You're coming through loud and clear, Dickie!'

Moore escorted Fallon off the trading floor. In the lift lobby, Simon Crouch hurriedly brushed past the two men. Fallon recognised the face and for a split second saw fear in Crouch's evasive eyes.

Memory became knowledge.

Max Fallon was suspended from work pending the results of his blood and urine tests. Two days later, once Richard Moore had received the analysis from the company doctor, he sent Max a brief letter that explained Fogle & Moore's uncompromising stance on drug abuse and that Max had been fired.

Max read the letter whilst sitting naked on the floor of his Chelsea flat. He had fully expected to be fired but the attached copy of his blood and urine test results made fascinating reading:

'Sample contains mixture of drug traces suggesting amphetamine and psycho-active stimulant abuse...lysergic acid diethylamide, 3,4-Methylenedioxymethamphetamine (ecstasy), mescaline, muscimol . . . dosage between 200–400mg based on analysis . . . combination of stimulants from organic and derivative sources.'

He tried to rationalize the information in front of him. The Soma was indistinguishable from the elixir of immortality. He had become the Soma after absorbing these chemicals. He had been on an extraordinary odyssey under oceans, through the clouds and beheld the Godhead. They had put something in his drink: something that had turned him into a god. The journey had been brilliant and spectacular and yet he was struggling: struggling to forge a true understanding of what he was about to become. He wanted to go back. His mother had been waiting for him at the top of the mountain: he wanted to see her again.

He consulted the books he had purchased at the British Museum. He found reading them difficult. He spent hours highlighting pages then had no recollection of what he had read. Max Fallon tried desperately to concentrate. He had to discover the essence of what he was becoming. He had to recreate the essence of the Soma.

He reread the results of his drug test: *'Mescaline, Muscimol . . . dosage between 200–400mg based on analysis . . . combination of stimulants from organic and derivative . . .'*

Max paused. *'Muscimol'*. A faint flicker of electricity sparkled across his exhausted brain like a firework illuminating wasteland. He had made a connection. He opened one of the books he had bought on the Soma legend and eventually found the section he had been looking for. He had underlined it. However, he had underlined the entire book.

Max decided it would help his concentration if he read aloud:

'Certain twentieth century studies, particularly Wasson's "Soma the Divine Mushroom of Immortality" have associated the Hindu plant deity Soma with the psychoactive mushroom Amanita Muscaria. There is evidence in the Rig-Veda that these mushrooms were used as part of religious services in ancient Hindu culture. It is believed that the hallucinogenic effects of their constituent chemicals including muscimol allowed the taker to experience vivid religious visions.'

There was a photograph of a strange red and white-capped mushroom on the opposite page. He knew what he had become. He began to see what he had to do.

14

Simon Crouch had fallen asleep in front of his television. He woke at 11p.m. and blinked in exhaustion at a football highlights programme. There was a knocking at his front door. He looked in surprise at his watch and turned on the hall light as he walked to the door. Max Fallon was standing under his porch light.

'What do you want?' asked Crouch, relieved that he'd put the chain on the door.

'I need to talk to you,' Fallon said, pronouncing each syllable with great care as if it caused him huge difficulty. 'About what you did.'

'I've got nothing to say to you. How did you get this address?'

Max smiled. 'Thought you'd ask that. I stole Liz's address book. You remember Liz. Our mutual receptacle.'

'Piss off.' Crouch was tempted to open the door and finish off what he and Aldo had started a week previously.

'No. Wait. Listen to me.' Fallon leaned against the doorframe as the world swam away from him. 'I need to know what you gave me.'

'I don't know what you're talking about,' Crouch snarled, 'now piss off.'

'You and your friend. Put something in my drink and since then I've been becoming.'

'Becoming?'

'Becoming . . . something.'

'Look. I don't work for you anymore. You are trespassing. Now piss off before I call the police.'

Max raised a finger and waved it admonishingly. 'I thought you'd say that. So I'm going to call them for you. You and your friend gave me drugs in my drink and hit me with sticks. You drove me somewhere and made me bleed. I probably deserved it for shafting your girlfriend so thoroughly but I'm going to call the police now.' He held up his mobile and made a great show of dialling:

'Nine . . . nine . . . nine.'

'What do you want?' Crouch asked.

Max smiled and nodded, cancelling the call. 'I want to know what you put in my drink. And I want to know where I can buy some more.'

'You're sick, man. You need help.' Crouch was beginning to become aware of an unpleasant smell about Fallon. He hoped the brown stains down Fallon's trousers were just mud.

'You sound like my father,' Fallon spluttered. 'He says I need professional help. He's an idiot.'

'Take his advice. I want you to leave now.'

Fallon was unfolding a piece of paper. 'You know what this is? This is a shopping list of all the things you put inside me.' Max read out from the report: 'lysergic acid diethylamide, Methy . . . methyl, methylenedio-something mescaline, muscimol.'

Crouch was unrepentant. 'You've got the wrong man, Max. I don't know what you're talking about.'

Max shook his head as the lights swam out from under his eyelids. 'It was you. I know it was you. I need to find what you gave me. You see, it took me somewhere incredible. My mother died when I was a kid. She was there. I saw her. I fucking spoke to her. I have to go back. I only learned a little of what I am.'

Crouch had heard enough. 'Ok. I'm closing the door now. I want you to go. I don't know what you want. As for Liz, you can have her. You deserve each other.'

Crouch slammed the door, his heart beating.

'I'll be seeing you,' came the voice from the darkness.

Fallon looked around at the cluttered London street with its cramped little houses and double parked cars. It was claustrophobic and beneath him. He needed space. He needed room to explore his becoming. He had time and money. He would complete the purchase of a property in Cambridgeshire. He would leave London. He no longer needed it.

The vast black canopy of night hung over him. He studied its formless chaos as if the detritus of his imagination had been projected massively across the void. Perhaps as the god

55

of the moon he could draw the disparate elements into order: imbue his scattering thoughts with purpose, make the planets themselves witnesses to his newfound divinity.

But first he had to find a way back. His brain ached with the ordinariness of existence. It screamed out for beauty and understanding. He had to find a way back: capture the lightning that had lifted him from the milky white ocean to the summit of perception. Capture it. Bottle it.

Maybe even share it.

The Scrambling of Brihaspati

15

Eight Months Later

29th April 2002, New Bolden

John Underwood sipped his first whisky in over a year and savoured its smoky taste. Jack Harvey watched him closely.

'Taste good?' Harvey grinned.

'You must stop asking stupid questions, Jack,' Underwood replied.

'I'm a psychiatrist. I get paid to ask stupid questions.'

'I thought this was a social occasion.' Underwood placed the glass back on the table and resisted the urge to pick it straight back up again. 'Haven't we done with all the "did you ever fancy your mother stuff"?'

Harvey smiled. It was good to have Underwood back. It hadn't been an easy year for either of them. 'It is a social occasion, John. And I know you never fancied your mother. I suspect you might fancy my wife, though.'

'Everyone fancies Rowena, Jack. I'd be mad if I didn't.'

Harvey nodded. He had been blessed with a beautiful wife and cursed with the perpetual terror of losing her. 'Listen. You've done very well, John. You've worked very hard at getting back.'

'Down to you really,' Underwood said dismissively. He toyed with the keys to his new flat that he had placed on the table in front of him.

'You're still too defensive, John. I only pointed you in the right direction. You did the rest.'

'Prozac and the eminent Dr Harvey did all the useful stuff. I was just a stoned spectator.'

'That is utter bollocks.'

Underwood liked winding Jack up. He'd been doing it for

ten years. He was learning to treasure his friends. He didn't have many left. Dexter maybe.

'Possibly,' said Underwood. 'I was trying to pay you a compliment.'

'Jesus. That would be a first. You must have gone mad.' Harvey knew that you had to give as good as you got with John Underwood.

'I'm serious. You kept me going. No one else bothered.'

'That is not true.'

'Ah, whatever.'

'Look,' Harvey leaned forward, 'you made a right bloody mess of things. You are not out of the woods yet either. Depression is like the tide – it will keep coming back.'

'Your analogies are getting predictable, Jack. I suppose I'm King Canute?'

'Just remember that we don't create and solve all of our own problems.'

Underwood fixed Harvey for a second with a cold gaze.

'Are you going to let me go back, Jack?' he asked.

'I'll drop a line to the Chief Super. I can't promise anything. They may not want you back.'

Underwood nodded. Jack might be right there. His relationship with Superintendent Chalmers had always been fraught. Besides, he mused, according to the rumours emanating from New Bolden CID, Inspector Alison Dexter was now doing a far better job than he ever had. Underwood noticed the dark lines around Jack Harvey's eyes for the first time.

'You look tired, Jack.'

'It's a stressful job. You know that.'

'Anything else? Problems with Rowena?'

Harvey chuckled. 'You analysing me now? Things must be messed up!'

'I'm only asking, Jack. You've not been yourself recently.'

Harvey shook his head. 'Rowena is great. Rowena is the light.'

'Too good for the likes of you,' Underwood said in mock seriousness.

'Probably.' Harvey thought for a second. 'We all have our problems, John. You had yours. I've got mine.'

'Erectile dysfunction?'

Harvey laughed out loud. 'Not yet!'

'Give it time.'

Harvey let his eyes wander around the busy little pub.

'Ghosts,' he said quietly, ending the topic.

They stayed another hour before the Bolden Arms became too crowded and the noise became too oppressive. It got to Jack first and he suggested an early departure. Underwood agreed and finished his whisky.

'I feel quite pissed,' he said with a tired smile. 'I'm out of practice.'

'Don't forget your keys,' Jack called out as Underwood began to pick his way carefully through the crowd. Underwood raised a hand in acknowledgement and returned to the table. 'Where would I be without you, Jack?'

'Standing out in the street all night,' Harvey observed.

A minute later they were crossing the lane outside the pub to the car park opposite. Despite the soporific effects of the whisky, Underwood noticed that Jack seemed suddenly nervous.

'Scared of the dark, Jack?' he asked playfully.

'Eh?'

'You keep looking around.' Underwood pointed. 'The car's over there.'

'It's nothing.'

Jack beeped his remote locking system and the lights flashed on his new BMW in acknowledgement. Underwood climbed inside. Harvey locked the car from the inside and started the engine.

'Nice motor this,' Underwood observed, 'you been moon-lighting, Jack?'

Harvey steered the car carefully onto the road and turned into the network of country lanes that unwound through Holtskill Forest down into New Bolden.

16

The rain was warm like spit. Stark enjoyed its touch: God was spitting on him. He was used to that.

The station was deserted. Most of the late commuters had hurried away to their brick-box dormitories and the late night minicab drivers had long since flicked away their cigarette ends and relocated to the city centre nightclubs. Stark planned to visit the clubs later. He had a new set of imported pills that were coloured like footballs. They were called '66's' after the world cup victory. The teenage lager brigade would gobble them up. It was fucking smart marketing. The irony was that the pills were made in Germany. Stark found that amusing.

Pills – ecstasy derivatives and speed – were his cash cows. That part of business was starting to do very well. New Bolden had a growing young population with bulging pockets and starved imaginations. The glitz of the London nightclub scene was an hour and a half away by train; too far for the average teenager seeking immediate gratification. In consequence, the clubs in New Bolden were teeming on Fridays and Saturdays and Stark had cornered the market. He supplied a couple of the club owners with coke and other recreationals. In consequence, he got special privileges.

Still, if the club scene paid for the little luxuries in Stark's life, the Car Wash was still a necessary unpleasantness. Behind the train sheds was a disused industrial estate: two hundred acres of low brick buildings with broken windows and deserted forecourts. The Car Wash was sheltered on three sides by the remains of a plastics factory and the derelict offices of a van-hire company. There was only one entrance big enough for cars. Stark liked it that way: less chance of unpleasant surprises.

The Car Wash was well known to local drug-users. Its secluded but easily accessible location made it a favourite. There was also a wide choice of derelict buildings in which to sample Stark's product range. Like any businessman, Stark had his regular clients and despite his developing business in the nightclubs he was too shrewd to desert his core markets. Pills paid for the little luxuries in his life but smack and weed were his bread and butter.

Besides, he had high hopes for the new batch of heroin his supplier in London had recently delivered; top notch smack from Colombia, Jamaica or some other dope factory. Lovely stuff. Even his dead eyed, skull-faced regulars would lose their fucked-up minds over this one. He'd been tempted to try it himself after hearing the rave reviews but he wasn't that stupid: not anymore.

Stark approached the Car Wash through the broken down buildings that had once been RT Plastics. The machines had long since been stripped away and even the glass had been taken from the windows. The derelict premises provided a secure, invisible route to the Car Wash. Stark waited inside the building and stared out intently into the darkened court-yard. He was expecting a couple of punters but none had arrived yet. He pulled up a wooden crate and sat down.

The rain grew heavier and rushed against the corrugated iron roof. Stark cursed quietly. Rain wouldn't deter the smack-heads but it would definitely put off the fair-weather middle class dope fiends. A shape moved outside in the yard. Stark caught his breath and strained his eyes for some point of recognition. The shadow moved closer: it was a man, hunched against the cold and rain. The figure found shelter in a dry corner of the yard and lit a cigarette. Stark recognized the gaunt face that was briefly illumined by the flash of match light.

'Bernie,' he called to the burning cigarette end. The glowing tip turned in Stark's direction and, after a moment of evaluation, moved soundlessly towards him. Stark pushed open what had once been a fire exit from the plastics factory and ushered the shadow inside.

'Jesus, I'm cold,' said the figure.

'You and me both, Bernie.'

Bernie's sunken eyes fixed him for a moment. 'It's different. I'm freezing from the inside out. Thank God for cigarettes.'

'They'll be the death of you, Bernie.'

'Don't make me laugh.'

Stark watched as Bernie reached inside his duffel coat and withdrew a small roll of notes. He placed it between them on the crate. Bernie's hand was small and scarred. It looked like a claw. Stark picked up the cash and counted.

'What's this, then?' Stark waved the roll at Bernie.

'What does it fucking look like?'

'There's forty quid here. That's not even half a measure.'

'So give me half a measure.'

'I don't deal in halves, mate. It ain't worth my time.'

'Course it is. Just cut the stuff.'

'I'm a businessman, Bernie. This is not a bleedin' soup kitchen. A measure is a hundred notes. It's the lowest unit of currency. You've never heard of half of half a "p" have you?'

'It's all money isn't it? Just take the money and give me your shit.'

Stark thought for a second: business was quiet and he doubted whether there'd be many more paydays in Bernie. He didn't normally make exceptions but the poor bastard was half-dead already. He might as well squeeze the last drop of blood out of the stoned.

'All right. Make it fifty quid and I'll sell you half a measure. I'm not gonna lose money over you.'

Bernie pulled a damp tenner from his back pocket and tossed it over. 'That's my dinner.'

Stark smiled as he opened his rucksack and reached inside. 'As a connoisseur, Bernie, you'll appreciate this.' He withdrew a small plastic envelope containing the heroin and handed it over. 'This stuff is vintage.'

'It's probably flour, knowing you.' Bernie snatched the envelope and, coughing horribly, hurried towards the door.

'Pleasure doing business with you,' Stark called out after him.

'Go fuck yourself.' Bernie crashed the door behind him and shuffled out into the rain.

Stark flattened out the five ten-pound notes Bernie had handed over and then inserted them neatly into his wallet.

An hour passed slowly. The rain showed no signs of

abating. Stark was down to his last two cigarettes. This was the shittiest part of the job: the waiting around. Dealing with junkies was miserable enough but waiting for them to appear was downright depressing. At midnight Stark decided to pack up. He called a minicab company on his mobile and arranged to be picked up at the main entrance of New Bolden station. He had fifteen minutes to get there: more than enough time. He was zipping up his rucksack and extinguishing a cigarette when a car's headlights swung into the courtyard.

Stark froze. Not many of his clients drove. It was most likely a squad car. He knew that the New Bolden police did regular drive-bys after dark. He shrank into the shadows and watched carefully. The car stopped directly opposite to his position. It was a Porsche 911. The driver didn't move. Stark peered out from the shelter of RT Plastics. It was odd. Perhaps the driver was looking for prostitutes. The area wasn't the exclusive preserve of druggies. The car door opened and the driver stepped out into the rain and extended his arms upwards towards the heavens as if stretching a troublesome back. He was tall. Beyond that, Stark couldn't determine very much.

The car door slammed. Stark heard the man's footsteps moving around the courtyard. Perhaps he was a client: a lawyer or a young farmer seeking some jollies after a hard day's exploitation. Business was slack – maybe it was worth the risk.

'You looking for someone?' he called at the figure. The footsteps stopped. There was a moment's silence before the darkness replied in a crisp, rasping voice.

'I was told I could buy stuff here.'

'What stuff?' Stark was uneasy but confident in his invisibility.

'You know, syringes, needles, some smack.'

'Who told you that?'

'A bar man at The Feathers. Shaun, I think.'

Stark knew Shaun McBride. He was reliable, a believer. In any case, the man didn't look like a copper.

Stark decided to chance it: one last punt before he hit the

clubs. He climbed out of his hiding place and pushed open the fire exit, walking out into the courtyard. The figure stood before him smiling.

'So what exactly were you after?' asked Stark.

17

Harvey dropped Underwood at his flat just before 11p.m.

Underwood unlocked the door to the small studio he was renting and flopped into an armchair. The flat was pokey and basic: telephone, sofa, armchair, bed, table. He hadn't unpacked his books and his record collection. It wasn't home. He wasn't really there.

He knew he had to occupy his mind until sleep came. The tide began to roll in when he became bored.

Busy.

Underwood looked at the small pile of envelopes on his dining table. The previous evening he had rearranged all his direct debits and bank details. That morning he had written out his shopping list for the month. He was King Canute, running out of ideas.

He decided to transcribe all the numbers saved in his mobile phone to the address pages of his diary. That would fill some time. As he began the task, he realized that there were significantly less numbers than there had been twelve months previously. The completion of his divorce from Julia had revealed the true allegiances of their 'mutual' friends.

Wankers.

Julia hadn't called him for some time now. He knew she was alone, living in Hertfordshire, that she had bought a little cottage, that she had a job in an office. He tried not to let the situation anger him. Julia had left him for a man called Paul Heyer, then promptly left Heyer to be on her own. He still wasn't sure whether he should feel insulted or complimented. He decided to return to his task and fill his mind with numbers. Words were pissing him off. Numbers were inert. Numbers didn't hurt.

Underwood was disappointed that the transcriptions only took him ten minutes. He reassured himself that it was important to keep hard copies of mobile phone numbers; that he had been livid when he had lost his old mobile. Still, he felt pathetic. Particularly so when he noticed that he had entered Dexter's number twice: once under 'Alison' and once under 'Dex.'

Pathetic.

It didn't make it any likelier she would call.

The starkness of the room was getting to him. His life had been cleared of ornamentation and elaboration. These were the bare bones of existence. They were rattling. He was frightened.

Keep busy.

He picked up a copy of the *New Bolden Gazette* and began to flick through the personal ads.

18

Detective Inspector Alison Dexter covered the scars on her wrist with her shirt cuff and stepped out of her Ford Mondeo into the hospital car park. It was late, long after midnight. But Dexter liked to keep busy. Sleep had become an uncomfortable, intermittent experience. Besides, if she was awake, she wasn't dreaming.

DC Jensen was waiting for her at the entrance to Accident & Emergency, her irritating prettiness illuminated by the blue light above the doorway.

'Evening, Guv. Sorry to drag you out.'

'What have we got?' asked Dexter sharply. She didn't like Jensen and had to work hard to disguise the fact, usually unsuccessfully.

'An old friend.' Jensen flipped open her notebook. 'Ian Stark.'

Dexter laughed an empty laugh. 'If I'd known that I'd have stayed in bed.'

'Doctors think he might have taken an overdose.'

'Good,' snarled Dexter. 'Poetic bleeding justice.'

Stark was notorious around New Bolden and well known to Alison Dexter. She had wanted to put Stark away for a long time. She had seen plenty of kids lying in the same A & E ward because of the drugs Ian Stark had sold them. Many of them hadn't come out again.

'What goes around comes around, I suppose,' Jensen added with a tired grin. Dexter noticed that Jensen had heels on. She decided to let the indiscretion go.

For now.

'Let's hope he doesn't make it,' she said.

They walked through the ward. Dexter looked at the usual collection of bloody noses and beer glass stitch-ups. She could hear some drunk shouting gibberish in one of the recovery rooms. She pitied the doctors and nurses. Nights in provincial towns always depressed her: the lager and piss, blood and vomit. The 'wannabe' alpha-males that got absurdly territorial about grotty birds in grotty pubs. It reminded her of tomcats spraying musk to protect their private patch of wasteland.

'So if it's an open and shut,' Dexter questioned her junior officer, 'why am I here?'

'You should probably speak to the doctor,' Jensen replied. 'This one might be a little complicated.'

The shouting was getting louder. It came from the last cubicle, curtained off at the end of the corridor. Dexter looked behind the curtain. Ian Stark lay writhing and screaming in apparent agony on a hospital bed. There were two nurses and a doctor trying to hold him down to prevent injuries. Dexter tried to make sense of Stark's words. It was nonsense; half-sentences and meaningless phrases. It was the product of a scrambled brain. Dexter also noticed there was blood all over Stark's t-shirt and a severe wound to his neck.

An exhausted looking young registrar saw the two police officers and nodded. He turned to the nurses who had finally managed to place Stark's arms in restraints. 'Take him off the Narcan. It's not helping. Keep his arms and legs secure. I'll be back in a second.' He turned and crossed the short distance to Dexter and Jensen. 'Thanks for coming. I'm the registrar – Nicholas Wells.'

'DI Alison Dexter. Tough night?'

Wells nodded. 'He came in about an hour ago. He seemed to be showing symptoms of heroin overdose. We know Ian Stark here. He was one of our regulars until six months ago. I have treated him on previous occasions when he has OD'd.'

'So what's the punchline?' Dexter asked. He was screaming. She no longer found Stark's plight gratifying – the noise was beginning to disturb her.

'The punchline is that I goofed. I gave him a dose of Naxolone. That's the standard procedure.'

'And he started freaking out?' Dexter looked at Stark again. It didn't look like a heroin overdose to her.

'Yep. It's made him worse. His heart will give way unless we can figure out what's going on. I still think he's OD'd but I'm buggered if I know on what. He's in agony and we're not helping.'

'Have you requested blood tests?' Jensen asked.

'Of course,' Wells looked irritated by the question. He brushed sweat from his brow with the sleeve of his white coat, 'but results take time to get in. He might not make it.'

'What about the blood on his shirt?' asked Dexter. 'It looks like he's been stabbed in the neck.'

'That's the other thing,' Wells coughed wearily. 'Someone, possibly Stark himself, has tried to cut his throat.'

Ian Stark was screaming again, burbling something through the waves of pain. Dexter listened to what he was saying. This time she understood the words but they made no sense.

19

He lay back naked on the cold roof. The dried blood on his hands and face was starting to itch. Fallon felt a profound sense of frustration. His attempt to rip order from chaos had been thwarted. His work had been interrupted by drunken voices emanating from the desolate factory buildings. He had not been able to remove the man's head. He tried not to allow his disappointment to translate into anger. The demons came at him mostly when he was angry. The lights were at their most disconcerting when his mind was burning with fury. Instead, Fallon concentrated on the distant lights in the night sky; trying to distinguish stars from planets and trying to draw those planets into the plane of his consciousness.

The moment was approaching. He would bring forth his progeny on earth. The ordered heavens would bear witness.

Relaxing at last, he scratched the black blood from his skin.

20

30th April
The following lunchtime, Alison Dexter sat in her office listening to pathologist Roger Leach's preliminary post-mortem report on Ian Stark. DS Harrison and DC Jensen leaned up against the glass wall of the office. Leach sat in the chair opposite Dexter, flicking through his own notes and the hospital registrar's report on Stark.

'Ian Daniel Stark,' he said. 'Male. Thirty-five years old. Known heroin addict. Admitted to New Bolden Infirmary last night after collapsing outside New Bolden railway station. Suspected overdose. Registrar Dr Nicholas Wells gave him small initial dose of Naxolone at ten-fifty p.m. then repeated the process after patient failed to respond. Naxolone wears off faster than heroin so Wells was probably right to repeat the dosage. He obviously made the assumption Stark was OD-ing.'

'A reasonable assumption given Stark's previous,' muttered Harrison.

'Patient deteriorated,' Leach continued, reading the words without expression, 'screaming, swearing, apparently hallucinating. The hospital started to suspect Stark had been poisoned. They received the results of their initial blood tests at about two a.m. The liver function tests – Prothrombin Time, Aminotransferases and Bilirubin – revealed extremely high levels of amatoxins. The patient finally lost consciousness at two-seventeen a.m.'

'The Accident and Emergency staff injected Stark with four doses of Penicillin G and Silibinin. Both these drugs are designed to inhibit the amatoxins from penetrating the liver cells. Too little too late. Stark died at four a.m. this morning. Cause of death was massive and total liver failure.'

'Goodbye and good riddance,' Harrison added.

'That does seem to be the consensus,' Leach agreed. 'However, there are two problems here.' Leach was getting uncomfortable, aware that Dexter's hard green eyes had been focussed intently on him since he had started speaking. She was like a lion watching from the undergrowth. 'Problem One. The levels of amatoxins in his system were extremely high. Normally, after a severe amatoxin ingestion, liver failure is unlikely to occur within the first twenty hours. This was no ordinary overdose.'

'Evidently,' she replied.

'We are working on a full toxicology report now. Initial findings show very high levels of various toxins: mostly cyclic octapeptides.'

'Come again?' asked Harrison, uncomfortably aware that Dexter was very quiet.

Leach pushed his gold-rimmed glasses back up to the bridge of his nose and squinted at his notes. 'Organic poisons. Amatoxins occur naturally.'

'Where?' Dexter asked sharply, always seeking the angle.

'Most commonly, in poisonous mushrooms.'

71

'Mushrooms?' Dexter couldn't help smiling faintly, 'you're telling me that Stark died from eating magic mushrooms?'

'No. I'm not really. I need to do some checking but the levels of amatoxin found in Stark's system were extraordinarily high. Once I have the full toxicology analysis I'll be able to be more specific.'

'Problem two?' Dexter asked.

'Problem two,' Leach continued, 'the damage to the neck. There is a twelve-centimetre incision on the front, left side of Stark's neck leading from under his left ear to his larynx. Some serious muscular damage. Amazingly none of the major blood vessels was severed.'

'Could the wound have been self-inflicted?' asked Dexter suddenly. 'If he was spaced out on some drug or other might he have tried to top himself?'

'I wondered about that too,' Leach replied, 'but the difficulty is that I think Stark was left-handed.'

'How do you figure that?' Dexter was trying to remember her previous encounters with Stark.

'He was a former addict. Most of the needle track marks – the scars from old puncture wounds – were on the inside of his right arm. That is consistent with a left-handed addict who regularly injected himself.'

Jensen was thinking about the significance of Leach's comments.

'So if he was left-handed,' she raised her own left arm to replicate the necessary movement across her own throat, 'he couldn't have cut himself from left to right.'

'It's unlikely,' Leach concluded.

Dexter sat back in her chair and crushed a yawn. 'Anything else?'

Jensen handed Dexter and Harrison a photocopied sheet. Leach shifted on his plastic seat as Jensen leaned across him.

'I'm sorry, Doc,' said Jensen, 'I only have three copies so you'll have to share with me.'

'No problem,' Leach replied, catching a faint waft of perfume. Perfume was against regulations. Dexter smelled it

72

too. It made the thin line of mascara under Jensen's eyes doubly unforgivable.

Oblivious, Jensen read from the sheet she now shared. 'Items recovered from personal effects of Ian Daniel Stark. Officers present DC Jensen and PC Evans. One wallet (black leather) containing five hundred and sixty pounds; one Nokia 3330e mobile phone (blue). Phone battery appears to be dead. There was thirty pence in change in his jacket pocket and a packet of chewing gum. That's it.'

'Any drugs?' Dexter asked.

'Nothing,' Jensen answered.

'OK,' Dexter had heard enough. 'You'll get us the tox report by tonight, doc?'

'Absolutely.'

Dexter stood and stared out of the window at the blue and white line of parked squad cars and the little square of grass behind New Bolden police station.

'Frankly, Ian Stark was a shit-eel and we are well rid of him. If he died because of his own drugs then so much the better. However, the neck wound makes this our problem. I'm going to check out Stark's flat this afternoon. Jensen, you can drive me.'

Jensen shot a cloudy look across the room at Harrison.

'Harrison. Take a SOCO team and check out some of Stark's old haunts. Start around the station. That's where he turned up bleeding. Aren't there some old factories nearby where all the junkies hang out?'

Harrison nodded. 'The Car Wash. Behind the station. We've picked dealers up there before.'

'Take Marty Farrell,' said Leach. 'He's the most thorough.'

'I know Marty,' Harrison said, 'he's a top man.'

'That's it, then,' Dexter concluded. 'Jensen, can you wait a moment?' The DC took a deep breath and turned to face Dexter as the others left the room. Harrison closed the door softly behind him.

'We keep having this conversation, don't we?' Dexter asked acidly.

'Guv?'

73

'Perfume. Make-up. Heels. Not here. Not on my team. Not ever.'

'Guv, I've hardly . . .'

'You look like a panda. Wash it off.'

Jensen bit her lip.

'Understood.'

'Go and get the motor. I'll meet you out front in ten minutes.'

Jensen passed Harrison on the way out. He had been hovering by the door. He winked at her. She ignored him.

'You don't need to be so hard on her, guv,' Harrison said as Dexter emerged from her office pulling on a waterproof jacket.

'Who asked you?' she shot back.

Harrison was tap-dancing on dangerous ground. He chose his words carefully.

'She's good at what she does.'

'And you'd know all about that,' Dexter snarled. Harrison's relationship with Jensen was common knowledge. No one at the station really cared about it anymore – except Dexter.

'Give her a chance and she might surprise you.'

Dexter resented the imposition and struggled – only half-successfully – to contain her anger.

'This is a police station. We are professionals. Jensen is not a stripogram, she is a CID officer and should make the effort to look like one. Since you've chosen to be defender of the faith maybe you should read the regulations too.'

Harrison mouthed an obscenity at Dexter's back as she left the office.

21

Jack Harvey sat in the consulting room that he had constructed in the extension to his house. He hunched over his computer typing up his conclusions regarding the treatment of John Underwood. His comments formed part of an email message to Chief Superintendent Chalmers at New Bolden Police Station:

'DI Underwood has made significant progress in therapy during the last twelve months.' he took a long drag on his cigar. *'His relapse at the end of 2000 seems largely to have been the product of his marriage breaking up. Underwood was at this time co-ordinating a full-scale murder hunt and seems to have been unable to cope with these combined pressures.*

'He has been receiving prescription anti-depressant medication and attended weekly therapy sessions with myself during the last year.'

There was a knock at his door and Rowena Harvey appeared.

'Hello darling, I'm off soon.'

Jack looked over his shoulder. 'You look fantastic,' he said.

'Hardly! This skirt makes my legs look enormous.'

'That's ridiculous.'

'That cigar stinks, Jack!'

'I'm allowed one vice.'

Rowena Harvey walked across the room and kissed the bald patch on top of her husband's head. 'What are you working on?' she asked.

He turned quickly in his swivel chair and slipped his arm around Rowena's waist, pulling her onto his lap. He gave her a long, hard kiss as she giggled. 'I know what I'd like to be working on,' he whispered.

'Jack! I've just got changed. I'm meeting Petra in ten minutes.'

'It only takes me a couple of minutes!'

'I can't.'

'Spoilsport.'

'When I get home tomorrow!'

'I'll be knackered by tomorrow. Pressure of work. Men of my age have to seize the moment. I might not be able to get it up tomorrow.'

'Now who's being ridiculous?' Rowena pulled away and kissed her husband's forehead. 'I'll be home in the morning.'

Then she was gone.

Jack turned back to his computer screen. The house was quiet now. The window rattled against its frame.

Ghosts.

He tried to concentrate. *'The symptoms and causes of DI Underwood's depression appear to have receded. In my opinion, he no longer poses a physical threat and would benefit from an immediate return to light duties.'*

Harvey looked around his little consulting room. He had an uneasy and powerful sense that he was being watched. His case files lined two walls, filling three bookshelves. Many contained private ghosts and personal horrors, including John Underwood's. Sometimes the ghosts liked to play tricks with him. His telephone rang suddenly. Then stopped. Harvey waited for a moment then continued typing.

'I would recommend a reduction in DI Underwood's consultations to one session every eight weeks. I have also decided to take him off of his course of anti-depressants. DI Underwood is an experienced and skilled officer and can still be an asset to the force.'

That was good enough. The Superintendent knew that Harvey and Underwood were friends. Harvey sensed his report was veering dangerously towards eulogy. He attached the Word file to an email and sent it immediately to Chalmers' office address. Next, he called John Underwood and left him a message on his answerphone.

As he hung up, the telephone rang immediately. He answered.

'Harvey.'

'Is she on her period, Jack?' asked the caller before the line went dead.

Jack Harvey ran to the window and looked outside. There was no one outside: no one visible anyway. His heart was racing. He had recognized the voice.

22

Jensen parked near one of the two central accommodation blocks of the Morley Estate. Dexter surveyed the grim expanse of concrete. It was a desolate place. Two miles northeast of New Bolden, the Morley was familiar to most local police officers. Dexter looked at the graffiti on the building walls, the upturned shopping trolleys and the rubbish that blew aimlessly past the line of steel garage doors. For a second it reminded her of Hackney, or of Broadwater Farm in Tottenham, or of some of the soulless council blocks in Leyton. Desperate.

'Let's get this over with,' she muttered as she opened the car door.

'Even the social workers call this place the "capital of cruelty".' Jensen observed as they approached the optimistically titled 'Hope House'. 'They get more calls out here than to anywhere else in Cambridgeshire.'

'I'm not surprised.' Dexter pressed the call button for the lifts. 'People get brutalized living out here.'

The lift door opened. It smelt of piss.

'There's at least half a dozen animal neglect cases out of this estate every year,' Jensen continued. 'Pig ignorance. Man buys puppy for girlfriend. Puppy gets big. Puppy gets irritating. Man argues with girlfriend. Puppy gets locked in a broom cupboard and forgotten about. Place starts to smell of shit. Neighbours complain.'

'It's a cruel universe.'

'Neglect's worse than outright cruelty, I reckon.'

Dexter said nothing. She knew that it wasn't.

Ian Stark's flat was tidier than Dexter had expected. It was small with one tiny box bedroom and a kitchenette adjoining the main living room. Jensen started checking cupboards. Dexter sat at a small desk and began to riffle through Stark's papers.

Electricity bill, gas bill, mobile phone bill. A five-hundred-pound mobile phone bill.

77

Dexter flicked through its itemized pages. Dealers lived via their mobile phones. It was a potential goldmine finding the bill. Stark's numbers could prove very useful when cross-referenced with the mobile operators' records.

'Nothing here except dirty laundry,' Jensen observed from a small airing cupboard.

'Try the kitchen,' Dexter replied, moving into Stark's bedroom. It smelt stale. There was a poster of a Ferrari taped to a wall with a girl in a bikini draped across the bonnet. On the bedside table Dexter noticed a pile of pornographic magazines and a clod of tissue paper.

'Charming,' she said quietly.

Instinctively, she opened the top drawer of Stark's bedside table. Inside was a Navy blue 2002 diary. She immediately turned to the page showing the previous day: 29th April. It was blank. She smiled to herself – that would have been too easy. Dexter flicked to the back of the diary and found pages of initials and phone numbers. Stark's client list seemed the most likely explanation. There were no full names.

She thought for a moment. What did Stark have lined up for the coming week? 30th April was left blank but there was a single entry for 1st May: 'MW. 2200. MCP. 07911 4112370.'

Dexter started. The number was familiar. She felt a cold hand reach inside her and tear something out.

'Guv, you need to see this,' Jensen called from the kitchen.

Dexter picked up the diary and hurried through into the living room. Jensen had placed a shoebox on the dining table. It contained a small amount of cash and some plastic bags filled with multi-coloured pills.

'What do you reckon they are?' Dexter asked.

Jensen held a bag up to the grey light of the window. 'God knows. 'E's I'd say at a guess. That's what most of the clubs round here specialize in. To be honest, I thought we'd find more than this.'

Dexter didn't agree with Jensen's observation. Stark wouldn't have left his entire stash of drugs in his own flat. He wasn't that stupid. 'Stay here, Sarah. There's something I need to do. I'll call for a team to help.'

'No problem.' Jensen suddenly realized that Dexter had never called her by her first name before.

On her way to the door, Dexter collected the itemized mobile phone bill from Stark's desk. Once outside the flat she ran down the filthy stone steps to the car park and unlocked her Mondeo.

Sitting in the passenger seat, she opened the diary again to 1st May.

'07911 4112370' *stared back at her.*

She turned to the itemized phone bill and ran her right index finger down the list of calls, trying to remain calm.

'07911 4112370' *stared back at her.*

Lastly, she opened the glove compartment of the car and withdrew her personal mobile phone. She selected the 'phonebook' option and scrolled down to 'M'.

'07911 4112370' *stared back at her.*

She sat back in her seat and looked out through the rain-specked windscreen. The sky was darkening outside as the clouds began to thicken overhead. The desolate spaces and litter-strewn alleyways of the Morley Estate stretched around her. In their misery, ugliness and futility Alison Dexter saw that she had been turned inside out.

23

Jack Harvey awoke with a start. He looked at his watch. It was late Just before midnight. He was still in his consulting room. His computer hummed efficiently in front of him. He had a terrible pain in his neck from where he had fallen asleep sitting upright in his chair. Jack tried to blink away his exhaustion.

The front door bell rang again. Just as it had to wake him up ten seconds previously. His immediate thought was of Rowena. Had she returned home early without her keys? Was his wife as forgetful as Underwood? Wearily, Jack rose from his seat and left his consulting room. He flicked off the light as he left and climbed the three steps into the main hallway of his house. It smelt of Rowena's perfume. The smell was reassuring and arousing.

'Who is it?' he called through the door.

There was only silence. Jack peered out through the frosted glass. It distorted his view but he couldn't see anybody outside. He was suddenly nervous and hesitated. He had a decision to make: open the door and find out who – if anyone – was outside, or remain inside and face a night of anxiety starting at every shadow and sound. He chose the former and opened the door. In a second he was engulfed by the wrath of the Soma.

Harvey regained consciousness half an hour later. He was aware of an acute pain across his shoulders. He was lying down on his consulting room table, his wrists tied painfully together beneath it. He strained hard but found that he was unable to move.

Max Fallon tore around the room in a fury. He pulled Harvey's case files down from the shelves and flung them to the floor. He tried to swat the demons from the air around him as they tormented him for his impotence. Paper spread and slid across the floor. Fallon grunted and mumbled obscenities in his frustration. He sat down at Harvey's computer and tried unsuccessfully to log in.

Eventually, he gave up and kicked out furiously at the PC monitor. At his fourth attempt his foot smashed through the glass. He stormed over to Harvey, desperately trying to blink away the lights that swooped and swirled behind his eyes.

'Where is it?' he spat the words at Harvey.

'Where's what? Get me out of here!' Harvey hissed back at him.

'My file. All those banal fucking notes you made during our so-called sessions. I want them now.'

'I destroyed them.'

'Bullshit.' Fallon grabbed Harvey's neck. 'Tell me where they are now!'

Harvey tried to remain calm. He knew Fallon was volatile,

that he was capable of violence. He would try to calm him down.

'Okay! Okay!' Harvey coughed for breath. 'The file isn't here. I keep my private client records elsewhere.'

'I'll bet you do,' Fallon sneered, 'bet the taxman would be interested in your little asides. Does that horny little wife of yours know that all the jewellery that drips off her has been paid for by the manias of the independently wealthy?'

'This has got nothing to do with Rowena.'

Fallon watched him closely for a second then started laughing. He laughed so much it hurt him. He sunk to his knees and crawled out of the room on all fours, tears coursing down his cheeks. He returned two minutes later carrying two large blue cool-boxes. He was still giggling.

Fallon placed the boxes in the middle of the room and pulled up a chair so that he sat close to Harvey's head.

'So how are you feeling, Jack? Still worried about going bald?' he giggled. 'Don't panic. Some women find it sexy apparently. Personally I think it looks bloody awful.'

'Max, you have to let me go.'

'Don't call me that. Don't call me Max. You should know better. I am not your friend, dickhead. Now, what did you write about me in those files?'

'Let me go and we'll talk about it.'

'No. Let's talk now, buddy boy. All those mind-numbing hours I spent in here while you poked at my mind and wondered how to spend my daddy's money. I explained my incarnation to you and you just sat there nodding and disbelieving. I thought that you might have the vision. I thought you might be the sage of the gods. You couldn't diagnose a headache. You did write down lots of things though. Now it's time to deliver. What did they say?'

'If you are a God, you'd already know.'

'You had no clue about me, did you? I bet you sat there writing sexy little notes to Rowena while you were supposed to be helping me.' He leaned in closer and whispered politely in Jack's ear. 'By the way, I'm planning to copulate with her once you're out the way.'

Max exploded into a high-pitched giggle. His saliva spat across Harvey's face. Jack struggled frantically to free his hands.

'I wrote that you had a drug problem,' said Jack, desperately playing for time.

'Brilliant!' Max spluttered through his hysterics. He bent down and opened one of his cool-boxes. 'What extraordinary insight. I know about the drugs. I told you about the drugs. Daddy didn't really get value for money with you did he, Jack?'

'You think that you are becoming some kind of god. You have the same recurring delusional fantasy.'

'Delusional? Hmmm. That's better. Keep going!' said Max as he continued to rummage in his cool-box.

'You're like a scratched record. You keep replaying the same loop in your mind. You have to break the cycle.'

'You still don't accept the notion that I have entered an alternative plane of consciousness: that I have unlocked the memory of my former divinity and translated it into certain knowledge.'

'No, I don't. Your father told me you had a drug problem. He told me you had lost your job after some psychological episode last summer. He believed it stemmed from the loss of your mother when you were a child.'

Max withdrew a clean syringe from the box, one of the twenty he had taken from the pockets of Ian Stark. He also withdrew a medicine bottle that was half-filled with dark cloudy liquid. He opened the bottle and drew its contents carefully into the syringe.

'What the hell is that?' Jack asked, suddenly terrified.

'If you truly understood me, Jack, you'd already know,' Fallon observed, pleased with himself.

'Max, stop this now.'

Fallon was staring at the syringe, mesmerized. 'It's interesting that you called it a drugs problem, Jack. Drugs aren't necessarily the problem. They can be the solution. You prescribe drugs to help people, right? Your sad little patients with manias and neuroses.'

'That's completely different.'

'Did you know that in many ancient cultures, tribal leaders used drugs as part of religious services?'

'Max, we've been through all this. Let me go and I'll promise to help you.'

'The theory is that the drugs activated a certain part of the worshipper's brain. This allowed them to transcend the mundane limits of the imagination, unlock the memories of our former existences and even behold the face of God. Guess what, Jack?' Fallon held the loaded syringe in front of Harvey's terrified eyes. 'Your flight is ready to depart.'

Fallon held Harvey's head steady and injected the contents of the syringe into the psychiatrist's neck.

'Welcome to mass, Dr Harvey. Only a benign God would allow you to take this journey. Only a generous God would let you see his face. Don't be afraid. I will be your guide on your journey to the godhead.'

Half an hour later, as Harvey began to spasm violently on the table, Fallon reached into his cool-box again. This time he removed the power saw he had found in a shed behind his house. Placing the saw on a table, Fallon began to whisper into Harvey's ear. Prompted and petrified, Harvey's mind washed in and out of consciousness. Unguarded, unable to filter Fallon's suggestions from reality, Harvey began to live the nightmare. And he started to scream.

An Unlikely Prophet

24

1st May

The bungalow was neatly arranged and smelt vaguely of lavender. There were lines of photo frames organized on the main mantelpiece. Many contained black-and-white photos, some of men in uniform.

PC Sauerwine sat on the edge of Mary Colson's two-seater sofa. The sitting room was becoming familiar to him now. This was, after all, his third visit in two weeks. His mates at the station thought he was gold-digging, trying to muscle in on the old lady's inheritance. That was harsh, he told himself. Mary was a frightened old age pensioner and part of his job was reassurance. Besides, she cooked a mean egg on toast.

'You spoil me, Mrs Colson,' he called out to the kitchen.

There was no reply. Sauerwine knew that she was slightly deaf, that she watched his lips closely when he spoke. He unclipped his radio and called in.

'Seven-eight-one in attendance at seventeen Beaumont Gardens. Clear in ten minutes.'

'Control to seven-eight-one acknowledged. Make sure you look under the mattress,' squawked the control centre derisively.

Bastards.

'That thing makes a right racket,' said Mary Colson as she shuffled in carrying Sauerwine's breakfast.

Two eggs sunny side up. Slightly overcooked today but no matter.

'You spoil me, Mrs Colson,' he repeated, hoping she hadn't heard the details of the radio message.

'Rubbish,' Mary said as she placed the tray on Sauerwine's lap, 'no one else looks out for me.'

'You've got your carer.'

'She doesn't care about me. Just her filling her fat stomach.'

'Well, with treatment like this, Mrs Colson, I might have to move in with you.'

Mary laughed out loud. 'Whatever would the neighbours think?' She sat painfully in her favourite armchair.

'That you'd got yourself a handsome man in uniform,' Sauerwine quipped, then panicked for a second as he remembered the black-and-white memories on the mantelpiece.

Mary smiled softly. 'It's a nice uniform,' she said.

Sauerwine ploughed into his eggs on toast.

'So,' he said between mouthfuls, 'these yobs who woke you up. What were they up to this time?'

'There were four of them. Gypsies,' Mary pointed out of the front window, 'gadding about like idiots setting off fireworks. Four in the morning. Bloody cheek.'

'I doubt they were gypsies, Mrs C, not in this neighbourhood.'

'They looked like gypsies,' she insisted.

'Caravans and campfires?'

'Don't you be cheeky. I know what I saw.'

'Did they wake you up, then?' Sauerwine asked sympathetically.

'I was awake.' Mary reached for a bottle of pills that sat on the coffee table. 'They're for my Parkinson's. They make me pee all night.'

'I'm sorry.' Sauerwine suppressed a smile.

'And they give me funny dreams.'

'Involving dashing young policemen?'

'You are a naughty boy,' said Mary. 'No. They give me nightmares if you must know.'

'What kind of stuff?' Sauerwine sipped his cup of tea wondering what eighty-eight-year-old women had nightmares about.

Mary looked uncomfortable for the first time. 'You know about me, don't you?'

'Know what?'

'About my abilities.'

Sauerwine frowned for a second then he remembered

88

something that one of his colleagues had told him about Mary.

'Oh yeah!' he remembered. 'You read fortunes and things.'

Mary looked a little hurt. 'It's more complicated than that. I used to do séances.'

'Like a medium?'

'Yes. I stopped after I made an old man scream.'

'How?'

'I told him his dead wife was watching us through the kitchen window.'

Sauerwine choked on his tea in amusement.

'It's not funny,' Mary rebuked. 'She was.'

'I'm sorry, Mrs C.' Sauerwine coughed to clear his throat. 'So what's all this got to do with your nightmares?'

'I'm not sure. It scares me, though.'

'It?'

'It's the same nightmare.'

'Tell me.'

Quietly, Mary Colson described what she called the 'dream of the dog-man.'

'Spooky,' Sauerwine conceded. He was beginning to get the picture. A frightened old lady has recurring nightmare, calls handsome young copper for reassurance. 'Don't worry about it, Mrs C. Dreams are dreams. They don't come true. It's like all that astrology crap. Everyday the newspaper promises me that something big is about to happen, that I'm about to meet someone special, that my life is going to change. I'm still here though. Plodding along like a carthorse. I don't see how Mars and Jupiter will help me win the lottery.'

'This is an important week astrologically as it happens,' Mary sniffed. 'I was reading about it: five planets of the solar system come into alignment.'

'Let me guess. The end of the world?'

'I hope not. It's supposed to be good for fertility.'

'Sadly that's not a big issue for me at the moment, Mrs C. The future Mrs Sauerwine has yet to make herself known.'

Mary seemed distracted by something and was staring into the space behind Sauerwine.

'Not in my experience,' Sauerwine continued. 'I used to dream of playing for Arsenal and look at me . . .'

'Do you know anyone called Christine or Christy?' Mary asked suddenly, cutting across him.

'I'm sorry?'

Mary frowned into the space. She seemed to be looking for something, sorting through the white noise in her head. 'Christine or Christy,' she whispered, 'one of the voices.'

Sauerwine felt very uncomfortable. The boys at the station would have a field day if they found out about this. Suddenly his radio squawked. It made him jump.

'Control to mobile. Fire brigade request assistance. Twenty-two Moorsfield. Possible fatality. Officers in transit.'

'They don't like the radio,' said Mary admonishingly, 'or mobile phones.'

Sauerwine stood quickly and drained the last drops of his tea. Moorsfield was only five minutes away. 'Gotta go, Mrs C. Duty calls.'

Mary wasn't listening. 'She's gone now. She had a message for you.'

'For me?'

'She's very proud of you.'

'You take care now,' Sauerwine called back as he opened the front door, 'thank you for my breakfast!'

Mary picked up a puzzle book. Sometimes it helped to blot out the whispering.

Sauerwine jogged down the front steps to his squad car. He knew Moorsfield well enough: smart, upper-middle-class housing. He rehearsed the route in his head as he started the engine and pulled away. *'Out of Beaumont Gardens, left onto Wallis Avenue down to Morton's roundabout, straight over then left at the lights . . .'*

At the junction of Beaumont Gardens and Wallis Avenue, Sauerwine slammed on his brakes and looked back at the square bungalow with its sad, scrap of grass and white net curtains. His own grandmother had died five years previously. Her maiden name had been Hannah Christian.

25

The call had come through at 7.45a.m. That was the way with Alison Dexter, Underwood had thought at the time, not 7.44 or 7.46. Their conversation had been brief and unsettling. Underwood had dressed rapidly and driven like a maniac to 22 Moorsfield; Jack Harvey's home address. He arrived seconds behind PC Sauerwine's squad car.

The house seemed pretty much intact and any flames had been extinguished. However, a dense black cloud of smoke hung over the street and, as he approached, Underwood could see serious flame damage to the Harveys' front door and extension. His stomach curled into a tight knot of anxiety. Two fire engines were parked at the front of the house. Instinctively, Underwood headed for the squad car parked behind the fire trucks.

Dexter saw him coming and waved him through the blue 'Police Line' tape that had sealed off the entrance to the Harvey's driveway.

'Hello, Dex,' he said, happy for a second to be caught once again in her green-eyed gaze.

'Good to see you, Guv.' She didn't have time to correct her error – Underwood wasn't 'Guv' anymore. 'I wish it could have been under happier circumstances.'

'Any more inside?' Underwood already sensed the worse.

'Wife wasn't. Staying with a friend. She's on her way over.' Dexter hesitated. 'She says Jack was there last night.'

'He was,' Underwood nodded, 'he called me. Left a message.'

'I'm sorry. Fire boys say there's a body in the office. Sir, there's some weird shit going on here.'

She was interrupted by a shout from the front of the house. A fireman was gesturing them over. Dexter ducked under the cordon. Underwood hesitated.

'Chief Super called me at home last night. They are putting you back on light duties, sir.'

'Stop calling me that, Dex,' Underwood retorted.

Dexter looked at him, half-frustrated and half-pitying. 'I'd appreciate your help,' she said simply.

'I'm not sure this constitutes "light duties".'

Dexter had run out of patience. 'Let's go.' She approached the fireman who had called them over. Underwood followed a step or two behind.

'What's the story?' Dexter asked.

'It's safe to go in,' the fireman wiped sweat away from his face with the cuff of his jacket, 'but be careful. The office is the first door off the hallway on the right. It's burned to buggery but what you need to see is in there.'

'Understood.' Dexter thought for a moment. 'Any idea yet on when the fire started?'

The fireman shrugged. 'We got the call at five thirty-eight. An hour, forty minutes before that maybe. It definitely started in the office, though. Have a chat with our boss man when you get out. I'll let him know.'

'Thanks.' Dexter pushed past him into the gloomy hallway. Water dripped from the walls. Steam and smoke hung in the air clagging her throat. She caught another sudden and sickening smell of burnt meat. Underwood retched suddenly.

The office was a desecration. The floor was covered with charred remains of Harvey's box files and patient records. Underwood wondered if his own neuroses and nightmares had been incinerated with everyone else's. He tried not to look at the blackened mess in the centre of the room that used to be Jack Harvey. Dexter approached the body carefully. 'We need the SOCOs in here now.'

Underwood nodded but remained at the door.

'Bloody hell,' said Dexter suddenly.

'What is it?' Underwood still couldn't bring himself to focus on the burnt lump that had once been his friend.

Dexter paused and tried to understand what her eyes were telling her. She crouched carefully and looked at Harvey's hands, still tied together under the table. She stood and turned to face Underwood. 'The head's missing,' she said through dry lips.

At last Underwood forced himself to look at the body. He was transfixed in shock and morbid revulsion.

'Someone tied him up, John.' Dexter continued trying to figure the situation out for herself. 'Someone has tied him up and cut his head off.'

'Get a proper forensic team in here now,' said Underwood, already halfway out of the room.

Dexter looked back at the body. The morning sun was shining through the heat-shattered window frame. Something caught her eye. Something glinted amongst the ash and rubbish on the floor next to the burned table and its hideous cargo. She looked more closely. There were three ten-pence coins neatly aligned on the floor. She resisted the urge to pick them up.

Underwood stood at the front of the house trying to rationalize what he had just seen. Something was gnawing at him. Something other than the loss of his friend and the terrible scene he had just witnessed. He felt as if he was missing something obvious, or that something obvious was missing.

'No one goes in there,' he said as Dexter rejoined him, 'except our people.'

'Absolutely.' Dexter considered the faces of the nearest group of uniformed officers. She needed a face she could rely on. 'Sauerwine! Get your arse over here.'

PC Sauerwine broke off his conversation with one of the firemen and hurried over to join them.

'Stay by the door,' instructed Dexter. 'No one is allowed in except the SOCOs from now on.'

'Yes, sir. I mean ma'am.' Sauerwine seemed agitated. 'Is it true that the body has no head?'

'Bad news travels fast,' Underwood observed darkly.

'Sorry, sir,' said Sauerwine as he turned to face Underwood, 'the fireman told me.'

'Keep it to yourself,' Dexter ordered the constable.

'Of course. Ma'am, this is going to sound strange. Could I possibly see the body?'

'Why, for Christ's sake?' Dexter was starting to regret calling Sauerwine over.

'I've had a weird morning, ma'am. It might be important.'

Dexter exchanged a glance with Underwood who shrugged.

'All right,' she said, 'stick your head around the door if you must but don't go into the office. Only the SOCOs go in there. What you see stays with you,' Dexter warned. 'Jack Harvey was one of us and he was a gent. I don't want to hear any bullshit jokes about the poor bastard at the station. If I do, I will have your bollocks rattling in my desk drawer.'

'I understand.' Sauerwine started for the door.

Dexter put her hand on Underwood's shoulder. 'You okay?'

'A bit freaked.'

Dexter hunted for the right words. 'John, what's left in there, that isn't Jack. Jack's gone. What's left behind doesn't mean shit.'

Underwood smiled faintly. He appreciated the effort. 'You've got things to do, Dex. I'll stay out of the way.'

'I'd appreciate any suggestions.'

Underwood watched her go. Dexter the dynamo was already throwing off sparks. He had missed her energy. He wondered if she was right. Whether what had been left behind really did lack any meaning. Do we cease to have meaning as soon as our heart stops beating? That seemed too simplistic. That made the matter merely an issue of timing and emphasis. Maybe we cease to have meaning the second we are born. That was simply another point on the same timeline.

Underwood knew he was a concentration of different pasts trapped in the present. Dexter was wrong. What gets left behind does have meaning. It has meaning because other people have to carry the burden with them. If that burden changes them, weakens or strengthens the carrier, then it also serves to redefine the present. There is no escaping the past. It has a stranglehold on us all.

Underwood started as Sauerwine re-emerged from the house. The young constable looked pale and shaken, his face drained of blood.

'Had your fill?' Underwood asked bitterly.

'It's pretty grim, sir.'

'It was my friend.'

'Sir, I really need to speak with Inspector Dexter.' Sauerwine shifted nervously.

'Why?'

'It's probably nothing.'

'Look son, Inspector Dexter is organizing a scene-of-crime investigation. Unless you have something important to say, I suggest you keep your head down and do what she asked you to do. Namely, guard the entrance to the office.' Underwood sensed something unusual in the constable's manner. The lad was shaken and clearly had something to say. Underwood paused for a second, considering his options. He decided to take the swallow dive.

'Tell me.'

Sauerwine looked surprised. 'Are you back with us then, sir?'

'Light duties. Counselling young officers could conceivably come under that heading I suppose.'

Sauerwine decided to risk humiliation: better to be battered by DI Underwood than castrated by DI Dexter. 'Sir, I've just come from an old lady called Mary Colson. She lives nearby.'

'Make your point.'

'Sir, if you'd asked me to describe what was in that office, I could have done so without looking.'

'You are talking in riddles, constable.'

'Mary Colson is a kind of fortune teller, a sort of amateur psychic. Palm readings, séances and stuff. Sir, an hour ago, she told me about a recurring nightmare that she has been having. People get their heads cut off.'

'Old ladies dream about death, constable. We all do.'

'Sir, she told me about people with their hands tied under a table.'

Underwood began to focus through the fog of his scepticism. 'What else did she say?'

'Lots, sir, mad stuff. She talks about a dog-man killing people.'

'A dog-man?'

'I know it sounds ridiculous but the way she described it was just like that fucking room.'

Underwood could see Sauerwine was upset. He relented

95

slightly. 'You do realize that this could make us look like total muppets?'

'Sir, she told me my dead grandmother wanted to speak to me. She got her name right, sir – almost – it freaked the shit out of me.'

Underwood thought for a moment. He needed to keep busy. Dexter was unlikely to let him get too involved in the organization of the investigation. Moreover, he needed to get away from the ruination of Jack Harvey. Perhaps he had come back too quickly. Terrible images were starting to flash up at him: monsters were starting to step off the escalator of his consciousness. Jack Harvey had evidently told the Chief Super that he was fit for duty. Perhaps it would be fitting to try and prove Jack right. Defy the malevolent gods.

'I'll speak to her,' he said eventually, 'give me the address.'

Sauerwine scribbled Mary Colson's details on a piece of notepaper.

'Okay. Listen to me,' Underwood immobilized Sauerwine with a fierce look, 'this stays with us. Half the force thinks I'm stark raving bonkers already. If it gets out that I'm investigating a murder by hassling old ladies, I might as well drive straight to the Job Centre. You stay here, do what Inspector Dexter asked you to do and keep your gob shut.'

'Yes, sir,' Sauerwine nodded. The weight had lifted.

Underwood walked briskly up the Harveys' drive. He could see Dexter embroiled in a conversation with two firemen. He decided to leave her alone and crossed between the two fire engines to get back to his car. Dexter saw him leave. So, from a safe distance, did a malevolent god.

26

New Bolden Council paid Doreen O'Riordan to make day visits to the OAPs on its care list. She ensured that the 'crumblies' as she called them ate regular meals and took their prescribed medication. It was poorly-paid work but it had its benefits and Doreen had learned exactly how to exploit them.

'You're getting fatter,' Mary Colson observed as Doreen placed a tray of tea and toast in front of her.

'Thank you, Mary, thank you so much,' said Doreen through gritted teeth. *I'll live a lot longer than you, though,* she thought.

'It's no wonder you can't find a man, looking like that,' Mary said disingenuously.

'The last thing I need is someone else to cook and clean for,' Doreen snarled, 'and since we're on the subject, you pissed all over the toilet floor again.'

Mary smiled.

'It's disgusting. There's no excuse for it,' Doreen continued bitterly, 'I shouldn't have to mop up your mess when you are quite capable of getting it into the pan. It's just laziness. You should have more self-respect.'

Mary looked down at the tray: two rounds of burnt toast and a cup of tea. 'I've had my breakfast already,' she said helpfully, 'you needn't have bothered.'

Doreen felt a wave of cold hatred crawl through her congested veins. 'You have to eat breakfast at nine o'clock in the morning. That's when you are meant to take your pills.'

'It's the pills that make me piss the toilet,' Mary replied.

Doreen sighed a frustrated sigh and returned to the kitchen. She lit a cigarette and took a long, inelegant drag.

'Don't you smoke in my house,' Mary called from the living room.

'Get stuffed,' Doreen muttered. She was hungry and looked around the little kitchen for sustenance. Doreen knew that Mary had a box of fudge. She also knew that the old bitch was getting better at hiding it. This time, it took Doreen nearly ten minutes to find it, stuffed inside the microwave oven that Mary never used. She opened the box and took a handful of fudge delighting in the way its hard edges softened to goo in her mouth.

'What are you doing?' Mary called through.

'Eating your fudge!' Doreen replied through a thick, sweet mouthful.

Mary was upset. 'You leave that fudge alone, fatty! That was a present.'

'From your policeman fancy man – I know. So you keep telling me.'

'You're too fat already,' Mary shouted in impotent fury.

Doreen gave Mary the finger from behind the kitchen wall. 'You can't eat it anyway. It's got nuts in remember?' Doreen spat back.

'It was a present,' said Mary sadly.

Doreen took a deep breath. Sometimes it was hard not to walk through and strangle the old bitch. Still, there were other forms of vengeance. First, she collected the money and shopping list that Mary had left for her. Then she placed the remains of the fudge back into the microwave and set it to cook for ten minutes. As she pressed the 'start' button, and Mary's fudge began to absorb 750 watts of radiation energy, the front doorbell rang.

'I'll get it,' said Doreen, walking through the living room. 'I'm on my way out.'

'Good,' Mary replied.

Doreen opened the front door.

'I'm looking for Mary Colson. I'm from New Bolden police.' John Underwood held up his ID for Doreen to inspect.

'What's she done now?' said Doreen with a nervous laugh: policemen made her edgy. 'I'm her carer – Doreen O'Riordan.'

'Who is it?' Mary Colson squinted out into the corridor.

'Another policeman, Mary.' Doreen touched Underwood's arm. 'Will you be needing me, officer? I was off to buy her shopping.'

'You're fine,' Underwood replied.

'I'll be off then.' Doreen left the house as Underwood stepped inside. He walked through the small hallway into Mary's living room and for a brief second took stock of the tiny, grey-haired woman huddled inside a red cardigan.

'Hello, Mrs Colson. I'm from the police. There's nothing to be alarmed about.'

'I know,' said Mary, 'you've got a kind face.'

'You're the first person that ever said that! Do you mind if I sit down?'

Mary studied her guest with keen eyes. 'You met Fatty Arbuckle, then?'

Underwood sat on Mary's sofa. 'Your carer?'

Mary laughed. 'I don't think anyone cares about me less!'

'Why do you say that?'

'She's a fat bitch. She steals my housekeeping money. She thinks I'm an idiot. That I can't add up. But I'm not stupid. I keep records. I've got her number all right.'

Underwood was concerned. He hated to see people being taken advantage of. 'Would you like me to have a word with her?'

'You know, sometimes she turns all my photographs face down on the mantelpiece. Just so I have to put them all up again. What kind of a person would do a thing like that?'

Underwood made a mental note about Doreen O'Riordan. 'Mrs Colson, I need to talk with you. It's about something you told Constable Sauerwine this morning.'

'He gave me some fudge last week,' said Mary, 'that fat cow's been eating it.'

'You told him about a dream you've been having. Do you remember? You said it was a nightmare.'

Mary suddenly became concerned, quiet.

'Why would you want to know about that? Something's happened, hasn't it? Sometimes my dreams come true you know. I can see things. I hear things too. The voices are around us all the time. I'm like a radio, I suppose! I tune in and out. Did he tell you?'

'Something did happen today, Mrs Colson. PC Sauerwine saw it and said it reminded him of your dream: of the things you described to him.'

'Well, I'm blowed.' Mary's eyes suddenly flashed with concern. 'Is he all right?'

'He's a bit upset, but he's fine. Could you tell me what you told him? Tell me about your dream.'

Mary's eyes flicked up at the ceiling as she extracted the nightmare from her memory. 'It's a sequence of images, really. A big, old house. A field underwater. There's screaming. A woman screaming. The screaming is the worst part of it. It gets worse and worse.'

'What else?'

'There's a man tied to a table and a big pile of bodies under a . . .'

'The man on the table,' Underwood interrupted, 'tell me about him.'

'He's tied to a table but his head is in a box.'

'How is he tied to the table?' Underwood asked.

'A rope I think,' Mary frowned. 'I can't remember.'

Underwood looked at his notebook. Harvey had been tied with masking tape. 'Were his feet tied up, in your dream?'

Mary shook her head. 'No. His hands are tied beneath him under a table.'

'What else?'

'His head is in a box.'

Underwood felt the hairs on the back of his neck stand up. He could see why Jack's dead body had freaked out Sauerwine. 'What about this pile of bodies you mentioned?'

Mary rubbed her eyes. 'It's just that, a pile of bodies. All of their heads are missing.'

'How many bodies?'

'Lots, I don't know.'

'A hundred? Two?'

'Five or six. I don't know. Maybe more, it's hard to say.'

'Where is this pile of bodies?'

'Outside. There's always children playing nearby. I can hear them shouting and laughing. And I want to shoo them away. But they keep getting closer to this horrible mess.'

Underwood was writing down as much as he could in his notebook. Elements of the dream certainly reminded him of Jack's death but much of it seemed vague and he was uncer-

100

tain whether any of it would be useful: even if Mary Colson did have some strange psychic power.

'Did he tell you about the dog-man?' Mary asked.

'Not really.'

'The dream always ends the same way. When the dog-man appears. He's horrible. He always wakes me up.'

'I don't understand. What is a dog-man?'

'He's got the face of a man. And the face rises from the ground until it's right over me. But his body is made of dogs.'

'What does this man's face look like?'

'Like a tramp. Dirty.'

'You said his body is made of dogs?' Underwood was beginning to feel rather ridiculous and had stopped making notes.

'It's like he's wearing a wedding dress. It sweeps down and away from him but the dress is made of dogs.'

Underwood really wanted to give Mary the benefit of the doubt. He realised that if Dexter had heard the old lady's comments she would have packed up her stuff, bitten her lip and left a long time ago. It was all too vague. Crazy nonsense. Sauerwine was correct to mention it but Underwood could not escape the conclusion that he had been wasting his time.

'Do you mind if I get a glass of water, Mrs Colson?' he asked.

The old lady nodded and Underwood walked through to the kitchen. As he filled a flower-patterned glass with tap water and took a glug, the microwave oven beeped three times indicating the end of its cooking cycle. He opened it and saw the liquid remains of Mary's fudge drip out on to the work surface. He felt a cold stab of fury and mopped away the worst of the mess with a tea towel.

On returning to the room Underwood looked more closely at Mary Colson: her eyes were closed and her head was tilted slightly to one side. Her face was screwed up into tight lines of concentration.

'Mrs Colson, can I ask you about Doreen O'Riordan?'

'Shush!' she raised an admonishing finger, 'there's somebody with us.'

101

Underwood felt a bead of sweat trickle down under his shirt collar. The flat felt suddenly stuffy. He wanted to leave.

'Who?' he asked.

'Shush! There's so many voices. It's hard to understand. It's these silly tablets I have to take. It's difficult to focus.'

Underwood noticed the bottle of pills next to the armchair. He wondered if Mary Colson had any idea what was going on.

'The man who died today,' she said quietly, 'he was your friend.'

Underwood felt his heart flutter. 'Yes, he was.'

Mary nodded. The raised finger still told Underwood to keep quiet.

'He's saying something,' she said.

'Where is he?' Underwood asked.

Mary opened her eyes. 'Standing right behind you.'

Underwood stood sharply and looked around the empty room.

'He's saying something.' Mary's lips moved silently, as if reciting a prayer.

Underwood remained standing a few feet away: suddenly unsure of himself.

'What's he saying?'

Mary seemed to relax in her chair and her eyes, previously unseeing, located Underwood.

'He said "don't forget the keys".'

Underwood stared at her in horrified silence. It was one of the last things Jack Harvey had said to him.

27

Three miles away, Rowena Harvey sat in shock in the back of an ambulance, her face streaked with tears. Dexter watched her closely. Rowena Harvey was a beautiful woman, much younger than Jack. Was there an angle here? Dexter wondered. Was Rowena Harvey playing them? Had she been humping some tennis coach or her aerobics instructor? Should she check Jack Harvey's life insurance policy for any irregularities or recent amendments?

Dexter suddenly remembered the brutalizing of Jack's body and cursed her own suspicious nature. It was too ridiculous to contemplate. Still, Rowena Harvey was an attractive woman. Dexter couldn't help but picture her in widow's black and for a single, surprising second imagined tasting Rowena Harvey herself.

Mad shit. Concentrate.

Jensen emerged from the back of the ambulance.

'Anything?' Dexter asked. *Back to business, Alison.*

'She stayed with a friend last night. Jack called her about ten-thirty to say good night. It checks out. She showed me her mobile.'

'Who is the friend?'

'Petra Longley.'

'The magistrate?'

'The one and only.'

Dexter knew the fearsome Petra Longley well. 'So much for my maniac boyfriend theory then.'

'Mrs Harvey wants to go and stay with her parents in Diss. She's in a bad way. Can we allow it?'

Dexter nodded. 'Take her yourself. She's not much use here. Try to get her talking in the car. Do it gently. See if she knows anything about Jack's patients, stuff he was working on recently.'

'Will do.'

'Call me if you get anything.'

Dexter turned away and headed over to Marty Farrell. One of the senior SOCOs, Farrell was engaged in an earnest conversation with Steve Polk of Cambridgeshire Fire Brigade.

'What have you got, Marty?' Dexter asked briskly.

'Early days, guv.' Farrell's restrained manner always had a calming effect. 'The body will be removed in the next hour. No sign of the head, though.'

'The president's brain is missing!' commented Steve Polk with a grin.

Dexter rounded on him. 'Stow it. He was a mate.'

Farrell interceded diplomatically, 'Steve and I were talking about the fire. How it was started, right, Steve?'

Polk took a deep breath and decided to be professional. 'Fire started in the office – that's clear from the pattern of heat damage. It's a guess at this stage but I would say the arsonist, the murderer, used an inflammatory fluid to get things going. Lighter fuel looks likely. Lots of paper in there – woof.' He mimicked a fire exploding to life with his hands.

'The weird thing, though, is that there isn't a single local source for the fire within the room,' Farrell added.

'I don't understand,' Dexter admitted.

'Usually, an arsonist will kindle a fire in say one corner of a room,' Polk explained. 'You know, a pile of paper or a rag soaked in paraffin, right?'

'Right,' Dexter agreed.

'Well, in this instance, it looks like the arsonist stood in the middle of the room spraying the fuel all around him. Then started chucking matches until one of them ignited the fuel.'

'Why do you say that?' Dexter asked.

'The centre of the room is the least damaged,' Farrell explained, 'and we've found matches lying around the edge of the room – lots of them.'

Polk took over. 'It's like a normal fire but in negative. Your average arsonist localizes a flashpoint then does a runner. This guy filled a room with fuel and started chucking lighted matches about.'

Dexter was beginning to see their point. 'You mean he wanted to be in the room when it all started to go up.'

'Yeah. It's like after he chopped the bloke's head off he wanted to be surrounded by fire. It can be quite hypnotic, watching flames crawl up walls, therapeutic even.' Polk was anxious to restore his credibility with DI Dexter who he had decided was a wriggler.

Dexter was only half-listening. She had remembered the knife wounds on Ian Stark's neck as he lay screaming in

Accident and Emergency two nights previously. Finding a quiet place, away from the fire trucks and the hubbub of the investigation, she called Roger Leach.

28

DC Jensen hammered the squad car out of New Bolden and quickly picked up the A11. The drive to Diss would take her no more than half an hour: A11 to Thetford then the A1066 to Diss.

Doddle.

She watched Rowena Harvey in the driver's mirror. The tears had stopped and she was staring, in stunned silence, at nothing in particular. Jensen remembered Dexter's instructions and decided to ask some questions.

'Mrs Harvey, I have to ask you something.'

Rowena Harvey stared blankly at her.

'Was your husband in any trouble? You know, did he have any financial problems?'

No response.

Jensen battled on. 'Had he been under any pressure recently? Any strange phone calls or visitors to the house? Anything unusual at all?'

Rowena Harvey was staring at her wedding ring as if trying to remember what it was. Jensen decided to lay off. It was a waste of energy.

'He was sad,' said Rowena quietly and suddenly.

'Sad?' Jensen resisted the urge to look over her shoulder. 'Do you know why?'

Rowena Harvey shook her head slowly. Jensen tightened her grip on the steering wheel.

Behind them, the incarnate Soma kept a watchful distance from inside the light show. He increased the intensity of his masturbation as the squad car turned left out of Thetford onto the A1066 and ejaculated into the empty crisp packet he had kept handy. He wiped himself and dropped it onto the already litter-covered floor of his Land Cruiser.

Jensen accelerated as the A1066 opened up between Thetford and Diss. Rowena Harvey had drawn her tanned knees up in front of her and sat huddled on the back seat. The car flashed past a couple of stud farms and then out into open countryside. A red triangular traffic sign warned of a sharp right turn ahead and Jensen began to decelerate. Suddenly she noticed the Land Cruiser that had filled her back window.

'What is this guy's problem?' she asked herself.

The Land Cruiser swung out to the right of the squad car and drew alongside. The bend loomed thirty yards ahead of them. Jensen slammed on her brakes as the two vehicles ran two abreast. Then, in a sudden and brutal movement the Land Cruiser swung into the driver's side of the squad car. Taken off guard, Jensen lost control. The steering wheel slipped through her hands and the car careened off the road, smashing with sickening force into a stone wall. Rowena Harvey was flung between the two front seats, hitting the dashboard in front of the gear stick. Jensen was thrown forward into the driver's side airbag then felt her neck whiplash as it was wrenched forward then back, smashing against the headrest.

Jensen was nauseous, struggling to retain consciousness. She was dimly aware of Rowena Harvey lying across the gear stick, her head wedged against the dashboard. She was also dimly aware of the green lights of the Land Cruiser reversing back towards her.

Ten minutes later a coach driver called Suffolk police and reported the wrecked squad car. It was empty.

29

At 9p.m. that evening, Underwood crept into the back of a packed incident room at New Bolden police station. A couple of heads turned at the sound of the closing door and registered their surprise. Underwood had not been inside the station for over a year. It felt strange to him: like the first day of school. Alison Dexter and Roger Leach nodded their acknowledgement: nobody else did.

'Let's get started,' Dexter announced loudly and crisply. The conversation ended abruptly. 'Most of you know what happened to Jack Harvey. You should also know that DC Jensen and Mrs Harvey are missing. Their car was wrecked outside Diss. No trace of them was found at the crash site.'

Underwood started. He hadn't known about the car crash. Clearly he wasn't fully back in the loop. Suddenly, he remembered what had been troubling him about Jack Harvey's office.

Dexter continued briskly, 'Jensen's car was found on the A1066. Uniform are sweeping the area, doing house to house enquiries, stopping traffic. So far we've got nothing. I don't believe in coincidence. It's fair to assume that whoever killed Jack Harvey has got Jensen and Mrs Harvey.'

There was a ripple of anxious conversation. Dexter didn't mind. She wanted them anxious. Anxious got results. Dexter shot a quick look at Harrison. His face was expressionless.

'Bearing in mind what happened to Jack,' Dexter announced, 'that makes it pretty bloody urgent we turn up something here quickly.'

Underwood watched the grey skies beyond the window. He remembered Jack Harvey's office – the little consulting room where he had laid back and opened the black box of his depression; the little consulting room with its cluttered shelves and crowded desk; the little consulting room with its large portrait photograph of Rowena Harvey hanging above the computer. The photograph hadn't been there when Underwood and Dexter had seen Jack's body.

The killer wanted Rowena Harvey.

'There's a lot of mad shit going on here,' Dexter was saying, 'and the murder of Harvey appears to be connected with the death of Ian Stark two nights ago.'

Underwood had often stared at Rowena's photograph during his sessions with Jack. Fantasizing, imagining himself

107

with her. Had the killer sat in the consulting room too, looking at the same picture, indulging his fantasies? Underwood looked sadly at the back of DS Harrison's head two rows in front of him. He knew DC Jensen was dead.

Roger Leach had risen to his feet. 'Two corpses in forty-eight hours. Ian Stark, the local drug dealer and thug, died at the Infirmary at 4a.m. on Saturday morning.'

Underwood withdrew a notebook from his jacket pocket. It was an old habit and one that he had neglected. Still, he thought, in his new regime of stable mental structures it seemed like a worthwhile discipline to restore.

'As DI Dexter says, the deaths are connected,' Leach continued. 'The details are unusual so I suggest you write them down.'

Underwood smiled. He hadn't been ahead of the game for over a year.

'There are three important similarities between the incidents. One. Infliction of severe damage to neck. The cuts on Stark's neck suggest he was attacked with something like an axe or a meat cleaver. He received serious muscular tissue damage but the wound was not fatal. Jack Harvey's head was severed completely. This time the pattern of tissue and bone damage suggests the killer used an electric saw. Something like a DIY power saw.'

'Bloody hell,' said Harrison softly. He was finding it hard to focus. His thoughts inevitably drifted back to Jensen. *Concentrate.*

'Similarity two. This is the clincher. We have now run full toxicology profiles on Stark and Harvey. The results are extraordinary but remarkably similar.'

'Specifics?' Dexter asked.

'Both victims have extremely high levels of organic toxins called amatoxins and phallotoxins in their bloodstreams. This is what caused the death of Ian Stark and would probably have killed Jack Harvey too if he hadn't also received fatal physical injuries. These poisons interfere with protein synthesis once ingested. This means that cells with particularly high rates of protein synthesis are most vulnerable to damage: particularly cells in the liver and kidneys. Enzyme levels increase within the liver. Glutamate oxalacetate transaminase and lactate dehydrogenase increase in concentration and lesions develop in the liver itself. This invariably leads to coma and liver failure. That's how Ian Stark died.'

Underwood was struggling to keep up. The complex terminology had confused him.

'The most likely sources of these toxins are poisonous fungi. Magic mushrooms for want of a better term. I have been in contact with someone called Adam Miller. He works at the University Botanical Gardens in Cambridge. According to him toxicology profiles suggest poisoning with a combination of Amanita Virosa and Amanita Muscaria mushrooms. The difficulty with this thesis is that the levels found in the victims greatly exceed those found in these particular fungi.'

'How great is the anomaly?' asked Underwood suddenly from the back of the room.

'As I understand it, we are talking about toxins levels four or five times greater than occur in individual mushrooms. I've arranged for Inspector Dexter to meet Dr Miller tomorrow so he can give us a better picture. Also, no traces of the fungi were found in the victim's stomachs or intestinal tracts. The poisons have been injected in some form of solution. The high concentration and the fact they were injected directly into the bloodstream explain why Stark experienced liver failure so rapidly,' Leach concluded.

Underwood tried to build a picture in his mind: a killer who injects victims with organic poisons before decapitating them. He made a mental note to ensure that he accompanied Dexter when she visited Professor Miller.

'Were there syringe puncture wounds in either of the victims then?' Underwood asked.

'Plenty in Stark. The burns to Jack Harvey's skin made it very hard to localize any puncture wounds though,' Leach answered.

There was a brief pause as the gathered police officers tried to absorb the strange information that Leach had imparted to them. Harrison broke the hiatus.

'What was the third similarity?' he asked. 'You said there were three.'

Leach nodded. 'Coins. Ian Stark had three ten pence coins in his pocket. There were also three ten pence pieces placed next to Jack Harvey's body.'

Dexter had been wondering whether to impart the additional piece of information she had on a scrap of paper in front of her. She decided to chance it. 'Uniform also found two ten-pence pieces on the driver's seat of Jensen's car two hours ago. That information is not to be discussed outside this room.'

Quietly, Underwood withdrew a ten-pence piece from his pocket and studied it for a moment, rolling it between his thumb and forefinger.

'In conclusion then,' Dexter cut through the chatter, 'I will be heading the investigation into the murders of Stark and Harvey. DS Harrison will be co-ordinating the search for DC Jensen and Mrs Harvey. Check the duty sheets and see which team you've been seconded to. I have asked PC Sauerwine to help us out in CID until we get Jensen back.' *Might as well try to end on a positive note, Dexter thought.*

The meeting began to break up. Underwood hovered for a second, uncertain what to do. Dexter approached him.

'What do you think?' she asked.

'You handled it well,' Underwood replied.

'I meant about Jensen and Mrs Harvey.'

Underwood looked at her. 'I think Jensen is dead.'

'Why?'

'The coins.'

'Explain.'

'Let's find an office. I'll walk you through what I think. If it's all right with you, I'd like to hear what this Botany bloke at the university has to say tomorrow.'

Dexter looked at her watch. Her stomach flipped. It was nearly time. 'John, I can't really talk now. I have to go and meet someone. But let's talk in the car tomorrow morning. I'll pick you up at eight.'

'Fine.'

Underwood watched her leave. He couldn't hide his disappointment.

30

Forty minutes later, Dexter sat in her Mondeo in a dark corner of Meadowview Car Park. The car park was a huge concrete tundra that extended behind New Bolden's Meadowview Shopping Centre. It was also – Dexter was convinced – the 'MCP' mentioned in Ian Stark's diary entry. Now she was keeping Stark's appointment for that night. The accompanying mobile phone number had told her who to expect.

Rain ran across her windscreen. The car idled quietly. Occasionally, Dexter flicked the wipers and caught a brief reflection of her features in the darkened glass. The image vanished as quickly as it had appeared. The English rain always knew exactly where to find her.

At 22.04 a Land Rover Freelander pulled into the Car Park and stopped about fifty yards away from her. Dexter leaned forward, peering through the glass, as Mark Willis emerged from the driver's side door. He looked around him suspiciously, then apparently satisfied, he shot a disgusted look up at the heavens and clambered back into the jeep.

Dexter hesitated, suddenly uncertain of how to proceed. She was in danger of losing control: a prospect that filled her with anxiety. She tried to make sense of her emotions. She recognized fear, resentment and, to her shame, excitement. For a split second she remembered a sunlit park, a grassy bank hard against her back, Mark Willis inside her, his stubble grazing the side of her face.

Fuck it.

Alison the Brave got out of her car into the rain and walked directly over to the Freelander. She tapped on the shaded glass of the driver's window. The window descended an inch electronically.

'Not tonight, love,' said Mark Willis from inside, 'I'm not paying for it.'

'Get out of the fucking car!' Dexter hissed. 'Police.'

She took a step back as the door opened. She knew exactly what Mark Willis was capable of. Willis flicked his cigarette out of the car. It sizzled for a second on the wet tarmac then died as Willis stepped outside. He was tall with cropped black hair and the wary eyes of the CID officer he had once been.

'What's the problem, officer?' he squinted through the dark and streaming rain at Dexter's silhouette. 'Can I see some identification?'

'You know me,' said Dexter firmly.

Willis's eyes focused on Dexter's face. He looked surprised for a brief moment before a slow smile crawled across his face. 'I don't believe it!' He advanced to kiss her but Dexter backed sharply away. 'Is that you, Sparrer?'

'Don't call me that name,' said Dexter, crushing her emotions.

'You'll always be my little cockney sparrer, Dexy,' he insisted.

'What are you doing here?'

'I might ask you the same question.'

'You're not a copper any more. I am. I work here. What's your story?'

Willis ignored the question. 'Of course!' Willis slapped his forehead in mock amusement. 'I forgot that you got rusticated, Sparrer.'

'I applied for the transfer.'

'Mmmm. Course you did.' Willis rubbed his chin thoughtfully. 'Nasty business that.'

It wasn't a subject Dexter wanted to dwell on. 'Ancient history,' she said, 'like you. Until now.'

'You know what they say: bad penny an' all that.' Behind his smile Willis was trying to work out how Dexter had found him. Plenty of other people were trying. He had to find out. 'Tell you what, Sparrer,' he said in the broken glass cockney of the Hackney Council Estate he'd never truly escaped from,

'I'm staying at a nice little hotel locally. Why don't you and me go for a nightcap. Catch up on old times.'

Dexter felt the idea wrench at her. 'I don't think so. Why are you keeping appointments with Ian Stark?'

So that was it. He'd batter Stark when he caught up with him.

'Never heard of him,' Willis sniffed.

'Don't insult my intelligence. He's a drug dealer. Like you are.'

'Sparrer, I'm hurt.' He clutched at his broken heart mocking her.

'He had an appointment to meet you here.'

'You've made a mistake.'

'Not me. Not this time. Stark is dead. Someone tried to chop his head off. Then who should crawl out from his rock but Mark Willis, copper gone bad, Hackney's shittiest export.'

'Am I a suspect, then?' Willis was thinking hard and fast. Stark was dead. That presented him with a problem and an opportunity.

'I haven't decided yet.'

'Arrest me, then.' He looked around the deserted car park. 'I don't see any uniform plods though. I might be a bit of a handful for a little Sparrer in the dark.'

'Don't tempt me.'

'To be honest, Sparrer I'm impressed,' he leaned back against the wet wing of the Freelander. 'Out here in the dark all by yourself. You don't have bad dreams any more then?'

'Fuck you.'

Willis was growing in confidence. He was beginning to see that Dexter didn't have anything on him; that she'd just come to have a look and get wet for old time's sake.

'Used to wake me up – all that screaming. Good job I was there to console you. Still, you liked a bit of CID pipe to cling on to in those days. Especially when bad Uncle Vince turned up in dreamland.'

Dexter struggled to contain her fury. 'I want you out of New Bolden tonight.'

'This shit-hole ain't big enough for the both of us, right?'

'Tonight! Or I'll stitch you up, I swear it.'

'Dunno, Sparrer. I've got some business on. Maybe I'll hang around for a few days. I thought you'd be glad to have an old friend up here with you. Word is you went a bit peculiar after you left the Smoke: cut all your hair off and started carpet munching. Must be tough being out here with all these in-breds.'

Dexter unclipped her police radio from her belt. 'Dexter to Control. Need immediate assistance. Meadowview Car Park.'

'Acknowledged,' squawked the radio back at her. 'Will despatch.'

Willis grinned. He knew when it was time to go. The last thing he needed was a wagonload of plods pulling out the side panels of his Freelander. He climbed back inside. 'I'll be off, Sparrer. You know my number if you get lonely.'

The engine roared to life and Willis reversed quickly. He honked his horn and flashed his headlights at Dexter as he pulled away.

'Control to Dexter,' the voice barked from her radio. 'Respond, please.'

'Go ahead.' She watched the Freelander disappear into the night.

'Mobile unit despatched. ETA five minutes.'

'Cancel it,' Dexter ordered. 'False alarm.'

'Acknowledged.'

Soaked and exhausted, Alison Dexter returned to her car and flopped inside. She started the engine. Warm air rushed across her face from the car's powerful heating system. She closed her eyes.

The warm air had rolled across her skin like his breath. It was a steamy Paris day and the Parc des Buttes-Chaumont had been busy all afternoon. Now in the orange light of early evening it was almost empty. She had loved the Parc for its steep undulations and eccentricities. Its winding grass banks and twisting paths created many private spaces. They had laid back and marvelled at the Parc's strange stone cliff faces, its gazebos and bandstands.

114

She had tasted the champagne on Mark's breath as his tongue had explored her mouth. She had writhed underneath him, her dress riding up to her waist. He'd pushed her knickers to one side and forced himself into her. The grass had felt cool against her back.

She had been vaguely aware of the hazy Paris skyline; of the distant Latino clatter of a marching band; of bees and after-shave; of pure uninhibited happiness.

Eight years later in the desolation of a rainswept car park, Alison Dexter wondered at her mixed emotions as she touched the place where Mark Willis's baby had grown inside her.

Willis had driven away from Dexter at speed then doubled back through a confusing maze of side streets until he could see the exit to the car park. He pulled over and watched.

Alison Dexter: the perennial spanner in the works.

He wondered how much she knew about his relationship with Stark, about his problems in London. He couldn't risk his location leaking back to London. Logic told him it was time to move on. He certainly didn't need any unnecessary attention from the Old Bill: least of all, Old Bill with hormones. He had to turn the situation to his advantage.

And yet, Ian Stark was dead. Willis didn't really care how his associate had died. What he did care about was the hundred and twenty grand Stark owed him. He had impor-tant debts to pay: quickly. There was an opportunity here. He guessed that Dexter didn't know the details of his transactions with Stark: after all, he mused, if she did know he'd be banged up by now. Stark was too smart to keep his business records and stock in his flat. Willis knew he would have to take some risks if he was to find Stark's lock-up. However, he knew exactly what was waiting for him back in London if he didn't.

He tensed as he saw the headlights of Dexter's Mondeo illumine the road ahead of him. He allowed her to pull well away from Meadowview and his position before he started his own engine. From a discreet distance, Willis followed Dexter back to her home.

31

Underwood took a long look at the single photograph he had placed on the mantelpiece in his living room. It didn't make him feel excited or aroused as Rowena Harvey's had once done. It just made him feel guilty: then angry.

Best to keep busy, he told himself.

It was 11.25p.m.

It had been an unsettling and terrible day. Jack Harvey was dead. DC Jensen and Rowena Harvey were missing. He was convinced Jensen was dead: the coins had told him that much. Rowena Harvey's fate seemed more ambiguous to him. Retrieving Julia's picture from the box where he'd buried it had reminded him of the missing portrait of Rowena.

The box had been Jack's idea. It had been part of Underwood's therapy. Jack called it the 'box of bad memories.' He had instructed Underwood to strip his life of the visible reminders of his former existence: tear down the wallpaper of his depression. So Underwood's photos, work files, music, even videos had all gone into the 'box of bad memories'. Jack's theory was that it would be impossible for Underwood to reconstruct himself while weighed down by the burdens of his failures. 'When you feel stronger, more confident, more able to face the past,' he had said to Underwood, 'you can choose some items from the box and bring them out again.' Julia's photograph was the first thing he had removed from the box. Now, he was unsure why.

Another issue had been troubling Underwood. Jack Harvey had appeared to be living well beyond his police salary. Underwood knew Rowena was from a wealthy farming family but the thought still niggled at him. Had Jack been moonlighting? Had it got him into trouble? He considered the notes that he had taken at Dexter's meeting. Leach's analysis had intrigued him. The victims had been injected with organic poisons, similar to those found in magic mushrooms.

Psychoactive drugs in concentrated doses.

Underwood felt as if he was fumbling for a torch in a

power cut. He was missing an obvious point. 'Concentrated doses.' Why had the killer taken such elaborate preparations to inject Stark and Harvey with these drugs? There were far more effective and straightforward ways of killing people. There were also more stimulating ways of making people suffer. If the motive behind the drugs wasn't to inflict pain or death, then what was it? Underwood paused for a moment. His mind liked to flip problems over. It was like turning the lights on and off: in the dark, your other senses become more finely attuned.

What then if the drugs were designed to have the opposite effect? To bring pleasure not pain, life not death. He continued to play with the idea: light instead of dark, understanding instead of ignorance. Understanding of what?

He was tired but knew that he wouldn't be able to sleep. The empty bed taunted him. Loneliness drove him on.

32

It was a night of bad dreams and fear.

Alison Dexter dreamed of the baby she had made and killed.

Mary Colson woke again from the dream of the dog-man in a cold and terrible sweat. The whispering kept her awake. At 4a.m. she went to the toilet. At 6a.m. she returned and poured water all over the seat and the bathroom floor for Doreen.

Mark Willis stared at the blue door of Alison Dexter's flat imagining the horror that awaited him if he failed to deliver £100,000 by Saturday. After an hour, he headed back to the anonymous security of his hotel room on the outskirts of New Bolden.

For Max Fallon it was a night of frustration. He was exhausted but sleep eluded him. The structure of his memory was crumpled. It had been an eventful day. He remembered taking Rowena Harvey and securing her to a bed that afternoon. He had marvelled at her beauty but decided to leave her at peace and expel his furies elsewhere.

He recalled a light omelette lunch followed by an unsatisfactory molestation of the spitting, writhing policewoman on the floor of the library. Her violence had irritated him. Decapitating her had been a blessed relief. Max had then driven to London to reacquaint himself with his old colleague Simon Crouch. There had been some sort of struggle. Max could remember an old lady, standing across the road with her shopping, watching them brawl in Crouch's crappy little garden. A screwdriver into Crouch's windpipe had eventually settled the dispute. The journey back had been even more stressful: roadworks on the M11 delayed Max's return to Cambridgeshire until nearly three in the morning. Aching and hard eyed, Max sat in his library admiring his handiwork.

As he drifted in and out of consciousness, the dilapidated manor house became a confusing, creaking terror. His mind had unexpectedly thrown him back to his former life at Fogle & Moore. He was a child playing on a slag-heap of facts and terminology that he no longer understood.

'A bond is a stream of cash flows,' he told his empty library. 'Price and yield have an inverted relationship.' Frustrated at the silence that greeted his announcement Max grew angry. He hated silences in business. Silences meant ignorance. This was basic stuff. He squinted into the library to see who was listening to his seminar. There was Liz, some crouching monkey from Settlements, some faces he didn't recognize.

Silence.

'This is so basic,' he screamed. 'As price goes up yield goes down and vice fucking versa. This is easy stuff. You people couldn't trade sausages, never mind bonds.'

There was a question from the floor. There was someone out there.

At last, a question!

118

He tried to make sense of a shape that was neither an arm nor a lamp. 'If eurobonds pay annually why do we price sterling bonds semi-annually?' said a voice he thought for a second was his own before realizing that it couldn't have been. He was stunned at the ignorance of the question.

'Because of the fucking gilt market!' he shouted. 'Gilts pay semi-annually so you price sterling bonds on the same basis and then convert to an annual yield.'

He stared angrily out of the window expecting to see Canary Wharf's sea of lights before him. All he could see was darkness.

'The sterling interest rate curve,' he said deliberately and slowly as if speaking to a difficult child, 'is inverted. Rates are higher in the short maturities reflecting . . .' he stopped, unable to remember what it reflected. He knew the sterling curve looked like a slide, though. He had played on a slide on the compound in India. His mother had waited at the bottom to stop him sliding off the sterling yield curve into her arms. He was dressed in a hat of plastic jewels and a belt of moonlight glitter. She had been so proud. He had won the prize.

His parents had always disappointed him. His mother had died and deserted him: his father had stayed alive and encumbered him. The old man's first visit to his new country house three months previously had been particularly disappointing.

Robin Fallon had sat in a wooden chair, shocked by the disintegration of his son. Max was laying stretched, pale and exhausted across a sofa. Books and strange sketches lay strewn across the floor. Robin had picked up a couple of the drawings and tried to decipher some logic through the scrawled obscenities, the souvenirs of his son's terrible journeys into the back of his own head. Robin screwed some of them up and then vainly looked around Max's dilapidated drawing room for a waste paper bin.

'This has gone far enough, Max,' he observed sternly.

Max was fiddling with a Rubik's Cube, marvelling at its strange colours and intricate possibilities.

'What is all this stuff?' Robin gestured at the mess that sprawled across the ancient carpet.

119

Max giggled to himself but didn't look up. 'Try to imagine the bible before it was copy-edited.'

Robin Fallon had looked at the rotting wood panelling on the walls of the drawing room, the broken bookshelves, the smashed electricity sockets and the fireplace stuffed with papers and rubbish.

'I want you to listen to me, Max,' he said angrily, 'this has to stop. Whatever it is you are doing to yourself – these drugs – it must stop now. If you aren't strong enough to stop by yourself, I will get someone professional to help you. You promised me after you left your job in London that you'd see someone. I insist that you see a psychiatrist.'

'You can't possibly understand what I am about to become,' muttered Max as he rotated the squares on his cube. He toyed with the idea of showing his father his research on the Soma; his identification and locating of the divine Soma plant itself. The moment died as two lines of red squares clicked together on his Rubik's Cube.

'No. I don't understand. You had a fantastic job and you managed to get sacked. You spent a fortune on a listed building that frankly should be condemned. As far as I can see, all you are becoming is a tramp.'

'Typical!' Max had fumed at the Rubik's Cube. He had completed four sides of the conundrum but still had a single blue square and a single red square in the wrong locations. 'Fuck it. That happens every fucking time.'

Robin Fallon sat in a filthy armchair. 'Would you like me to speak to Richard Moore? Perhaps I could get your job back. He owes me some favours.'

'You speak to that puffed up arsehole and I'll never forgive you,' Max hissed with rage.

Robin felt a cold wave of despair crash down upon him as Max hurled the incomplete Rubik's Cube into the fireplace.

'Someone keeps changing the stickers around,' Max grumbled. 'It's the only explanation.'

'What are you talking about? Who?'

'Someone comes in here and switches the coloured

120

stickers around. The thing is fucked now. It's like a lobotomy.'

'A lobotomy?'

'Yes,' said Max warming to his theme. 'Like someone cuts a cube out of your brain then puts it back in the wrong way. It looks like it should work but all the connections get mixed up.' Max stared through the lights at his father. The old man's head had become a swirling mass of blues and greens that had erupted from nowhere. Like clouds rotating around a planet. It reminded Max of something, a scrap he had read. It was a provenance. A revelation. The cube of brain had been slotted back correctly. Suddenly, beautifully, everything made sense. He decided to keep his epiphany to himself.

'All I need,' said Max, blinking away the strange colours that swam across his field of vision, 'is understanding.' Max had a bottle of his elixir in the pocket of his soiled jogging bottoms. 'I can make you understand but you won't like it. Memory is knowledge. I can help you make the transition. Then you'll see for yourself.'

Robin saw an opportunity. 'Max, if it's understanding that you want, I have a friend who can help you.'

Max turned his back on his father and stooped to retrieve his Rubik's Cube from the fireplace.

'Did you ever meet Jack Harvey?' Robin continued. 'He's a police psychiatrist. He works in Huntingdon.'

Max laughed hysterically. 'A policeman! That's fantastic. What's he going to do? Wheelclamp my cerebellum?'

'He's a psychiatrist. A very good one. He helped me after your mother died. Maybe he could understand you – what you are becoming – better than me.'

Max went quiet for a second.

Perhaps this policeman was Brihaspati, the sage of the gods. Perhaps he could be a mouthpiece, translate the teachings of the Soma into a language mortals could understand, refract the divine light into some sort of obvious fucking rainbow.

'Okay, I'll see him.'

Robin Fallon was relieved. 'I'll arrange it. Jack isn't

supposed to do private consultations but I'll sort something out.'

'Chequebook psychiatry. That's a fucking riot!' *Max was laughing again.*

'Believe what you want.'

Max watched as the lights danced away from his father's face and the turquoise clouds began to dissipate.

'Here endeth the lesson,' *he shouted as his father left the room.*

Max stopped the playback in his mind. It was disturbing him now. He knew that he no longer had to deal with such contempt masquerading as paternal concern. Pain was surging up behind his eyes like a building electrical charge. He looked around the derelict room and wondered whom he had been talking to. He couldn't see anybody. He lifted Jack Harvey's head from his lap and considered it for a moment. The sage of the gods had disappointed him. Fallon blinked in discomfort. The lights had become more aggressive, more persistent. The memory of his father's visit had awoken them. They had started to assume forms. There were terrible shapes and demons. He tried to swat them away as they ghosted across his field of vision. He sank to the floor as they nibbled at his head. They were the Assura: demons bent on sucking him dry of the divine Soma juice. Harvey's head fell to the floor with a dull thud.

Max sank to his knees and then rolled in agony on the dusty floor of the library as they tore holes in his head and swam into his throat and down into his stomach. The pain was everywhere. He shuddered and retched as he felt the demons laying eggs under his skin; as they writhed and stung at his stomach like a bellyful of electric eels. His skin bubbled and itched as the eggs hatched and the larvae scratched and wriggled through his flesh, feeding on the blood of the Soma. The fluid would make them immortal. He couldn't let that happen. He had to fight them now before they became too powerful.

Max screamed and bellowed in fury, trying to tear the irritations from his body. Suddenly, the demons were gone and the lights retreated to the edge of his field of vision. He began to relax. He would piss the eels out of his system later.

Max collapsed into an armchair and waited for dawn.

33

2nd May

Alison Dexter was working at her desk by 7a.m. The night had been long and tortuous. She was glad when it was over. She wanted to fill her head with information to blot out the memory. She read through Ian Stark's papers, his diary and his mobile phone bills. Dexter justified this by reminding herself that Stark had been murdered and that checking through his records was a legitimate investigative procedure. However, the more time she spent, the more she came to focus on Mark Willis's phone number. The same way she had stared at her mobile phone for six months of her life waiting for the same number to appear.

Mark Willis was a blister on her soul that stung. In her mind, she had tried to turn him into an abstraction: an example of what can happen when you let your guard down. Now he had become a reality again. She had to get a clearer understanding of his relationship with Stark, figure out exactly why he had come to New Bolden. That was another legitimate investigative procedure, she told herself.

Dexter picked up her phone and called the number of CID at Leyton Police Station in East London. She knew the number well. She'd been on the other end of it for three years.

'McInally,' grunted a hard London voice.

'Early start, Guv?'

'Who's that?'

'Alison Dexter.'

There was a brief pause as Chief Inspector Paddy

123

McInally absorbed the information. 'Fuck me!' he boomed eventually.

'I don't do charity work.'

'Sexy Dexy! I don't believe it.'

'Don't call me that, please.'

'How's life up in bandit country?'

'The usual. Cattle rustling, sheep shagging, ritual decapitations.' Dexter smiled. Her old boss had a curious knack for cheering her up.

'Read about that,' McInally observed. 'Nasty. Some junkie?'

'It's early days, guv,' Dexter replied.

McInally laughed out loud. 'In other words, you haven't got a Scooby!'

'Learned from the master, didn't I?'

'You are a cheeky bastard!' McInally's voice softened. 'Ah. We miss you, Dexy. When are you coming back to civilization?'

'No time soon.'

'That's a crying shame.'

'Guv. I need some information. You could be the man.'

'Ask the oracle.'

Dexter took a deep breath. 'Mark Willis.'

'Go on.' The humour had gone from McInally's voice. Willis was a running sore for him too.

'I've heard a whisper up here that Ian Stark – the first murder victim – was mixed up with Willis. Drug shit. I'm trying to tie up some loose ends.' It was only a slight lie.

McInally slurped some coffee. 'You sure that's all? I'm not a dating agency.'

'Do me a favour, guv. He's nothing to me.' That was a bigger lie. Whenever Willis became entangled in her life, Dexter always found herself becoming entangled in deceit.

'Mark Willis,' McInally sighed. 'Why won't that name just go away?'

'Tell me about it.'

'Well, Alison, he's become the professional toe rag that he always showed the potential to be. Willis has become quite a big fish since you went rural.'

'How so?'

'Pills. Ecstasy. Smack. You name it. He's made some heavy-duty connections in London and overseas. He supplies drugs in bulk to club pushers. We're talking big numbers. All over the East End and into Essex and Kent. At least until recently.'

'I don't understand.' Dexter was making notes.

'Dexy, I like you and I trust you. This goes no further. Right?'

'Understood.'

'Willis is in trouble and has gone AWOL.'

Dexter bit her lip anxiously. It bled slightly.

'You heard of the Moules?' McInally continued.

'Of course. Casinos and shit?'

'Casinos, money laundering. The list's as long as the Romford Road.'

'And Willis is involved.'

McInally snorted. 'You could say that. He owes them. Owes them big apparently. Word is up to a hundred thousand.'

'Jesus.'

'He always liked to talk the big game. Well, it's blown up in his face large style. Gambling debts.'

'Idiot.'

'Dexy, I'd crucify that bastard with blunt nails for what he's done. But even I wouldn't wish Eric Moule on him.'

Dexter agreed. 'Nasty.'

'That may be the understatement of the new century.' McInally was beginning to sense that Dexter wasn't playing entirely straight. 'Alison, if that wanker turns up on your patch I want to know about it. I need to have a long, intimate chat with him about a number of issues.'

'You'll be the first to know, guv.'

'Come home soon, Dexy,' McInally shouted. 'There's a cup of tea and a bacon sandwich waiting here for you.'

'You're a gentleman.'

'Only where you're concerned.'

Dexter put the phone down. She felt herself welling up with tears. Only Paddy McInally could make her nostalgic for Leyton High Street. She looked up and noticed Underwood was standing in her doorway.

'You okay, tiger?' he asked uncomfortably.

'Fine.' Dexter was surprised to see him and checked her watch. 'I thought I was picking you up at eight?'

'Couldn't sleep.'

Dexter suddenly looked very small in her chair. 'Sleep would be nice,' she said quietly.

'Do you want to hear about these coins, then?' Underwood entered the room.

'Coins?'

'The coins found on Stark, Harvey and in Jensen's car.'

Dexter remembered. 'Sorry, I'm being dense. Three tenpence coins on Stark, three found next to Jack and two on Jensen's car seat.'

'The killer's signature.'

'Calm down, John!' Dexter reached into her pocket and pulled out a handful of coins. 'I've got six tens and twenty here. No ones chopped my head off. Could be just coincidence.'

'You said yesterday that you don't believe in coincidence.'

Dexter sighed. Underwood's memory was full of trivial detail and irrelevancies in the places where police procedure and details of the criminal law should have been. 'Go on then,' she said, 'let's have it.'

'It's not coincidence. Jack is murdered and decapitated. We find three ten-pence pieces next to his body.'

'Why is that so significant?'

'Look at a ten-pence coin,' Underwood gestured at the pile of change Dexter had place on her desk. 'What do you see?'

Dexter saw what he was driving at. 'The queen's head. Isn't that a bit bleeding obvious, though?'

Underwood crossed round to Dexter's side of the table. 'Let's say you were a murderer with a real hard-on for chopping people's heads off.'

'Hard to imagine that, but I'll try.'

'Let's also say that you were collecting a specific number of heads for some fucked-up reason.'

Dexter smiled thinly. Underwood had a peculiar way of expressing himself.

'Hypothetically, three heads,' he continued.

'Go on.'

Underwood arranged three of Dexter's coins in a straight line on the table. 'So you need three heads. Three heads equals three coins. We found three coins by Jack Harvey. Next, you need two heads.' He removed one of the coins. 'Two heads equals two coins. We find two coins on the driver's seat of Jensen's car. On the next victim, we'll find a single coin. I guarantee it. It's a countdown.'

Dexter pulled at her short black hair, as if trying to straighten out the kinks in Underwood's logic. 'What about Ian Stark? We found three coins on him. He still had his head.'

'True but there were severe injuries to his neck. Maybe the killer tried to decapitate him but was interrupted or bottled it and forgot about the coins.'

Dexter's eyes never left the coins in front of her. 'Then there's Rowena Harvey. Why not leave a coin for her?'

Underwood frowned. 'The killer took a photograph of Rowena Harvey from Jack's office. I don't think he plans to kill her. Not yet anyway.'

'Why does he want her, then?'

Underwood didn't want to think about that.

Dexter didn't seem convinced. 'I'll get my jacket. Let's go meet the mushroom man.'

Underwood nodded his acknowledgement as Dexter left the room. He stared at the coins intently. He replaced the third ten-pence piece and arranged the coins in a row, aligned left to right across the desk.

The heads were all pointing the same way.

34

Two miles away DS Harrison stood contemplating the derelict buildings that surrounded the Car Wash. A forensic team had identified traces of Ian Stark's blood at the scene the previous evening. The area had been cordoned off and the entrance to the enclosed square of tarmac had been blocked with a squad car. Harrison watched as the SOCOs clad in their strange white protective suits investigated every inch of the Car Wash and the smashed up surrounding buildings.

Harrison wondered if Sarah Jensen was tied up or lying dead in a similar building nearby. He racked his brains for an angle, a way of finding her. He had seen the looks on the faces of his colleagues in the Incident Room. They all thought she was dead. In his darkest moment, when he had awoken the previous night and reached out for her in the empty bed, so had he.

'There's not much here, mate.' Marty Farrell, the senior SOCO had joined him.

'It's been raining for two nights,' Harrison observed angrily. 'What did you expect?'

Farrell decided to concentrate on the basics. 'We found the blood traces in the centre of the tarmac. No evidence that the body was dragged anywhere. All blood patterns are concentrated in that area.'

'So what does that tell us?'

Farrell thought for a second. 'If you'd just cut someone's throat you'd have blood all over your hands and your clothes most likely. You'd probably want to drive home, right?'

'Agreed.'

'I reckon the killer drove in from Station Road. I reckon he drove right in here. Did the job on Stark and drove away.'

'You're speculating.'

'Maybe. But if he'd walked away from here we'd expect to find traces of Stark's blood near the exit or on the pavement out front. There's nothing.'

'So he drove off? So what? How does that help?' Harrison was frustrated. They seemed to be making no forward progress.

'Easy, mate,' said Farrell. 'I'm just thinking out loud. Now our friend Stark was no mug, right? He was an experienced pusher.'

'Yep.'

'If the killer drove in, then it's unlikely he caught Stark off guard. You know, crept up on him in the dark.'

'Go on.' Harrison felt a flicker of interest.

'I don't know, mate. It just feels odd. There are police patrols up here regularly at night. Why would Stark not do a runner when the headlights shone through the entrance?'

'Maybe he knew it wasn't a police car. Maybe a squad car had just gone through. I can check the uniform patrol schedule for that night. See which cars were in this area.'

'A car comes in that for some reason he knows can't be a police car. Why would he risk it, though? Why expose yourself if you're as canny as Stark?'

'Money, I suppose,' Harrison mused. 'If he thought he was going to make a killing. No pun intended.'

'Right. Put all that together and what have you got? A car pulls up that can't be a police car. Stark thinks he going to make a pile of cash so he comes out of the dark.'

Harrison felt a tingle of excitement. 'Marty, you are a genius. He drives a flashy car. A sports car or a Roller or something big that stinks of money.'

'It's just speculation, mate. He might have pedalled up on a frigging unicycle.'

It was something. Harrison needed a break. It wasn't much but it was a start. He would check the patrol schedules and see if any of the squad car drivers had seen any incongruously expensive cars around the station the night Stark was killed. If that turned up nothing, he would get some plods to start questioning late night commuters at the station. For the first time since Jensen's disappearance, Harrison felt a flash of positivism.

35

Dexter parked on Trumpington Road, stunned that she had actually managed to find a convenient parking space in

Cambridge on a weekday. The University Botanical Gardens are situated just to the south of Cambridge, away from the overcrowded little streets, the hubbub of tourists and shoppers. In the summer, the gardens became cluttered with students and picnickers stretching out across its lawns and surrounded by wine bottles and unread books. At nine in the morning, it is usually deserted and Underwood found the Gardens' quiet beauty particularly therapeutic.

'Where are we meeting this character?' Underwood asked, inhaling a deep breath of pine-scented air.

Dexter consulted the map she had downloaded from the internet. 'By the rock garden, in front of the greenhouses. Leach arranged it all. We need to take a left here.'

They turned off the main walkway. There was a small lake to their left. Ahead, through the trees Underwood could see a sculpted outcrop of grey rocks. Sitting on a wooden bench about twenty yards ahead of them was Dr Adam Miller. Underwood judged Miller was in his mid-thirties. He had long chestnut coloured hair tied back in a pony tail and was eating an enormous roll, the contents of which were gradually spilling out on to his lap. Miller threw occasional lumps of bread to the increasingly agitated ducks that had gathered by the edge of the lake.

'Dr Miller?' Dexter asked.

Miller looked up and hurriedly placed his roll on the bench, dusting himself down.

'Shit! You're early!'

'I'm DI Dexter, this is DI John Underwood.'

'Sorry to disturb your breakfast,' Underwood added.

'No worries,' Miller grinned.

'What part of Australia are you from?' asked Dexter appraising Miller's accent.

'New Zealand.' He noticed Dexter's embarrassment. 'Don't worry. Everyone thinks I'm an Aussie. You want to talk mushrooms, right?'

'Poisonous mushrooms,' Dexter clarified.

Miller gestured to the row of white-framed glasshouses

130

behind him. 'Let's go over to the oven. I've got some stuff set up for you.'

'The oven?' asked Underwood.

'That's what we call the glasshouses. You'll figure out why when we get inside. Shall we go?'

They walked along the gravel pathway. Miller had a breezy charm that Underwood liked. 'Nice place to work,' he observed.

Miller nodded. 'Can't beat it. The Gardens have been part of the University since eighteen thirty-one. I guess even you Brits can figure out how to do something right given a hundred and seventy years!'

'You obviously haven't been on one of our trains,' Underwood replied.

Miller opened the door to the glasshouses and the three of them were instantly engulfed by heat. 'Welcome to the oven, guys!' Noting their uncomfortable expressions Miller added, 'Don't worry. This is the tropical house. I've reserved us a little experimentation lab. It's air conditioned.'

They walked down the central aisle and Miller gave them a brief guided tour. 'Like I said, the Gardens were set up in eighteen thirty-one by a guy called Professor Henslow. He taught Charles Darwin. We're in the tropical house now. Beyond the central atrium are the succulents and carnivorous plants with the cacti down the end. However, we are booked into Lab Three which is down here on the left.' They crossed the high vaulted courtyard area and turned right into a shaded corridor. The temperature dropped suddenly and Dexter shivered as the film of sweat on her back began to chill her skin.

'Here we go.' Miller unlocked a grey door and they were inside Lab Three. There were colourful printed diagrams of plants pinned up on two walls. Miller placed his keys on a desk in front of a blank white board and gestured them over to the central work area. There were two metal trays filled with earth containing planted mushrooms.

'A word of warning before we start,' Miller said. 'Don't touch any of these. Bad idea. So, what do you need to know?'

Dexter looked at the fungi. There was something vile about

131

them that made her uncomfortable. 'Dr Miller, what we discuss today is confidential. We need your expertise. However, you cannot repeat what we discuss today to anybody. Do you have a problem with that?'

'None whatsoever,' Miller smiled. 'To be honest after the telephone conversation I had with your colleague Dr Leach I was fascinated. Glad to be of assistance.'

'Leach faxed you the toxicology reports he produced on the two victims?' Underwood asked.

'He did. Both victims had lethal levels of amatoxins and phallotoxins in their systems. I guess he explained to you how that can be fatal.'

Dexter consulted her notes. 'He said that the poisons attack the liver and kidneys. That they induce liver failure.'

'Right. Amatoxins are cyclic octapeptides. Nasty little poisons. Ingestion of even a small amount can be deadly. Zero point one milligrams of poison per kilo of body weight can be fatal, particularly if the victim is very old or very young. Basically, you ingest five to seven milligrams of amatoxins and you are in for a very bad couple of days. That amount can be present in a single mushroom of about fifty grams.'

Dexter was making notes. 'The first victim, Ian Stark died of liver failure six hours after he was admitted to hospital. Assuming he ingested the poisons on the same day that's rather an accelerated timetable.'

Miller nodded. 'It is. If he had eaten a single mushroom containing amatoxins, his deterioration would have taken place over three or four days. There are some treatments that can inhibit the poison's attack on the liver cells: the hospital gave him Penicillin G and Silibilin, right?'

'Eventually.' Dexter tried to recall the details. 'They gave him Naxolone to start with. They assumed it was a heroin overdose. Stark wasn't given Penicillin and Silibilin until about four hours after he was admitted.'

'If he'd eaten a single mushroom, that should still have given him a reasonable chance,' Miller explained. 'The issues as I understand them are that the levels in his system were extremely high. Something like zero point five milligrams per kilo of body weight. That's a fatal dose. And that there were no traces of fungi in his digestive tract implying the toxins were introduced directly into the blood stream.'

'Direct injection speeds up the process?' Underwood asked.

'No question. There have been experiments performed on lab animals that show amatoxins introduced intravenously can cause death within two to five hours.' Miller pulled on a pair of latex gloves. 'You wanna see some black magic?'

'Go ahead,' Dexter replied.

Miller picked up a scalpel from the work surface next to one of the trays of fungi. He selected a large yellow-capped mushroom and sliced off a small section from its cap. Then he placed the section on a square piece of newspaper and pressed down on it firmly. Having done so, he placed the mushroom section in a clear plastic bag and dropped it into a bin. 'This is called the Maixner Test,' he said as he retrieved a small bottle containing a clear fluid from a shelf behind his desk. 'It's the standard test for the presence of amatoxin.'

He unscrewed the lid of the bottle and, using a glass pipette, dropped a tiny amount of the fluid onto the stained newspaper. He then placed the paper in the sunlight to dry. 'This liquid is hydrochloric acid,' he said as he replaced the bottle. 'It reacts with the amatoxin residue left by the mush-room and . . . well, you can see already.' He pointed at the newspaper. The stain was already turning light blue. Over the next two minutes the blue became more vivid and obvious. 'Cool, isn't it? That means "don't eat me".'

Dexter was intrigued. 'Based on the toxicology reports can you suggest why the levels of toxin were so high in the victims?'

'My guess would be that whoever injected the victims with this stuff has managed to create a concentrated dose of fluid derived from several mushrooms,' Miller replied.

'Can you identify the types of fungi based on the toxicology profile?' Underwood asked; he was beginning to sense an angle that they could exploit.

'I'm way ahead of you guys!' Miller grinned. 'I can't be one hundred per cent accurate given the likelihood that the killer has mixed and concentrated residues obtained from several fungi. However, my best guess is that he has used combinations of these two babies.' He pointed down at the two trays on the work surface in front of him.

'This brute is called the Amanita Phalloides or European Death Cap.' He looked at the tray of mushrooms with a mixture of awe and respect. 'Looks inoffensive enough, right?'

Dexter nodded. The mushrooms were about ten centimetres high with a wide smooth cap that was a strange kind of yellowish-green colour. The section Miller had cut for the Maixner Test had been from one of these mushrooms.

'And that's part of the problem,' Miller continued. 'These are often mistaken for edible mushrooms. Trouble is they contain very high levels of amatoxins. Ingest enough and you are dead meat. There's no effective antidote as yet.'

Miller pulled the other tray closer to them as Underwood and Dexter bent over to investigate. 'You recognize these?'

The tray contained six mushrooms of the same genus. The caps were blood red but covered with crusty white scales. The stalk was white with a small veil just below the cap.

'They look like the mushrooms that grow in woods in fairy stories,' Dexter observed, pleased with herself.

'That's right. These are called the Amanita Muscaria or Fly Agaric. The white flecks on the cap are the remains of a membrane that once covered the entire cap and stalk. Powerful hallucinogenic fungus, this one. It contains a poisonous alkaloid called muscimol. The Fly Agaric has had a long association with mankind. People were tripping out on this baby long before the sixties.'

'You are saying that poisons from both these mushrooms were present in the bodies of Stark and Harvey?' Underwood asked.

Miller nodded. 'That's my estimation based on the toxicology profiles.'

'Do these things grow in the UK? Or has this guy imported them from overseas?' Underwood was working the angle now, it was becoming clearer to him.

'They aren't common in the UK but they do grow indigenously in certain areas,' Miller thought for a second. 'As a basic rule the European Death Cap tends to grow in mixed forests – you know, deciduous and coniferous. The Fly Agaric prefers birch forests or clumps of birch trees in mixed forests. You know, I could probably find a list of likely sites. I'm sure the University must keep records of that kind of thing.'

Underwood was impressed that Miller had seen the angle too. 'That would be enormously helpful.'

Dexter's mind was working through other possibilities. 'Do these toxins degrade over time? I mean is the killer digging up these mushrooms immediately before he uses them or is he using stuff he's stored up for a while?'

Miller whistled softly. 'That's a smart question. You should be a mycologist. There's not a huge amount of research literature on that subject. However, I have read some case studies. There are cases of people who have had amatoxin poisoning after eating fungi they have frozen. There was a case of an old guy – in France I think – who defrosted a European Death Cap eight months after picking it. He died. Should have been more careful. My view is that amatoxins degrade slowly. It's possible that your killer could have harvested these things months ago, extracted what he wanted from them and then frozen it. That's not what you wanted to hear, is it?'

Dexter shook her head.

Underwood's mind was racing. He remembered the notion that had occurred to him the previous evening. The idea that the fatal effects of the fungi were not the killer's only motive for using them. 'Why do people eat these things then?' he asked Miller. 'What do they get out of having these hallucinations?'

Miller shrugged. 'Many different types of mushroom contain powerful psychoactive agents – chemicals that produce powerful hallucinations. I mentioned earlier that the Fly Agaric contains muscimol. Other mushrooms contain Ibotenic Acid or Psilocybin. They have similar effects to ingesting LSD.'

Underwood frowned. The terms meant nothing to him. He

was interested in the effects. 'How do those chemicals induce hallucinations? What do they do to the brain?'

'That's a tough one. You should really ask a neurologist. Basically, your brain receives millions of pieces of information every second, right? Your sensory organs and nerves are constantly feeding data to your brain about your body, your external environment and so on. Now, your brain has the capacity to filter that information and make sense of it.' Miller noted their blank expressions. 'I'll try to demonstrate. Close your eyes for a second.' As Dexter and Underwood nervously obliged, Miller looked around him, picked up a plastic biro and hurled it at the glass window. It clattered to the ground a second later. 'Your brain just told you that the sound you just heard was a pen or a plastic object hitting a window, right?'

'Pretty much,' Underwood agreed.

'But, if the filter in your brain was switched off, that sound might appear to be anything. It might be the sound of the end of the world or of all your bones breaking. And you would believe it.'

'Sounds terrifying,' Dexter observed. She liked to be in full control of her senses.

'It can be,' Miller agreed, 'it can make the mind very vulnerable to suggestion. Variants of Ibotenic Acid have been used as truth drugs in the past.'

'You mentioned that the history of these fungi goes back further than hippies and the sixties?' Underwood observed.

'God, yeah! Ethnomycologists have shown that the recreational use of psychoactive mushrooms has been linked into human civilization for thousands of years.' Miller peeled off his gloves and walked over to a sink to wash his hands. 'My advice is steer well clear of them. Reality is underrated.'

The Box of Bad Memories

36

Alison Dexter dropped Underwood back at New Bolden Police Station shortly after 10a.m. After leaving him, she headed for the Morley Estate. She received an update from Harrison about the search for Jensen and Rowena Harvey via her car phone.

'Marty Farrell's team is sweeping the Car Wash for forensics.' he said. 'They haven't come up with much yet. Rubbish mainly. We're checking what they bagged up for prints but I don't hold out much hope.'

Dexter agreed. 'I can't imagine whoever did that to Stark and Jack would be daft enough to leave a print behind. There was nothing on either body.'

'Absolutely. The only half-interesting thing that came out of it was a suggestion that Marty made.' Harrison had explained the theory about the killer driving an expensive car.

'It's not much to go on, mate.' Dexter respected the logic of Harrison's idea but didn't see how it would help.

'I know. I've checked the uniform patrols for that night. None remember seeing any unusual cars. We're still running enquiries around the site of Jensen's car crash. It's open farm-land though: hardly any houses. Nobody saw diddly-squat. Suffolk Police have been stopping traffic on the A1066 but so far zero.'

'I'm sorry . . . ' Dexter struggled for the right words. 'Jensen and I didn't get on but . . . well, you know.'

'Yep.' Harrison didn't want to develop that line of conversation. 'County HQ at Huntingdon have said we can have the use of their EC135 chopper for a couple of days.'

'Is that going to be helpful?' Dexter asked. She knew the latest police helicopters were great at traffic control but she couldn't see where one would add much value in a manhunt.

'Probably not,' Harrison conceded. 'But apparently it has

new thermal imaging equipment. It might help us locate a body in open ground.'

Dexter could hear the edge of desperation in Harrison's voice and decided to cut him some slack. 'Fine. If they've offered it, we'll take it. It's your show. You run it as you see fit.'

'Thanks, guv. I'll be in touch.'

Dexter was relieved he hadn't asked her where she was going. It took her fifteen minutes of weaving through traffic before the stone bulk of the Morley Estate rose on the horizon ahead of her. She had determined from Ian Stark's paperwork that he rented two garages at opposite ends of the estate. Dexter was convinced that the bulk of Stark's drugs and business details were hidden in one of them. She sensed that was why Mark Willis was in New Bolden and she was determined that he wouldn't get hold of them.

She drove to the east side of the estate first. There were two teenagers sitting at the roadside next to their mountain bikes. Dexter registered that the bikes looked new and beyond the means of fourteen year olds living on the Morley. Still, she drove past. She had more important matters at stake.

She pulled up at the entrance to a square of twelve garages arranged in two rows of six. Stark rented number five. She found it and saw it was padlocked. Dexter had expected this and retrieved a bolt-cutter from the boot of her car. She was vaguely aware that the two teenagers were now riding their bikes in circles watching her from a safe distance. She wasn't concerned. Big estates are very territorial and the locals recognize outsiders instantly. She was an oddity.

It took considerable force to snap through the padlock and chain and Dexter was sweating with effort by the time she rolled up Stark's garage door. As the door immediately showered her with dirt and detritus, Dexter sensed she had picked the wrong garage. Stark obviously hadn't been inside for a while. Carefully, she stepped inside brushing leaves and muck from her hair.

The dismantled remains of a motorbike lay strewn across the floor and there was a powerful, sickly smell of engine oil.

Dexter crouched and opened a heavy canvas bag that was bulging next to the small inspection pit. It contained tools: screwdrivers and engine spanners. She moved on to the back of the garage. There were rows of paint tins arranged along the back of the wooden workbench. She used a screwdriver to prise open each of the lids in turn and to her immense disappointment found only paint.

'What do they say about great minds?' asked Mark Willis from the garage door.

'What are you doing here?' Dexter asked, suddenly feeling very vulnerable: she had been backed into a corner.

'I might ask you the same question.' Willis smiled his tiger smile. 'Is this an official visit?'

Dexter leaned back against the workbench and closed her grip around a steel hammer. 'I don't have to answer your questions smartarse.' She realized she had left her radio in the car.

Idiot.

'So this is Starkey's lair, is it? Not very salubrious.'

Willis hadn't moved but Dexter could sense his eyes were scouring the room, just as hers had.

'I don't know what you're talking about.'

'I'm not an idiot, Sparrer. You didn't come here to strip the engine of that Kawasaki, now did you?'

'What is it you want, Mark?' Dexter could feel her anger rising, she was struggling to keep control. 'Stark owed you something, did he?'

'You might say that.' Willis was inside the garage now. Dexter was becoming increasingly uncomfortable.

'You're in a bit of trouble, I hear,' Dexter said, having decided to take the offensive.

Willis looked at her, through her. His smile had gone. 'What have you heard, Sparrer?'

'Just that you've finally lived up to your reputation as the East End's leading idiot.'

Willis grinned suddenly and wagged a finger. 'You're very naughty. For a second there I almost thought you knew what you were talking about.'

'I know about you, a hundred grand, the Moules.'

Willis froze and stared at her in sudden fury. 'How the fuck?' He thought for a second, 'Oh, you've been speaking to Big Daddy McInally, I suppose. Should have guessed that. You shouldn't pay any attention to him. He just wants to put his cock in your mouth.'

Dexter let the insult wash over her. 'He was very keen to know your whereabouts.'

Willis stepped closer. 'Yeah but you didn't tell him did you, Sparrer? I can see it in your eyes. Your eyes give you up every time. You're a lousy liar.'

He was too close. Dexter swung the hammer out from behind her in fury. Willis saw it coming and grabbed her wrist, twisting it away from her painfully until the hammer fell from her grip. He pulled her close and kissed her hard, trying to force his tongue into her mouth. Dexter jerked forward. She cracked her knee up hard in his crotch as they clashed heads. Willis recoiled sharply, wiping blood from his mouth.

'Pussy,' he said, giggling, 'you taste of pussy. You *have* gone peculiar.'

'Come near me again and I'll fucking kill you.'

Willis shook his head, 'It's a pity we didn't work it out, Alison. We had some laughs.'

'Your choice,' she said. Her fist was still clenched. 'It was your choice.'

'Yeah,' Willis was smiling again, 'it was, wasn't it?' He shot a final look around the garage. 'I guess I'll be off, Sparrer. There's nothing here for me.'

'I'm on your case, Mark. If I see you again I will nick you. And McInally will be driving up the A10 looking to put your head in a vice.'

'I don't think so, Sparrer. You had your reasons for getting out of London on the hurry up. It would be a pity if some of those reasons came up here looking for you.'

'Don't threaten me, you piece of shit.'

'Bear it in mind, Sparrer. Before you have me nicked by some plod for a parking on a double yellow, just bear it mind. Your nightmares must be worse than mine.'

142

Willis left the garage and jogged over to his parked Freelander. Despite his confidence that Dexter wouldn't give him up, he was irritated. He was running out of time and still had to find Stark's stash.

'Got any pills, Mister?'

Willis looked around. There were two teenage boys a few feet behind him. They were standing on the pedals of their bikes ready to make a quick getaway. Willis smirked at the irony.

'You've got the wrong man, lads,' he said. 'Now piss off.'

The bikers turned sharply and pedalled off hard, realizing they had made a mistake. Willis suddenly realized he had made one, too.

'Wait! he called out. 'Come back!'

But they were gone.

Dexter sat on the floor of Ian Stark's garage in a cold fury. She felt like a butterfly pinned to a wooden board. She tried to understand the mass of feelings that Mark Willis provoked: loathing, fear, excitement, frustration, loss. He was a cancer in her heart. When she had swung the hammer at him, Dexter had fully intended to do him damage. Now she felt ashamed. Would it ever stop, she wondered? Would there ever be a day when she woke in the morning without his name flickering across her half-conscious brain?

She stood and brushed herself down. She closed Stark's garage door behind her and sealed it with police tape retrieved from the boot of her car. She looked out across the desolate estate: the towering loneliness of its accommodation blocks. And for a moment, she remembered how Mark Willis had made her love him.

Alison Dexter had joined Leyton Police Station in 1992. Three years later she was promoted to Detective Constable and had started working for McInally in CID. As the only woman in the group, she had been hassled from the outset. It had begun with suggestive sexual comments and flirtations, then steadily deteriorated into insidious bullying. Only McInally and Willis had let her do her job without inter-

143

ference. Detective Sergeant Mark Willis gradually became her self-appointed mentor.

As the two grew closer the suggestive comments and jibes started to evaporate. McInally was highly respected throughout the department as being fair-minded and vastly experienced, but Mark Willis was feared. He had a reputation as a hard man. He had received two warnings for the use of excessive force in interrogations in his first year as a Detective Sergeant. Once the rumours started that Dexter and Willis were an item, the other CID officers started to leave her alone.

Two months after they had started sleeping together, Dexter had been called to her mother's flat late at night. The next door neighbour had called Alison's mobile number after hearing screaming. Willis had driven her to the council estate on the edge of Walthamstow and waited in the car while Alison went inside. Her stepfather, Vince Stag, had beaten her mother unconscious: the culmination of a drunken row.

'She deserved it,' Vince had snarled as Alison tried to rouse her mother.

'Stay back!' Alison had shouted as Vince had lurched at her.

'She's always pissed up,' Vince slurred. 'She's come in swearing, calling me every name under the bleedin' sun.'

'She needs to go to hospital, Vince, you stupid bastard.'

'They can keep the filthy bitch.'

Alison leapt to her feet and threw herself at her stepfather. However, despite his drunken state Vince was still strong and alert and his first calculated punch had sent her sprawling with a burst lip.

'You enjoy that, did you?' he snarled. 'Thought you would have learnt your lesson.'

'Arsehole.'

'I always thought you might have enjoyed it really. Girls like it when a bloke cuts up a bit rough. It's an animal thing, innit?'

'I'll have you, Vince. You're going away for this.'

'Must have been hard for you listening to me screwing your old ma. Fancied a bit yourself, I guess. Like mother like daughter. Still, wouldn't have been right, would it? A father and a daughter.'

'You're not my father, Vince.'

'No. We're still trying to work out what happened to that prick, aren't we?'

Dexter hadn't heard Mark Willis coming up the stairs to the living room. Suddenly he was standing in the doorway. He absorbed the situation instantly, noting Alison's cut lip as it dribbled blood across her chin.

'Watch out!' said Vince, laughing and waving his whisky bottle at Willis, 'the cavalry's arrived.'

Willis had crashed into Vince without warning, knocking the bigger man to the ground and raining furious punches down on his head. Vince had smashed his whisky bottle against the floor and slammed it into Willis's leg, drawing blood. It was a desperate gesture. Willis quickly reduced Vince's head to a bloody, snotty mess. He finished the confrontation sharply and brutally, smashing Vince's head into the television screen.

Alison had watched the beating with cold, voyeuristic pleasure. It gave her a charge of sexual excitement as the man who had wrecked and scarred her childhood was reduced to a snorting unconscious heap. Willis had stood over the fallen man with his fists clenched. Alison had desperately wanted him to finish Vince off. But Willis had turned to face her and smiled. They were bound in blood. She knew in that moment that he would protect her.

Starting her car in the rain outside Ian Stark's garage on the Morley Estate, Alison Dexter cursed her stupidity.

37

At approximately the same moment, Mary Colson called the police station. She was nervous, disturbed by a night of bad dreams and anxiety. She had seen the bodies again, piled high in the dark while children played nearby. She had seen the dog-man rising from the ground, his arms and legs snarling and barking. And she had seen herself inside a box as John Underwood had closed the lid. She knew she was going to die.

Mary didn't bother to remonstrate with Doreen O'Riordan for being an hour late. Nor did she mention the ten-pound note that had mysteriously vanished from her money jar. She was starting to feel a terrible tiredness in her bones, a rising sense that she had seen and experienced enough, that staying alive would be less natural than dying. She sat quietly, and waited for her friends to arrive.

'You've not eaten your breakfast again,' Doreen nagged, noticed the untouched tray on Mary's lap.

'I'm not hungry.'

'You look like you've lost weight,' Doreen observed with a smile.

'You don't.'

'Why don't you have a bite of toast?'

'I'm not hungry. I'm not supposed to eat toast anyway. You know that. Why can't I have some fruit? It hurts to swallow toast.'

Doreen did know that. 'I can't do your exercises with you until you've had your breakfast.'

Mary shrugged. 'They're a waste of bloody time. Imagine making an eighty-eight-year-old woman do exercises. How ridiculous!'

'It's not done for my amusement, Mary. It's for your Parkinson's. Exercise will strengthen your joints and your muscles: make it easier for you to get about.'

'I can get about.'

'Of course you can.' Doreen decided not to fight. She withdrew into the kitchen and sat on one of Mary's hard wooden chairs. She took a travel brochure from her carrier bag and allowed herself the satisfaction of a quick look. The hotel she had chosen was on the west coast of Corfu, just outside Paleokastritsa. She touched the glossy half-page photograph of the crystal blue sea and green clouds of olive groves.

Only a few weeks to go.

She had already paid the one-hundred-and-fifty-pound deposit. Soon she would need to pay the remaining nine hundred pounds. She wasn't unduly worried: she would have saved the money by then. The Odyssey Hotel looked beautiful, staring out across the Ionian Sea with its back to the mountains. Doreen read the description in the brochure to herself although she already knew virtually every word: 'Follow in the footsteps of the mighty King Odysseus to our Ionian Paradise. This well-appointed four-star hotel is a sun lover's dream. Soak up the rays in the day by the conveniently sized swimming pool and in the evening relax to the music of the Lazaros band at the "Acropolis" bar. Make your dreams come true on your very own Greek Odyssey.'

Doreen wondered what her dreams were. One had always been to travel abroad and now she was on the verge of achieving that. Uncertain, she looked down the hotel's list of attractions: pool, gymnasium, restaurant, snack bar, air conditioned rooms with balconies, hair drier and tea making facilities. She imagined herself sitting on her balcony with a glass of white wine and a box of chocolates in the warm shades of early evening. That would be a dream. Far away from blank, damp Cambridgeshire with its cantankerous old ladies and wet toilet tiles.

Underwood and Sauerwine arrived half an hour later. Sauerwine had received Mary Colson's message via an amused control centre. He had told Underwood on the latter's return from Cambridge. Doreen made them both a cup of tea and remained in the kitchen listening, suddenly nervous at the regular police visits as her dream neared its realization. She sucked on a cigarette as she concentrated.

'Are you feeling all right, Mrs C?' Sauerwine asked. 'We were worried about you.'

Mary Colson was watching a television programme about apes.

'Don't you think it's sad, Mr Underwood, about them killing all the gorillas?'

'I hadn't thought about it to be honest,' Underwood conceded

'Chopping all their forests down so they've got nowhere to live. It makes me very angry.'

'Ah,' Underwood noticed the documentary, 'I see. Yes, it's a terrible thing.' He shifted in his seat. 'Can I ask why you called us, Mary? Was it something else about . . . about my friend? The one who died?'

Mary Colson reached into her handbag and withdrew a sealed white envelope. 'I've written some things down for you both.' She was coughing quite badly, irritated by the smoke drifting from the kitchen.

'What things are these, Mrs Colson?' Underwood took the envelope from her but didn't open it.

'My dream,' she said, 'it was clearer last night. I felt closer to it. I understand it better now. The dog-man has killed other people. Not just your friend.'

Underwood looked down at the envelope. 'What have you written, Mrs Colson?'

Mary rubbed her tired eyes. 'After I woke up this morning, I wrote down all the details I could remember. It was a terrible dream. Worse than before. Your friend was in it. And a woman. I've never seen her in my dream before. I forget things as the day goes on. I get tired very easily these days. So I wrote it all down for you.'

'That's very kind of you, Mrs C,' Sauerwine thanked her, 'and don't you worry about being tired. You've always got more energy than me!'

'The planets haven't made you any more virile, then?' Mary joked.

'Not that I've noticed.' Sauerwine turned to Underwood. 'Mary's my personal astrologer. There's some planetary alignment thing this week. Mary reckons it's good for the old love life.'

Mary had stopped smiling. 'He's coming for me now,' she said quietly.

'Who, Mary?' Underwood asked. 'Who's coming for you?'

'I was in the dream, Mr Underwood. The dog-man is going to kill me too. I was inside a box.'

'Now, Mary, you listen to me,' Underwood said crisply, 'no

one is coming for you. You are safe here. No one knows about your dreams except PC Sauerwine and myself. We will make sure that no one else sees the notes you have made.'

'You promise?'

'I promise. You have any fears or concerns, you just call the station and we'll have a car here in a couple of minutes.' Underwood knew that the control centre would love him for making that pledge.

'I'm not afraid of dying,' she said, her gaze floating up to the window. 'I know my brothers and my son will be waiting for me. You know, my mother used to say that life is like a lullaby: a pretty song that sends us to sleep. I used to like that idea but my dreams aren't pretty anymore. I don't want to go to sleep now.'

'Come on now, Mrs C, we'll look after you.' Sauerwine crossed the room, took Mary's empty tea cup away from her and held her hand as she started to cry.

Underwood left them for a moment and walked through to the kitchen. Doreen started as he opened the door.

'Mrs O'Riordan?' he asked.

'Ms,' she corrected, stubbing out her cigarette on a saucer.

'Ms O'Riordan, Mary is rather upset today. She had a bad night's sleep. You may want to keep a close eye on her for the next hour or so.'

'That's why I'm here.'

'Yes,' said Underwood, 'it is. Planning a holiday?' He gestured at the brochure on her lap.

Doreen was suddenly flustered. 'Greece. Corfu.' She pronounced it 'Cor-phew'. Underwood found that immensely irritating.

'Well deserved, I'm sure,' he said dryly.

'I can't wait.'

'Mrs Colson seemed to be a little upset by your smoking.'

'Oh.'

'Maybe you should avoid smoking inside in future.'

Fucking old bitch.

'She should have said,' Doreen said tartly.

Underwood looked around the small kitchen. 'You know,

149

Mary was asking about her fudge. She wondered what had happened to it.'

Doreen shrugged, 'She's got you looking for it now, has she?'

'Oh no,' said Underwood. 'I know what happened to it.'

Doreen remembered that someone had cleaned up the microwave. She'd assumed it had been Mary.

'You do all Mary's shopping do you, Doreen?' he continued.

Doreen was nervous now. She was being escorted into a minefield. 'Unless it's my day off or a weekend. Then there'll be another carer on cover.'

Underwood smiled. He'd expected that. Doreen O'Riordan was no mug. 'Perhaps you could do me a favour.' He rubbed his chin thoughtfully. 'Mary is worried that her money is going missing. She thinks it's being stolen. Now, you know what these old folks are like – forgetful, aren't they? But maybe you could give me your duty schedules and any till receipts for the last month or so. That would show when you did her shopping and when one of the other carers covered for you, wouldn't it?'

'It should do.' Doreen was already trying to think of a way out. 'How would that help?'

'I could cross-check with Mary's records. See what she thought had been spent and what the reality was. If I had your duty rotas I'd know who had done her shopping on certain days.'

'She keeps all the till records then?' Doreen asked in surprise.

'Oh yes,' said Underwood, 'she keeps records.'

Half an hour later, in Dexter's office, Underwood opened Mary Colson's envelope and read the details of her latest dream. He noticed the date at the top of the first page and was reminded for a second of his own mother. The tenth anniversary of her death was approaching.

'Dear Mr Underwood, I am very sorry about what happened to your friend. But now we are friends and I hope that this might help you. Yours, Mary Colson.'

Underwood felt a twinge of guilt. He hadn't regarded Mary Colson as a friend. Maybe he had forgotten how to recognize them.

'First there is a man tied to a table. His hands are bound underneath him and his head is in a box. This was your friend: I know that now. He has spoken to us already. His spirit is restless. I told you his message about the keys. He has also appeared in other parts of my dream. There's a woman too, crying in the dark. She's terrified, screaming.'

Underwood found Mary's words more disturbing when written out in front of him. He didn't like to think of the dead sending messages: standing in massed, whispering huddles around him. Underwood had long since given up on hopes of salvation. The death of his parents and the implosion of his private life had eradicated any last vestiges of his Catholic belief system. He found the idea of an afterlife, of sharing eternity with all the spirits he had disappointed, utterly depressing. He had reconciled himself to death by imagining it as nothingness: a return to the same state of blissful unawareness we enjoy prior to birth. Underwood regarded awareness as a curse: becoming aware of things was, for him, a prelude to becoming disillusioned with them. That was why he opposed capital punishment: better to let the bastards rot in boredom.

He stopped drifting as he felt the tide lapping at his feet and tried to focus on Mary's letter:

'Then there is a pile of bodies: people hidden in different darknesses. They are together but separate. They are inside but outside. It's like a room with no building around it. There are children playing nearby. Maybe there's a school. I can hear them laughing and shouting. They are running in and out of the trees. Sometimes I can hear loud cracks like stones being smashed or gunshots.'

151

Underwood paused for a second. He had two problems: the first was that he had no evidence that there were bodies waiting to be found. Jensen and Rowena Harvey were missing but even though he sensed Jensen was dead it was standard procedure to assume abductees were alive until proof was found to the contrary. However, he reasoned, if his theory about the coins was correct, that the killer was counting down, then he could easily have dumped them somewhere together. Maybe the countdown was already complete.

His second problem was that Mary's dream was still vague. It gave him no real sense of where to look. *'Inside but outside. It's like a room with no building around it.'* Underwood was frustrated. The statement could mean anything. Maybe Mary had imagined a cellar: a building that had been demolished above the surface but whose basement remained. It seemed the most plausible explanation.

'But where?' He looked again at the page in front of him.

'There are children playing around the trees nearby. Maybe there's a school. I can hear them laughing and shouting. Sometimes I can hear loud cracks like stones being smashed or gunshots.'

Underwood discounted the idea of children playing: it was too vague. It could have referred to a school, or a playground, a field, anything. He focused on the last sentence of the section. *'Sometimes I can hear loud cracks like stones being smashed or gunshots.'* That was potentially more useful. Perhaps, Mary had seen a quarry in her dream. Underwood felt a spark of excitement. A quarry might have underground chambers that resembled a *'room without a building.'*

He reached into Dexter's drawer and withdrew her road atlas of Cambridgeshire. His finger quickly located three quarries: Melbridge Clay Pits, Little Elstead Gravel Quarry and Paxton Gault Stoneworks. He hesitated. He knew at least two of the three were still working quarries and the more he thought about the logistics of moving four or five bodies the less viable leaving them in a quarry seemed.

It would take the killer time to move and conceal so many bodies. He would not want an exposed area. He would want the privacy afforded by woodland or deserted buildings. Still, he would give the names of the quarries to Harrison to check up on.

'*Like stones being smashed or gunshots.*' He paused. What if the latter half of Mary's statement was correct? That the area was located near to the sound of gunshots. Underwood racked his brains. Where would you hear gunshots? On farmland possibly but that would only be intermittently; on organized shoots for game birds maybe.

Organized shoots.

He looked back at Dexter's map. There were two major rifle ranges that he knew of in the county. He wrote down the locations of both. The remainder of Mary's letter was disturbing and unstructured. It seemed merely a collection of strange images that lacked clarity and meaning.

'*I know, Mr Underwood, that the dog-man is going to kill me. You see, it happens in my dream. I fall to the floor and the dog-man rises above me. I feel a terrible pain in my head.*'

Underwood skipped through the next two paragraphs, which developed the image in greater detail. However, the conclusion of Mary's account drew his full attention.

'*The dream ends with me in a box. That's how everything ends, I suppose. Your friend is in the box with me. I try to get out but I can't. Then the lid closes. The thing is, Mr Underwood, that it's you who closes the lid on the two of us. I have had the dream for months without knowing who finally buries me. Now I know that it will be you. I knew it was you when I first met you. I find that reassuring. As I said, you have a kind face.*'

Underwood folded the letter up and placed it in his inside jacket pocket.

153

38

Dexter returned to the office shortly before lunchtime. She had driven home and tidied herself up; washing her face and trying unsuccessfully to scrub the redness out of her eyes. Underwood got up from her desk as she arrived and politely moved out of her way. Dexter dropped her radio and mobile phone on to her desk.

'Everything okay?' he asked.

'Marvellous.'

'Sorry I was using your office,' he said. 'It's just, well, I don't have one anymore.'

'Not a problem.' Dexter's eyes were glazed and unfocused. It was unlike her. Underwood was concerned. He decided to concentrate on business.

'If you've got a moment, Dex, I'd like to run through what we've got so far.'

'That won't take long.'

Underwood smiled. Dexter was in there somewhere: under the fog of unhappiness her redoubtable spirit still glowed. 'I'm not so sure. We're building a clearer picture of the "how", it's the "why" we're not so hot on.'

Dexter pulled open a drawer and took a bottle of mineral water from her desk. Her head was throbbing with dehydration. She unscrewed the cap and took a large and grateful glug. 'Two deaths, two abductions,' she said. 'We know that the two murder victims were injected with some mixture of organic poisons. The most likely sources for those poisons were the mushrooms our friend Dr Miller showed us.'

'Amanita Muscaria and Amanita Virosa,' Underwood added.

'Whatever. Does that matter?'

'I think it might.'

Dexter shrugged. 'So they are injected with this crap. It kills Ian Stark and would probably have killed Jack if the killer hadn't cut his head off.'

'I don't think the injections were designed to kill the

victims,' Underwood observed.

'What, then?'

'I'm not sure. That's the key to all this. The "why" that we are missing. The murderer wants to send them on some sort of trip before killing them.'

'Why did he cut Jack's head off? That's another "why" we haven't figured out yet.'

'Maybe he wants to take the symbols of their knowledge, of their intelligence away with him.' Underwood was struggling now, his ideas were still fragmented. 'You know, like a trophy. It's the coins that bother me.'

'How so?'

'If I'm right and they do represent some form of countdown. We still don't know what he's counting down to.'

'You're saying that he's collecting heads in anticipation of something?'

Underwood still hadn't figured it through properly. 'Maybe. By the way, I've asked HQ at Huntingdon to send you a list of all the police referral cases that Jack has been working on.'

'Why to me?'

'Two reasons: you're in charge and I'm one of the cases.'

'Okay. You think this fruit might be one of Jack's patients?'

'It would make sense.'

'There's another element here which I haven't discussed with you.'

Dexter raised a quizzical eyebrow. 'Go on.'

Underwood took a deep breath and told Dexter about Mary Colson and her dream of the dog-man. To his surprise, Dexter didn't laugh him out of the room.

'You say she has been specific? Specific about things she couldn't have known?' Dexter asked.

'Enough to freak the shit out of me. She knew about Jack's hands being tied under the table, she knew he was my friend, she said something about "remembering my keys": Jack said much the same thing the last time I saw him.'

'And she says there's more bodies?'

'About half a dozen.'

155

'Bloody hell.' Dexter thought of Rowena Harvey and Jensen.

'She's described a possible location. It's vague but I've given some suggestions to Harrison.'

'Do you believe in this stuff, John? All this psychic business?'

'Never encountered it before. The Met have used psychics in some cases, haven't they?'

'Yeah, as a last resort,' Dexter said darkly.

'Well we don't have a huge amount else to work with, do we?' said Underwood patiently. 'Look, Dex, if we do use Mary Colson, you need to be okay with it. Ultimately, if we catch this nutcase, no one will worry too much how we did it. On the other hand, if we don't catch him . . .'

'Everyone will say "why did you waste time talking to some cranky old bird?" And my arse will have a target stamped on it.'

'Something like that.'

Dexter thought for a second. 'Our priority is finding Rowena Harvey and Jensen. We have to assume that they are alive until we find evidence to the contrary. If this person is working to a timetable – counting down to something – we need to work quickly. We haven't got a lot of information to work with. I say let's use what she says.'

Underwood nodded. 'You want to hear the rest of it?'

'I'm all ears,' she said with the ghost of a smile.

Encouraged, Underwood related the dream of the dog-man.

39

It was a beautiful sunset: orange and white swirls reaching across the dizzying East Anglian sky. Max Fallon found himself sitting on the riverbank at Ely watching a university women's boat crew paddling back after a training session on the fens. He had little idea of why he was there. He lay back on the camp grass and listened to the vague quacking of ducks and the gentle slapping of oars on the water. The moon was starting to emerge above him.

He knew that the moment of his final incarnation was close. He couldn't see its twisting, momentous, approaching beauty through the glowing fuzz of clouds and sky but he sensed its inevitability. The idea was enervating. Rowena Harvey would be the willing vehicle for his chariot ride to immortality. He had already investigated her body in great detail, tracing her skin for blemishes, washing her in the morning. It was testing his reserves of self-control to the extreme. However, the moment had to be right and the moment was now a mathematical certainty.

Max found the thought arousing. He sat up and watched the women's boat crew. They had pulled up opposite him on the other side of the river and were leaning forward, releasing their feet from the strapping that fixed them to the boat. Max liked their light-blue Lycra body suits and the way their hair had become damp with sweat. He started with surprise as he felt a hard inside his jogging bottoms. It took him a minute of ecstatic confusion to clarify that the hand was his own.

The crew hauled the fibreglass rowing eight from the water and carred it inside the boathouse. The large wooden door clanked shut behind them. Max cursed his frustration. He became irritated with the cold grass and the exposure. He decided to walk back to his Land Cruiser. He had parked close to the river, next to a tea shop. An old Labrador retriever lay on the pavement in front of the entrance. He noticed its eyes tracing his movements.

Max froze when he arrived back at the car. He sensed a powerful but familiar smell emanating from inside. He looked through the glass and saw four grain sacks: two on the back seat, one in the passenger seat and one rammed up at the rear window.

'Whaaaafuck?'

He looked at the Labrador. It had the face of an old man: some inbred old fool.

'What did you say, you wanker?' Max called out to it.

157

The Labrador's ears twitched at the cry. It stood and sauntered over.

'I don't have time for a conversation, pal,' Max insisted,
'someone's filled up my car with shit.'

The smell was strong and nauseating. Max looked around
him.

'Did you do this? Is this your idea of a joke?' he asked the
dog which had sat down directly in front of him. 'I'm
laughing. Ho – Ho – Ho.'

The dog had picked up the smell too. It was scratching at
the rear door of the Land Cruiser, becoming agitated. Max
climbed inside and fiddled with the grain sack in the
passenger seat. He peered inside.

'Oh hello, Liz,' he said as recognition and awareness began
to trickle back into his brain. 'Sorry to disturb you.' He retied
the bag.

Now he remembered. He had driven the car up to the fens
to dispose of the bodies he had collected. He had developed
them already and so had no use for the remains. Besides, he
had reasoned, it was important to keep the house tidy for
Rowena and the baby.

'Woof!' shouted the dog, suddenly disturbed at the terrible
aroma.

'What?' Max replied confused. 'What are you talking
about?' The lights were stretching around his eyeballs the way
tired limbs are stretched after waking.

The dog growled, contorting the features of its old man
face, and backed away from the jeep as Max slammed the
door and started the engine. 'Woof!'

'You're not making any sense, mate,' Max shouted at the
golden shape. 'You old missing-link country cousins should
spend a bit less time playing banjos and take some fucking
elocution lessons.'

'Woof!' The Labrador turned sharply and ran into the tea
shop.

'The rain in Spain stains mainly on the brain,' Max called
out in his plummiest accent. The shape had gone. Max was
irritated. 'Fucking inbreds.'

He drove around Ely's tight, narrow streets for twenty minutes passing the cathedral twice before arriving back at the car park. He peered through his windscreen at the river in frustration and felt a sudden rush of panic: the town was enclosing him, its exits shutting around him. Even the tea shop had closed.

It took him another fifteen minutes to break free of Ely and he found himself racing south towards Cambridge and New Bolden through the bleak and desolate fens. He tried to remember how he had planned to dispose of the bodies. Max was certain that he had constructed a plan. He could recall reading a guidebook and consulting a map of Cambridgeshire.

Arriving at Ely had disorientated him. Had he planned to drop the bodies into the river? Or sink them into some soggy fen? The idea was tempting now as he cut through the watery fields of North Cambridgeshire but somehow it didn't ring true. He had chosen somewhere secluded. He was sure of that. It had been somewhere private that he had read about and for some peculiar reason he had missed the location and ended up watching the river in Ely. His memory was fragmented. It threw up distorted images rather than information.

Max tried hard to concentrate as the bodies shifted restlessly in their seats.

'Don't blame me,' he muttered at them, sensing their irritation. 'I don't hear you bastards making any helpful suggestions.'

A dark green smudge suddenly stretched across the horizon to his right. Max frowned, trying to identify it. It was a line of hedgerows enclosing a sprawling area of undulating marshland, pockmarked here and there with thick clumps of pine trees and entangling bracken.

'That's it!' he cried, smacking the steering wheel in delight. 'It's all right,' he shouted over his shoulder. 'You can stop moaning. I remember now. That is why I am a director and you are monkeys. There are leaders and followers. There are gods and mortals. Some people make a plan and implement it.

Others just come along for the ride. You lot are just passengers. I've been carrying you for too long.'

The Land Cruiser accelerated, overtaking a dawdling tractor and roaring through the twilight. In the near distance, terrible shadows stretched across Fulford Heath.

40

Rowena Harvey lay blindfolded, gagged and terrified in darkness. Her forehead still bled gently from the accident despite the presence of a crassly tied bandage. She was aware that she was unable to move. In her first moments of consciousness she wondered if she had been paralysed in the car crash. Then, gradually as her senses began to orientate themselves, she realised that she could flex the muscles in her arms and legs although she seemed to be restrained, tethered to a bed. Cold air nibbled at her skin and she realized, in a sudden flash of terror, that she was naked.

She strained at her ties, uncertain of whether she was alone in the room. She tried to push the cloth gag out of her mouth with her dry tongue. The sensation made her feel sick. After a minute of exhausting effort she sank back and considered the hopelessness of her situation. She was naked and trapped. Her husband was dead. No one was coming to save her.

Rowena Harvey tried to remain calm and gather her thoughts. She tried to draw moisture into her mouth and began to work again on pushing out her gag.

41

Dexter's telephone rang at 8.30 that evening. Underwood had been reading the post-mortem reports on Stark and Harvey, allowing his mind to wander in realms of terrible possibilities. The shrill cry of the phone in the dimly-lit office had made him jump.

'CID,' Underwood said after a moment's hesitation.

'Is John Underwood there?' It was a male voice: loud, confident and vaguely familiar.

'Speaking.'

'John, it's Paddy McInally down at Leyton CID.'

Underwood was taken by surprise. 'Hello, Paddy.'

'How have you been, mate?'

'I'm fine. I've been off ill for a while. Just started back. Your star student has been running the show in my absence.'

'It's Dexy I wanted to talk with you about, John,' McInally said.

For a terrible gut-wrenching moment Underwood thought Dexter was heading back to London and that DCI McInally was reclaiming the prize he had lost four years ago. 'What's the matter?'

McInally seemed uncharacteristically hesitant. 'This is between us, mate. It doesn't get back to her.'

'Understood.'

'She called me today. Asking questions about one Mark Willis. You heard of him?'

'No,' Underwood replied.

'Good for you. He's a toe-rag. Used to be my Detective Sergeant when Dexy was down here. He went bad. Started dealing the drugs he was supposed to be fucking confiscating. We chucked him out in 'ninety-five.'

'That's when Alison made Detective Sergeant.' Underwood remembered from her file.

'You always were sharp, John. Willis got the boot and Dexy got upped.'

'So what's the problem?'

'He's a proper villain now. Big time drugs right across East London. Dexy is interested in him. I'm wondering if he's turned up on your patch.'

'Not that I've heard,' Underwood admitted. 'I still don't quite understand your concern.'

'They were an item once, John, for a year or so before Willis got fired.'

Underwood felt a sudden inexplicable twist of jealousy. He was disappointed he hadn't outgrown himself. 'Oh.'

'She caught a lot of flak when she started in CID. He sort of adopted her. They got close and it all kicked off. You know how these things happen?'

'Of course,' said Underwood, still feeling horribly let down.

'Willis, being the toe-rag that he is, started jerking her around. We found out he was shagging a couple of WPCs on the quiet. The station got to hear of it before Dexy. Took the piss. It tore her up, mate. Worse than I thought it would. She talks tough but she's soft as shit underneath.'

'She wants to be taken seriously,' Underwood observed. 'It must have been a nightmare.'

'It's worse than you think. I found out from one of her so-called mates that she was pregnant.'

Underwood rubbed his eyes sadly. 'Oh Christ. What did she do?'

'Got shot of it and I don't blame her.'

'I'm beginning to see why you called now.'

'We've all got an Achilles heel, John. Mark Willis is Alison Dexter's. If he appears on the scene she'll need help. He always had a way of getting at her. He's a devious, dangerous little wanker. He also owes the Moules best part of a hundred grand. He's cat food if he doesn't turn up the dosh. Under that sort of pressure he's capable of anything.'

'I'll keep an eye on her, Paddy. Thanks for letting me know.'

'She's the best copper I ever worked with, mate. If Dexter blows up there's no bleeding hope for the rest of us.'

'You got that right.'

Underwood felt alone and exhausted as he put the phone down. McInally was right. Dexter was the rock. If she crumbled he would have no foundation stone to build upon. It wasn't even worth contemplating.

He felt a sudden, desperate longing for comfort.

42

Alison Dexter returned to the Morley Estate in darkness. This time she made sure that she hadn't been followed. Ian Stark's other garage was in the south-east corner of the estate. The lighting was poor and Dexter could see why Stark had chosen it: she felt comfortably invisible as she forced entry to the garage with her bolt-cutter. No dirt or leaves fell off the garage door as she opened it.

She shone her torch around the bare walls and checked her police radio was safely in her pocket. The garage was empty apart from a steel filing cabinet and some tools. Dexter picked up a hammer and a screwdriver and rested her torch on the ground next to the cabinet. She carefully placed the screwdriver under the lip of the locked top drawer and hammered it halfway inside. Then using all her weight she leant on the handle of the screwdriver, twisting back the lip of the drawer about an inch. She withdrew the screwdriver and shone her torch inside.

Bingo.

Dexter closed the garage door behind her to inhibit the noise she was creating. Next, she rummaged through Stark's tools to find a piece of equipment likely to inflict greater damage on the filing cabinet's locking system. She settled for a masonry chisel and went to work. The lock was resilient and it took Dexter an hour of furious industry to break through its mechanism. Eventually, a mixture of brute force and leverage forced the top drawer open fully.

Inside Dexter counted twenty separate kilo bags of cocaine. They were accompanied by dozens of plastic bags filled with pills; thousands of them. She sat back on her haunches, pouring with sweat. This was what Willis had coming looking for. At last she had the bastard by the balls. Working quickly, conscious that her endeavours might have attracted unwelcome attention, Dexter opened the garage door. A minute later, after checking she still alone, she reversed her Mondeo inside.

She loaded all the drugs into the car boot except for a single bag of cocaine. This she split open, spreading its contents across the garage floor. She withdrew a piece of paper from her inside jacket pocket and wrote a brief message on it. Dexter then left the message wedged under the burst bag of drugs. It was a calculated insult. She hoped it would sting.

After rolling her Mondeo forwards for a couple of yards, Dexter closed the garage door firmly then relocked it with a new padlock. Flushed with the effort and success of her operation Dexter then drove at speed across the Morley and around the New Bolden ring road. The journey took about fifteen minutes. Dexter parked up at the side of the Bolden Canal, a stagnant stretch of waterway behind a new industrial estate. She was careful to stay away from the CCTV cameras that some of the corporate residents had attached to their high metal fencing.

Dexter had a very clear objective. She removed the bags of cocaine and pills from her car boot and, one by one, poured their contents into the brown water. The process gave her enormous satisfaction. It was like blood letting. She was bleeding out the poison Mark Willis had injected into her system. Technically, she was destroying evidence. However, the thought no longer concerned her greatly. Ian Stark was dead and gone; his operations had ceased. There was no way that she could link the drugs directly to Willis: the only evidence she had was the appearance of Willis's name and number in Stark's diary. In any case, she had no desire to see Willis in prison. He knew too well how to play the system and beat it. Better to destroy the stuff completely and put it beyond temptation's reach. She also wanted to see the look on his face when he found out she had liquidated his hundred grand investment.

Dexter knew that she had lost her focus. Willis had clouded her vision as he always had done. She had needed him once. He had seemed to be the protective force she had once craved and needed. She resolved to break from her past. After all, she reasoned, one of her motivations for transferring to New Bolden had been to escape the quicksand of bad memories that had once threatened to engulf her completely. It was time to make good on her bullshit. She needed closure.

New Bolden was a small town with a small town mentality. It had frustrated her when she had first arrived. Still, Dexter thought as she accelerated away from the industrial park, it was a blank canvas. She could paint on whatever life she wanted to. The yellow glare of the streetlights flashed past the car as she headed home to her little flat near the police station. To Alison Dexter it seemed every glowing lamp was a bad memory and she was determined to leave them all behind her.

43

Underwood felt himself sliding into the whirlpool. He was clawing for a handhold on walls of water. His conversation with Paddy McInally about Dexter had unsettled him. He knew McInally relatively well. They had met and spoken at great length about Dexter's transfer from Leyton to New Bolden four years previously. The circumstances had been difficult and complex. Underwood had initially been hesitant about allowing Dexter to join him. However, McInally had convinced him. He had said losing Dexter would be like someone sawing his arms off. Underwood now understood what the Londoner had meant.

He tried to make sense of his feelings. He had spent months with Jack Harvey learning to isolate and control errant thoughts and emotions. Why had the conversation upset him? Alone, in the still unfamiliar silence of his bare flat,

Underwood surprised himself. He was jealous. Jealous that DCI Paddy McInally knew Alison Dexter better than he did. Jealous that McInally still saw fit to extend a protective arm around his former detective sergeant.

That was the root of it. He wondered if it was some primordial instinct. Did he labour under the primitive misapprehension that Dexter was his emotional property? Underwood was frustrated at the absurdity of it. He knew he had no right to be possessive of someone he had never possessed. How could he possibly have upset himself over some incident in Dexter's past that had happened eight years previously? He looked at the photograph of Julia he had placed on the mantelpiece. He had felt fury at his wife's betrayal: blind, white anger. Over time, that anger had melted into loneliness and a realization that he had created the problem himself.

Dexter hadn't betrayed him. She had been more supportive of him than anyone, with the possible exception of Jack Harvey. Perhaps he had built an image of her in his mind that suited his own purposes. That Dexter was the flawless professional he had never been. That she had willingly plugged logic and electricity into his tired and scattered mind. That she looked up to him as some kind of patriarch. Maybe he had filled in the blanks in Dexter's past to suit his own imagination; to make her into an idea he could control.

The realization made Underwood feel ashamed. He was tired of his imagination. It had driven him to the edge of madness. It had dropped him cruelly into an empty flat that he was frightened to decorate. It was now trying to twist Alison Dexter into a shape he could possess. Underwood remembered something Adam Miller had said to him: 'reality is underrated.' He didn't need to make up anything about Alison.

He decided to risk a glass of whisky. His mind was a jumble. His conversation with McInally had distracted him from focusing on the murder investigation and the hunt for Jensen and Rowena Harvey. Mary Colson's dream was beginning to tighten its grip on his thoughts. If, as Colson had suggested, there were potentially five or six victims awaiting

166

discovery, the inquiry was at risk of becoming trapped in minutiae. Underwood knew that forensic and post mortem evidence was critically important but he also had an uneasy sense that time was short. The priority had to be locating Jensen and Rowena Harvey. To do that, Underwood knew that they had to look for some kind of logic underpinning the killer's actions.

Let's imagine Mary Colson is correct, he mused, and that there are five or six victims. Let's also assume that the killer has removed each of their heads. Why would someone collect heads? What did the heads represent? The personalities of the victims possibly: perhaps taking the heads was a kind of trophy hunt, a control trip, predator and prey. Then there's the drug issue. Did he inject his victims with drugs to elevate their minds in some way? To change their perception? Change their perception of him maybe. Was the killer trying to redefine himself in the perception of his victims? It seemed to be almost a religious . . .

Underwood's train of thought suddenly derailed as he noticed that he had a message on his answerphone. He poured himself a small whisky and pressed play. His ex-wife's voice, crackly and electronic, emerged from the machine:

'Hello, John, it's Julia here. It's about ten o'clock. Just calling to see how you are. I saw the headlines in the paper about the killings in New Bolden. I wondered if you were involved in the investigation. I hope . . . well, I hope not to be honest. Things are going well for me. I'm set up now in Stevenage. Work is hard but I'm still enjoying it so that's the main thing. The, er . . . the other reason I called was just to let you know that I hadn't forgotten about tomorrow. I know it's a difficult day for you. I'll try and light a candle for your mother once I get back from work tomorrow. There's a Catholic church near me. I just wanted you to know that I was going to do that. If you need to talk tomorrow, or any time really . . . well, I'd better go or I'll use up your whole tape. Take care.'

Underwood downed his whisky in a single gulp. In his darkest moments through the previous year he had often imagined placing a shotgun in his mouth: two sawn-off barrels. He had imagined biting down hard on the metal shaft and then blowing out all the frustration and anger out of the back of his brain. The image flashed back at him and he struggled to banish it. His ex-wife was lighting a candle for his dead mother. What was that supposed to mean? He was uncertain how to react. Should he be grateful? Why had she decided to tread on his brain now? Was she being spiteful or trying to confuse him?

His mind filled with questions like a sinking ship filling with water. He was angry. Underwood reached up and retrieved Julia's photograph from the mantelpiece. After a moment's consideration, he dropped it into the cardboard box by his television.

Body and Blood

44

Dr Adam Miller had worked through the night at the Cambridge University Department of Botany. He had prepared a thorough analysis of both the Amanita Muscaria and Amanita Phalloides mushrooms including large photographs of both species that he had downloaded from the department's database. He had found his discussion with Dexter and Underwood stimulating. Although his mycological research still held the same curious fascination for him that it always had, Miller felt that his life had been drifting into the abstract. Research papers and lectures were interesting enough but he enjoyed the challenge and human interaction of fieldwork. However, in the UK that invariably meant trudging through soggy marshes and forests in the pouring rain and fog with a group of half-interested natural science students in tow. Still, until his dream job appeared at a West Coast American University, he would have to content himself with wellington boots, traffic jams and trudging across dank fens.

The challenge of applying his knowledge to a practical set of problems – and a murder hunt at that – was too good an opportunity to refuse. He knew that the police were mainly interested in the natural distribution of the two Amanita species that he had identified. However, he had resisted the immediate temptation to dive directly into the university's distribution records. The methodical approach, he reasoned, would be to write brief profiles of the fungi in question first. That in itself could provide valuable insights into possible local distributions.

He was keen to keep the report as non-scientific and jargon free as possible. He also determined that he would attempt to relate his analysis closely to the issues in question: why had the killer chosen the two species in question and where might possible sites for those species be?

He completed his report shortly after 7.30a.m. as sunlight began to find its way into his cluttered office on the second floor of the Department of Botany. As his printer began to spit out the pages of his report, Miller picked up one of the colour photographs he had downloaded of the Amanita Muscaria. Its deep red cap and white crusts made it hypnotically beautiful to Miller. It was as physically beautiful as its chemical signature was complex. Miller had only ingested Amanita Muscaria himself on one occasion: a drunken, youthful visit to Amsterdam. A night of anxiety and distortion had ensued as he watched his body slowly dissolve into a wash of unfamiliar colours and sounds. He had then endured an unfortunate gastro-intestinal reaction and spent a day being treated in a Dutch hospital for chronic diarrhoea and stomach muscle spasms. It was not an experience that he wished to repeat. However, the strange mushroom had fascinated him and he had concentrated his post-graduate research on the chemistry of toxic fungi.

Once the report was fully printed he placed it into a plastic folder for his own records. He then emailed the report in its entirety to Inspector Alison Dexter's address at New Bolden Police station. After a brief phone call to ensure the document had arrived and to offer further help should it be required, Miller left the department and walked through Cambridge to his favourite café for a large and unhealthy breakfast.

45

Alison Dexter called Underwood into her office and handed him a photocopy of Miller's report.

'I haven't read it yet. I need to speak with Harrison first,' she had told him. 'We've got one of county's helicopters today. He's taking it over to the crash site and then checking out some of the locations you gave him yesterday.'

'Based on Mary Colson's dream?'

'Yep. As you said, we've got sod all else to go on. Help yourself to the office until I get back. You can walk me through the report.'

'Thanks,' Underwood replied without obvious emotion.

As she left the room, Dexter realized that Underwood had steadfastly refused to look her in the eye during the exchange.

Sitting at Dexter's desk, Underwood noticed the date on Dexter's calendar. It had been ten years to the day since his mother's death. Ten years had flashed through his fingers. He would give himself a quiet moment later. He picked up Miller's report and sipping a coffee, began to read:

'Profiles of Amanita Muscaria and Amanita Phalloides: prepared for Cambridgeshire Police by Dr Adam Miller, May 2002.'

Catchy title, Underwood mused.

'Toxicology profiles provided by Cambridgeshire Police (May 2002) suggested lethal levels of amatoxin poisoning in two male adults. Detailed analysis of these profiles confirmed this hypothesis.

Toxin Identification: High levels of alpha-amanitin in both victims indicated the strong possibility of Amanita Phallcides ('Death Cap') ingestion. Alpha-amanitin is a cyclic-octapeptide that prevents protein synthesis in human cells. This makes human liver and kidney cells particularly vulnerable to its effects. 0.1 mg of alpha-amanitin per kilogram of body weight is usually considered a potentially fatal dose. This equates to a total ingestion of 7–9 mg. A single Amanita Phalloides mushroom of average size contains between 40–100 mgs of alpha-amanitin.

It should be noted that both victims contained significantly higher levels of alpha-amanitin ingestion than the

0.1 mg per kilo danger level. Victim A contained approximately 4.5 mgs per kilo. This suggests a total ingestion of 360 mg based on victim's body mass. Victim B contained approximately 5 mgs per kilo. This suggests a total ingestion of 375 mg based on victim's body mass. Clearly, the extremely high levels of alpha-amanitin imply that the ingestion was not accidental.

Blood and urine samples from both victims also showed high concentrations of Ibotenic Acid and Muscimol. These are powerful hallucinogenic substances found in various mushrooms of the Amanita genus, most notably the Amanita Muscaria ('Fly Agaric').

The large dosages found in the victims (and the absence of mushroom remains in their digestive tracts) suggest powerfully that some solution – or solutions – containing the above chemicals was introduced to the victims intravenously. This is a plausible if unusual hypothesis: Ibotenic Acid and Muscimol are both water-soluble, alpha-amanitin is lipid-soluble and water-soluble.'

Underwood wondered how the extraordinarily high doses would have disrupted the victim's brain functions. He thought especially of Jack Harvey whose clarifying logic and humour had hauled Underwood back from the brink of suicide. He hated to think of Jack's last thoughts being scrambled and meaningless. He read on, underlining sections of Miller's report which he found particularly interesting:

'**Descriptions:** Amanita Phalloides mushrooms have a broad, convex cap of up to 15 cm diameter. The cap may be slimy and varies in colour from dark green to yellow. It usually emits a pungent aroma. The stalk is white and up to 18 cm in height and 3 cm in width.'

Underwood looked at the photograph that Miller had provided and confirmed the details before moving on:

'The Amanita Muscaria is highly distinctive. The cap is

blood red and covered with white or yellow crusts or warts. It is usually between 6 and 30 cm in diameter. The stalk is white, up to 15 cm in height and 2–3 cm thick.'

Underwood flipped forward a couple of pages. There were more pictures of the two mushrooms from various angles and some complex details relating to how the mushrooms reproduce. He was looking for possible distribution patterns and was pleased to see that Miller had not disappointed him:

'**Distribution:** Both mushrooms grow indigenously across the United States, Central and South America, Japan and other parts of South-East Asia. They are also commonly found in Scandinavia and Siberia. It should also be noted that both the Death Cap and Fly Agaric grow indigenously within the United Kingdom.

'The most likely sites for finding these mushrooms within the United Kingdom are broadleaved, mixed and coniferous woodland areas between the months of May and November. The Amanita Muscaria is often found within birch forests or on clumps of birch trees in mixed forests. Both mushrooms can also be found within pine and fir forests. Recent evidence suggests that locating these fungi on open grassland, parkland and artificial habitats is becoming increasingly difficult.

'Specific areas of mixed, broadleaf and coniferous woodland include Wareham Forest in Dorset, the New Forest in Hampshire, woodland areas with the Yorkshire Dales National Park, Sherwood Forest in Nottinghamshire and in the coniferous forests of Northern Scotland.

'**Incidence in Cambridgeshire Region:** There are few records of either mushroom occurring in the Cambridgeshire region. Given the nature of the county's soil and the scarcity of appropriate woodland areas this is hardly surprising. There have been reports of Amanita Muscaria incidences on Holme Fen and in Monks Wood but these appear to have been made some years ago.

'However, it is worth noting the proximity of Thetford Forest, in Suffolk which is less than a twenty-minute drive from the New Bolden area. The forest is a state-planned natural development site planted largely with Corsican Pine. It also contains a number of birch and oak trees both of which provide suitable habitation environments for both of Amanita mushrooms under discussion. It should be noted that botanists from the university have identified samples of both fungi in this area: namely, in Wangford Glebe (1997), Brandon Park (1999), Thetford Warren (1999) and Santon Downham (2000).'

Underwood blessed Adam Miller. The information might not ultimately prove to be useful but it had given them a solid line of inquiry at last. Miller had identified the toxins that had been present in Ian Stark and Jack Harvey. He had identified the specific mushrooms that matched the toxicology profile and now even given a possible local source for those mushrooms. When Dexter eventually returned to the office Underwood paraphrased Miller's report for her benefit.

'Sounds like we should get a team up to those sites,' Dexter said after absorbing the details. 'I'll speak to the Suffolk plods and arrange it.'

'It might be worthwhile to get Miller up there, too.'

'You think that's necessary?'

'Could you tell one fungus from another?'

'Fair point. I'll call him. Sounds like he's done us a favour.'

'We still haven't figured out why, though,' Underwood said quietly. 'Why inject people full of this crap when you are going to kill them anyway?' His eyes moved quickly across Dexter's body and down on to the photographs in front of him.

46

It was a clear, chilly morning. The dew clung to DS Harrison's shoes as he crossed the grass lawn behind the county police headquarters in Huntingdon. He headed for the two police helicopters that were being prepared for take off about a hundred yards away. One was scheduled to fly down to coordinate the police response to a rush hour accident on the southbound M11 near Cambridge. The other had been assigned to him by County Headquarters to assist in the search for DC Jensen and Rowena Harvey.

The two pilots were deep in conversation and only noticed Harrison's approach when he ducked instinctively under the rotor blades of Airborne A.

'You don't have to do that when they're not moving!' one of the pilots called out.

'Force of habit,' Harrison replied.

'I'm Tony Payne, this is Gary Dennis. You must be DS Harrison.'

'That's right.'

'You're flying with me, mate,' Payne continued. 'Gary's off to direct traffic.'

The other pilot smiled at the insult. 'I hope you've packed a parachute, Sergeant Harrison.'

Payne grinned at Harrison as Gary Dennis climbed into the pilot's seat of Airborne A. 'He's a mouthy git. You've flown in the chopper before?'

Harrison nodded. 'A few times. Can't say I'm a big fan.'

'We'll be fine. It's a nice clear day. Not much of a breeze. Might be a bit foggy up in the fens but that should burn off. Might get a bit bouncy as I swoop in and out of telegraph cables. Only joking.' They walked the short distance to Airborne B. It was a dark blue helicopter with yellow trim and markings. Payne opened the pilot's door and withdrew a clipboard from his seat.

'Fantastic looking machine,' Harrison observed.

'It's a bit tasty,' Payne agreed. 'EC135. Mission Pod underneath contains a video camera with downlink and a state-of-the-art thermal imaging camera. I guess that's what you're interested in?'

'That's right. I want us to start at the crash site beyond Thetford and then work back towards Huntingdon. I have a couple of possible sites for us to check out.'

Payne checked his flight plan. 'First one between Burwell and Waterbeach, second one a couple of miles south east of Ely.'

'That's it. I want to use the thermal imaging equipment over those two sites.'

'What we looking for?'

'Bodies.'

Payne looked doubtful. 'The infra-red is sensitive but if the bodies have been exposed for more than twenty-four hours the chances of us picking anything up are pretty small. It's more effective for tracking live suspects.'

'I understand that, but it can give us a snapshot of a wide area and that might help us narrow our search.'

'True enough.' Payne looked back towards the main building blocks. There was a slight figure jogging across the grass in a blue flight suit. 'That's Janet Stiles. She'll be working the cameras for us.'

The helicopter rose above Huntingdon approximately fifteen minutes later. Harrison gripped the handholds next to his seat as Payne swung north-east and headed out across Cambridgeshire. The rotors were surprisingly quiet. Harrison leaned forward between the two front seats and spoke into his headset microphone.

'I thought there'd be more noise.'

'This is a surveillance platform,' Stiles acknowledged. 'It's meant to be quiet.'

Payne pointed out of his side window. 'We're going to follow the A1123, then trace the A11 until we're over Thetford. There's airbases at Lakenheath and Mildenhall so we'll keep south of those on our way up.'

Harrison watched as the strange patchwork of fields unfolded below him. Tiny uneven scraps and shapes: it was as if someone had shattered the countryside into thousands of fragments and painted each a different shade of green. He suddenly felt remote. As the vast flatlands of Cambridgeshire opened out beneath him, scarred only by the clustered grey villages and snaking lines of tarmac, he began to understand the enormity of his task.

The huge green expanse of Thetford Forest sprawled across the horizon less than twenty minutes later. Harrison recognized the A11 and the low white roofs of Thetford's industrial estates.

'The accident happened on the A1066, between Thetford and Diss,' he told Payne and Stiles. 'I'd like to do a thermal sweep of the surrounding fields. It's mainly open farmland. We've done house to house checks but the area's too big to search on foot.'

'Acknowledged.' Stiles began to adjust the control panel of a monitor on the left hand side of the cockpit instrument panel. 'Can you take us down to five hundred feet when we are over the crash site, Tony?'

Payne nodded and the helicopter swung eastwards over before dropping to low altitude over narrow, twisting line of the A1066. Stiles manipulated the control of the Forward Looking Infra-Red Camera underneath the EC135 and began to sweep the camera slowly across the fields. Images began to appear on her monitor screen. Harrison squinted at the strange white outlines and differential heat patterns trying to make sense of them. It was a painstaking process. Two hours later, Harrison conceded that they had drawn a blank.

'Where do you want to try next?' Stiles asked. She was already beginning to believe the search was a futile one. However, she knew that one of the missing women was a copper. She also knew from gossip in the staff canteen in Huntingdon that Harrison was living with her. She decided to keep her thoughts to herself.

'Site two, is near Cambridge between Waterbeach and Burwell,' Harrison said, checking his own map.

'There's not much there,' Payne commented as he banked

the helicopter south-east and climbed to 1000 feet. 'Why do you want to check it?'

Harrison hesitated. Underwood had given him the last two sites as possible locations. The inspector's rationale had been curious. He wondered how much he could tell the aircrew without destroying their enthusiasm for the search completely. 'We had a tip-off. The suggestion is that the bodies may be located in a wooded area near a rifle range. There are two major private ranges in the county. Sites two and three cover the areas surrounding both of them.'

'What kind of tip-off was that?' Stiles asked, looking over her right shoulder at Harrison.

'Trust me, you don't want to know.' Harrison decided not to share his knowledge: that the two sites had been chosen on the basis of an old lady's dream and a very shaky set of assumptions.

Ten miles to the east, in his semi-detached house near Downham Market, William Bennett was having great difficulty mobilizing his family. His wife Sylvia seemed to be inventing housework deliberately to delay their departure and his twin daughters Isobel and Imogen appeared to have an addiction to sleep. He was certain that they were feigning their exhaustion.

William wanted to get outside while the weather was favourable. He had spent an hour the previous evening preparing the family picnic in order to facilitate the logistics for the following morning. Now, the supposed time advantage he had created was being eroded by familial inertia.

'We really need to get going,' he told Sylvia agitatedly as she cleaned the inside of their oven. 'The weather may not hold and then the picnic will be ruined. I've done jam sandwiches for the twins and a tuna fish sandwich for you.'

Sylvia was fighting a losing battle but she continued stalling. 'It's only a twenty-minute drive, Will. What's the urgency?'

'The urgency is that if it rains there's a high chance the heath will get waterlogged. Then I won't be able to check

180

whether there's anything of interest. It could be an important archaeological site, Sylvia.'

Sylvia sighed. William's passion for local archaeology was becoming something of a bore to her. His growing collection of apparently meaningless rocks was a particular source of irritation. Especially when he insisted on washing and drying his 'finds' in her kitchen.

'Why is this such an important discovery, Will? Why is it any different from all the others?'

Bennett sat on one of the kitchen chairs. 'You've heard of the Lingheath Flint Mine near Thetford?'

'Of course.' Sylvia often felt as if she was living there.

'Well, the stones and soil marks I found last week on Fulford Heath were very similar to the rocks discovered at Lingheath. Now, the Lingheath mines produced flint that was used in the making of weapons – you know, gunflints and so on – from the eighteenth century. The evidence I've found suggests there may have been another flint mine operating in the area near Fulford. Perhaps not as important but historically significant nonetheless.'

'A flint mine? Historically significant?'

'Absolutely. During the Napoleonic Wars the mine at Lingheath was a major supplier to the British Army. Don't you thinks that's interesting? That the guns fired at Waterloo had flints that came from a local mine? If I'm right and there was another mine at Fulford, then who knows? Maybe flints from there were used in guns fired during the American War of Independence.'

Sylvia shrugged. 'It's your day off, William, wouldn't you rather be resting?'

It was a training day at the local primary school where William was headmaster. He had devolved his training responsibilities to his deputy with the governors' approval. It was an opportunity to test the theory he had been developing at weekends and school holidays.

'Come on, Sylvia,' William insisted, 'how often do we get a chance to go out together as a family? It'll be fun, I've done the picnic already. If I don't check the heath out properly

181

soon, the university will have students traipsing all over it dropping crisp packets and cola cans. It's my theory, after all. Don't you think I should get the credit for it?'

Sylvia looked at her husband – already dressed in his clean wellingtons – and felt a forked stab of guilt and pity. It was wrong of her to belittle his hobby. At least he wanted to involve her and the twins.

'Okay,' she conceded, 'I'll get the girls up. But I want to you promise that if it rains we are coming straight back again.'

William Bennett nodded and kissed her on the cheek. 'I'll put the stuff in the car.' He collected the sandwiches and bottles of drink from the fridge and placed them in a cool box. Before he started to load his car, he made one last check of his holdall: camera, ordnance survey map, notebooks, pens. He was ready and felt a buzz of excitement at the prospect of unearthing new evidence for his local history monograph.

47

Mark Willis drove slowly around the Morley Estate: a shark in shallow water. He was furious with himself for letting the two teenagers go after his altercation with Alison Dexter the previous evening. They were a possible information source squandered. In his current predicament information was money. And money was life. There was a small shopping precinct at the centre of the Morley. It contained a dismal parade of shops and a rather downtrodden doctor's surgery. Willis decided it was a good place to wait. He parked and bought himself a cheese ploughman's roll wrapped in plastic film from the Quik-Shop mini-market. It cost eighty-nine pence and tasted like rubber. He washed away his disappointment with a coke, enjoying the sugar rush. He returned to his car and waited.

Alison Dexter hated him. He had seen the fury burning in

her pebble-hard green eyes. However, he had also seen some-thing else, something pathetic. The same vulnerability that had attracted him eight years previously was still lingering there: it was an edge of desperation and loneliness. After a while that vulnerability had come to bore him. She had started to get clingy and possessive.

Their trip to Paris had been a mistake. It had given her a hope that he knew he could never realize. She had started holding his hand, talking about the future, about how they could manage their relationship at work. He had found that her serious manner suddenly revolted him. He felt crushed, that his options were starting to vanish. The night they had flown back into Heathrow together he had felt an over-powering urge to get away from her. He had called a friend from his mobile in the gents' toilet at baggage reclaim and engineered an escape plan. The same friend called him back five minutes later and Willis had feigned a sudden work crisis. He had put Alison into a cab with fifty pounds – 'The least I can do, Sparrer' – then driven alone away from Heathrow into the West End. The sense of relief had almost overwhelmed him. He had pulled an Irish nurse at a Leicester Square nightclub and spent the night working out his frus-trations on her.

Mark Willis had suddenly been cut free. He had loved the excitement of his job and his independence but his increas-ingly claustrophobic relationship with Dexter was draining his spirit. He resolved to start enjoying himself again: get jiggy with a few birds, make a bit of cash on the side. He knew how the system worked. He also knew how to exploit its weaknesses. Dexter had found out about him a couple of months later. That had been unfortunate. Her reaction had been far worse than he had anticipated. Still, he reasoned, that was proof that he was well shot of her. She was far too keen.

Willis snapped out of his musings as a mountain bike whipped past his parked car. He recognized its rider and started his engine. He trailed the bike around to the far side of the estate. Its driver dismounted at the front entrance of

183

a particularly dirty block of flats. Willis pulled up alongside in his Freelander and wound down a window.

'You still after some pills?' he called out.

The boy looked at him. His eyes were watery and his face pock-marked and pale. Willis recognized the symptoms. 'I'm a friend of Starkey's,' he added. 'I can do you a better deal than him, though.'

The boy leaned his bike against the wall of the flats and walked over cautiously. 'You a copper?' he asked.

Willis laughed. 'Do I look like a copper?'

'A bit.'

'Listen,' Willis reached inside his jacket pocket and retrieved a handful of yellow tablets, 'see these? These are called submarines. They'll blow your mind. I'm a big fan myself.'

'What are they?'

'Like speed. They'll give you a right fucking buzz. Give one to a bird and you are laughing.'

'How much?'

'Free to the right person. What's your name, sonny?'

'Joe.'

'Tell you what, Joe. Let's do each other a favour here. I'm looking for Starkey's lock-up. Would you know where that is?'

'You sure you're not a copper?'

'Absolutely.'

Joe shifted nervously in his worn Adidas trainers. 'He had a garage.'

Willis groaned inwardly. 'I know that. Over behind Hope House.'

'No,' Joe pointed in the opposite direction, 'I saw him using a garage over the other side, behind the precinct.'

'Could you show me?' Mark handed over the pills. Joe placed these into his trouser pocket.

'Okay.' Joe climbed back onto his bike and led Willis to the far side of the estate.

They found Stark's other garage within five minutes. Willis saw the shiny new padlock on the door and was immediately suspicious. The lock also looked much too easy to break. He knew that Stark was more cautious than this. Sensing a trap, he looked around the cluster of garages carefully before attempting to smash open the padlock. Satisfied that he was not being observed, Willis opened the boot of his car and withdrew the hammer that he sometimes carried in the pocket of his leather jacket for protection.

'Why are you still here?' he snarled at Joe.

'Do you need any more help, mate?' the teenager asked, wondering if there were more pills up for grabs. 'I could keep lookout.'

'You do that,' Willis muttered, eyeing the padlock.

'I'll wait by the road,'

'Loser,' Willis muttered under his breath.

He brought up his right arm and smashed the hammer down repeatedly on the lock. It snapped at the third impact and Mark Willis hauled open the garage door. He instantly knew he had been shafted. He saw the filing cabinet with its wrenched-open drawers and the bag of cocaine that had been emptied all over the floor. He checked inside the cabinet and found nothing. Then stooping down, he picked up the piece of paper Alison Dexter had left for him. He unfolded it, expecting a triumphant, sneering witticism. She had only written: '!'

Willis screwed the note up and threw it on the floor. 'Fucking bitch!' he shouted, throwing his hammer out through the open garage door. 'That fucking bitch!' She was playing a game. He could see what she was up to. He knew her too well. She wanted to make him grovel, beg for her forgiveness and charity. Well, he wouldn't demean himself.

He tried to clear his head to concentrate, focus on the reality of the situation. She had not done this officially, he told himself, she deliberately left the cocaine to make sure he knew she'd taken it. The garage had not been properly sealed either. The malicious little bitch had done this off her own back just to spite him. Mark Willis had seen enough. He was sick of games and the petty resentment of a childish

185

little woman. He lived in a bitter fucking reality and time was running out.

As he returned to his car, Joe came jogging back round the corner. 'All done, mate?'

Willis didn't reply. He opened the car door of his Freelander. Joe stopped him. 'Any chance of some more Scooby Snacks? I did keep look out for you.'

'What?' Mark Willis turned to face him with cold contempt.

'I helped you out big time. Wouldn't want me to get all talkative with the old bill, would you?' Joe made a point of looking at Willis's licence plate.

Willis nodded slowly and closed the car door. Suddenly, and with brutal strength, he butted Joe in the face. Blood erupted from the younger man's face as he stumbled backwards and fell into the garage. Willis was on Joe before he could stand up. He smashed his fist hard onto Joe's nose and then his jaw.

'You want some extras, pal?' he hissed. 'Some fucking scoobies? Well here you go.' He entwined the fingers of his right hand in Joe's hair and forced his face into the dirty pile of cocaine that Dexter had left lying on the garage floor. Joe's front teeth cracked against the unyielding concrete and he grunted and coughed as Willis ground his nose into the ground.

'Little word of advice, Joe,' Willis said as he took a pinch of cocaine for himself with his free hand. 'In future, don't get involved.' Willis slammed Joe's face into the concrete one last time and decided that every cloud did indeed have a little silvery lining.

48

The picnic on Fulford Heath had been a marginal success. The twins had enjoyed their jam sandwiches but a light spattering of rain had ruined Sylvia's mood. William Bennett

186

knew he would have to work quickly, before her patience began to drizzle away completely. She was already sitting in the car listening to the radio. William suspected that if the gathering black clouds dispensed their load, Sylvia would simply drive off and leave him.

He was working in an area about 100 yards away from the car. He could see the twins playing with their water pistols. Their blonde heads bobbed around as they dodged each other's fusillades. He had collected a number of flint samples from the area he suspected had once been a mine. He had also found a number of shallow indentations scooped in the uneven soil that he suspected had once been the entrances to mine shafts. He photographed each of these in turn and marked them with a small plastic tag for future reference.

He had almost completed his survey. He could hear the distant 'phut . . . phut' of gunshots from Fulford rifle range in the distance and the muffled thudding of a helicopter about a mile away. There were still two large earthworks and a ditch that he wanted to investigate. These were located behind a sprawling expanse of tangled hedgerow. Seeing their father disappear from sight into this area, the twins ran over to join him, squirting each other all the way.

William Bennett noticed something odd between the larger earthwork and the ditch that drained water from the heath. He moved closer to investigate. He could see tyre tracks, thick tracks that had left indentations gouged into the soil along the line of the ditch. They extended past the hedgerow for fifty yards in the direction of the road. He clambered over the first grass-covered mound and looked down into the ditch. He could see four grain-bags lying in the muddy water at the bottom of the gully.

'Phut . . . phut . . . phut,' said the rifle range.

'Thud . . . thud . . . thud,' replied the helicopter.

'What the bloody hell is that?' Bennett whispered to himself.

The hedgerow crackled slightly behind him.

'Daddy, Daddy!' called the twins.

'I'm here, guys, I'm just checking something.' Bennett swung his legs over the earthwork and gingerly lowered himself into the ditch.

'What is it?' asked Imogen.

'Can we see?' asked Isobel.

'*Phut . . . phut . . . phut,*' *said the rifle range.*

'*Thud . . . thud . . . thud,*' *replied the helicopter.*

'No, you stay there please.' Bennett advanced through the ditch.

'What can you see, Daddy?'

'I'm not sure, I think some naughty man has been dumping his rubbish here.'

'Yuk!' said Imogen. Bored, she turned and squirted her unsuspecting sister in the face with her water pistol.

Isobel screamed and the two exchanged giggles and shots.

'*Phut . . . phut . . . phut,*' *said the rifle range.*

'*Thud . . . thud . . . thud,*' *replied the helicopter.*

William Bennett crouched over the first of the four bags. It was tied at the neck with string. It stunk. Bennett hesitated. Holding his breath, he untied the string. Warily, he lifted the coarse edge of the grain sack and found himself confronted with the ragged, black tangle of flesh and sawn bone that had once been Liz Koplinsky's neck. He gasped for air and stumbled backwards falling painfully in the ditch. Panicking, he hauled himself back up and, ignoring the terrible pain in the wrist that had broken his fall, screamed at his daughters to get back to their mother.

Fifteen minutes later, County Headquarters radioed the discovery to Airborne B. Harrison was stunned when he heard the news: they were less than a mile south of Fulford Heath at the time. Stiles had been working the infra-red camera over a wooded area adjacent to the Fulford and Ely Gun Club. At Harrison's instruction, Tony Payne accelerated away from the position he had taken over the woods and headed north towards the open ground of the heath and the family salon car parked on the muddy access road. Harrison sat back in his chair as the EC135 dropped from the sky and bumped down on the rough ground. He tried to focus on being professional; on treating what he found on the heath as dispassionately as possible; on overcoming the shock of the coincidence. Then he realized their presence in the area was not coincidental at all.

Underwood had been right.

49

Mary Colson was afraid and disorientated. She had slept poorly again and had found it impossible to eat anything. She was also discovering that her daily sparring sessions with Doreen O'Riordan were gradually wearing her down. The realisation that this situation was precisely what Doreen was seeking had upset her even more. She had also been switched onto more powerful drugs to control the symptoms of her deteriorating Parkinson's disease. The side effects were unsettling. Mary sat in her armchair all afternoon. She had begun to feel uncomfortably warm and was finding it painful to swallow her tea. The doctor had warned her what to expect from her worsening symptoms. She could cope with the physical difficulties but found the erosion of her powers of concentration and reasoning distressing. Mary had begun to find herself standing in certain parts of her house with no recollection of why she was there.

Worst of all were the hallucinations. Mostly these came in the form of voices, some immediately identifiable, others curious hybrids born of her imagination. This upset Mary. She was becoming unable to use her gift. She found that the spirit voices she had once heard were becoming absorbed and corrupted by her aural hallucinations. It had become harder for her to distinguish between them at precisely the time that her mental powers had started to wane at an alarming speed.

'As you know, Mary,' she heard the doctor say, 'Parkinson's is a progressive neurological disorder . . .'

'I'm eating your fudge.' Doreen's voice swam out of the kitchen.

'Leave my fudge alone,' Mary heard herself say.

'As the nerve cells in the brain degenerate, you'll find it harder to get around the house . . . your muscles will feel stiff and uncomfortable . . .'

'The natural habitat of the gorilla has been critically eroded by deforestation and hunting . . .' said the television that wasn't turned on.

'You can't eat that, Mary,' Doreen's voice reminded her of an irritated school teacher, 'it's got nuts in it.'

'The degeneration causes a shortage of a chemical called dopamine in the brain . . . this makes it harder for your brain to send and receive messages from your muscles . . .'

'It's got nuts in it,' Doreen insisted.

'The man who died today was your friend, Mr Underwood.' Mary remembered that she had said that herself.

'Yes he was.' Underwood's voice floated over from her sofa.

'I'm prescribing you a more powerful dopamine agonist to compensate for this.' Mary heard the sound of tearing paper as the doctor had removed a prescription form.

'Remember the keys?' asked Underwood's dead friend.

'Ready for your box, Mary?' asked a voice that she didn't recognize.

'It's got nuts in it,' Doreen said.

Mary Colson tried hard to concentrate the conversation away. She looked around the empty living room and realized that she had to try and keep her brain occupied. However, this time her puzzle brain seized on particular words hidden in the jumble and built conversations out of them. The jumble on the page seemed to become projected into the room, a melange of nonsense broken only by occasional words that she recognized. She put the puzzle book away.

Perhaps she could do something around the house. Mary decided to open the kitchen window: she was sweating beneath her cardigan and felt that a breeze might help her.

The shaking in her arms and legs had abated over the previous hour and she felt confident enough to try it. Shuffling the short distance to the kitchen was easier than she had expected and Mary felt her confidence and mood increase. The volume of the voices began to recede and as she fumbled open the kitchen window the cooling breeze on her face calmed her agitation. Then, she noted with annoyance that Doreen hadn't bothered to take her rubbish out to the front of her house.

'It's bin day tomorrow,' she heard herself say. 'Don't you forget, Fatty.'

'Eat your breakfast,' Doreen had muttered.

Mary tried to lift the bag. It wasn't heavy. There was a slight drizzle in the air but she felt strong enough and confident enough to perform the task herself. She dragged the bag through to the front hall and unlocked the door. She peered outside and gingerly stepped down onto her front pathway, after ensuring her door was left on the catch: she had been caught out like that before.

She heard a dog bark. Halfway down her pathway, Mary felt a terrible flash of fear.

'The dream always ends the same way,' said her own voice from inside the house, 'when the dog-man appears.'

The dog barked again, louder this time. Mary squinted out into the fuzzy near distance. She couldn't see anyone but then her vision was poor. She struggled to the front of her garden and left the bag by her front gate. Now she could see movement: two shapes walking towards her.

'The dream always ends the same way . . .'

One of the shapes was a man, the other was a large dog jumping around him excitedly. Mary felt a rush of panic and terror. She turned and tried to hurry back to the house, her weakening nerve cells misfiring in her agitation. She stumbled and fell against the cold, damp concrete. It struck her face before she had time to put her hands out in front of her.

'Ready for your box, Mary?' asked the voice again.

She lay on her side as the world blurred around her. She

191

could see the green fuzz of the grass, the grey sky falling in on her and the face of a dog. She could smell its breath, feel its tongue rough and wet against her face. There was a man standing above her, peering down at her. She could taste blood in her mouth. She accepted the darkness gratefully.

50

Fulford Heath and the surrounding lanes had been closed off. A group of ramblers were watching the police vans and squad cars arrive from the edge of the police cordon. The EC135 police helicopter stood forlornly at the edge of the heath. The rain began to fall with greater strength and regularity. Underwood looked around the desolate land, its rough grass and clumps of entangling hedgerow. It was a fitting site. Mary Colson had been right to have nightmares about it. The scene of crime officers and forensic investigators worked methodically around the ditch that had contained the four bodies. Underwood found their spectral white overalls disturbing.

Dexter joined him. 'Are you as freaked by this as me?'

Underwood nodded. 'The old lady was right.'

'So were you. You figured out the rifle range.'

Underwood didn't feel any satisfaction. 'How many bodies?'

'Four,' said Dexter, 'two male, two female.'

'Any ID on them?'

'Nothing. All four bodies are naked. None had any personal effects with them. All four have been decapitated.'

'Jensen?'

'It's impossible to say at the moment, but one of the female bodies appears to be of the right build and age. Harrison is convinced that it's her.'

'We have her prints on record presumably?' Underwood asked.

'In her file. I'll make sure Leach gets a copy.'

'What about the others?'

'Middle-aged male and a younger male of between thirty and forty. Jensen – if it is Jensen – and another woman of approximately same age.'

'Twenties to thirties?'

'Right.'

Underwood was curious. The victims were not natural selections. Serial killers tended to prey on groups of similar social, sexual and ethnic background. The two male victims intrigued him. Both were potentially difficult targets: potentially physically strong and experienced. He remembered Jack Harvey was also in reasonable physical condition before he was murdered. Why would the killer choose such potentially awkward victims? Unless . . .

'He knew them,' Underwood said abruptly. 'He knew all of them.'

'Jensen?'

'She was with Rowena Harvey. The killer obviously knew the Harveys. Jensen just got in the way. He's killing people he knows, for a specific reason. Identify the bodies and we'll catch him.'

'That is easier said than done. Two are badly decomposed. Without the heads we won't be able to use dental records. We'll just have to wait for the post-mortem results. Maybe one had some particular disease or surgery that could help us when we cross reference with missing persons. It'll take time though and it may not produce anything at all.'

'Fuck it.' Underwood felt his stomach knot in frustration. He knew Dexter was right but he kept thinking of Rowena Harvey.

'There's one other thing,' Dexter said. 'This won't cheer you up but it might give us some encouragement. In the sack containing the middle-aged man we found five ten-pence coins. In the sack containing the female victim – not Jensen – we found four coins. In the sack containing the younger man we found a single coin. Now if you combine that with the three coins we found on Jack Harvey and the two in Jensen's car . . .'

'Five, four, three, two, one,' said Underwood quietly.

'It's a countdown. You were right. That's something, isn't it?' said Dexter, trying to encourage him. 'Something we can work on.'

'No,' Underwood replied quietly. 'It means we've run out of time.'

Dexter turned as Marty Farrell approached them from the direction of the ditch.

'The bodies are being moved now, guv,' he said to Dexter, 'we're taking them to Addenbrookes. Their resources are better than New Bolden's. I'll call Leach and send him there.'

'Thanks, Marty,' Dexter replied. 'Anything else?'

'We've got tyre tracks, pretty good ones, heading to and from the ditch. Mr Bennett, the guy who found the bodies comes here regularly. He swears blind that the tracks weren't here last week. It's a good bet they belong to our man.'

'Anything we can go on?' Underwood asked.

'We're taking photos and casts now. There's a good impression of the tread. We'll certainly be able to match tyre type.'

'What about the car?' Underwood continued. 'Will we be able to ID it based on the tracks?'

'Maybe. It's early days but given the dimensions we've got – you know, the distances between the left and right tyres, between the front and rear axles, and the depth of the tyre impressions in the mud – I'd say we're looking for one of those fuck-off great jeep things or a people carrier. Sorry, I wasn't trying to be funny.'

'Didn't Harrison figure that the killer drove a flashy motor?' Dexter asked.

'He did,' Farrell conceded. 'Is he all right, by the way?'

Dexter shook her head. 'Would you be?'

'No. I guess not.'

'Thanks, Marty. When you get more on the tyres will you let me know straight away.'

'No problem,' Farrell nodded at Underwood and walked back towards the ditch.

Dexter could see Harrison sitting in the passenger seat of one of the parked squad cars.

'I'm going to speak to Mary Colson again,' said Underwood. 'She got us this far, maybe I can get something else out of her.'

Dexter agreed. 'I should stay here.'

'Absolutely.' Underwood looked at Dexter for a moment, remembering his conversation with McInally. 'Dex, is everything else okay?'

Dexter turned in surprise. 'You my pastoral carer now?'

'No. I just wondered. You've been under pressure. It can get tough.'

Dexter was taken aback, touched by her former boss's concern. She was uncertain how to respond: opening Pandora's box and releasing Mark Willis for Underwood's assessment was unthinkable to her. She was also aware that Underwood had registered her hesitation.

'Let's get going,' she said eventually. 'We've got lots to do.'

Conversation over. Underwood turned sadly and headed towards his car. Dexter had never been good at hiding her emotions and he could read heartbreak in her eyes.

51

Max Fallon had just given Rowena Harvey her evening bed bath and taken his time applying moisturizing cream to her body. She had writhed violently and screamed into her gag, to his immense irritation. The woman appeared to have no sense of the great task for which she had been chosen. Max was finding it increasingly difficult to contain himself. However, the great day was looming and soon his incarnation would be complete. His eyes lingered on Rowena Harvey's naked body. She was ripe for motherhood. It could all have been very different. He sat on the edge of the bed as a sunny day a month previously reared brilliantly in his memory.

He had sat in his convertible Porsche 911 outside the main entrance of the Fogle & Moore building. It was 8.30 on a Sunday morning in early April and the streets around Canary Wharf were deserted. He knew where he was but felt strangely disorientated. The buildings seemed unfamiliar, uneasy at his presence.

Under the milky ocean something is not quite right

They were temples of the Gods, thrown out of the water by the churning of the ocean. Their colours were shifting in the brilliant, white light of his divinity. The deserted glass temples still echoed with the screams and laughter of his incarnation.

Max lay back in his seat and watched the sunlight bounce off the windows of the Canary Wharf Tower, race across Cabot Square and ricochet off the mirrored glass of the Morgan Stanley building. He was faster than the beams. He waited for them at each point of their triangulation. He was, after all, a God.

He was the Soma. Created at the churning of the ocean. Deep under the milky ocean he was forged by forces beyond human comprehension.

'Who are you talking to?' said a female voice above him. A face silhouetted in the sunlight that he had left trailing in his wake. The face moved away, Max slid down the sunlight and tried to focus.

Liz Koplinsky tried to open the boot at the front of Max's Porsche.

'This is locked, buddy!' she called out.

Max said nothing and Liz eventually climbed into the car and slung her overnight bag into the space around her feet. Max watched her closely for a second, waiting for the lights to recede. When Liz's face emerged she was just as beautiful as he had remembered.

He would fuck her. She would incarnate his divinity.

'Are we leaving this place any time soon? I'm on holiday as of now,' Liz said impatiently. 'Four weeks! Bring it on, buddy. I hope this sunshine lasts. Danny's been running the floor since you left. He's relocating me to head trading in Frankfurt . . .'

Max floated away as she babbled.

'. . . it's kinda scary I guess but the Krauts aren't making jack shit. Their margins are way down. I'm going in like the 82nd Airborne to kick some ass. Hey! Are you listening to me?'

Max watched as the lights grouped and accelerated into the air, high above the car, spiralling like brilliant fireworks until they arced down suddenly into the splashless water.

'Fucked up or what?' he asked.

'Excuse me?' Liz laughed at the unusual comment.

The Porsche roared to life as Max mumbled a reply. They sped out of Canary Wharf and rumbled east past the Millennium Dome. Max realized as they drove past that it was a scrotum dangling between the hind legs of the Isle of Dogs.

'How long will it take to get there?' Liz asked as she placed her Armani sunglasses on the top of her head.

Max's erection was starting to hurt him. It wouldn't go away and now it hurt. It was as if someone had thrust a hammer into his perineum.

'An hour. There's a bottle of champagne under your seat.'

'You're kidding?' Liz reached between her feet and retrieved the bottle. 'Champagne at nine in the morning?'

'Who gives a toss? Drink it.'

'You swear too much, Maxy.'

'That is not the fucking point.' Max missed a gear and the car groaned its frustration back at him. 'The point is it costs two hundred big ones a bottle and I bought it for you.'

'I'm touched,' said Liz sarcastically.

'Besides,' said Max as they jumped a red light, 'it'll help to take the taste away.'

'What taste?'

The Porsche swerved across the dual carriageway as Max reached inside his jogging bottoms and pulled out his erection.

Liz laughed. 'You are too much.'

'I'm serious.'

'And you can't ask me any better than that?'

'I'm a God.'

'Yeah, the unemployed God of Bullshit.'

197

Liz peeled the foil from the top of the champagne bottle and flicked the cork out of the car with a gratifying pop. She took a deep swig of the champagne and unbuckled her seat belt.

'You don't deserve this,' she said, leaning over.

'Just fucking get on with it.' Max was irritated. The lights rushed past the car and were tap dancing on the road in front of him. He squinted them away, looking for signs to the M11.

'Hey! Will you stop swearing at me?' Liz's smile had vanished.

'I'm sorry.'

Liz leaned over again. She slipped one hand under his balls and bent down to take his dick in her mouth. She recoiled suddenly. 'When did you last take a shower?'

Max was confused. 'What do you mean?'

'You're a little ripe down there, honey.'

He was horrified at this affront to his divinity.

'I've got an idea.'

Liz picked up the champagne bottle and poured a small amount over Max's penis. He gasped as it fizzed at him. Liz reached over again and this time took him into her mouth.

'Better?'

Liz grunted her approval. He held her head down on him. The Porsche raced towards the M11, drifting from left to right across the empty street. A few people watched the car as it roared past. Max didn't care. He was laughing too much, laughing at the absurdity of a god with a genital hygiene issue.

They arrived at the house at 10.30. Liz was impressed.

'Wow! When was this place built?'

'About seventeen-fifty.'

'Shit. That's older than America.' She scrunched across the gravel drive and looked around. 'You need a gardener, Maxy. I think Vietcong might be hiding in these bushes.'

'I used to have a gardener,' said Max thoughtfully. 'I can't remember what happened to him now.'

'He probably got lost in the herbaceous border. This place has got huge potential though.'

Max looked at the sad old house. Its crumbling stonework

and faded façade. Liz was right. The building was in decay
but it would soon be rejuvenated. And its location was
perfect. Max had reaped the harvest.

'Are you on any birth-control pills?' he asked suddenly.

'I'm sorry?'

'Do you want to have children?'

'You're asking me now? On a driveway?'

'Do you?' Max studied her face closely.

'Boy, you are full of surprises. "Want" – yes. "Can" – no.'

'I don't understand.'

'Premature menopause. The egg store is dried up. I can't
have kids.'

'You can't have children?' Max was struggling to concentrate. The lights were contorting Liz's face into something
disgusting.

'You asked. I told you.' Liz approached him and put her
arms around his neck. 'Is that a problem?'

Suddenly she revolted him. Her breath. Her perfume. Her
body. She was a horror. She could not have children. She was
merely a useless receptacle. He resented her barrenness. He
mourned for the progeny of Soma that had already died
uselessly inside her.

'So,' she said, 'are you gonna give me the big tour or are we
gonna get all maudlin in the driveway?'

He led her inside and showed her the main hallway with its
huge staircase and the oil paintings that lined the walls of the
corridors. Without interest he showed her the library with its
giant east-facing window and high ceiling. Max was rapidly
drained of enthusiasm and after only the briefest of tours, he
decided to take Liz up onto the roof.

There was a small steel ladder in the huge attic space that
led onto the roof via a hatch. It took Max an irritating half-
minute to fumble open the padlock. Once he had done so,
they both stepped outside.

'God! It's beautiful up here!' Liz observed.

'You can see forever,' said Max.

Liz squinted out at forever.

'Well,' she said, 'you can see the motorway.'

199

Max didn't find her amusing. Liz picked her way across the flat roof, enjoying the view of Thetford Forest to the east. She curled her nose suddenly.

'Can you smell something?' she asked, looking back over her shoulder.

Max didn't move. All he could smell was her putridness.

'It sure does stink.' Liz looked around her. There was a bulging grain sack lying a few feet to her right. 'I think it's coming from here.' She approached the bag cautiously. She was close to the edge. Max came over to join her.

'What the hell is in there, Max?' she asked undoing the string tie around the neck of the bag.

Max laughed. 'Funnily enough, that's the gardener.'

Liz stepped back as the bag fell open, spilling its black and bloody contents over her feet. Max grabbed her and in a swift, powerful movement, flung her over the edge of the building.

Liz Koplinsky only started to scream a split second before she crashed through the roof of the old conservatory seventy feet below.

Max leaned over the edge and peered out at forever. He reached into his pocket, withdrew four ten-pence coins and tossed them into the air.

And so Rowena Harvey had no sense of how lucky she was. Her involvement in his grand plan had so nearly never happened at all. If Liz Koplinsky had not failed him, then Rowena Harvey would only have been a spectator to history rather than an active participant. And yet she still had no understanding of the great duty for which the Soma had selected her. He mused upon how the situation could be rectified. His remaining phials of elixir were of considerable potency. He did not wish to inflict any physiological damage upon the bride of Soma. Perhaps there could be some compromise solution. Max giggled at his unintentional pun. Kissing Rowena Harvey on the forehead and on each nipple before he left, Max hurried downstairs from the master bedroom. The kitchen was located in the basement of the old house, two flights of gloomy stairs below him. It was a chaotic mess of dirt, mushrooms and litter. Max kept the phials of his elixir and clean syringes in the fridge.

He considered his options. The intravenous introduction of the elixir was out of the question as the risks were too great. The toxin concentration was dangerous and Fallon usually mixed his own blood into the elixir. Much as the idea of a needle piercing Rowena Harvey's skin excited him, he did not want to damage her permanently.

His own preferred method for ingesting small quantities of the Soma was to drink the urine he had expelled and bottled during some of his most kaleidoscopic transformations. Max's research had alerted him to the fact that many of the magical components of the Soma lived on after passing through the body. He checked his stocks of urine. He counted six one-litre bottles on the kitchen draining board. It was a possibility. However, he felt it unbefitting that the bride of Soma should enjoy her first visit to the Godhead by partaking of his divine piss.

Max sunk to the floor in silent hysterics. His hands touched the soil that was strewn across the floor. 'This is the dirtiest fucking taxi I've ever seen,' he roared, tears of mirth streaming down his face. It took him ten minutes to calm down. Eventually, Max struggled to his feet and tried to formulate another plan.

Oral ingestion! Of course.

He staggered about the kitchen stunned by the simplicity of his idea: he would make Rowena Harvey an omelette. Had not Zeus assumed the form of a swan before the rape of Leda? Had not Jupiter visited Aegina in the form of a great fire before her impregnation? He knew now that he was writing his own mythology. The Soma would visit Rohini in the form of an omelette.

'Now,' he said to the head he had been washing in the kitchen sink. 'Ingredients?'

Max looked around him, trying to make sense of the detritus and litter scattered around him. 'This taxi is a fucking mess,' he giggled, 'I shall report you to the Hackney Carriage Association of London!' He found an old frying pan in a cupboard under the sink, it was blackened and ancient but functional.

'Milk, eggs, onions, fat and mushrooms!' he clapped his hands together in excitement, 'Mushrooms we got!' He picked a particularly juicy-looking Fly Agaric mushroom from his bread bin and chopped it up on a wooden carving board. He emptied it into the frying pan. Then Max's culinary slide ground to a shuddering halt. He had no milk, no fat and no eggs. He cursed in frustration. He would have to go shopping.

He explained this difficult set of circumstances to Rowena Harvey after an energy-sapping ascent of the east staircase. She lay perfectly still, but watched him wide-eyed with terror.

'So eggs will be my priority,' Max announced as he read off his scrawled shopping list. 'Eggs will make you strong. I'm going to get some little surprises for you too. Seeing as you're such a good girl.' He sat down on the bed next to her and ran his index finger in circles around her tummy. 'You've got little blonde hairs under your belly button.' He stared at her nakedness for a moment, savouring what was to come, before hurrying out of the room.

He climbed into his Porsche and spent an irritating five minutes trying to fumble the keys in the lock. Eventually, he realized that he was trying to start the wrong car and switched to his Land Cruiser. It started immediately. Max roared out into the early evening. He knew there was a twenty-four-hour superstore just north east of New Bolden, about ten miles from his house. He manoeuvred the jeep onto the A10 and accelerated towards New Bolden. His mind fixated on Rowena Harvey. The prospect of impregnating her and siring the lunar race on earth was almost too much for him to bear. He somehow had to make it through one more night without pre-emptively debasing her.

He arrived at the superstore shortly after 6p.m. It was vast, white and intimidating. Max felt highly conspicuous. He chose a shopping trolley instead of a basket as he felt it would be a more effective means of hiding the erection that had ambushed him in the car park and which he now couldn't get

202

rid of. He made a mental note never to wear his jogging bottoms again in public. He was a Divinity. He was the Soma. The Soma must have dignity.

'Eggs, milk, fat,' he repeated to himself as he pushed the trolley up and down the aisles. 'Eggs, milk, fat.'

Finding the eggs was easy. He selected twelve large barn eggs. The milk took him half an hour to locate. He chose three large plastic containers of semi-skimmed, pleased that he could subsequently use them for the urine of the Soma. He accosted a female shop assistant next to the cheese counter:

'I'm trying to find the fat,' he announced.

'You mean cooking fat?' the assistant asked, taking a small step backwards after catching a waft of Max's body odour.

'I'm specifically after omelette fat,' Max clarified politely.

'Try the second aisle on the left.'

Max shambled off in the suggested direction. There was a bewildering choice of fats: sunflower fat, olive fat, low calorie fat. He became confused and settled for olive fat. On the way to the checkout Max passed a large display of disposable nappies. He realised how remiss he had been. He had made no preparations. And Rowena could hardly be expected to go shopping in her condition. He placed a couple of multi-packs of nappies in his trolley, along with baby talcum powder, some small tins of baby food, a packet of rusks and a rattle.

The girl at the checkout wore a red shirt and a badge that said Janice.

'Hello, Janice,' said Max Fallon.

She appraised him with tired, hope-starved eyes and smiled an empty smile. She whisked Max's shopping through the electronic eye. He watched her, hypnotized by the beeping machine.

'You should try to keep the intervals between the beeps constant,' he advised, 'that way you would almost be playing music.'

'You what?' Janice frowned.

'You know: beep . . . beep . . . beep . . . beep . . . land of hope and glory . . . beep . . . beep . . . beep . . . beep . . . monarch of the sea,' he sung.

'Thirty-eight pounds sixty-two please,' Janice held out her hand.

Max gave her a screwed up fifty-pound note he had found in the pocket of his jogging bottoms.

Max had to concentrate hard through the sudden light show that emerged behind his eyes to locate the driveway to the old hall. He shifted his new possessions down to the kitchen and happily made up Rowena Harvey's magic mushroom omelette. He included four eggs. He wanted to keep her strength up. He was careful to fry the mixture at a low heat so as not to degrade the vital elements within the blood-red mushrooms that garlanded his creation. He was delighted with his work.

Max carried a tray upstairs to the bedroom. It contained his omelette, neatly folded over on a surprisingly clean white plate, a flower he had stolen from a display at the supermarket, a tape recorder, a rattle and a glass of urine.

He pulled down Rowena Harvey's gag to feed her. She screamed. And screamed. And screamed. Max allowed Rowena to wear herself out. He contented himself with a relaxing drink as he enjoyed the views out of the bedroom window towards the distant bulk of Thetford Forest. Finding a house that so suited his purposes in such an ideal location had been incredibly lucky. He considered it two million pounds well spent, even if the place was falling to pieces. Eventually, Rowena stopped screaming, and Max returned to the bed. He sliced a portion of his omelette and placed it onto a fork. Rowena turned her head away.

'Now come on, Rowena, have a little piece. You must be starving.' Fallon plucked the piece of omelette off of the fork and forced it into Rowena's mouth. He clamped his hand over her mouth and nose until he was satisfied that she had swallowed it. Then he repeated the exercise until she had eaten half of his creation. He picked up the tray and placed it on the bedside table.

'Look,' said Max excitedly as he replaced the gag, 'a flower for you and a little rattle for our baby.' He shook the blue and red rattle before Rowena's bewildered and petrified eyes.

'I have to go now,' said Max. He pressed play on his tape recorder after noticing Rowena's eyes were rolling and losing focus, her pupils dilating. 'Listen to the tape, Rowena. It will take you to the Godhead. Don't be surprised to find me waiting for you.'

Max left the room as his own voice came onto the tape recorder, reading extracts from the Rig Veda and explaining how he had come to be the Soma. He headed downstairs in a state of high excitement. He found two fifty-pound notes in his favourite jacket and decided to drive back to the service station he had passed on the A10 an hour or so previously. He had heard on his radio that roadside relief was a growth industry.

52

Underwood arrived at New Bolden Infirmary shortly before 9p.m. He had driven directly to Mary Colson's house after leaving Dexter at Fulford Heath. Finding the cottage empty, he had driven back to New Bolden police station and found a message waiting for him for PC Sauerwine. Entering the hospital gave Underwood a twinge of apprehension. The proximity of death and illness had always reminded him of his own mortality. He crossed the main reception and took a lift to the second floor. Mary Colson had been moved from Accident and Emergency to a recovery ward once the extent of her wounds had been gauged. He found her in the last bay of ward 2F. Sauerwine sat at her bedside, his dark blue uniform incongruous in the bleached, colourless surroundings.

'Thanks for coming, sir,' Sauerwine said as Underwood approached. 'Much appreciated.'

'No problem. What's the story?' Underwood looked at the frail figure sleeping beneath the plain sheet, remembering the death of his own mother.

'A neighbour was walking his dog down Beaumont Gardens and saw her fall over. He called the ambulance. Sounds like an accident. She was taking out her rubbish and slipped. Apparently she's been switched onto new medication recently: it can make you feel nauseous. Doctor reckons she got dizzy and lost her balance.'

'What's she done to herself?'

'She badly bruised her right arm and her ribs. Bashed her head as she fell over. It's a miracle she didn't break anything. She was in a lot of pain, though.'

'How long have you been here?'

'An hour or so.'

'You're a good egg, Sauerwine.' Underwood frowned slightly. 'You say a man was walking his dog outside?'

'Some old codger, I've got his details. Seemed a decent sort. He's worried we're going to have his dog put down.'

'Why? Did the dog have a go at her?'

'No. There's no scratches or bites on her but he reckons she stumbled when she was trying to get away from the dog. He's mortified. You know what these old folks are like. Will you want to speak to him?'

Underwood shook his head. He recalled Mary's dream. Mary had foreseen her own death at the hands of a dog-man. She had interpreted that the dog-man had also been the murderer of Jack Harvey. Perhaps she had conflated the images, Underwood mused. If Mary did have an ability or gift to see in to the future it seemed plausible that she might have muddled the messages: associated her own pain with that of Jack's.

'She's been right all along,' Underwood said quietly. 'What she's told us has been accurate: generalized, muddled but accurate.'

'I heard about the bodies on Fulford Heath. I was on my way up here when I got the call about Mrs C.'

'She said the bodies would be underground but outside. They were. She said she could hear gunshots in the background. Fulford Heath is next to a rifle range. She said there'd be five or six bodies and we found four. Include Jack Harvey and Ian Stark and that makes six.'

'So far,' Sauerwine added.

'There won't be any more,' said Underwood confidently. Then he thought of Rowena Harvey. 'At least I hope not.'

'Why do you say that?'

Underwood ignored the question and sat down next to Mary Colson. 'What state is she in? Is she going to be able to talk to me?'

Sauerwine shook his head. 'She's on tranquillizers. She's out for the count. To be honest, I was about to head up to Fulford Heath and see if I could help out. Hospitals depress me.'

Underwood nodded. 'I'll stay here for a while.'

Sauerwine collected his notebook and radio from Mary's bedside table and left the ward. Underwood tried to focus on the basic facts of the case. He found the silence of the ward helpful. So far they had found six bodies. Five had been decapitated. Victims had been both male and female and of various ages. Both Farrell and Harrison had suggested the killer drove a large expensive car. The tyre tracks on the heath appeared to confirm that he drove a large vehicle. That made sense to Underwood. There was one anomaly Underwood recalled: all the bodies had been found outside except Jack Harvey's. Jack had been attacked in his own home. The killer had taken pains to burn all of Jack's records. Had he been trying to erase Jack or his own previous identity? Underwood was becoming increasingly convinced the killer had been one of Jack's patients.

Underwood had been aware that Jack was living beyond his means: a beautifully furnished house and office, a new expensive car. Perhaps Jack had been doing private consultations in addition to his police work. It was against regulations but an understandable lapse. There was a possibility that the killer was wealthy. Had he been paying Jack inordinate amounts for treatment? Underwood's mind collided with a brick wall. It made no sense. Why would anyone financially secure pay a police psychiatrist for treatment when they could afford specialist attention? Through the dim light of his exhaustion, Underwood saw a possible reason.

Mary Colson shifted slightly in her bed. Underwood wondered if Julia had lit a candle for his own mother as she had promised. He felt a pang of guilt that he had not done so himself. When he had tried on previous occasions he had not found it a helpful process. It had made him feel like a hypocrite. He leaned his head back against the wall and, tired of his own mind, drifted into a light sleep.

He dreamed of Julia. She was in church. It was dark. He was blowing out candles as she lit them. They had walked down the aisle together. Julia had knelt in front of the altar. He could hear a baby crying. He looked around. The noise grew louder. He looked again. There was a baby lying on the altar table. He walked up and considered the child's face. The baby was screaming, gasping away its life. Alison Dexter was standing beside him. She was screaming too.

53

4th May

He awoke at 6a.m. and realized he had been crying. His eyes stung. He looked down and saw Mary Colson's hand resting on his. She seemed to be trying to wake up: her eyelids struggling to roll back the heaviness that the tranquillizers had given them. Underwood leaned forward.

'Mr Underwood?' her voice was dry and almost inaudible.

'Hello, Mary,' he said softly.

'Did you remember the keys?'

Underwood nodded.

'Your friend wants to know about the keys.' Her grip on the top of his hand tightened slightly as Mary tried to wake up.

'I know, Mary, you told me.'

'Good,' she whispered. 'He's been talking about a box.'

Underwood felt his hackles rise in fear. 'Jack told me to put things – things that made me sad – in a box.'

'He wants you to open it.' Mary's eyes were open now. She was becoming more alert and aware of her surroundings. 'I'm in hospital.'

'You fell over yesterday. You banged your arm and your head. Do you feel all right? Can I get you anything?'

Mary smiled faintly. 'I'd like a cup of tea.' She patted his hand softly. 'You're a good friend.'

Underwood stayed until Mary had been served breakfast. He decided to refrain from informing her about the bodies on Fulford Heath, judging her condition to be too weak. After Mary had sipped her tea and made a half-hearted effort to eat some porridge, she lay back on her pillows and drifted back to sleep. Underwood left a brief note saying that he would return to see her in the evening. It was by no means an act of entirely selfless generosity. Mary's description of the location of the bodies was uncannily accurate. Underwood realized that the old lady still provided the only real insight into the investigation. However, there were other issues drifting through his consciousness. As he drove away from the Infirmary, Underwood's mind inevitably came to focus again upon his own mother. Ten years before he had driven from the same hospital never to see her again. He knew that in many ways he had been a frustration and a disappointment to her: particularly, his failure to produce children. Their relationship had become fraught in the months leading up to her death: as the cancer had taken control of her body, Elspeth Underwood had become irrational and spiteful. He knew she had been in great pain and he remembered the terror that had grown behind her eyes. Her fear had been translated into bitterness. She had criticized him for ancient indiscretions; accused him of deserting her if he arrived late for visiting time at the hospital; crushing any sympathetic comments with savage fatalism. His rational mind had long accepted and tried to box the memory. However, Underwood knew in the darkest, most childish and selfish part of his soul, that he still resented the manner in which his mother had left him.

Mary Colson's hospitalization and her warmth towards

him had come as a sharp contrast. She had called him her 'friend'. The simple gesture had a deep reverberation with Underwood. He had come to believe that with the collapse of his marriage and his lapse into depression he had lost the ability to build new friendships. Mary's affectionate nature engaged him. She had accepted the inevitability of her death stoically: 'I'm not afraid of dying,' she had told him in reference to her vision of the dog-man, 'but not like that.' Underwood wondered whether his own mother might have felt the same way about her own disease but merely lacked the courage to say it. He had always been the focus of his mother's love as a child. Perhaps her bitterness stemmed from the fact that the son she had worshipped had been unable to save her. The thought filled him with pity.

Underwood made a sudden decision. He left the ring road and drove directly into New Bolden town centre. He passed the grey carbuncle of the police station and headed south on Argyll Street to the residential district known locally as the 'Hawbush'. Here he parked outside St Joseph's Roman Catholic Church. He sat quietly in the car for four or five minutes before going inside.

The church was a plain brick structure built in the early 1950s. Underwood pushed open the door. He tried to stymie his usual feeling of sceptical resentment by focusing on the job in hand. The church was being prepared for mass. Underwood wanted to be well clear of the area before any hocus-pocus began. He asked a woman arranging flowers on the left-hand side of the nave for directions to the devotional candles. He found the stand almost immediately, noting that none of the candles had been lit. He checked his watch: it was still early. The fact that his candle would be the first of the day made Underwood feel even more uncomfortable.

He struck a match, enjoying its gratifying flare, and lit a single candle. Developing an appropriate thought to accompany the act proved difficult. Instead, Underwood found himself recalling his mother's face on his wedding day. It had been a curious mixture of pride and despair: pride in her son's happiness, despair at his coming of age. The candle flame glowed in front of him. The priest drifted into Underwood's field of vision, preparing the altar table for mass. Underwood remembered his embarrassment at being forced to take communion during his childhood, loathing the hypocrisy of undertaking an act that meant nothing to him. It had pleased his mother though. The priest smiled over at him. Underwood nodded an acknowledgment and decided to leave.

St Josephs was attached to a nearby Roman Catholic School and as Underwood headed back towards the west door, he noticed a display created by the children along the wall. He found himself slowing slightly to absorb their brightly coloured renderings of biblical stories and characters.

'My favourite Saint is Saint Francis,' one piece began, 'because I love animals and Saint Francis could talk to them. I have a dog called Mac and a hamster called Chuckles and I speak to them all the time.'

Underwood smiled. Another display exhibit was entitled 'Twenty Questions About Church'. He read on, 'What is mass? Mass is very important in the Catholic Church. It commemorates the Last Supper. We believe that the bread and wine turns into the blood and flesh of Jesus Christ.'

Another child had copied out an extract from a religious text in beautifully flowing calligraphic writing: 'For not as common bread and common drink do we receive these; but in like manner as Jesus Christ our saviour, having been made flesh and blood for our salvation.' Underwood had seen enough. Churches and hospitals were his two least favourite places and he had supped full of both. He hurried back to the car, shivering in the cold morning air. Unlocking the door, Underwood began to assimilate some of the extracts he had read and a terrible logic started to emerge.

The killer of Harvey and Stark had injected them full of some curious mixture of drugs before killing them. These drugs induced hallucinatory experiences and visions. Underwood had already sensed that the drugs were not designed solely for the purpose of killing the victims. There were much easier ways of achieving that. He reasoned that the drugs were intended to change the victims' perception of their environment or their captor. Did the killer want to be changed in the perception of his victims into someone or something else? Dr Miller had mentioned that certain chemicals in the drugs had been used in the past as truth serums; that they made the taker vulnerable to suggestion.

Underwood thought about the Catholic Mass. The idea of change was important to several religious belief systems. In the Catholic Mass the communion bread and wine is thought to physically convert into the flesh and blood of Christ: '*Jesus Christ our saviour, having been made flesh and blood for our salvation.*' Were the drugs injected into the victims as some bizarre Eucharistic ritual? Was the killer enacting some form of transubstantiation, changing himself in the minds of his victims from the mundane to the spiritual? Or by forcing the mixture into their bodies was the killer compelling them to share in his vision, to become one with him?

It didn't quite hang together but Underwood sensed he was close to discovering something. The Holy Communion was a passive act where the receiver willingly takes the Eucharistic elements into their body. The killer's actions were aggressive. He was forcing his will onto his victims. He was injecting them with his drugs forcibly and presumably in the face of resistance. It was a penetrative act: a rape of the perception. For the first time Underwood began to see the crimes in a sexual context. The killer was forcing his own vision into the minds of his victims. He wanted to create change; to forge a new mode of perception. Underwood felt a cold rush of anxiety as he thought of Rowena Harvey. He was beginning to see why the killer wanted to keep her alive.

The key was in the nature and history of the mixture. The killer had created a specific fluid that he believed was somehow synonymous with himself. During their meeting in the botanical gardens, Adam Miller had mentioned that the Amanita Muscaria mushroom had been used recreationally in ancient human civilizations. Underwood suddenly realized that he needed to find out how and quickly.

He could feel the pieces of the puzzle were dropping into place. The killer was most likely a patient of Jack's: not an official police referral but a private client. The killer was wealthy and drove a large jeep or people-carrier. He was trying to change the perception of his victims: make them alter the way he appeared to them. The Amanita Muscaria mushroom had been deliberately selected by the killer. The mushroom had a long history and was closely interlinked with certain ancient civilizations. And the killer was collecting heads. He now had at least five. He had completed his countdown. Underwood started his engine and accelerated away from St Josephs.

Counting down to what?

He needed to talk with Dexter and go through Jack's personal effects and the remains of his records. Underwood had a growing conviction that God was hiding in the details.

Interlocking Orbits

54

Doreen O'Riordan nervously fingered the fat that overhung her belt. She had learned from PC Sauerwine that Mary Colson had been committed to hospital. However, her anxiety did not spring from genuine concern. DI Underwood's request that she provide him with all Mary Colson's recent shopping receipts had filled her with a cold panic. Particularly, she thought bitterly, because she had readily agreed to do so. With the advantage of hindsight, Doreen realized that she should have fronted the policeman then: she should have just shrugged and said that she threw away all Mary's receipts. Instead, she had panicked and buckled under the pressure of his suspicion.

She had stayed up late trying to assess the extent of the problem. Now, in the hard light of morning, her situation seemed no better. She had been assigned to Mary Colson six months previously and had been shopping for her twice every week during that period. Doreen didn't keep accurate accounts of the money she had short-changed from Mary's housekeeping. She knew that she hadn't taken any money in the first three weeks of her association with Mary Colson. She had wanted to assess how alert the old bitch was before she started lifting the odd ten-pound note from her change. So during those three weeks Doreen had been scrupulously honest. As she had become confident in Mary's deteriorating mental state her policy had changed. So, she told herself, she had been stealing from Mary for roughly five months; say, twenty weeks.

Doreen did some quick mental arithmetic: two shops per week for twenty weeks amounted to forty shops. Assuming that she took about ten pounds from Mary's change each time she went shopping for her, the total she had stolen had to be in the region of four hundred pounds: approximately half the cost of her holiday. Doreen had also taken smaller amounts from some of her other patients but Mary had been her major source of extra revenue.

Her problem was that Mary had fooled her.

'That old bitch tricked me,' Doreen thought bitterly.

She knew that she had to assume the worst: that Mary Colson had kept records of exactly how much she had given to Doreen and how much she had received in change. Doreen ate a bun and stared out of the bedroom window at the yawning desolation of the Morley Estate. Was she right to think the worst, though? Mary had never seen any of the receipts – Doreen had always been careful either to throw them away or keep them – so how could Mary have known she was being short-changed?

There was only one possible explanation. Doreen usually left the shopping bags on Mary's sideboard so the old bitch could unpack them herself. Maybe Mary had added up the price tags on the shopping as she packed it into the cupboards. That way she would end up with a total and be able to subtract it from the amount she had given Doreen then compare the figure with the change she had received. Doreen hesitated. 'Surely the old bitch wouldn't be that bloody-minded?'

She would. The more Doreen thought about it, the more she came to suspect that Mary Colson had set her up. She thought of her holiday, suddenly jeopardized. She thought of her balcony 'overlooking the crystal clear waters of the Ionian Sea'; she thought of 'soaking up the rays by the conveniently sized swimming pool' and of relaxing in the evening 'to the music of the Lazaros band'. Now that conniving, cantankerous old bitch was trying to spoil her dream. Doreen couldn't help crying.

She knew that she had to concentrate. She was determined. She would not sacrifice her dream and besides, it was Colson's word against hers. Doreen walked through to her little kitchenette and made herself another strong, sugary coffee. Assuming the worst case – that Mary had kept her own records of the money she had handed over – Doreen considered that she had three obvious options. Option one was to give the money back to Mary and apologize. She had absolutely no intention of doing that. Option two was to provide DI Underwood with a mass of till receipts, some genuine and others from her own shopping. She could try to confuse him by highlighting certain items on some of her own till rolls and claiming that they had actually been bought for Mary. It was an attractive plan: she couldn't believe a busy CID officer would waste his time checking through dozens of old till receipts. Then there was option three. She could go back to Mary's bungalow while she was away and place some of the money she had taken in various points around the bungalow. Then, if DI Underwood did check the receipts against Mary's own records and discovered a shortfall, Doreen could claim that Mary was actually hiding money around the house and deliberately trying to drop her in trouble.

She settled on option three. It would be a calculated loss to guarantee her holiday. She opened the biscuit tin containing her holiday money. How much money would be enough to create the necessary impression without compromising her holiday? She settled on eighty pounds. She would put thirty under Mary's mattress and fifty in an envelope in one of her cupboards. It meant that she would have to reduce the amount she had set aside for spending money on holiday but she was prepared to take that risk. She was staying full-board at the hotel so she wouldn't have to worry about buying food. Besides, she told herself, perhaps a nice gentleman would buy her drinks at the Acropolis bar in the evening.

Doreen was absolutely determined that her dream would not be spoiled. She gathered together a mass of receipts and highlighted various items. Once satisfied that the result would be utterly confusing, she placed them in a manila envelope and wrote 'DI Underwood' on the front. She would drop them at the police station next time she was in town. Doreen decided not to write an explanatory note: Underwood hadn't asked for one. All he wanted was the receipts, so that was what she would give him.

Pleased with her morning's work, Doreen allowed herself the luxury of a second Chelsea bun to accompany her cup of coffee.

55

Underwood arrived in CID to find Dexter, Leach and Marty Farrell in an office waiting for him. They all looked exhausted. Leach seemed especially tired, his face gaunt and his eyes sunken and black. Dexter waved Underwood in to join them.

'I was wondering where you were,' she said crisply.

'At the hospital,' Underwood shot back, 'with Mary Colson.'

'Roger and his team have been working through the night with the pathology staff at Addenbrookes. He's going to run through the initial findings on the four bodies we found yesterday. Marty's been checking up on possible tyre and car matches with the tracks found on the Heath.' Dexter paused for a moment. 'Jensen's fingerprints match one of the bodies.'

'Shit.' Underwood thought of Harrison. Dexter read his mind.

'I've told Harrison to take time off. He wants to work through it. He'll be back in this afternoon. Do you want to get us started, Roger, before we all fall asleep.'

'Indeed.' Leach had preliminary post mortem reports on the four victims in front of him. 'Now, I should say that the information I'm about to give you has been compiled in a rush. More detailed tests on the four cadavers will continue through the week. Bearing in mind that we are still missing Rowena Harvey and I realize that there is a time pressure, I've concentrated our initial investigations on building a preliminary physical profile of each victim and attempted to ascertain a time of death for each victim.'

'The quick and dirty analysis?' Underwood asked.

'Exactly. I guess it's helpful to assess the corpses chrono-logically.' Leach frowned through his exhaustion. 'By that I mean, I've considered each case in the order in which we believed they were killed. Make sense?'

'Go ahead,' Dexter said.

'Victim A. Male, Caucasian. Head had been severed completely from the body. Five ten-pence coins found with the corpse. I would estimate his age at being between forty-five and sixty years, his body weight around one hundred and seventy pounds and his height at roughly five feet seven inches. Remaining body hair was dark brown. In many ways, he's the most interesting of all the cadavers. We estimate he was killed between three and four months ago.'

Dexter whistled softly. 'How can you tell? You can't make an assessment based on body temperature for a body that's been dead for so long, and presumably he was in a bad way.'

Leach looked Dexter in the eye. 'You sure you want to know?'

'Of course,' came the assertive reply.

'The body was in an advanced state of decomposition. We call it butyric fermentation. The body is drying out. Fluids ferment. Most of the flesh and hair is falling away and mouldy. Butyric acid produces a powerful cheesy odour. Do you all know what forensic entomology is?'

'Bugs,' said Underwood grimly.

Leach nodded, 'One of the ways we can estimate time of death is by studying insect activity on the corpse. Once decay begins after death various different types of insects are attracted to the remains: blowflies, fleshflies and so on. They lay eggs, eggs hatch into larvae, which feed off the rotting flesh. We can work out from the type of insect, and the stage in its development on the corpse, when the person in question died.'

Underwood remembered why he wanted to be cremated.

'For example, we found larvae of an insect called Piophilia Casei in the abdominal cavity of victim A. It's more commonly known as the Cheese Skipper.'

'Charming,' Dexter observed.

'Now,' Leach continued, 'the presence of Cheese Skipper larvae in the corpse is interesting. It means that the victim died a minimum of two months ago. Usually the presence of Cheese Skipper larvae occurs three to six months after death. I would suggest that the state of decomposition and the early stage of the larval development imply death at the front end of that time scale: say three months ago. I would also suggest that the body has been kept outside.'

Underwood shuddered. Leach's comments had reminded him that death, like life, was a process not a single event.

Dexter tried to sum up the information. 'So the victim was a middle-aged man, heavy build, dark brown hair, who most likely died at the end of January or beginning of February.'

'Correct. Victim B then.' Leach turned over a page on his clipboard. He had been working on the bodies all night and was feeling the strain. 'Female, Caucasian. Again the head was severed completely from the body. Four ten-pence coins found with this corpse. I would estimate age between twenty and thirty-five years, body weight around one hundred and ten pounds and height at roughly five feet five inches. The distinguishing thing about this body was that a number of bones were broken: including both arms, a number of ribs and the pelvis. We also found fragments of glass embedded in the flesh of both arms. It looks like she died in an accident: went through a window at high speed.'

'Time of death?' Underwood asked, staring at his own notes.

'Again, we backed up the physical analysis with an ento-mological assessment. Organs and soft tissues were beginning to liquefy, skin was breaking away and the abdomen was bloated with gases. However, on the cadaver we discovered a high proportion of blowfly pupae. Blowflies lay eggs on flesh within a day of two of death. However, these pupae were in their final stage of development. Bearing in mind the typical life cycle of a blowfly, I'd suggest the victim was killed eighteen to twenty four days ago. In a few days we can give more accurate findings.'

'Why the big time lag between victims?' Underwood asked.

'He kills the first one three months ago – so end of January or beginning of February – and then waits two months until the next one.'

Leach shrugged. 'That's for you lot to figure out.'

Dexter turned to Underwood. 'Maybe he was out of the country. Maybe he was in prison. Maybe we've arrested this prick for something else. We let him out after two months and he carries on killing.'

'Maybe,' Underwood agreed, *or maybe he was receiving treatment.*

'Victim C we have now confirmed from fingerprints was DC Sarah Jensen. The body was cold but rigor mortis had passed. Green stains to the abdomen showed the start of putrefaction suggesting time of death was thirty-six hours or so prior to the discovery of the body.'

'Makes sense,' Dexter nodded. 'Cause of death?'

'As yet unknown but there were two needle puncture wounds at the base of her neck.'

'What about the last victim, then?' Underwood asked suddenly. 'If you're doing this chronologically he must have been topped pretty recently.'

'Victim D. Male, Caucasian.' Leach replied, 'Head severed and absent like the others. A single ten-pence coin was found with the corpse. Aged between twenty and thirty five years, body weight around one hundred and sixty pounds, height roughly six feet. Remaining body hair was mousy blonde. This was the only body in a state of rigor mortis: it was cold and stiff. He died sometime between eight and thirty six hours prior to his body being discovered. Again, there were needle puncture marks on the neck.'

Underwood stood and tried to reconstruct the full chronology on the office white board. 'So first we have Victim A, a middle-aged man killed around the beginning of February. Then, for reasons unknown we have a gap of two months until Victim B, the unidentified woman, is attacked eighteen to twenty-four days ago.'

He drew a timeline on the board with a blue marker pen.

'Next, Ian Stark is attacked on 29th April and Jack

Harvey is murdered the following evening. Jensen and Rowena Harvey are abducted on 1st May. The bodies were discovered yesterday afternoon.'

'Busy week,' Farrell observed.

'Very,' Underwood agreed, 'the thing that interests me is the gap of two months between Victim A and Victim B. I'll bet you that this guy was a patient of Jack's and he was being treated in that period.'

Dexter could see the logic in Underwood's argument. 'So what do we do? Pretty much all of Jack's files and his computer were destroyed. We've looked at the official referral cases he was working on from County and drawn a blank.'

'I need to go though Jack's personal effects. There may be something we've missed. Can you arrange for me to have access to his house, Dex? I may need to go back there.'

'Shouldn't be a problem.'

Underwood returned to his chair. He wondered whether to tell the group about his notion of change: that the killer was altering the perception of his victims. He decided that to do so would muddy the waters. This meeting was about detail. He would work through the logic of the idea himself.

'Marty,' Dexter continued, 'what can you tell us about the tyre tracks on the heath?'

Farrell leaned forward in his chair, 'Better news there, I think. We've been able to narrow the type of vehicle down significantly. If you remember DS Harrison had suggested the killer might drive a large, expensive vehicle. Once we'd taken the dimensions and tyre impressions from the heath we calculated the size and weight of the vehicle in question. Now, once we had the details I compared them with the specifications of some of the most popular off-road vehicles and jeeps. We got a match.'

'Let's have it, then.' Dexter felt like they were making progress.

'Most likely it was a Toyota Land Cruiser.'

'Nice one,' Dexter was relieved. She had suddenly remembered that Mark Willis drove a large Land Rover Freelander.

'How can you be sure?' Underwood asked.

224

Farrell checked his notes. 'We derived three estimated numbers based on the tracks on the heath: wheelbase, tread and vehicle weight. We estimated wheelbase at two-six-eight-zero millimetres. The Land Cruiser two-point-eight litre long wheelbase jeep has a specification of two-six-seven-five millimetres. Tread we calculated at one-four-seven-seven millimetres. That was pretty much spot on. The same Land Cruiser has a front tread of one-four-seven-five millimetres and rear tread of one-four-eight-zero millimetres. We worked out gross vehicle weight based on the depth of the track impressions on the soil. We calculated a range of between two-seven-fifty and twenty-nine-hundred kilos. Again, that is consistent with a two-point-eight litre Land Cruiser with a long wheelbase. We also made rough projections of vehicle length and width. These are consistent.'

'Good work Marty, it gives us something specific to work on at last,' Dexter said.

'The forensic team from Huntingdon came up with most of this. I can't claim much credit,' he replied.

'We should tell the traffic plods and the house to house investigation teams to look out for that version of the Land Cruiser. Can we get a picture from somewhere?' Dexter asked.

'Already done,' Farrell replied, sliding a colour sheet across the table.

'We'll circulate this.' Dexter paused and thought for a moment. 'Knowing our luck, every farmer in East Anglia is driving one of these things. We need to try and narrow down the search. Can we get lists of Toyota garages and dealerships in the area? Maybe if they have ownership records we could cross check them against known violent offender lists.' It was a useful idea but Dexter realized it would be a vast under-taking and her resources were already stretched.

'There may be another way,' Underwood observed. 'Check with dealerships and garages for service and MOT bookings. As our boy seems to have gone off the rails over the last three months, it's a fair bet that if he had previously scheduled an MOT or service for that period, he missed the appointment.'

'Especially if he was driving around with a body in the boot,' Farrell observed.

'Absolutely.'

'It only works if he had the jeep booked in during that three-month time period,' Dexter commented. 'There's nine other months in the year.'

'It's something,' Underwood said simply.

Dexter nodded and decided to bring things to a close. 'This is what's going to happen from here. Roger is going to complete the post-mortem examination of the bodies and provide detailed blood test results and toxicology profiles. In the meantime, I'll assign a couple of uniforms to check the physical profiles of the three unidentified victims against missing persons lists.'

Leach nodded. 'Agreed. Give us twenty-four hours.'

'Marty,' Dexter continued, 'give PC Sauerwine the details on the jeep and on local Toyota dealerships. He can trawl through sales and service records in the way that John suggested. I'm meeting Adam Miller from the university and driving up to Thetford Forest. He's going to take me round some sites where these magic mushroom things supposedly grow.'

'I'd like to speak to him when you get back,' said Underwood.

'No problem,' Dexter replied. The meeting broke up. Farrell and Leach left the office. Underwood stayed behind.

'It's a lot to take in,' Dexter said.

Underwood nodded. 'We're making progress, though. The problem is our procedures take time. It's like trying to catch a cheetah by lining up a bunch of people in a field and walking very slowly towards it.'

'We'd catch it eventually, though.'

'Once everything was already dead.' Underwood watched as Dexter yawned. Her eyes watered slightly. She wiped them dry with the cuff of her shirt. 'I spoke to your old gaffer the other day,' he said softly.

Dexter's ferocious green eyes zeroed in on Underwood for a head shot. 'McInally? What for?'

226

'Calm down. He called me. He was concerned about you and some bloke called Willis.'

'What else did he tell you?' Dexter snapped, anxiety and fury crawling up her throat.

'Nothing,' Underwood lied. 'He asked me to keep an eye on you. Said you might be paddling in a bit deep,'

'He had no right. I can look after myself.'

'I thought that once about myself. Look where it got me.'

Dexter saw the concern in Underwood's eyes and felt her anger recede slightly. She had been thinking intensely about the Mark Willis situation. She had enjoyed seeing his name appear on her mobile three times in the previous hour. She sensed he was nearby, waiting for an opportunity to confront her, to vent his fury. He was wriggling on a hook of her creation. Alison Dexter had decided to purge her past, quickly and brutally. The scars that had suddenly become visible on her newly exposed wrist reminded her why. Willis had already made her destroy one life. One was enough.

'There's nothing to worry about, John,' she said, adjusting her cuff, 'it's under control.'

Her office intercom suddenly squawked to life. 'Inspector Dexter, this is front desk.'

'Go ahead,' she replied.

'There's a Dr Miller in reception.'

'Thank you.' Dexter looked up. 'Time to go.'

56

Mark Willis managed to climb into Dexter's flat through her bathroom window. He guessed that she had left the smaller, top window open to air the bathroom after her morning shower. There were still small patches of water on the white-tiled floor when he clambered in. Leaving the small window open had enabled Willis to reach down into the bathroom and lift the main window catch. It had all been remarkably easy.

He had laughed at Dexter's idiocy. Ground floor garden flats were soft targets for burglars. A copper should have known better. His initial amusement and pleasure at gaining access so easily was marred by the sudden realization that if Dexter had concealed his drugs in the flat, she would have locked the place down as tight as a snake's arse.

He decided to check the place out anyway. He was sick of Dexter chucking obstacles in his way, he had resolved to take the initiative. At best, he would retrieve his drugs and retire, at worst he would take immense satisfaction in trashing her apartment.

He looked around at the little white bathroom. It came as no surprise to him that Alison had adopted a minimalist approach: white curtains, white bath, blue and white tiles. Willis remembered from her flat in Leyton that she despised frills and ornamentation. He unscrewed the top from a bottle of shower gel and smelled it: lemon and lime.

Willis left the bathroom and walked out into the hallway. There was a picture of Dexter in uniform with her class at Hendon Police College hanging on the wall. Their names were printed underneath the photograph. He read along the second row: *'left to right, Davis A. L, Dering J.F, Dexter A. G, Dolton S.'* She looked pleased: she'd even managed a smile for the cameras.

'Happy days,' Willis muttered to himself.

He unhooked the picture from the wall and smashed it on the floor. Moving on, Willis rooted through the cupboards in the hallway and found little of interest: suitcases, boots, water proof clothing. The kitchen told a similarly blank story. He found a packet of rice in a cupboard and emptied it over the work surface. He immediately cursed his haste: it would have been much better to drop it all over the living room carpet. Dexter's fridge was bare apart from six small bottles of Stella Artois beer, a pint of milk and a strawberry-flavoured yoghurt. Willis took a bottle opener from a drawer. He fancied a cold beer.

Dexter's living room had crème walls and was tidily furnished. Willis slumped onto her sofa. There were two shelves of books and a rack of CDs next to him. He scanned the CDs, half-amused at her taste in music.

'Always the rocker, Sparrer,' he muttered. Some of the names were familiar to him, from the time he had spent at Alison's previous flat: The Jam, The Clash, Guns 'n' Roses, The Rolling Stones. Willis remembered Alison for a second dancing around her bleak little Leyton kitchenette, cooking a risotto to 'Town called Malice.' He banished the thought.

The beer disappeared rapidly and Willis returned to his work. He checked under and behind the sofa and knocked over Dexter's computer table. Her papers spilled onto the carpet. Irritated by now, Willis walked through to her bedroom. He half expected to see her old West Ham pillowcase on the bed but was disappointed: white pillows and duvet cover.

'Christ, it's like being in hospital,' Willis observed.

There was a pile of clean clothes, neatly folded on a wicker chair. He kicked them over. Willis was pleased to find her underwear drawer first of all, spending some time trying to find knickers that he recognized: he was unsuccessful but was reassured to find her taste in undies hadn't changed. He stuffed a thong in his pocket for old time's sake. Her clothes cupboard proved more interesting. Lying beneath a row of immaculately pressed shirts and sombre suits, Willis found a pile of black diaries and pulled them out to investigate further. The first was marked 1984, the last 2002. He opened 1984 randomly and read out loud: '*22nd September. Sick of school. Tired of being treated like a five-year-old. Can't wait for college.*'

Willis closed the book. He was surprised. Despite the time he had spent with Alison Dexter, he had never realized that she had kept a journal. He didn't think she was the type. And yet here was a record of her entire adult life. Presumably, there was also a complete record of their relationship and their unfortunate break-up too. That would make interesting reading. He selected 1994 and flicked through until he found August.

'*23rd August. Just back from Paris. Fantastic weekend.*

229

Great hotel. Mark spent a fortune. Went up the Eiffel Tower. Saturday night we had dinner on a river boat: amazing views. It's so beautiful. Sunday, we had a great picnic and sex in the park! I've always wanted to do it outside. Got back to London late. Mark had to go into town on work. Pity it ended like that. He must be knackered. X'

Willis smiled to himself. He had indeed been knackered: and by the time he'd finished with Staff Nurse Siobhan at five in the morning he'd been completely exhausted. He thumbed forward a month or two, trying to remember when Dexter had found out about his daily trips to the boiler room with WPC Otham.

'15th October. Working GBH case. Busy as hell. Got in late again. Mark ignoring me. Can't think what I've done wrong this time. Bad feeling. Trying to ignore it. I'm late.'

Willis frowned at the last comment, his brain scrambling for an explanation until the penny clanked into place. He flicked forward, looking for a similar reference.

'31st October. Bought home pregnancy kit. Result positive. Doctor's appointment Saturday morning. Haven't told anyone. Panicking.

'2nd November. Pregnant. It's official. What the fuck am I going to do?'

There were no entries for the following week. Willis felt a cold sweat breaking out on his neck. Dexter had never told him she was pregnant. He asked himself if he would have done anything differently if he'd known: an answer eluded him.

'17th November. Cut myself. First time in years. Totally alone. Petrified. Doctor told me baby due on May 20th. It's real. It's going to happen. Despair.

'18th November. It's a girl. I can feel it. There's a little girl growing inside me. Bought a book of baby names at lunchtime. Must be going mad. I think I like "Zoe".

'20th November. Spoke to Mark. He admitted he's fucking Otham amongst others. Whole station knows. Couldn't tell him about baby. Wanted to kill the bastard. I'm a fucking laughing stock. Told Gillian though. She says get rid of it.'

230

Willis nodded, he remembered DS Gillian Read. She was eminently sensible.

'Good advice, Gillian,' he said quietly.

'21st November. Mum called. Had to tell her. She cried. Told me to have abortion. Said she didn't want me ending up like her. Can't bear it. Cut myself.

'28th November. Appointment booked. I'm terrified. Rather kill myself. Need to go into hospital.

'1st December. Done. Horrible. Hardly slept. Dreamed of a baby crying: crying because she's alone, crying because she'll never know her name. Feel ashamed.'

Willis sat back on the bed and tried to absorb what he had just read. Alison had been pregnant with his baby in 1994 and not told him. Alison had wanted to have his baby. Alison had an abortion. He looked deep into himself to try and identify what he was feeling. Was it anger? Resentment? Betrayal? After a moment, he decided it was relief.

Mark Willis finally understood where Dexter's hatred of him came from. But did it really change anything? He considered his situation. The basic facts remained the same. If he didn't produce one hundred grand quickly he was a dead man. Alison Dexter had stopped him retrieving the drugs that would have saved his neck. She knew what had happened to them.

He opened the 2002 diary, turning to the current date: 5th May. He needed to get her alone. Now he had the information about the baby it could work to his advantage, force her to drop her guard. There was no entry. He had two choices: wait for her to return to her flat or try to intercept her at New Bolden Police Station. He elected for the former option, at least until the beers in the fridge ran out. Then, on instinct, Willis turned forward two pages in her diary to 20th May.

There was a two-word entry:

'Zoe's birthday.'

57

Underwood retrieved the steel box containing evidence gathered from the crime scene at Jack Harvey's house. He took the box into Dexter's office, clearing a space for it on her desk. Each evidence bag had been labelled with the location it had been discovered and the number of the Scene of Crime Officer that had logged it. Underwood considered each bag in turn.

The first contained a group of envelopes found in a metal box next to Jack's desk. Underwood put on a pair of sterile gloves and removed them from their clear plastic container. There were two white envelopes from the County Police Headquarters in Huntingdon. They each contained a pay slip: one for March and one for April. Underwood wasn't surprised to learn that Jack had earned more than him. Still, he reasoned, after some mental arithmetic it didn't explain how Jack had managed to afford his relatively extravagant lifestyle.

He flicked through the next group of envelopes: there was a warranty agreement for Jack's new computer, an advertisement for a credit card, some fliers for forthcoming medical books. It was all fairly uninspiring stuff. Then at the bottom of the pile, Underwood found Jack's bank statements. He read back through the itemized list of transactions, noting that, like his, Jack's police salary had been paid on the last Friday of each month.

Underwood quickly found what he had been looking for: two substantial deposits. The first had been made on the 7th of February: a cash deposit of ten thousand pounds. Exactly the same amount had been deposited on the 8th of March. Underwood whistled softly.

'What were you up to, Jackie boy?' he asked the empty room.

It was an unsettling amount of money. Jack had clearly become entangled in something serious. Underwood tried to work out a logic underpinning the information he had discovered. Twenty thousand pounds paid in two instalments in the space of four weeks. To Underwood, it seemed like payment for services. No other explanation seemed to fit the evidence. Underwood confirmed that both payments fell into the two-month gap between the first and second victims. Assuming Jack had been hired by the killer or, as Underwood was coming to believe, an associate or relative of the killer, it was clear that they were seeking someone with access to considerable wealth.

'Not only wealth,' Underwood told himself, 'but also liquid wealth. Cash.'

He replaced the envelopes into the evidence bag and continued to sift through the contents of the box. Most of the other paperwork that had been salvaged from the fire had been burned almost beyond the point of usefulness. Underwood could decipher occasional fragments of typed text or handwriting that suggested he was reading a patient report but it was a hopeless task. Besides, he was aware that Dexter's team had already checked up on all Jack's official patient referrals. The bank statement underlined that whatever he had been up to was very much on an unofficial basis. Underwood knew Jack was too canny to mix up his records.

Jack's computer had been destroyed in the fire and the floppy discs that had survived had yielded nothing of interest. Underwood was gradually coming around to the belief that Jack had kept records of his unofficial activities secured elsewhere. He removed Jack's wallet from an evidence bag. It had been discovered in the inside pocket of his sports jacket which had been hanging in the hallway outside his office. Underwood removed each of Jack's credit cards one by one and smiled softly when he saw the unflattering photograph on Jack's driving licence. He could find nothing of value.

The final bag in the evidence box contained Jack's keys. Underwood looked at them briefly: he recognized the remote electronic lock and keys for Jack's new BMW. There was a Yale key that he guessed opened Jack's front door, a window key, what looked like an old shed key and two smaller keys which Underwood guessed opened a garage door or a padlock.

He dropped the keys back on the table with an irritated 'clonk'. He was beginning to lose hope that they would find Rowena Harvey alive. They had built a vague chronology of events and Underwood was starting to understand the killer's modus operandi but there were still too many missing links. He reminded himself bitterly that they had turned up virtually no insights at all without the prompting that Mary Colson's dream had provided. His encounters with the old lady had been profoundly disturbing. She had shaken his long held belief that death was simply oblivion. The idea that the human spirit continued in some other form after life ceased was not one he found attractive. Mary Colson had scared him witless with her quiet assertion that Jack Harvey's ghost had been standing directly behind him.

Underwood looked around the CID department. He could see Farrell and Sauerwine discussing the best way to tackle the Toyota car dealerships, and there were a couple of uniformed WPC's on telephones following up on information derived from house to house enquiries. He found their presence comforting.

He looked back at Jack Harvey's keys and remembered the last drink he had enjoyed with Jack a week previously. Underwood had been ambushed by the strength of his whisky and had slipped into a near drunken state very quickly. He'd even managed to leave his own keys on the table in the pub. Jack had reminded him about them: 'don't forget your keys', he had called out.

Underwood distractedly bit down on a fingernail as he picked up Harvey's key ring again.

'Don't forget your keys!' He could still hear Jack's voice as it rung out across the crowded pub.

He remembered that Mary Colson had uttered the phrase in their first meeting. She said that Jack's spirit had asked about Underwood's keys. It had freaked him out. A few hours previously she had repeated the exact same sentence as she emerged from the fog of her tranquillized night's sleep. Underwood suddenly corrected himself. She hadn't repeated the exact phrase. She had said, 'Did you remember the keys?'

234

He wondered for a second if the difference was important. Mary had also said that Jack wanted him to 'open the box'. That was something new. She had not referred to a box in their previous conversations. His box of bad memories had been Jack's idea, Underwood had assumed that she had been referring to that.

The keys clinked as Underwood shifted them between his fingers. Gradually, a cold realization swept over him as if iced water had been poured down the back of his neck. Jack Harvey had been with him: screaming noiselessly at him all the time. Underwood had finally heard him.

58

Max Fallon stood on the flat roof of the crumbling, old house marvelling at the cold beauty of the universe he had created. Nor was its beauty random or chaotic like the mess of human ideas. It was mathematical and exact: expanding mathematically, contracting mathematically. Just as the human form developed in life and receded in death. He only had a matter of hours to wait now. At 11.27 that evening he would inseminate Rowena Harvey with the seed of the Soma and the lunar race would be born on earth.

He knew that she was fortunate. In legend, the Soma had possessed some twenty-seven wives: the daughters of Daksha. Max lay down on the hard surface of the roof, ignoring the dry crusts of bird shit that flaked against his naked skin. He blinked at the vast blue expanse above him, wondering at the possibilities posed by having twenty-seven wives. Max couldn't remember why he hadn't indulged the vision more regularly. He distinctly recalled dictating this aspect of the Soma myth into his tape recorder. Perhaps it was time, in the long hours before the insemination of Rowena Harvey, for him to re-familiarize himself with the details of his previous existence.

He dusted himself down, picking small pieces of stone and mess from his skin. Fallon kept his tapes in the library of the old hall but before he retrieved the story of Daksha, he hurried down to his kitchen and selected a solution he had derived from two Amanita Muscaria mushrooms. He unscrewed the bottle and poured the mixture into a glass of water. That way Fallon hoped to ensure he could absorb the essence rapidly into his system without encountering any of the risks posed by intravenous injection.

Returning to the library, Max eventually found the 'Daksha' tape from his collection and placed it into his tape recorder. He settled on to the chaise lounge, smiling as his own voice emerged from the machine.

'Daksha was named as a Lord of Creation,' said the recording, 'he fathered several daughters by his consort Prasuti.'

Slowly as the words washed over him, so the corners of the room seemed to soften and warp as the muscimol began to impair his perception. The tinny electronic voice became indistinguishable from the divine voice in his head. He was beginning to remember the patterns of his former existence.

'Twenty-seven of Daksha's daughters became wives of the Soma,' said the voice. 'Twenty-seven beautiful, virginal maidens.'

The Soma writhed under the heat of their bodies as they crawled and slid across him: their eager, inquisitive hands exploring his nakedness, tongues painting delicate circles on his skin. He found himself struggling away from them. Surprised at his own reluctance, Max tried hard to hear his voice through their breathless incantations. It was difficult, he was being sucked down from reality and drawn into the whirlpool of bodies. As he was starting to panic, he saw Rowena Harvey's face floating in front of him.

'Soma invoked the fury of Daksha by favouring only one of his daughters, Rohini.'

Rowena . . . Rohini . . . Rowena . . . Rohini.

The name held a massive significance. It could not be coincidence. Just as Rohini had spelt the death of hope for Max

Fallon the child, it now signalled the birth of beauty for Max Fallon the man.

Max engulfed the image of Rowena Harvey, entwining his arms and legs around her to prevent her escape and to protect her from the jealous wrath of her sisters. He would make her part of himself. She would overcome her terror of the Soma. She would mother the lunar race on earth.

'In his fury,' the voice continued, 'Daksha cursed Soma with consumption.'

Snapped from his reveries Max began to remember why he had only played the tape on a single previous occasion.

'The Soma seemed to be doomed to a terrible and protracted death: drowning in the mucus of his own lungs.'

The suggestion was a powerful one and it worked havoc in Max's vulnerable brain. He felt himself turning inside out; he saw his limbs and skin fold inwards and disappear. He was sliding into his own lungs, inexorably sinking into a sea of blood and mucus. He found himself unable to breath as he drew the sludge inside. It burned like larva. He tried to reach out, to tear through the mucus-soaked lung lining and pull himself out into the air.

Max coughed violently and uncontrollably. He fell to the floor of the library and came to rest on his hands and knees, hacking mucus onto the wooden floorboards. The movement in his throat made him heave and he spewed muscimol-laced vomit, feeling its strange heat rolling down across his face. The room span in every direction. Max hauled himself to his tape recorder and threw it against the wall. The voice abruptly crashed to a halt.

Max slowly began to relax into the light show. He needed air.

59

Dexter had driven with Adam Miller to Thetford Forest. She found his company and enthusiasm engaging: a pleasant relief from the scowling anxiety of Underwood and Mark Willis. It had been a straightforward journey taking only twenty minutes up the A11. Dexter had been impressed that Miller had taken a genuinely enthusiastic but not unhealthy interest in the progress of the investigation.

'It's weird,' he observed. 'The guy has gone to a lot of trouble. I mean, injecting people with Amanita extracts. It must mean something important to him.'

'That's something I wanted to ask you,' Dexter said as they turned onto the B1105 at Elveden under the dark canopy of Corsican pine trees. 'Does it take a great deal of knowledge to do what he's done? Is it difficult to identify these things in the wild and know how to treat them?'

'You're wondering if this guy's a mycologist like me?' Miller seemed amused at the idea.

'It's called clutching at straws,' Dexter replied without emotion. She meant it.

'It's hard to say. Judging from what you've told me and from what I've read in the toxicology profiles, the guy is clearly pretty smart and fairly well-informed. Is he a professional though? I doubt it. The sort of information that he'd need is easily accessible. There are hundreds of internet sites and books he could look up. There's a huge amount of detail available on the Amanita Muscaria, for example.'

'The red and white one? Why?'

'It has a long history. It's readily recognizable. It makes you hallucinate and if you treat it properly it won't kill you.'

'Have you ever taken one?'

'Are you going to arrest me?'

'Not unless you refuse to answer my questions.'

Miller smiled. 'I took one once: a few years ago in Amsterdam. It wasn't a pleasant experience.'

'Why?'

'The hallucinogens affect different people in different ways. Your mood and outlook can affect the way your body treats the experience.'

'Not my cup of tea at all,' Dexter frowned. 'I'd never put that shit inside me.'

'Very wise.'

'What about the other one,' Dexter asked, 'the Death Cap?'

Miller thought for a second. 'That's a little trickier. There's plenty of literature on them but they are very easy to mistake in the wild. It's what makes them so dangerous. The killer would need to be fairly clued up about them.'

Dexter pulled up in a layby. 'Here we go, according to your map. Site one is along that footpath.'

'Can I ask what we're looking for exactly?' Miller asked, 'I mean, I can take you to the various locations where the university had recorded samples of these Amanitas but there's no guarantee that you'll find any. It's early in May. Most of them won't appear till later in the summer. And as I told you, it's quite conceivable that your guy harvested the things last November and has been storing them in a freezer. The toxins are pretty stable over time.'

'True enough.' Dexter opened the car boot and took out an evidence collection kit. 'But if we do find that some of the sites have been interfered with we might be able to turn something up: discarded litter with a fingerprint, shoe impression on the soil, dead body.'

'Bloody hell.' Miller looked at Thetford Forest with sudden trepidation.

'If we do find anything significant, I'll call a forensic team in anyway. Don't worry, I'll hold your hand.'

Miller seemed surprised. 'You didn't strike me as the type.'

'What's that supposed to mean?' Dexter asked.

'I'm just joking.'

The first site was on the edge of Wangford Warren. Miller pointed out a cluster of silver birch trees amongst the Corsican pines. He checked his notes.

'Okay. University research student found Amanita

239

Muscaria at the base of the central birch.' He walked forward and checked the surrounding area. 'Sorry, Inspector, there's nothing here.' Miller extended his search pattern around the immediate area and found nothing. Whilst he was mushroom hunting Dexter looked for signs of human interference. She too drew a blank.

'The second site's about a mile north east,' Miller announced when he returned. 'You happy to walk?'

'Of course.' Dexter was slightly affronted at the question.

'Your shoes are not ideal for this terrain,' Miller explained, pointing at Dexter's smart black leather shoes.

'They'll do fine. You just try and keep up.' Dexter was rather enjoying herself. The air was clean and the woods didn't scare her in the daylight.

The second location was around the base of a beech tree, just south of Brandon Park. Dexter pointed out a semi-circular fungus with a red-brown cap attached to the bark. 'What's that?'

Miller knelt to inspect it, 'Nothing very exciting. It's called Tinder Fungus. Ganoderma Applantum. It grows all year round. There's more over there.' He pointed to another larger example at the base of a pine tree.

'Any sign of the two we're after?' Dexter asked.

Miller shook his head. 'Have a seat, I'll do a quick circuit. Amanita Muscaria was recorded here three years ago.'

Dexter sat down on a tree stump and watched Miller wander between the trees, his eyes exploring their bases and surrounding undergrowth. She closed her eyes, feeling the exhaustion draining from her brain. Dexter wondered if she would drop dead when it reached her heart or whether it would just get pumped around her system and drag her down even further.

'There's a condom over here!' Miller called. 'It looks older than me.'

Dexter rose and walked over. She bagged the offending item and labelled it.

The next two hours passed quickly but without success. They found some litter at a site near Santon Downham and a beer can west of Thetford Warren. Dexter collected all the items and placed them into evidence bags. She would arrange for all the items to be fingerprinted. However, she was beginning to sense failure.

The final site that Miller had selected was in the north-east corner of the forest near the village of Weetling.

Miller had lost none of his enthusiasm. He pointed out a clump of tall plants with yellowish flowers.

'See those?' he asked.

'The weeds?'

'They're not weeds. It's called Wood Spurge or Euphorbia Amygdaloides. My daughter calls it Wood Spew. She says it's the colour of sick.'

'How old is she?' Dexter asked.

'Eight.'

Dexter suddenly wanted to change the subject but Miller had produced a photograph from his back pocket.

'Cute, isn't she?'

Dexter had to admit that she was: blonde curly hair and wide brown eyes.

'I didn't think you were married,' she said. 'You don't wear a ring.'

'Separated. Her mother lives in the USA. California. I keep trying to get an academic post over there. I could get to see Isabella more often. My current situation is a long way from ideal.'

'Isabella's a nice name,' Dexter conceded. *So was Zoe, she told herself. Zoe would have been eight in three weeks' time.*

'She's "Izzy" really or "Dizzy". She hates being called Isabella.'

Miller knelt at the foot of a small group of silver birch trees. Dexter looked out beyond the trees to the open fenland that bordered the forest. To her left, she saw the B1112 stretching round towards Feltwell and Hockwold cum Witton, to her right she could see the tiny clustered villages of Yaxford and Methwold.

'It's growing on me, this place,' she said to Miller.

'Like a fungus?'

241

'I used to think it was bleak, but it's peaceful I suppose. It takes time to learn to appreciate open space.'

'Too cold for me, I'm a sunshine boy.' Miller leaned in closer to consider a clump of material at the base of a birch tree. 'Hey! Come here!'

Dexter turned and walked over. 'What is it?'

Miller pointed at three white rings on the ground. 'Amanita Phalloides has a white volva that encases the base of each mushroom.' He opened his equipment box and removed a small trowel. He scraped away some of the dirt. 'Typically, most of the volva is underground. There you go.' He had excavated one of the samples. It looked harmless enough: a pale, white bulb coated in brown dirt.

'Is it definitely one of the two we're after?' Dexter peered at it.

'I'd say so. The stalk and cap have been cut off. Can you see? There's a clean incision been made across the base of each stalk.'

Miller found a bottle of hydrochloric acid from his equipment box and dropped a small amount on to the remains of one of the mushrooms. 'Remember the Maixner Test?'

'The test for amatoxins,' Dexter nodded. 'It should go blue, right?'

Two minutes later it did. Dexter suddenly felt a twinge of excitement. 'Okay. How sure are you that these are the right mushrooms?'

'Eighty per cent sure that they are Amanita Phalloides, but there's no way of being sure until I've analysed samples in the laboratory.'

'Understood.' She decided to take a chance. 'I'm going to get a forensic team up here right away. They might come across something we can use.'

'These have been cut fairly recently,' said Miller, 'you can tell from the . . .'

He paused. Alison Dexter was already on her mobile phone.

60

DS Harrison returned to New Bolden CID at 3p.m. He needed to focus, to clear his head of emotion and fill it with information. He realized that the only way he could help Sarah Jensen was to find the man who had killed her. The images of the bodies he had discovered in the ditch on Fulford Heath were still hovering at the front of his mind. That was not the way he wanted to remember Sarah.

He had spent the morning clearing her stuff from the shelves of his bathroom, packing her clothes into a suitcase. The smell of her in his flat had been upsetting. It was if she was lingering behind, taunting his failure to protect her and Harrison had felt unable to bear it. Sarah Jensen's possessions now sat without purpose or warmth in a black bin bag and a suitcase next to the front door of his flat just as her body lay in a metal drawer in the mortuary at Addenbrookes Hospital. The process had not been helpful. The flat felt violated to him and he knew that he would have to move out eventually. Aggression was starting to boil in his veins. Harrison had always believed that the first step away from despair was anger. So he tried to channel his loss into creative fury.

The CID floor was eerily quiet when he arrived. Dexter's office was deserted and even the seconded uniform officers had disappeared. He hoped that meant there had been progress made in the case during his brief absence. He found Sauerwine working at his desk. The constable looked surprised by his sudden appearance.

'Hello, sir, I wasn't expecting you. Sorry for taking your desk.'

Harrison nodded. 'What have I missed?'

Sauerwine cleared his throat. 'There have been a few developments. Inspector Dexter called a few minutes ago. She thinks they've found a location in Thetford Forest where the murderer might be harvesting the poisonous mushrooms. Suffolk Police are sending a forensic team to the site.'

'Why aren't we?'

'It's in their patch and our resources are stretched after . . .' Sauerwine hesitated, 'after the discoveries on the Heath.'

'Anything else?'

'DI Underwood has gone back to Jack Harvey's house. I'm not sure why. He didn't say.'

None of it sounded particularly promising. Harrison pulled up a swivel chair and sat down next to Sauerwine. 'Fair enough. So what are you working on?' He gestured at the list of phone numbers scrawled on a piece of paper in front of the detective constable.

'Forensic reckon the tyre tracks on the Heath were made by a Toyota Land Cruiser: two-point-eight litre engine, long wheelbase model. I'm calling the local dealer network and trying to get hold of any sales and service information.'

Harrison didn't feel any satisfaction that his hunch about the killer driving an expensive car had proved half-correct. He tried to remain focused. In truth, he had expected something more expensive after his discussion with Farrell at the scene of the attack on Ian Stark: a TVR, a Porsche or a Mercedes.

'DI Underwood had an idea about looking for owners that have missed scheduled services or MOT appointments in the last three months,' Sauerwine added, sensing Harrison's attention was drifting away from him.

It made sense, Harrison thought. Underwood had always been adept at spotting possible logjams in information flows: like a bear waiting at a waterfall for leaping salmon. However, it was a short-cut approach and therefore a risky one. He sensed Sauerwine was struggling.

'Need a hand?' he asked.

'That would be helpful, sir. It's taking longer than I expected. They're not being very forthcoming.'

'Let's divide the list. You work from the top down, I'll work from the bottom up. We'll tell them to photocopy their sales and service records for that model by say five p.m. tonight. Then we'll send squad cars round to pick up the paperwork and bring it back here. If they give us any grief, tell them we'll send a team to check the logbook and sales record

244

of every car on their forecourts. That should get the bastards moving.'

'Yes, sir.' Sauerwine paused for a moment, choosing the right words. 'For what it's worth, sir, I'm very sorry about DC Jensen. She was a good laugh.'

Harrison couldn't look the young constable in the eye. Instead, he stared fixedly at the page of numbers in front of him. 'It's worth a lot, mate,' he said eventually. 'She was. We just have to concentrate on doing our jobs properly. Let's get hold of this bastard before he can hurt anybody else.'

Sauerwine collected his papers and moved to an adjacent desk. Harrison tried to focus away the memories that were suddenly flooding back to him. He consoled himself with the thought that when they finally caught the bastard, he would make sure the custody sergeant vanished for half an hour so he could spend some quality time alone with him in the cell. He looked over at Jensen's desk, still cluttered with her personal effects.

It was distracting him. Someone would have to clear it.

61

Underwood removed the protective blue police taping from Jack Harvey's front door and unlocked it. He felt a certain sense of trepidation. It wasn't merely the thought of what had happened in the house a few days previously that jarred with him. Nor was it to do with the terrible images of Rowena Harvey's fate that his imagination was throwing up for his consideration. Moreover, it stemmed from the growing and uncomfortable sense that Jack was watching everything he did.

The stench of smoke still hadn't left the house. Now, after nearly a week, the hallway smelt acrid, acidic. Underwood moved with care into Jack's office. The forensic team had stripped most of the room; bagged and tagged all items of interest. Underwood was unsure of exactly what he was seeking. He wondered whether Jack had concealed a strongbox or a safe somewhere around the house; somewhere that the forensic teams had missed.

Based on Mary Colson's comments about the keys and on opening the box, Underwood had gradually come to the realization that the box of bad memories was real. It wasn't just a psychologist's trick. He had given the box a physical life based on Jack's advice, burying photographs, CDs and other reminders of his previous life with Julia. Perhaps, Jack had done the same thing. One of the keys on Jack's keyring looked like it would unlock a padlock. Underwood was convinced that Jack Harvey had a box of bad memories too; that it had a tangible, physical existence; and that it was still somewhere in the house.

But where?

He knew that the Scene-of-Crime team had been through the main house in great detail; seeking out tiny pieces of evidence, looking for DNA trace material. The fire had destroyed most of the contents of Jack's office and the search teams had found only fragmentary remains of his patient records. Underwood decided to leave the office and downstairs rooms of the house. He knew that these would have been searched exhaustively and that Jack would not have placed any sensitive material in an easily accessible ground floor location.

He headed upstairs. The main bedroom smelt vaguely of Rowena Harvey's perfume. He found it vaguely arousing. Underwood looked through the cupboards and drawers and checked the corners of the carpet for any loose areas. Finding nothing, he examined the bathroom. For no particular reason, Underwood found himself reading the labels of Rowena Harvey's array of toiletries: cleansing lotion, daily moisturiser, shampoo. He was slightly disappointed to find a bottle of self-tanning lotion: he had always believed Rowena Harvey's tan had been entirely natural.

The killer wants Rowena Harvey, he thought to himself, the killer sat in Jack's consulting room staring at her framed photograph. He probably met her too, when he visited the house. The killer wants her sexually. He has probably already raped her. Why wasn't she killed with the others? What else does he want to use her for?

He gave up on the bathroom and moved on. Searching the other three bedrooms and the loft space took Underwood just over an hour. Eventually he walked down to the Harveys' kitchen and poured himself a glass of tap water. The view over the back of the house was impressive. The garden covered approximately an acre and was lined with thick clumps of dark green conifers. Underwood noticed that Jack had installed a water feature in the centre of the lawn since his last visit. It was a little waterfall effect, with water pumped from the mains supply, splashing over a neat rainbow of round stones. He looked around for the control switch. There seemed to be little point in powering a waterfall that no one was ever likely to see. Underwood realized that the switch had to be located in Jack's shed.

He knew that the SOCO team had examined in the shed and found nothing of interest. He could see their evidence tag stapled to the wooden door as he approached across the lawn. The control for the waterfall was just behind the door on the right hand side. Underwood flicked it into the 'off' position and, stepping back outside, heard the feature babble to a halt. He absorbed the sights and smells of the garden, feeling a sudden rush of pity for the Harveys. There was the stone barbecue where Jack had sweated over steaks in the summer; there was the white plastic sun lounger where Rowena Harvey had given a veneer of authenticity to her chemical tan; there was the patio where they sat together and drank chilled glasses of Chardonnay in the evenings.

Underwood smiled as he remembered how Jack had cursed the cost of installing the patio. Rowena had insisted on rippled stones supplied by a company in Cumbria.

'Cumbria, for Christ's sake!' Jack had moaned to him. 'It's not like we don't have rocks down here, is it?'

Underwood saw that Jack had used two of the leftover paving blocks in the area adjacent to his water feature. He walked over. It didn't look right. The plain grey blocks seemed incongruous with the coloured stones within the feature itself. He doubted whether Rowena would have approved of such a cumbersome arrangement. Underwood stood on one of the slabs and felt it move very slightly beneath him. He stepped off and crouched down to look. One of the two slabs was firmly secured into the soil, the other seemed to be sitting unevenly on something. He retrieved a spade from the side of the shed and levered the offending slab, shifting it a couple of inches to the left. Underwood inspected the space underneath. The slab had been resting on a padlocked metal box. He dragged the stone onto the lawn and, with a considerable effort, hauled the box out from the soil.

Underwood hurried back into the house with his prize. Sitting at the kitchen table, he checked the size of the padlock. There were two keys on Jack's key ring that conceivably could have opened it. The second one did. Inside was an A4 manilla envelope and a significant amount of cash. Underwood flicked through the wad of money, estimating it amounted to about five thousand pounds. Then, trying to retain his focus, he withdrew the contents of the envelope.

It contained a collection of notes scrawled in Jack's handwriting, and two pages that seemed to have been photocopied from an encyclopaedia.

Underwood read the notes first of all.

'Session 1: Home. 3rd February 2002. Patient arrived late. Physical condition scruffy and unkempt. When I asked why his clothes were so filthy he replied that he had been gardening. He seemed to find this very amusing. Also appeared to resent my questions. Answers were guarded and often abrasive. Showed no interest in discussing his family of career history. Inability to concentrate, physical lethargy, defensive attitude are indicative of some form of narcotic addiction.'

Underwood read on. The notes seemed surprisingly general

248

to him. They seemed to be the basis for a more detailed analysis. He wondered if Jack was sending regular, more detailed reports on his client to a third party. There were no names either, he mused, nothing specific. Odd.

'Session 2: Home. 13th February 2002. Patient's physical appearance has deteriorated over the past week. Wore same clothes as in previous consultation and gave the strong impression that he hadn't changed in the intervening days. Arrived late. He is still reluctant to discuss details of his problem. When questioned on drug dependency, patient burst into hysterical laughter. I was unable to get any sense out of him for approximately five minutes. Seems to have little sense of self or of the consequences of his actions. Towards the end of the session, patient lost all engagement with me and began to describe a strange list of images that seem to have religious overtones.'

'Session 3: Home. 23rd February 2002. Physical appearance shocking. Patient was unshaven and filthy. Excrement smeared down back of his trousers. When questioned about his physical condition, patient replied that he was "of the earth" and launched into a stream of expletives. Appears to be unable to cope with reality. I asked him if he wanted medical help and he laughed at me. Patient appeared to be in the afterglow of a hallucinogenic trance: he claimed that there were lights in the back of his head that "chased him around the house" and that there were "demons everywhere". Patient continually drank from a plastic bottle that appeared to contain urine. More worryingly, he seemed fascinated by the idea of decapitation. He asked me, as a doctor, what I thought would be the optimal method. Judging by the total disintegration of his personality and apparent self-destructive tendencies, I assumed this indicated suicidal tendencies: the removal of the head being often equated with the excision of the problem or the erasure of the

249

hated personality. When I asked if he had thought about killing himself, patient giggled and replied "no, just you". Some of the hallucinatory and physical symptoms appear consistent with abuse of Lysergic Acid Diethylamide. Recommend hospitalization before patient inflicts damage on himself or on other people.'

'Session 4. Home. 5th March 2002. Physical appearance has improved. Patient appeared cleaner and had changed clothes since our previous meeting. He seemed more responsive to questioning. He revealed that he believes he is becoming an incarnation of a Hindu god. Presumably, this is a retreat into some childhood fantasy picked up during time in India. He refuses to answer to his name and responds only to the name "Soma". This is apparently the deity he believes that he is becoming. I asked him if his transformation had a purpose. I also asked him if he was trying to become a God so as to restore the life of his mother: who can turn back time except God? etc. He called me a "fucking charlatan". He said that I could not be "Brihaspati" if I asked such idiotic questions. (I later learned that the character "Brihaspati" was the sage of the gods in Hindu legend.) Patient then launched into a long and complex account of his transformation. He said he had been "forged at the churning of the ocean", that he had "distilled the elixir of immortality" and that he would be the "sire of the lunar race". Obviously, there seems to be little logical base for his thinking and I imagined it to be the product of whatever drugs he had ingested during the previous twenty-four hours. Patient also began to ask me a series of questions about my wife. He became especially excited when he learned her name was Rowena. I left the room briefly to get a glass of water. When I returned, I found that the patient had taken down a picture of Rowena from above my desk and was kneeling on the carpet masturbating over it. When I reprimanded him, he rolled onto his back and giggled

250

hysterically. The sessions are unproductive. The patient needs to be hospitalized and have an intensive course of addiction therapy.'

'Session 5. Home/YXH. 15th March 2002. Patient did not arrive for scheduled appointment. Called his home and mobile number and received no reply. Fearing he had injured himself I visited.'

Underwood stopped. Jack had finally dropped his guard and given a specific detail: 'YXH'. Was it a person or place?

'Patient was standing naked in the driveway when I arrived. He was holding what appeared to be a large knife or cleaver. I remained in the car. He stared at me for some time with no apparent sense of who or what I was. He seemed to be in some form of trance. After approximately ten minutes he returned to the interior of the house. Fearing for my own safety I returned home and contacted patient's father. Informed him that the patient was beyond my help. That long-term hospitalization was the only realistic option. Father replied that he would handle the issue henceforth and that my involvement was over.'

Underwood felt a spark of grim satisfaction. The picture was emerging. The patient's father had organized Jack's involvement. He had suspected a concerned third party had been involved for some time. He also began to wonder if the middle-aged male corpse that they had retrieved from Fulford Heath was the murderer's father. He also noted that the accounts tallied chronologically with the timeframe implied by the post mortems conducted by Leach. The first murder had taken place around the beginning of February. The sessions with Jack seemed to end in mid-March. The second murder – the woman with glass fragments embedded in her body – had been dated to early April.

The kitchen clock suddenly chimed for five o'clock,

making Underwood jump. The dead house was unsettling him; as was the growing recognition that Mary Colson's unusual abilities had again steered him a step closer to the killer. He could feel the dead watching him, anticipating his next move. Underwood briefly read the two photocopied pages that gave details of the Soma legend and of Brihaspati, the sage of the Gods, before deciding to leave the house.

'YXH' was now the key. He needed to talk to Alison Dexter.

He gathered his papers and left the house, double locking the door behind him.

The house fell quiet again. Rowena Harvey's perfume drifted faintly down the stairs. Water lay still in a film across the coloured rocks of the water feature. The kitchen clock ticked pointlessly and the central heating timer clicked the boiler on. The photographs on the living room wall stared out at the emptiness.

The emptiness stared back.

62

Alison Dexter realized as she drove back towards New Bolden that Adam Miller had been correct on two issues. Firstly, he had apparently located a site from where the killer could have harvested his poisonous mushrooms. Secondly, her shoes had indeed been totally inappropriate for trudging about in the woods. Her feet were soaked and her shoes and tights caked in mud. She had left the scientist at the final site after the forensic team from Suffolk police had arrived. It was possible that they might find something useful: a discarded item containing a print, maybe even an impression in the soil. The ground was certainly soft enough, as her ankles and footwear uncomfortably proved.

She needed to be at the station. Information was going to start flowing through the department quickly: Leach's full post-mortem results, details from Sauerwine's investigation into Toyota dealerships and hopefully data from the forensic team in Thetford Forest. She wanted to be the focal point for the investigation: allow the data to filter through her. If it was going to be a long night, she needed to change. Dexter turned off the New Bolden ring road and headed for her apartment.

As soon as she unlocked her door and walked inside, Dexter's instincts told her that something was wrong. Maybe it was an unfamiliar smell or a sense of disruption to her ordered world. Then she realized, her Police College graduation picture was smashed on the floor. Cautiously, she moved down the hallway trying to keep as quiet as possible. She passed the kitchen and shot a quick glance at the mess of rice and litter that had been spread across the work surface and the floor. Just as she was about to open her bedroom door, Mark Willis emerged from the bathroom behind her and, using all his weight, dragged her through the doorway, flung her on to the bed and fell heavily on top of her.

She fought violently against him, her hands scratching and tearing at his eyes. She could smell beer on his breath. After a moment or two she drew blood and Willis lost patience. He slapped her hard across the face and clamped his hand down over her nose and mouth.

'Sssshhh!' he whispered. 'Or I won't let you breathe.'

She bit at his hand and he slapped her again.

'Don't worry,' he slurred, 'I'm not going to try and slip you one.' He grabbed one of her breasts and squeezed hard. 'Although I'm glad to see that you've been looking after yourself.'

'What do you want?' she hissed before the hand could cover her face again.

'I want my drugs, Alison. You took them. They belong to me. I want them back.'

'I haven't got them.' She was working on an exit strategy. His body weight was keeping her legs pinned. If he moved slightly she could swing her knee up into his crotch.

'I know you haven't, I've been looking around. Nice flat,' he observed, 'like a cell.'

'Well you'd know, wouldn't you?' she snarled.

'That was uncalled for, Alison. Give me my drugs and you'll never see me again.'

'I don't have them.'

'I know you took them, I know you've hidden them. If I don't get them back, I'm going to hurt you. And you know I'm good at that.'

'The only thing you're good at is screwing people over.'

'Harsh words coming from you, Sparrer.' Willis smiled a malicious yellow smile. 'You never even told me I was gonna be a daddy.'

Dexter realized for the first time that her journals were scattered across the room. She felt herself go limp as if her final ounce of fight had suddenly fled from her body. He had violated her. The past she had tried so hard and secretly to rationalize lay in disorganized and exposed heaps on her bedroom floor.

'Little Zoe's going to be eight in a couple of weeks,' he continued, 'or at least she would have if you hadn't got her sucked out.'

'Go away,' Dexter whispered quietly.

'You see, Sparrer. You're not the Pollyana Perfect everyone thinks you are. At least I've never killed anyone. Then there's the issue of your rural anonymity. There are people in London who'd love to know where you're hiding. Maybe I'll put the word out. Maybe someone really scary will come to visit.'

Dexter was cold, numb with shock. 'Go away now and I'll give you your drugs tomorrow.'

'Why not now?'

'That's the deal,' she whispered, staring directly up at the ceiling. 'Take it or leave it.'

Willis thought for a moment. 'Where and when?'

'I'll send you a message.'

'Don't mess me around, Sparrer. I'll know if a cart-load of plods is waiting for me.'

'I'll send you a message.'

'See that you do.'

Willis climbed off of her and took a step back. He watched

her for a second lying perfectly still on her bed. 'You know,' he said, 'it's getting me all nostalgic seeing you lying there, Sparrer.'

She said nothing. Willis grinned, collected his beer from the sideboard and left.

Five minutes later, Alison Dexter stood up and collected her past from the different corners of the room. She put the journals back in their correct order and stacked them back in her cupboard. The mud on her tights had dried and crumbled onto her duvet and white carpet. The telephone was ringing in her living room. She didn't hear it.

63

Rowena Harvey gradually awoke from a nightmare that had seemed to last days. It had been a state of near consciousness of strange dreams and images: terrifying and enlightening. All the time the strange electronic voice had droned at her, conjuring dark shapes from her imagination. She had tried to fight but had found the powerful suggestions impossible to control.

She gradually began to remember the details of her abduction and the face of the man who had taken her. She recalled the pain of the car crash that still nagged at the side of her head. There were other images too floating in her mind: being dragged upstairs and tied down, lying naked while he washed her with a sponge, screaming into the masking tape gag that she still wore, the man feeding her some terrible omelette before she'd sank into oblivion.

Who was he? What did he want?

He hadn't raped her but she felt a cold terror that he fully intended to do so. She knew that she had to try and free her hands, at least try to get away. Rowena Harvey tried to open her eyes but they felt so heavy, as if she was trying to lift the world with them. The lights of the room swam between her half-closed lids, uneven shapes that made no sense. She was aware that her legs itched but couldn't see why. She also gradually became aware that she was not alone in the room. The man was in there too, talking to her, the same haunting, prompting voice that had driven her nightmares.

'. . . a little bit of foam . . . a scrape and hey presto!' the voice said happily.

Rowena managed to open her eyes a little more. She could see the outline of his body in front of her. She could hear water splashing too.

'. . . fortunate to have been incorporated in the incarnation.'

He was shaving her legs. Rowena Harvey could feel the razor dragging across her skin. She looked down and saw her entire body was covered in shaving foam. He was shaving off all her body hair. She screamed and threw every ounce of strength into freeing herself of the bindings.

'. . . you move around I'm more likely to slip and cut you, aren't I?' the voice warned sternly, 'the blood of the lunar race should not be spilt so stupidly.'

Max Fallon checked his watch. It was only a matter of hours now. Darkness was already stretching across the East Anglian sky beyond the windowpane. As the planets span beautifully and gigantically into alignment above him, he and Rohini would bring forth the lunar race on earth.

64

Underwood found an envelope waiting for him at the front desk of New Bolden CID. It contained a mass of receipts and for a moment he had no idea who had left it for him. Then he remembered his conversation with Doreen O'Riordan. He crammed the bulging envelope into his inside jacket pocket. He had really made the request to try and frighten the woman into behaving more respectfully towards Mary Colson. He hadn't expected her to be so bloody-minded as to provide him with hundreds of receipts. Still, he could be bloody-minded too when necessary.

He found Sauerwine and Harrison together in CID, sifting through two huge piles of photocopying.

'Service and sales records?' he asked.

Harrison nodded. 'It's all a bit of a mess. Some of the dealerships have given us records for all the two-point-eight litre Land Cruisers they've sold or serviced, others have given us details on completely different models. It's taken us since five just to identify relevant records.'

Sauerwine placed his left hand on one pile. 'These are relevant. Hopefully.'

Underwood pitied them. Examining documents in detail had never been one of his strong points. He found he could focus intensely but only for short periods before his mind wandered into minefields of its own creation.

'I found something that may be relevant in Jack Harvey's papers,' Underwood said. 'The letters Y,X,H are important. It may be a short form of the killer's name, it may be something to do with his address, it may even be his car licence plate.'

'Postcode?' Sauerwine volunteered.

'Worth checking out,' Harrison nodded. 'At least it gives us something to focus on.'

'Where's Dexter?' Underwood asked, seeing her empty office.

'Supposedly on her way,' Harrison replied. 'She's late in.'

Underwood felt a stab of anxiety. He recalled his conversation with Paddy McInally and realized that he had done little to help or investigate Dexter's own situation. She always gave him the impression of total self-sufficiency: of almost resenting his interference. Dexter seemed to take any offers of help as a professional and personal affront. He sensed that McInally's relationship with her was more affectionate than his own. They were both East-End types, Underwood consoled himself, perhaps it was natural for them to have an affinity.

He tried to remain focused on Rowena Harvey. Jack's

257

notes had given him an insight into the killer's frame of mind. The drug addiction seemed to have eroded the murderer's sense of identity. Underwood vaguely remembered reading an article a few years previously about LSD addiction amongst rock stars in the sixties: notably, the manner in which excessive use of the drug gradually undermined an individual's ego and destroyed their idealization of the self. It seemed plausible to him that a mind weakened by usage of the drug or its close relatives might try to create a new identity as the old one evaporated.

He flicked through the papers he had discovered at Jack's house. The killer believed he had become a Hindu deity, the Soma. Why had he assumed that identity? Underwood thought for a moment and then remembered a fragment of his conversation with Adam Miller from a couple of days previously.

'Have we got a contact number for Miller?' Underwood shouted across the room to Harrison and Sauerwine.

'We've got a mobile,' Sauerwine replied. 'He's being driven back to Cambridge, I think.' The police constable read out Miller's number from a photocopied sheet Dexter had left on his desk.

Underwood dialled and impatiently waited for Miller to pick up.

'Hello,' said Miller after three rings.

'Doctor Miller, it's John Underwood from New Bolden Police.'

'Hello John,' Miller replied. 'I've just got back from Thetford. You're not going to send me back up there, are you?'

'No. Did the forensic team find anything?'

'Not while I was there. I think they got fed up with me. They sent me home in a squad car.'

'Adam, I need to ask you something. When we met you in Cambridge, you mentioned that some of these mushrooms have a long history; that they were used by ancient cultures. You called it "ethno-something-or-other"?'

'Ethnomycology,' Miller confirmed. 'The Fly Agaric

258

mushroom – the amanita muscaria – certainly has a colourful history.'

'In what ways have they been used?'

'A variety of ways. In the nineteenth century, Western European visitors to Siberia observed Koryak tribesmen ingesting the Fly Agaric before going hunting. They believed it actually increased their physical strength and reflexes. There is also evidence that in certain ancient cultures the Fly Agaric was used to induce religious visions. It also made the takers susceptible to mind control, of course. Religion has often been used as a means of exerting social and political control through history, so that makes sense to me.'

'What about ancient Hindu religion? Have you heard of something called the Soma?'

'Absolutely,' Miller replied. 'I'm impressed! You've done your homework. The Soma was a Hindu god: the God of plants and the moon, I think. There was a famous piece of research by a guy called Gordon Wasson which equated the Fly Agaric mushroom with the god Soma.'

'I don't understand.'

'Look, I'm no expert on this stuff but as I recall in the Soma story the God is synonymous with juice of the Soma plant. If you drink the Soma you live forever, that kind of thing.'

Underwood looked back through Jack's consultation notes. 'An elixir of immortality?'

'That's it. If you drank the Soma you passed through the gateway to the Gods.'

'Thank you, Adam,' Underwood said quietly. 'Very helpful.'

'No worries.'

Underwood dropped his phone back onto its rest. He could see Dexter had entered the CID department. She stopped to talk to Harrison and Sauerwine. Underwood looked out of the window. It was a clear night, the moon glowed powerfully through the darkness. Miller had said the Soma was the god of plants and the moon. Something was niggling at the back of Underwood's mind.

'Sauerwine!' he called out. The PC broke off from his

conversation with Dexter and hurried over.

'What's up, sir?' he asked as he arrived at Underwood's desk.

'When we were at Mary Colson's house you said something about planets. Something to do with horoscopes.'

'Not exactly horoscopes, sir. It was a joke. I used to moan to her about not having a girlfriend. She liked to wind me up. She said there was some planetary alignment this week and that it was good for the sex drive. You know, it's supposed to improve your fertility. As I say, it was a joke really.'

Underwood felt a terrible sinking feeling in his stomach. He found a newspaper on an adjacent desk and flicked through to the horoscopes page.

He ignored the absurdly generalized selection of predictions and scanned down to the note at the bottom: '*Remember tonight at 11.27 GMT the five inner planets come into orbital alignment with the sun. This is the first major astrological event since the full planetary alignment of 2000.*'

It couldn't be a coincidence. He looked at his watch. He had less than two hours to find Rowena Harvey. Dexter joined him at his desk.

'What news?'

Underwood looked at her closely. 'Your eyes are red.'

'I'm knackered,' she replied.

'I'm not an idiot, Dex.'

She ignored his comment. 'What's all that?' She pointed at the papers in his hand. Underwood handed them over.

'I found them at Jack's house, buried in the garden. They're his consultation notes on our boy. No names unfortunately. He thinks he's become some Hindu god called Soma. I spoke to Miller. The Fly Agaric mushroom was apparently seen as containing the essence of this Soma.'

Dexter read through the notes at speed.

'He is one sick puppy,' she observed quietly. 'How did Jack get involved in all this?'

'Money,' Underwood said bitterly, 'twenty-five grand by the looks of it. Whoever this fuck-up is he's got some wealthy connections.'

260

'How did the SOCOs miss this stuff?' Dexter asked, her eyes never leaving the page.

'It was under a paving stone. It's forgivable.'

Dexter shook her head. 'Not by me.' Her eyes fixed on a piece of information.

'What's this "YXH" reference mean?'

'I don't know. Maybe it's a short form of the killer's name. The notes seem to imply it represents a person or a place.'

Dexter bit her lip as she tried to concentrate. It seemed vaguely familiar to her.

'If it is a place,' she reasoned, 'then the "H" could stand for Hotel.'

Underwood nodded. 'Or hospital. Maybe even "House".'

Dexter looked back down at the page. Her mind was frantically sifting through the litter cluttering her consciousness: Mark Willis, her flat, her ruined shoes, Adam Miller, Thetford Forest, Feltwell and Hockwold cum Witton. Then she suddenly saw what she had been looking for; like a little girl finding a photo in a cluttered drawer or recognizing a face in an unfriendly crowd.

'Bloody hell, John,' she said simply, 'I know where he is.'

65

The God Soma sat, naked and cross-legged in the woods near the front entrance to his driveway. He enjoyed the damp pressure of the soil against his bare skin. He was the Soma. He licked the red and white cap of a Fly Agaric mushroom as if he was tasting his own blood. The lights were beginning to creep at the corners of his eyes like insects crawling out from under stones. He wasn't afraid. The moment of his incarnation was approaching, rumbling across the heavens with a pirouetting inevitability.

He had brought his watch outside with him. It would be essential that he did not lose his sense of time. He had set the alarm for 11.15. That would give him adequate warning to marshal his thoughts and return to the library in time to penetrate Rohini at precisely 11.27. He had already moved her downstairs from their bedroom. It had been a tricky process: she had kicked and fought against him but ultimately he had secured her to the wooden table in front of his eager disciples. He had brought a knife with him to free her of her bindings; to allow her to succumb to his touch freely. Now he had only to enjoy the rotating heavens until the moment arrived.

Alison Dexter's Mondeo raced north out of New Bolden just ahead of the spinning blue lights of the police squad car that she had requested as back up. Underwood gripped his armrest nervously as they passed ninety miles an hour.

'I'm still not sure that I understand how you figured this out,' he said, his eyes never leaving the onrushing road.

'Miller and I found a site in Thetford Forest this afternoon. There were a bunch of mushrooms that matched the ones used by the killer. They had been dug up recently. The site is on the edge of the forest and faces west across fenland. From that point you can see, three or four villages. One of them is Yaxford. Look at your map.' She tapped the Ordnance Survey map Underwood had resting on his lap.

'Yaxford Hall,' he noted.

'Y,X,H.'

'We shouldn't really go charging in without a warrant,' he observed.

'You want to explain that to Rowena Harvey?' Dexter asked.

'I know.' Underwood checked his watch. 'We haven't got long.'

'Look, we'll just knock on the door and see what happens.'

The two cars roared through the Cambridgeshire night, splitting the silence of the vast and sombre fens, throwing blue and yellow light into the void.

The Soma found himself at one with the soil. It was a profoundly beautiful experience, the white wash of the stars above him, the gentle rushing of the wind against his face. He saw that his limbs were fizzing and disappearing, his corporeal form was vanishing before his eyes. He was becoming the essence, the very juice of life itself. He was melting into the soil like rainwater and erupting forth into the red and white beauty of the plant god. He sensed his erection grow from his body just as the plant god grew from the soil. The lights were strong in his eyes: spectacular spirals of blue. He could hear the rushing of the ocean that had been his amniotic fluid. Shapes began to emerge through the kaleidoscope; hard edges appearing from the cornucopia of formless elements. The shapes became recognizable to him. The Soma felt fear and fury rise from the ground and engulf him.

Dexter turned into the gravel driveway of Yaxford Hall and pulled up. The squad car stopped behind her. She unlocked her door and stepped out into the cold night air. PC Steven Evans, the driver of the squad car, wound down his window.

'I want you two to wait here,' Dexter told them. 'Keep your car parked on the drive. You're blocking the entrance so he won't be able to make a bolt for it.'

'Would you like one of us to go in with you, ma'am?' asked PC Dawson from the passenger seat.

'Inspector Underwood and I will go up to the main house. Stay sharp. If we call you, come running.'

'No problem.'

Evans and Dawson unclipped their seat belts and climbed out of the Volvo. Dexter returned to her car. The old house loomed large and impressively above them as they drove up to the main door. It was an eighteenth century country manor house with a flight of stone steps leading up to the front door which was flanked by two crumbling stone pillars.

'Jesus,' Underwood breathed. 'This place is huge.'

'Doesn't look like anyone's at home,' Dexter observed peering through the windscreen. 'There are no lights on.'

Underwood looked up at the crumbling stonework façade of the house. 'The front door's open,' he said.

Dexter nodded. 'There's torches in the boot.'

They got out of the car, nervously checking the blackness around them for any signs of movement. While Dexter removed two power torches from the rear of the car, Underwood noticed two vehicles parked at the side of the house: a Porsche 911 and a Toyota Land Cruiser.

'Is that what I think it is?' he asked.

Dexter shone her torch at the jeep. 'Yep. It's a Land Cruiser.' She unclipped her radio and leaned against the side of her car.

'Evans, this is Dexter.'

'Go ahead, ma'am,' came the crackling reply.

'This is the place. Get onto control and have them send a SOCO team and some extra plods.'

'Will do.'

'We're going to check the building. Check in every five minutes.'

'Understood.'

Underwood was facing the black mass of the building apprehensively.

'You ready?' Dexter asked.

He checked his watch. It was after 11p.m. He hoped they were in the right location.

'Let's get this over with.'

The torch beams illuminated the steps and the gaping dark mouth of the doorway. Underwood and Dexter approached cautiously, watching their footing on the cracked and uneven stonework. Stepping inside the entrance hall Underwood immediately noticed the smell of death and decay. It made him shudder. They surveyed the gloomy hall with their torches. Underwood tried a light switch. Nothing happened.

'I don't fancy this,' Dexter muttered suddenly. 'This nutcase could be anywhere. Getting ready to shoot us full of that mushroom shit.'

'I know.' Underwood took a step forward. 'But we haven't got time to piss around.' He jumped slightly as his torch beam illuminated a stag's head mounted on the wall. The two shaky circles of light drifted across a series of oil paintings that stretched up the stairway.

'You think we should split up?' Dexter asked without enthusiasm. 'We'd search the place more quickly.'

264

Underwood didn't fancy the idea of creeping about in the dark by himself, nor stepping backwards onto a loaded needle. 'No. Two sets of eyes are better than one.'

Dexter was relieved. She shone a torch down the stairs that led to the basement. 'Shall we start downstairs then?'

PC Evans called through Dexter's message to the control centre then rejoined Dawson outside the car. His fellow officer was shining his torch into the dense clump of trees and hedgerow that ran parallel to the driveway.

'You see anything?' Evans asked.

'I thought I could hear something moving around,' Dawson replied.

'Probably a badger, mate.'

Dawson swung his torch in a sweep across the lawn. 'This is a big gaff. Must be twenty acres.'

'Easy,' Evans agreed.

'Bugger to maintain, though.'

Evans turned away and looked hard into the woods. 'Can you hear that?'

'What?'

'A kind of beeping.' Evans craned his neck in the direction of the sound. 'Coming from over there.'

Dawson could hear something too, a vague electronic noise. 'What is it? A mobile phone?' he whispered.

Evans shook his head. 'That's a watch alarm, mate. You go down the drive and cut back into the woods. I'll go in here, flush him down towards you.'

'Shouldn't we call in?'

'Just get a fucking move on,' Evans hissed.

Dawson jogged down the drive for about thirty metres then vanished into the trees. Seeing him disappear, Evans lit his own torch and stepped into the trees. He could hear the beeping ahead of him. Twigs cracked underfoot as he approached. He strained his eyes to see into the darkness either side of his torch beam. Something slammed into him from below and to his right. Evans felt the breath squeezed suddenly from his lungs as he was driven hard into a tree. The Soma rammed his knife into Evans' abdomen and savoured

265

the warmth of blood as it entwined his wrist. The policeman fell wheezing to the ground, fumbling for his police radio. The Soma picked up the handset himself and retreated into the woodland.

Dawson could hear the beeping more loudly now; he pushed his way through the dangling branches and leaves, tracking his torch across the ground. After a moment, he saw the watch lying amongst the grass clumps and dirt. He knelt and using a pencil from his pocket lifted it from the ground. It was a digital diver's watch. The time was 11.01.

'Stevo?' he called into the woods. 'I've found it.'

No reply came. He unclipped his radio. 'Stevo, can you hear me?'

The Soma brought a rock down against the back of the constable's head with ferocious enthusiasm. Dawson slumped forward, face down in the dirt, blood trickling from a dirty wound on the crown of his head. The Soma removed his police radio.

Inside the house, Dexter stopped in her tracks. 'Did you make that out?' She asked Underwood after Dawson's call for Evans had spluttered through their radios.

Underwood wasn't listening. They had found the kitchen. He shone his torch into the huge work area. There was rubbish and soil everywhere. Broken glass crunched under foot. Dexter joined him and looked at the scene of chaos. She noticed there were two blue cool-boxes sitting amidst the detritus; she kicked the lid off one: it was stained black with blood. Underwood found the same residue in the second box. On the work surface was a pile of mushrooms. Dexter looked them over but didn't touch anything: she already had bad dreams.

They left the kitchen area and after checking the remaining utility rooms in the basement, headed back upstairs to the ground floor. The smell was powerful again, twisting and nauseating. Underwood gestured Dexter towards a drawing room. She looked inside. Rubbish spewed from the fireplace across the floor. Dexter's torch also highlighted audio cassettes scattered around the room.

266

She jumped as her foot kicked against something hard; she looked down as a Rubik's Cube rolled awkwardly away from her.

Underwood moved further down the main corridor, pushing open a heavy oak door. His eyes took a moment to adjust the darkness. The room stank: Underwood knew he had located the source of the smell. He froze as he heard shuffling and swung his torch towards the far end of the room. There his torchlight picked out the shape of Rowena Harvey's naked body strapped to a table with rope.

'Dex!' he shouted, stumbling across the room towards Rowena. Rowena Harvey's eyes were alive with terror before she recognized Underwood above her. He untied her hands from beneath the table and tore the gag from Rowena Harvey's mouth. She was hysterical with panic. Dexter entered the room and hurried over. She sat Rowena Harvey upright on the table, removed her own jacket and placed it around her bare shoulders.

'Rowena,' Underwood said, 'it's me. Look, it's John.' Rowena stared at him without any obvious sign of recognition. 'Where is he?' Underwood asked. 'Where is the man who took you?'

Rowena Harvey shook her head slowly, her entire body quivering with fear.

'Let's get her out of here,' Underwood ordered. 'She needs a doctor.'

'Agreed.' Dexter stepped back then suddenly span around clutching her neck. 'What the fuck was that?'

'What?' Underwood snapped as he helped Rowena Harvey to her feet.

'Something just fucking landed on me.' She looked at her hand and saw a dark circle of blood. 'Shit, I'm bleeding.'

Underwood suddenly shone his torch up towards the ceiling. Jack Harvey's severed head stared back at him. Dexter's torch then illuminated Sarah Jensen's head, also hanging about a metre from the ceiling directly behind Jack's. Together, the two narrow beams of light traced the grisly line back across the room. Five human heads dangled on ropes from the ceiling. There were five heads hanging in a line and staring directly at the spot where Rowena Harvey had been tied down, like coins aligned on a table.

'Oh my God!' Dexter breathed.

'We need help,' Underwood replied. Staring up at the ceiling was making him feel nauseous, as if he was seeing the sky swirling above him.

Dexter unclipped her radio and brought it close to her mouth, her eyes never leaving the ceiling.

'Evans. This is Dexter. Have we got an ETA on the support yet?'

There was silence.

'Evans or Dawson. This is DI Dexter. Respond please.'

Static crackled from the radio. Then a voice she didn't recognize hissed through the white noise.

'Under the milky ocean,' came the icy reply, 'something is not quite right.'

Dexter felt a rush of fear and flashed her torch around the room.

'Time to go,' said Underwood.

They helped Rowena Harvey to the door and Dexter checked that the corridor was clear before they crossed the entrance hall to the front door. It was locked. Dexter frantically rattled at the handle.

'It's jammed, for Christ's sake,'

'Try the windows.' Underwood looked around him, shining his torch into the gloom, trying to anticipate the ambush that he knew was coming.

High above them, leaning over the oak banister on the first floor landing at the head of the grand staircase, the Soma looked down on his people in amusement.

'They're nailed shut.' Dexter gave up heaving at the sash windows. 'We'll have to smash them. I need a chair or something.'

The Soma stepped down from heaven, dressed in a tall hat bedecked with jewels and a belt of moonlight glitter. He slipped gently through the clouds and entwining spirits towards the chaotic earth. He passed his father halfway

268

down the staircase, ignoring the hideous kink of bone where the old man's neck had broken. He floated towards the noise, clutching the elixir of immortality in his hand.

'In the library,' Underwood instructed Dexter. 'There's a chair behind the door.'

Reluctantly, Dexter hurried back through the darkness of the corridor. Underwood remained with Rowena Harvey in the hallway.

'Get me out of here,' she implored.

Underwood heard a creak above him and looked up, his torchlight penetrating the darkness and illuminating the face of the descending Soma: a needle glistened in the sudden light. He advanced to the foot of the staircase. Rowena Harvey started to scream. Dexter emerged from the library hauling a wooden desk chair.

'Get to the car,' Underwood snapped as she came alongside him. 'Get her out of here.'

'Welcome to the incarnation of the lunar race,' announced the Soma, raising his arms in joyous benediction to the strange new figures below him.

'What about you?' Dexter asked.

'Just get on with it,' Underwood hissed, beginning to climb the stairs. The Soma had come to a halt on a small landing halfway between the first and ground floors. He ran his hands along the frame of his favourite oil painting, savouring the sensuous touch of the carved wood. He wondered how he should treat his new disciples, imagining the delight in their eyes at the moment that he took Rohini. A man was standing before him, awash with colours at the heart of the light show.

'Don't you kneel before your God?' asked the Soma.

Underwood watched the figure closely. He could see the syringe held tightly in the killer's right hand and tried to anticipate the angle of the attack.

'Why do you insult a power you cannot understand?' the Soma asked in fury.

'I understand,' Underwood replied, 'you are the Soma: God of the moon.'

The Soma paused and felt a sudden surge of joy. Truly they were his disciples. Angels sent to bear witness to the insemination of Rohini. Below them, there was a crash as Dexter slung the chair against the sash window. Fragments of glass exploded across the ground outside. However, most of the wooden frame remained. She wrenched the chair from the window and repeated the movement. The Soma watched impassively.

'I have come to help you,' Underwood said. 'You cannot complete your task alone.'

'I am a god,' hissed the Soma angrily. 'What the fuck would you know?'

'If you are a god,' Underwood replied, 'make time stop. It's after eleven-thirty. The planets are moving out of alignment. You are too late.'

The Soma tried to assimilate the information. Chaos was returning to the brief order of the heavens. Demons had come to delay him. This was not an angel.

'You see,' Underwood continued, 'you can't make time stop. So you can't be a god. Your transformation is incomplete. You can hang heads in a line like the planets hang in the sky but you have no control over time. You are not a God. You are a man. And you've failed.'

Another crash resounded from the hallway. Dexter had finally split the interconnecting struts of the window frame. She broke away the splintering wood and, once she had created an adequate space, grabbed Rowena Harvey and pushed her through. There was blood on her hands from the smashed glass but she felt no pain.

The Soma lunged at Underwood and the two men fell to the floor. Underwood used both his hands to grab at the syringe. In the darkness he misjudged the movement and the needle punctured the palm of his left hand, pierced the flesh and emerged from the top of his hand. He felt the contents of the syringe empty harmlessly over the skin of his left arm. Infuriated, the Soma engulfed him in a rain of punches, spitting and hissing his fury. Underwood tried to block the blows with his undamaged arm but soon realized that he was

270

unable to defend himself. He wasn't trying to win the fight, merely create time for Dexter and Harvey to get away. As the punches grew in ferocity Underwood found himself beginning to lose consciousness.

Sensing victory, the Soma stood in naked triumph. The assault had disorientated him and he steadied himself as he rose from the stairs, nausea sweeping across his drugged mind. Underwood blinked through the blood at the image of the figure standing above him. Behind the man was a large oil painting. The picture seemed somehow familiar. It showed a hunting scene: a horse rider clad in scarlet at the head of a huge pack of hounds. The Soma staggered back against the picture as he tried to balance himself: to Underwood's battered consciousness, it seemed as if the two images had become fused. The pack of dogs seemed to be flowing from the man's body. Through clouds of distorted vision and pain Underwood realized that Mary Colson had not foreseen her own death. She had foreseen his.

A car engine started outside and Underwood allowed his eyes to close. The Soma, having cleared away his dizziness, left him on the landing and headed downstairs.

Dexter allowed herself a final look over her shoulder at the house. Rowena Harvey sobbed in the seat next to her. She felt a terrible guilt about leaving Underwood behind. She hesitated for a moment, on the point of unbuckling her seat belt and returning inside. Then she saw the naked figure of the Soma emerge from the front of the house and rush towards the car.

She started the engine and crunched into first gear. Gravel sprayed from behind the car as the wheels slid. She pulled away, checking in her mirror as distance began to open up between the car and its terrible pursuer. The Mondeo accelerated down the twisting drive for a few short seconds. Dexter's eyes lingered too long in the rear view mirror. Too late, she saw the police squad car directly in front of her, blocking the exit to the drive.

'Fuck!' she shouted, slamming down hard on her brakes.

The Mondeo crashed into the Volvo at thirty miles an hour. Dexter and Rowena Harvey were flung forward. The Soma skipped in delight and sprinted hard across the gravel, ignoring the pain as it dug and tore into his feet. Stunned from the impact, Dexter saw the shape running towards them in her mirrors. She tried to clear her mind and forget the pain. She had to act quickly. She had no weapons. She was uncertain how long it would be before help arrived.

Make a decision.

Dexter slammed the car into reverse gear and pressed down hard on the accelerator. The Mondeo wrenched away from the Volvo and surged backwards. The onrushing Soma had no time to react. Dexter closed her eyes as the impact came, she heard his legs break and winced as his body thumped down on the roof of the car before sliding onto the driveway. Her heart was pounding. She unlocked her door and stepped outside.

The Soma lay on his back on the gravel, staring at the sky he no longer controlled. Dexter saw that both legs had been mangled, twisted out of shape by the force of the impact. She looked into the staring blue eyes. They blinked and looked at her. The Soma was alive. *Satisfied that he no longer posed a threat, Dexter ran back to the house.*

Fifteen minutes later, Underwood woke to find himself surrounded by people: ambulance men, uniformed police officers. He found his position, lying flat out on the stairway, an embarrassment. He tried to sit up but a strong hand restrained him.

'Stay put, mate,' said one of the paramedics.

'I'm fine,' Underwood replied.

'You've got a needle through your hand. Stay still while we take it out.'

'Be careful,' Underwood warned. 'There's poison in the syringe.'

'We know. Don't worry.'

Underwood winced as he suddenly became aware of intense pain.

'You all right, guv?' Dexter was crouching over him now. He was pleased to see her.

'What happened?' Underwood asked as the paramedics worked on his injured hand.

'I got him.' She thought for a second. 'Well, the Mondeo got him.'

'Is he alive?'

'Yep. Broken legs and some busted ribs but he'll live. We're sending him to Accident and Emergency at Addenbrookes. I got two uniforms going with him.'

'Rowena?'

'She's okay. Evans was stabbed in the stomach. He's in a bad way. Dawson was cracked on the back of the head. He's conscious.'

Underwood winced as the needle was slowly drawn out through the flesh of his hand. He concentrated on the picture of the dog-man hanging a few feet above him.

66

The ambulance rattled at speed through the flatlands north of Cambridge. Max Fallon's acid-soaked brain tried to seek explanations for the disastrous events of the night. It was hard for him to see beyond the excruciating pain in his legs and chest. He was gasping for air: dragging oxygen from a face mask into his lungs. His broken bones shifted agonizingly with every bump of the ambulance. To Fallon, the pain manifested itself as colours: white in his chest, red in his legs. Those colours were blinding and bright; they mixed with the green eyes of the car that had reversed into him, that had cut the universe from beneath his bleeding feet.

He was being punished. Daksha had cursed the Soma with consumption for favouring only one of his daughters. He tried to remember how the story had finished. Daksha's daughters had begged their father to be lenient and the creator-god had mitigated his punishment: the lunar god's disease would be intermittent, reflected by the waxing and waning of the moon.

The pain was growing more acute. The colours became more vivid and frightening as Fallon's body was swathed in great washes of fire and light. He realized that there was no one to plead for leniency. His pain would be perpetual. There would be no mitigation.

67

Alison Dexter eventually returned to her apartment shortly before three in the morning. She checked the outside windows carefully before entering. The flat was empty. She had cleaned up some of the mess that Willis had created earlier in the day but was unable to contemplate going to bed until the flat was immaculate again.

She vacuumed the splinters of broken glass from her hall carpet and brushed up the rice that Willis had thrown across the kitchen floor. After an hour of agitated domestic labour, Dexter allowed herself the luxury of a shower and wrapped herself in her favourite dressing gown. She knew that it would be difficult to sleep. The dramatic events of the day would take a long time to be filtered out of her mind. Besides, she still had work to do.

Dexter knew that Mark Willis had become an addiction. She had fallen for him at a vulnerable moment in her life: a time when she was struggling through a painful transition. For a time, he had softened the edges of her world and given her the protection she had always lacked. Then she had become addicted to not being with him. For eight years, she had allowed her mind to wander into dark places with him during her weakest moments. The memory would give her an emotional hit and she would place him back in a safe part of her mind where she could control him. She wondered if she had relished the controlled pain; if thinking of him had been the psychological equivalent of cutting her arms. Seeing him again had thrown her game into chaos.

Mark Willis was a black hole in her mind: a fixation that sucked in sanity and offered nothing in return. Dexter retreated to her bedroom and found her latest journal. She wrote down the day's events tersely and accurately. She realised that she was ordering her thoughts to try and conjure a solution to the problem: like a mathematician progressively resolving stages of some impossible equation. She began to understand that her memories of Willis had been based on an unreal idealization of the man. Dexter bitterly recalled a moment after Willis had left the force. She had discovered by accident that the Parc de Buttes-Chaumont, the location of her most treasured memory, was itself an unreality. The steep verges and grass-covered enclaves were in fact sculpted onto the remains of an old quarry and landfill site.

Dexter had come to the understanding that the memory was built on shit: her mental construction of Willis had been artificial: the daughter she killed was conceived on a rubbish heap. She knew that it was time to excise Willis from her life once and for all. She had written two phone numbers into her police notebook after Willis had left her in tears the previous evening.

Now, with exhaustion tightening its grip on her beleaguered mind, Dexter drifted to sleep wondering which one she would call.

Burial

68

The following afternoon, Underwood sat in CID at New
Bolden Station sipping a steaming coffee from a polystyrene
cup. His wounded hand was bandaged tightly and his bruises
ached. He had found that his damaged ribs prevented him
from lying down comfortably. Once he had realized this grim
fact in the early hours of the morning, he had resolved to
ignore medical instructions and spend the day at work. Sitting
bolt upright was just about tolerable and he wanted the
distraction of work to numb his discomfort.

Harrison sat opposite him reading through some of the
notes Dexter had made that morning based upon paperwork
they had discovered at Yaxford Hall.

'So tell me about him,' Underwood instructed.

'Maxwell   Fallon.   Aged   thirty-eight.   Unemployed.
Formerly, Director of Bond Trading at Fogle & Moore
Investment Bank. Fired for gross misconduct in August 2001.
This wanker was clearing over a million a year.'

'Unbelievable,' Underwood muttered.

'Most people don't see that in a lifetime.' Harrison returned
to the notes.

'Bought Yaxford Hall in September 2001. Sold his apartment in Chelsea at roughly the same time.'

'Next of kin?'

Harrison checked through the pages. 'It doesn't say.
Although it seems the body on the stairs was his father. We
found a driving licence and credit cards in the deceased's
trouser pocket. Looks like a strong, positive ID.'

'Do we know anything about the father?' Underwood
asked.

'He was quite a big fish,' Harrison replied, 'Robin Fallon.
Born nineteen forty-four. Eton and Trinity Cambridge.
Twenty years in the Foreign Office. Worked in Pakistan, the

279

Philippines and was deputy Ambassador to India from 'seventy-six to 'eighty. Retired from the FCO in nineteen eighty-four and became the director of various companies. He's in *Who's Who?*'

Underwood thought for a moment. 'Jack Harvey was at Trinity, Cambridge. He'd be about the same age as Robin Fallon.'

'Interesting,' said Harrison. 'I'll check if they were there at the same time.'

'It would explain why Harvey got involved in this mess,' Underwood said sipping at the scalding coffee. He looked through the glass wall of Alison Dexter's office. Dexter had not emerged from her room for nearly two hours. She sat with her back to them, scribbling notes onto a pad with her telephone jammed between her right ear and shoulder. It was unusual for Dexter to isolate herself from the buzz of the office. He sensed something was wrong.

'Do you want to hear what else we found?' Harrison asked, noticing Underwood's attention was drifting.

'Of course.'

'Obviously there were the five human heads in the library. The only ones that have been positively identified so far are Jack Harvey and Sarah Jensen.' Harrison tried to sound matter-of-fact although the image and his emotions still tore at him.

'I'm sorry,' Underwood said flatly.

Harrison nodded. 'The others have not yet been formally identified. Based upon age and sex of the victims, Leach reckons they'll match up with the bodies we found on Fulford Heath. We also found some personal effects amongst the rubbish on the floor of the library: a wallet, some credit cards and a Fogle & Moore Photo ID card. We've made some provisional guesses as to the identities. You want to hear them?'

'Go ahead.'

'One of the heads belonged to a middle-aged man. That fits the profile of Victim A the Heath. Fallon apparently had a caretaker living on site at Yaxford Hall. The wallet we found belonged to one Roger Dean. Driving licence gives his date of birth as 23rd June 1948. It's a fair bet that Victim A was Roger Dean.'

Underwood remembered the chronology of deaths that Leach had explained. Victim A had been killed at the end of January or beginning of February. 'Is Dean on a missing persons list? If it is him, he's been dead for some time.'

'Not on any of ours,' Harrison replied. 'If he lived at Yaxford Hall, there's a chance that he wasn't missed.'

'Unlikely but possible, I suppose,' Underwood commented. 'What else?'

'Victim B from the Heath was a woman. One of the heads in the library belonged to a young female. Best guess is that we are talking about an Elizabeth Koplinsky. That was the name on the Fogle & Moore ID card that the SOCOs found. The picture resembles the head in the library. I spoke to a personnel manager at the Bank. Koplinsky left work four weeks ago. She was about to be transferred overseas and had a month off. She was only reported missing when she failed to turn up in their Frankfurt office last week.'

'Tell me about the other guy, Victim D,' Underwood asked.

'Well, by a process of elimination, we think his name is Simon Crouch. We found two credit cards and Amex and a Visa in that name. I checked him out too. Guess what?'

'Another Fogle & Moore employee?'

'He resigned at the end of last summer.'

'Victim D was killed recently right? In the last week?'

'Correct.'

'Have you located next of kin for these people?'

'Working on it. Like I said, personnel at Fogle & Moore have been helpful.' Harrison thought for a moment. 'Interesting that he didn't decapitate his father.'

'Robin Fallon. The body on the stairs. Broken neck?'

'Yeah. Seems a waste. You'd think it would have saved him some effort,' Harrison muttered bitterly.

Underwood couldn't explain the anomaly. He was concerned that Harrison was sinking. He feared that the memory of Sarah Jensen and the inexplicable destruction of her life was beginning to overwhelm his Detective Sergeant. 'Don't strangle yourself looking for logic. Sometimes logic just breaks down.'

Harrison looked at him, surprised by Underwood's insight. 'What's left then? How else can you explain this kind of shit?'

'Emotion. Insanity. Chaos. Take your pick.'

'All I know is that we have enough evidence to see this sick bastard banged up for the duration of his sorry life,' Harrison replied, clenching a fist in anger.

Underwood shrugged. 'If this ever gets to trial.'

'You saying there's a Mental Health Act issue here?'

'Fallon will need to have a full psychological assessment,' Underwood explained, wondering who would perform the task now Jack Harvey was dead. 'Having spoken to him and seen first hand what he's done, I'd say there's a good chance he'll be sectioned and deemed unfit to stand trial.'

'That's a joke,' Harrison hissed. 'These weren't crimes of passion. These were planned. He was in control. He's still responsible.'

'I hear you, but I suspect the psychologists will see it differently.'

'Hospital's a soft option.'

'Would you want to be pumped full of tranquillizers and strapped to a bed in a secure mental hospital for the next twenty years?'

'You know what I mean. He should been chucked in a very dark hole and left there. Why should we treat him? He's killed seven people. If he is mad then let him live with it. That should be part of his punishment.'

'Let's wait and see what happens.'

Harrison seemed agitated. 'Sir, I'm still curious. I don't understand. Why decapitate the bodies and string the heads up in a line? What was he trying to say by doing that?'

'He saw himself as a god. He believed that he was living the myth of this Soma figure; that he was about to father the lunar race on earth. The timing was important. Last night the five inner planets Mercury, Venus, Earth, Mars and Jupiter came into alignment. He attached great significance to this.

282

The Soma was the moon god. Fallon believed the planetary alignment portended the conception of his offspring. I think that by murdering the victims and removing their heads, he believed that he was drawing each of the planets into alignment. Each head represented a planet. One by one he strung the heads up into a line; one by one the planets are pulled into alignment. I think he believed that, as a god, he was pulling the strings of the cosmos.'

'Jesus,' Harrison breathed, despairing that Sarah Jensen had been brutalized for such an insane purpose.

'The drugs were designed to alter the way he was perceived. He wanted his victims to see him as a god, not as a man. He wanted them to celebrate in his transformation: become his disciples if you like.'

'I see what you mean,' Harrison said bitterly. 'A trial is going to be unlikely.'

'Very.'

Underwood saw that Dexter was finally off the phone and he walked over to her office. She jumped as he knocked on the door and stepped inside.

'Everything all right, Dex?'

'Why wouldn't it be?' she snapped defensively.

'You're very quiet.'

'I'm very busy.'

'It's more than that.' Underwood sat down opposite her. 'Look, I'm hardly perfect but you can talk to me.'

Dexter seemed ruffled by his directness. 'There's nothing to talk about. You and Paddy McInally can relax. Your little girl's untwisted her knickers.'

'Then why the attitude?'

'I'd just rather be alone, John,' she said wearily. 'The last few days have taken it out of me.'

He decided to bite the bullet. 'Mark Willis is a thug. He should be inside. If he's up here and you know where he is, we should bring him in. It's that simple. Whatever has happened between you in the past is over. Don't let it crush you.'

'It's not a problem anymore,' she said. 'And frankly I'd appreciate it if you and McInally respected my judgment on

283

the matter. I don't need you all buzzing around me like wasps. I don't need protecting.'

'No,' Underwood said quietly, 'I guess you don't.'

'And shouldn't you be resting?' Dexter observed, a little less abrasively.

Underwood clicked the office door shut behind him.

Mark Willis was sitting in a café opposite the front entrance to New Bolden Police Station. There were two off-duty traffic policemen eating sausage sandwiches at the table next to him. He ignored them, preferring to concentrate on his full English breakfast and his view of Dexter's car. He felt his mobile phone vibrate in his trouser pocket and withdrew it immediately. He had received a text message and was interested to see it was from Dexter. Placing his knife and fork carefully on the table, he read it to himself:

'Norbury Services M11. Southbound Car Park. 10p.m. tonight. Take what you want and go.'

Mark Willis couldn't help but smile. He slipped the phone back into his pocket and returned to his fried eggs enthusiastically.

69

Doctors moving over him. White coats and unfamiliar inquisitive faces. His hands were tied down. Memory was no longer knowledge. The two had become jumbled and smashed out of order.

Max Fallon remembered a stiflingly hot evening in India some thirty years previously. He was sitting in the back of his parents' Land Rover as it bounced uncomfortably through the North-western outskirts of New Delhi.

His father was driving. His mother was chattering in the passenger seat. She wasn't wearing a seat belt. She never wore a seat belt. The show at the English School in Shiv Vihar had been a great success. He had won a prize. His costume had been the best.

'What's the best way back at this time of night, darling?' his mother was saying.

'I'm going to cut through the Rohini district and pick up the Rohtak Road. We should be back in Chanakyapuri before midnight,' Robin Fallon replied.

'I'll never find my way round this city.' Elspeth looked out at the cluttered pavements and maze of twisting side streets. 'It's too confusing.'

'You'll be fine.' Robin Fallon half turned in his seat. 'You already know your way around, don't you, Max?'

'Not really, daddy,' Max heard himself say.

'Where do we live?' Robin Fallon asked his son.

'Chanapooey,' Max said.

'Chanakyapuri,' his father corrected. 'And where's your school?'

'Shiv – something.'

'Shiv Vihar.'

'Well done baby,' his mother had said with a smile. 'You'll be my navigator.'

'Yes, mummy.'

'You did so well tonight Maxy, I'm very proud of you,' she had said.

'Was my costume easily the best, mummy?'

'Oh definitely!' Elspeth exchanged a smile with her husband.

'Did I really look like a god?'

'I would say so,' Robin Fallon replied. 'You should thank your mother for making such an excellent costume.'

'Thank you, mummy!'

'It's a pleasure, darling!'

The Land Rover turned right and headed south, parallel to a tributary of the Yamuna River. The lights of the city glowed on the black water.

'That's Rohini up ahead,' Robin Fallon explained to his wife, pointing at a row of houses ahead of them. 'We'll cross the river there.'

'Home soon, baby,' Max heard his mother say to him.

The Land Rover suddenly lurched to the left. Max remembered being thrown against the cold glass, then he felt the sensation of falling forwards, his mother screaming, his father wrestling with the steering wheel, the car sliding down an embankment and sliding into water. Max saw himself flailing against the hard edges of the car, fighting for breath, then suddenly climbing free through the darkness as if he was scaling the side of a vast black mountain under a vast black ocean. He remembered lying on a hard road with faces swirling above him, voices shouting in a language he didn't understand. He remembered his father clambering from the water. He remembered his mother had died. His mother had died in Rohini.

Doctors moving over him. White coats and unfamiliar inquisitive faces. His hands were tied down. The memory had gone.

70

In another hospital, a dream changed that afternoon and the dog-man receded into the waters of oblivion. As the white lights of the recovery ward softened around her, Mary Colson rose above the quagmire of her pains and drifted.

She dreamed she was back at home, in her favourite armchair at 17 Beaumont Gardens. The room was wonderfully familiar, like falling into the arms of her husband. She allowed her eyes to wander along the mantelpiece, absorbing the faces of her friends and family long gone. There had been a time when she had resented outliving them all; when she had hated the idea of going on alone. Now it no longer troubled her. She had been the keeper of their memories. She had stood in the light of wisdom and experience and drawn conclusions about their personalities and lives. Time had been a luxury not a torture.

She heard voices and imagined she was standing at a family party: words and fragments of conversation billowed around her. She heard her husband's soft north-eastern accent, her sister's musical laughter, her mother and father, babies burbling and crying. She was happy to be home.

The tea trolley came by at 5.30p.m.

But Mary Colson was dead.

71

Alison Dexter checked her watch. It was half past nine. She only had half an hour to wait. She wondered if she should feel nervous: a sense of anxiety at what was about to happen. However, having examined the situation from every conceivable angle during the previous day she eventually surprised herself. She felt nothing at all.

The night had filled with fog beyond her window: like smoke in a glass. It reminded her of the noxious haze that always hung in Paddy McInally's office at Leyton nick. CID had been filled with chain smokers and the stench had clung to her hair and on to her hands. Every night she used to spend an eternity scrubbing the stink from her skin in the bath; after a year of exposure she felt that she had become permanently stained with nicotine: like the once white walls of a pub or like McInally's teeth. Mark liked to watch her in the bath. He'd sit on the toilet seat with a glass of red wine and just watch.

She crushed the memory and kicked it away.

Mark Willis drove as fast as he dared through the swirling white mist. The terrible conditions had scared most other traffic away but he sensed that the prize was close. Inexorably he accelerated until he could see beyond the bonnet of the car.

The sign for Norbury Services suddenly loomed out of the mist. He indicated left, swinging across two empty lanes onto the slip road. Ever suspicious and deliberately early, he reduced his speed and drove his Freelander around the entire car park checking for concealed squad cars. Willis had an imported addition to his car radio that allowed him to hear local police radio chatter over their Mainscheme VHF radio network. It seemed to be a quiet night: the only incident of importance was a crash near Newmarket. Willis parked next to an articulated lorry and listened for a moment to the radio chatter. It almost made him nostalgic:.

'. . . RCIU on scene,' a voice squawked. 'AMBO in transit.'

Willis smiled at the terms. The plods loved their jargon. 'RCIU' was Road Crash Investigation Unit, 'AMBO' was police shorthand for an ambulance.

'. . . Pedestrian injury,' the same voice continued, 'Mobile unit has one on board. You are not required.'

'Acknowledged despatch,' replied a female office.

Willis could picture the scene. Some half-witted local failing to stop at a junction most likely. Some poor bastard trying to get home ends up in a wheelchair for the rest of his life. 'One on board' meant that the squad car at the scene had a prisoner in the vehicle.

'Rather him than me,' Willis mused, looking suspiciously out into the murk.

But there were other memories too, Alison Dexter told herself, terrible scarring memories. 20th November 1994. She had spent an entire working day trying to bury her fear in paperwork; to push the baby inside her to the edge of her consciousness. It hadn't worked. Irritated and exhausted, she'd gone to wash her face in the ladies' toilet. The cold water shocked her into a terrible state of panic. She had studied herself in the washroom mirror, wondering how long it would be until the baby began to show.

Dexter had decided to buy a Coke from the dispenser adjacent to the coffee room on the CID floor. She had cracked the can eagerly and, enjoying the sugar as it massaged her mind, had rested her head against the refrigerated dispenser. There was raucous male laughter emanating from the coffee room. Dexter tried to ignore it. She found that men in general and male coppers in particular seemed to enjoy repeating the same conversation over and over again: 'so and so got pissed . . . so and so got laid . . . so and so fucked up.' To begin with she didn't notice the words of the discussion, concentrating instead on the blissful cool of the drinks machine against her forehead. Then by some terrible osmosis their meaning began to sink in.

'. . . porking her for months!'

'You're joking!'

'I can't believe you don't know . . . I thought you're supposed to be a fucking detective!'

Dexter recognized the voices; DS Horton and DS Payne. She turned slightly to hear their words more carefully.

'He's a disgrace,' Payne announced.

'She's a dirty little slag, apparently,' Horton replied.

'I'm not surprised. She's got that look.'

'Yeah, you're right. Willis says she screams the place down.'

Dexter froze in horror. Fury boiled in her throat: Willis had been talking about her; telling his idiot mates what she was like; as if she was a piece of meat, as if she was a Spitalfields whore. Dexter threw her coke in the nearest bin and stormed into the coffee room.

'You fucking bastards,' she screamed at Horton and Payne. 'I'll report you both. I'll make your lives a fucking misery. There's rules against talking the way you just did. This isn't the fifties. I am a police officer, not some slag for you all to laugh at.'

'Have you finished?' Horton asked.

'No, I fucking haven't. If I ever hear you talk about me like that again I will personally put you on the ground.'

'We weren't talking about you,' Horton said with a smile.

'What?' Dexter felt the ground falling from under her.

'Your little squirm with Willis is old news. He's been boffing Otham for the past two months.'

Dexter knew Katie Otham. She was blond and cheaply decorated.

'So if I was you,' Horton advised, 'I would go away and have a little cry. Then try and keep your mouth shut and your legs together.'

289

It was past ten. Willis decided to check around outside. He got out of the Freelander and strolled through the damp air towards the lights of the service station. There weren't many people around. He began to wonder if Dexter had merely been winding him up: raising his hopes only to dash them by failing to appear. He discounted the idea: it wasn't her style. Dexter was a more sophisticated animal. In any case, he truly believed that some sick little part of her soul enjoyed their encounters. Willis entered the service station café. A group of tired looking lorry drivers studied him blankly. There was a pretty teenage girl serving behind the counter: Willis bought a cup of coffee and a chicken sandwich.

'Busy night?' he smiled.

She looked up from the cash register surprised by his attempt at contact.

'Yeah, I'm knackered. That's two twenty please.'

Willis handed over the money. 'Girl like you shouldn't be working here late on your own. Not with all these muppets about.' He gestured at the group of lorry drivers.

'I'm all right.'

'Bet your boyfriend doesn't like it.'

She handed over his receipt and change.

'He thinks it's better than getting a job himself.' Her smile was thin and humourless.

Willis saw her life in a moment. She would have a layabout boyfriend with a beer belly. He'd rest a beer can between his legs while he watched the football. They lived in a shitty little flat that stunk of chips. She'd reluctantly do her duty on her back after Match of the Day. Maybe she'd have girls' night out once a fortnight and screech about cocks in some tacky theme pub in a city centre. He suddenly found her very unattractive.

He took a seat that overlooked the car park and settled down to wait, aware that she was watching him closely.

Dexter had fled from CID with tears streaming down her face. She had crashed out of the building into the anonymity of the street. Cars and buses thundered past her. Rain streamed over her face hiding her tears. She tried to make

290

sense of the desolation inside. Now she had learned the truth. The truth had been that Willis had been doubling up on her for months. The truth was that he was shagging WPC Otham while she had vainly tried to telephone his empty flat. The truth was that his casual indifference to her hadn't been casual at all: it had been calculated and callous.

'Alison? Are you okay?' DS Gillian Read had followed her out of Leyton police station.

'I'm fine,' said Dexter without making eye contact.

'Look, I know what happened, sweetheart.' Read put her arm round Dexter's shoulders. 'Why don't we go inside?'

'How can I go back? They're all laughing at me.'

'The only way to stop them is show that it hasn't hurt you.'

'But it has.' Dexter's tears felt hot on her face, her eyes felt ready to explode. 'I'm pregnant.'

'Oh sweetheart.' Read enfolded Dexter in a hug. 'Is it his?'

'Of course.'

'What are you going to do?'

'I don't know.' Dexter watched the universe spinning out of control around her.

'Does he know?'

'I haven't told anyone yet.'

'You have to get rid of it.'

'I can't.'

'Alison. You are not a little girl. Think about the realities. You can't let this happen. Who can you talk to about it?'

'My mum, I suppose,'

'Talk to her then. Don't throw your life up the wall for a prick like Willis.'

Dexter nodded. She suddenly felt very cold. 'Let me go back and get my coat. I'm going home.'

'Alison, listen to me. If you are going back up there you have to be hard. Harder than you've ever been. Never let them see they can hurt you. If you let that happen you are finished.'

'I'll be fine.' Dexter wiped her face dry as they stepped back into the building. It was time for Alison the Brave.

She ran the gauntlet of stares as she returned to CID. Horton smirked at her from his desk. Even some of the

291

*uniformed coppers seemed to find amusement in her dishev-
elled appearance. Dexter collected her coat from her desk and
crossed the office floor to Willis's office. He was on the telephone when he saw her coming and waved her away. She
ignored him, stormed directly into his office.*

*'You fucking arsehole,' she said. 'You miserable little
prick.'*

*Willis promptly hung up the phone. 'What's your
problem?'*

'You are fucking Otham.'

*Willis shrugged. 'Amongst others. What's the big deal? We
ain't exclusive.'*

'Yes we are,' shouted Dexter. 'I am very bloody exclusive.'

*'You need to grow up, Sparrer. You're a decent time-filler
but nothing more than that.'*

His words tore her soul into shreds.

*'You don't mean that. You helped me. You helped me here
and with Vince.'*

*'Must have been fanny-happy. You're a good squirt,
Sparrer, I'll give you that.'*

*She stared at him in utter despair. The man was beneath her
contempt and his baby was growing inside her. Dexter turned
on her heels and left the office. The rest of Leyton CID had
enjoyed watching the showdown. Many of the police officers
were caught out by Dexter's sudden departure and urgently
tried to create an impression of business as she walked past.
Before leaving the department, Dexter turned to face them.*

*'Seeing as you've all taken an interest,' she shouted across
the floor, 'that little prick couldn't make a taxi come.'*

*Horton and a couple of male coppers grinned. Two WPCs
bit their lips and exchanged 'oh my god' expressions.
Emerging from his office with DS Read, Paddy McInally
laughed out loud.*

*It was a small victory. Alison Dexter cried all the way
home.*

Willis was getting annoyed. It was 10.30p.m. and she still
hadn't shown. He extinguished his cigarette into his coffee
and left the café. He was sick of playing stupid games. He

would drive to her flat, kick the door down and beat her senseless until she gave him his drugs. He'd already taken an hour out of his day to place a personal ad over the phone in the *East London Advertiser* and the *Evening Standard*. It had simply said, 'Primal Cut. Alison Dexter, New Bolden, Cambridgeshire.' He had paid extra to ensure that the details were located in a shaded text box and that the advertisement ran for a month. He wanted the information to be visible. Dexter had left London in a hurry in 1996. He felt London deserved the chance to catch up with an old friend.

Willis pushed open the door of the gent's toilet and approached a urinal. He had been desperate for a piss for ten minutes but had been reluctant to leave his vantage point in the café. He unzipped his trousers and stared at the white-tiled wall as he emptied his bladder. The door opened behind him. Willis ignored it, concentrating on the job in hand. Suddenly he sensed someone step up quickly behind him. Before he had time to react, Willis felt his head being wrenched back then slammed forward into the unyielding tiles. His nose broke just as he lost consciousness.

Willis' attacker hauled him to the exit and made a quick call on his mobile phone. Two minutes later, Willis had been loaded into the back of a Ford Transit. The white van rumbled out of Norbury Services and headed at speed down the M11 towards east London. Willis regained consciousness quickly: he tasted blood in his mouth and his tongue felt the jagged edges of his broken teeth.

'What's going on?' he tried to sit up but fell back sharply after a fist slammed into his face.

'Lie there, you little cunt,' snarled a voice charged with the fury of a south London council estate.

'Who are you?'

'If you don't shut your mouth, I'll tear your tongue out,' said another voice.

Willis tried to do some calculations: two men in the back of the van and a driver. At least three people had taken him. A cold and terrible realization began to dawn on him.

'Where are we going?'

'London town,' said the first voice.

'Why?' Willis was desperate.

'You owe someone money.'

'Eric? Do you mean Eric Moule?'

The same fist hammered into the side of his head. Willis felt nauseous, unable to make sense of what was happening to him.

'Mr Moule,' the voice said. 'To junkie cunts like you he's Mr Moule.'

There it was. Eric Moule had found him. Willis tried to think fast. He knew that unless he found a way out quickly he was dead.

'Tell Mr Moule I can get his money,' he spluttered.

There was some laughter in the van.

'It's too late for that, dickhead.' One of the men leaned closer to Willis's face. His breath stank of whisky and cigarettes. 'Do you want to be cremated or buried at sea?'

More laughter ricocheted around the inside of the van as it bumped at high speed along the motorway.

'Listen, I've got money. Turn the van around and I'll take you there. My girlfriend has it. She's a copper. She's been pissing me around. If we go there, you can make her give it to you.'

'I don't think so,' said the whisky and cigarettes. 'We've got a nice evening planned for you, sunshine. To be honest, I'm quite looking forward to it. Mr Moule will be popping over the water to say hello as well. He takes a personal interest in this kind of transaction. He may even offer you a glass of wine.'

'Why? What are you talking about?'

'When he's watching you eating your own bollocks off a plate. He might offer you a drop of Lambrusco to wash 'em down!'

'I think you'll find that Mr Moule is more of a Bollinger fan, Lenny!' the driver shouted out.

'Yeah! That's right, mate. What do you say then, Willis? A drop of Bolly to wash down your bollies?'

'How did you find me?' Willis asked. 'How did you know I was there?'

Lenny, Mr whisky and cigarettes, considered the question.

'Well, I'll forgive your impertinence given the circumstances. Let's just say a little bird told us.'

The van bounced and rattled along the deserted motorway as Eric Moule's men started work in earnest on Mark Willis with fists and pieces of metal.

Alison Dexter turned off the light as she left her office in New Bolden police station. She stepped quietly down the stone staircase to the entrance hall and nodded goodbye to the desk sergeant as she left the building. It was a surprisingly cold spring night and she drew her jacket tightly around her to protect against the grasping fog. Before she opened her car door, she withdrew a piece of paper from her pocket. Feeling nothing other than cold satisfaction, Alison Dexter tore it into small pieces and threw the fragments of Eric Moule's phone number into the night.

72

Five days later, early on a grey morning, PC Sauerwine rang the doorbell of Doreen O'Riordan's flat in the Morley estate. He heard a creak behind the door, sensing that she was appraising him through the security peephole. He tried to look as unthreatening as his navy blue uniform would permit. He wanted to speak to her. It was important that she let him in. On the other side of the door, Doreen hesitated and cursed her bad luck. It was the first day of her holiday: her flight left in nine hours and she hadn't finished packing. She had believed that the police had decided to leave her alone, that she would be able to escape into her dream for a fortnight. The doorbell rang again. She slipped the chain onto the door and opened it a few inches.

'Yes?' she asked Sauerwine through the gap.

'Miss O'Riordan. I'm PC Sauerwine. We've met before at Mary Colson's house. Can I speak with you, please?'

'Is it urgent?' Doreen asked. 'I'm very busy. I've a plane to catch.'

'It won't take a moment.'

With an irritated sigh, Doreen unclipped the chain and opened the door. She led Sauerwine through to the living room. It was cluttered and untidy with colourful magazines heaped in slithering piles. There was a portable plastic foot spa in front of a sofa that was laden with piles of clothing. A suitcase gaped open on the floor: Doreen's summer clothes were organized inside.

Doreen folded her arms and stared at Sauerwine. 'Let's hear it, then?'

'Hear what?'

'What's she been making up about me now?' Doreen had decided to brazen it out, play the outraged innocent.

'If you're talking about Mrs Colson, I'm afraid to say that she died at the hospital a couple of days ago.'

'What can I do for you then?' Doreen showed no visible emotion other than mild irritation.

'It's about the receipts that you handed in to Inspector Underwood. I've been going through them.'

Doreen felt that it might help to muddy the waters further. 'Yes, I couldn't find them all.'

'There's more?'

'I can't be expected to keep all the receipts I get,' Doreen smarted. 'Do you know how many old people I look after?'

'I do, actually.' Sauerwine checked his notebook. 'Six.'

'Five now.' Doreen perched on the edge of the sofa and looked into her suitcase wondering if Sauerwine was about to slam the lid on her dream.

'I've been through the receipts, Miss O'Riordan,' Sauerwine continued, 'and to be honest I'm confused. There's all sorts of stuff. For example, there's one in here for two CDs. Correct me if I'm wrong but Mrs Colson didn't have a CD player.'

'Not that I'm aware of,' Doreen said flatly.

'Right. So how do you suppose it got mixed up with all the others?'

'No idea. Mistake, I guess.'

'There's lots of others: receipts for sun lotion, t-shirts, wine.'

Doreen shrugged. 'I must have muddled them up.'

'Makes it very hard for us to check them doesn't it?'

'Yes,' said Doreen smiling sweetly. 'I suppose it does.'

Sauerwine had run out of patience. 'I'll be straight with you, Miss O'Riordan. I know you have been stealing money from Mary Colson. I imagine you have also been stealing money from the other old people in your care. Mrs Colson kept a rough record of what she gave you in housekeeping. I've been through all of these receipts. I've discounted all the goods listed that were clearly not for her. I've mentioned some of those already. By my calculations, which may be inaccurate of course because you failed to provide the proper receipts, there's a shortfall of about three hundred pounds.'

'She used to keep cash hidden around the bungalow,' Doreen responded. 'She probably forgot she had the money.'

'I found eighty pounds in her flat yesterday. That still leaves two hundred and twenty or so unaccounted for.'

'I'm afraid I can't help you. I'd have a look round there myself but I'm off on holiday this afternoon. I need to get the bus to Stansted at midday. Still, now she's gone I suppose it doesn't really matter anyway. So if you wouldn't mind letting me get on.'

Sauerwine smiled and put his pocket book in his pocket. 'Tell you what Miss O'Riordan, I can see you're busy so I'll do you a deal. Give me the two hundred pounds now.'

'Why should I? I haven't got it. Even if I did have, she's dead.'

'I'll be frank, Doreen. If you don't give me the money you've taken now, I will be forced to arrest you and take you in to the station for questioning. That is a long and tedious process. We can hold you for a long time before we have to charge you. Your plane will be long gone by the time you get out. There are funeral expenses and Mrs Colson left a will. Her savings are to be divided between two animal welfare charities.'

297

'I don't have two hundred pounds,' said Doreen with an edge of desperation, she was only just holding back the tears.

'I think that you do. We have already spoken to the council Social Services department. If you make life difficult for us, I will be forced to hand over the full details of our accusations. Chances are you'd lose your job, Doreen.'

'It's not fair,' she had started to cry.

'It's not your money. I'm offering you a deal: a quick fix. Don't be an idiot.'

Doreen saw her holiday dream hanging in front of her by a thread. She frantically considered her options. There was only one thing she could do. She reached into her flight bag, which was sitting on her dining table, and withdrew an envelope. Inside was her holiday spending money: four hundred Euros. She counted out three hundred and handed them over to Sauerwine.

'That's the only way I can do it,' she said. 'You'll have to get it changed. It's about two hundred quid.'

Sauerwine took the cash from her. 'You've done the right thing. It's the easy option.'

'Some bloody holiday I'm going to have.' Doreen felt her nose running as the tears coursed from her eyes. 'Two weeks in Greece with only sixty quid to spend.' She pictured herself sitting alone at the Acropolis bar with only a cold cup of coffee to accompany her through the evening.

Sauerwine was on his way to the door. 'We'll be keeping an eye on you, Doreen. When you get back, of course. Don't let me find out that you've been ripping off anyone else. Next time I won't be so accommodating.'

He turned and headed for the door.

'What are you getting out of this?' Doreen asked bitterly. 'Who made you her bloody guardian angel?'

Sauerwine thought for a moment. 'She made me breakfast,' he said, 'I owe her one.'

'You owe her one?' Doreen spluttered wiping away the snot and tears with her sleeve, 'You didn't have to carry her bloody shopping home in the rain. You didn't have to listen to all her nasty little bullshit. I was cleaning her piss off the bathroom floor while you were having your breakfast. She fucking owes me one.'

She was shouting now, bellowing her loneliness into the dark corridor.

But Sauerwine had gone.

73

After his injuries had been treated, his broken limbs set in plaster, Max Fallon was transferred from Addenbrookes Psychotherapy Unit to Wooton High Security Psychiatric Hospital on the edge of Cambridgeshire and Northampton-shire. Here he underwent a week of psychiatric assessments from David Pike, a Home Office psychiatrist, and two independent psychiatric experts from London.

Alison Dexter and John Underwood drove to Wooton to hear their conclusions. After passing through security control Dexter parked opposite the main reception area.

'This place gives me the creeps,' Underwood said as they got out of the car.

'Looks more like a factory,' Dexter observed. 'One of those nineteenth-century textile mills.'

They passed through an extended and tedious signing-in process and two more security checkpoints inside the main building before David Pike met them at the foot of the main stairway and escorted them up to the observation ward.

'Fallon is a curious case,' Pike said, brushing dandruff from his shoulders. 'Completely unbalanced.'

'I think we figured that one out ourselves,' Dexter replied.

'Of course.' Pike led them into the observation ward. There was only one occupant. Max Fallon lay securely fastened in his arm restraints, staring in a cold unblinking gaze at the grey ceiling.

'He's sedated now,' Pike continued. 'Interviewing him has been a virtual impossibility.'

'Why?' Underwood asked.

'He seems unable to speak. He won't reply to questioning. He refuses to eat. We have had to feed him intravenously as he seems incapable of chewing his food.'

'Has he had an episode, you know, a stroke or something?' Dexter asked.

Pike shook his head. 'No. We have run a series of scans and blood tests. His brain chemistry is unusual: he has been eating psychoactive drugs as if they were smarties for months. However, he has not lost motor control. In fact he has started spitting.'

'Spitting?' Underwood looked at the pathetic figure tied to the bed.

'We had two female nurses working with me here, I have had to move them to a different ward. He became agitated in their presence and started to spit,' Pike explained with unpleasant enthusiasm.

'Any idea why?' Dexter asked.

'I've read the notes made by Jack Harvey during his consultations with Fallon,' Pike said. 'Also the report that you kindly provided Inspector Underwood regarding the crime scene at Fallon's house and his attempt to impregnate the female victim he abducted. Based on that, I would say the spitting has a sexual connotation. The spit represents ejaculate. I'd keep your distance if I was you,' Pike warned Dexter.

'Thanks for the tip,' she replied grimly.

'Is there an office or somewhere that we can talk?' Underwood asked.

'Sure.' Pike gestured towards the steel door.

Fallon heard noises, snippets and abstractions of conversation wash over him. He had no clear idea where he was. His legs seemed to have fossilized into cold, white stone. His arms had somehow been immobilized. Perhaps he had become a statue of himself: a great, stone devotional colossus of the Soma. Truly then, he was immortal. The stone god: a great conscious, omniscient statue. He would accept fossilization for perpetuity. His dry, staring eyes watched a spider descending from the grey stone sky. It edged ever closer. The

300

Soma slowly opened his great stone mouth and waited to receive the messenger.

Underwood sat opposite Pike in the small meeting room outside the observation ward.

'What's the bottom line, then?' he asked.

Pike paused before he answered. He was choosing his words carefully. 'The report that the independent advisors and myself will be handing over to the Crown Prosecution Service will say that Fallon is not mentally fit to stand trial.'

'Shit,' said Dexter bitterly.

'He has no sense of his own identity. He is unable to form answers to questions. I have to answer two or three basic queries in a case like this. One: is he fit to plead his case? The answer to that is a clear "no". Two: was the suspect mentally disordered at the time of committing the crimes? The answer to that is a resounding "yes". Three: Was his mental condition such that he had no conception that what he was doing was criminal or morally wrong? In my professional opinion the answer to that is also "yes".'

'The point is that he was mentally disordered because he knowingly took drugs that altered his perception of reality,' Dexter argued.

'No. The point is that the drugs so dissolved his conscience and identity that he had no idea what he was doing.'

'I'm sorry, I just don't buy that,' said Underwood. 'The crimes were ordered and planned. That requires a degree of mental discipline and organization. If that's the case he is criminally responsible.'

'Look,' Pike said. 'We can argue this if you want to but the basic fact is that Max Fallon is mentally imbalanced. He is not fit to enter a plea. He has no idea of who he is. Wherever the drugs have taken him, he's not coming back in a hurry.'

Underwood sat back in his chair and let out an exhausted sigh. Pike was probably right but it still felt like a defeat.

'Think about what these drugs have done to him,' Pike continued. 'Have you ever poured salt onto a snail?'

Dexter nodded.

'Looks terrible, doesn't it. The salt attacks the moist

membranes of the animal: they bubble and and fizz and turn into pulp. Now Mr Fallon in there has done a similar thing to the surface of his brain. It's bubbled and it's fizzed and now it's pulp.'

'That is a disappointment,' Dexter said after she had absorbed the image. 'He killed two coppers. They were friends of ours.'

'I'm sorry, but the law affords him protection too. A trial would be a shambles. His mind is so stewed the prosecution could suggest almost anything and he'd have no idea whether he'd done it or not. Frankly, he'd have no idea where he was or why he was there.'

Underwood and Dexter left a few minutes later under a cloud of disappointment. Pike returned into the Observation Ward and sat down in a chair next to Fallon. He looked at his patient closely and felt a thrill of excitement: it was like having a shark in a fish tank. Fallon's mouth had closed. The great God Soma had consumed.

'Is that what you've done, Max?' Pike asked him quietly, poking the shark with a stick. 'Did you put salt on your brain?'

Fallon turned his head slightly to focus on the source of the voice.

'Did you put salt on your snail brain and make it bubble in its shell?'

The image skewered Fallon's consciousness: it terrified him. There were snails inside his head. He could feel them crawling across the grey undulations of his brain. The salt was making them froth, making them drive their sucker feet further into his mind. He opened his mouth and screamed silently.

David Pike sat back and smiled in satisfaction.

74

Doreen O'Riordan sat alone on a concrete balcony high above the shimmering grey Ionian Sea. The heat of early evening was making her sweat. She could hear music drifting up from the Acropolis Bar. It was a Greek Theme night with dancing and a traditional buffet. However, the extra cost – 25 euros per person – had deterred her from attending. She was running low on cash. She made do with a cheese sandwich and a packet of crisps. She watched the sea and wished away the loneliness of time.

75

The small party of mourners walked up the driveway to the Harveys' house. The front door was open in anticipation of the group. Rowena had arranged for a simple wake. She had only moved back into her redecorated house the previous day and was almost relieved to have it filled with people, regardless of the occasion. Reconstructing her life was going to be difficult. Keeping her mind occupied was a vital first step.

Jack's funeral had been an uncomfortable experience for Underwood. Two things had troubled him: the first had been the irksome knowledge that Jack's remains inside the black coffin were charred and desecrated. Underwood had wondered grimly whether the earth would accept such a pitiable sacrifice. He then thought of Mary Colson and her insistence that Jack's spirit had been present at one of their meetings. Was Jack watching them now? Underwood mused. Was he passing amongst them as they trudged back along the gravel pathway to the car park? Had he peered into the hole as his coffin had been lowered?

The second unnerving element had been the presence of his ex-wife.

Rowena Harvey had invited Julia Underwood to the funeral. The pair had been friends before Julia left New Bolden the previous year. Underwood had watched her closely during the brief service. Now as he poured himself a whisky in Rowena Harvey's living room, he tried to excise her from his thoughts, to expel the lingering doubts from his mind. He had told himself in the long and miserable months of his estrangement that letting her go was the best way he could help her. Now, confronted with the woman he had loved for most for his adult life, quietly beautiful in a straight black suit, he felt confused. Half of him wanted her: half of him hated her.

'Nice service,' Dexter observed from behind a glass of red wine.

Underwood remembered the wind drifting through the trees during the burial, like the tide hissing back across sand.

Underwood shivered. 'Never liked cemeteries,'

'I don't think you're meant to like them, John,' she replied.

Underwood looked around him, studying the photographs and ornaments that were all that remained of Jack Harvey.

'Funny to think we'll all end up like Jack. I can't imagine dealing with eternity. The last forty-odd years have been long enough,' he observed.

'I'm not being buried,' Dexter asserted. 'Cremation for me. I don't fancy rotting in a box.'

'Death is a process. Let's hope consciousness isn't invited.'

'I'm not taking the chance. Burn me, please.'

Underwood watched Julia enfold Rowena Harvey in her arms. He remembered how that felt.

Dexter saw his gaze shift from Julia to the carpet and then back again. 'Why don't you go and have a word? I don't mind waiting around.'

'I don't know what to say.'

'You'll think of something.' Dexter turned away from

him and pretended to study the painting of Rowena Harvey that had been re-hung in the living room after its recovery from Yaxford Hall.

Underwood walked across the room, holding back until Julia had finished her conversation with Rowena and was standing alone.

'It was good of you to come,' he volunteered.

'I felt I had to,' Julia replied. 'I hope you don't mind.'

'Of course not, he was your friend too. I should have invited you myself.'

'I understand. Rowena said you were hurt, when you found her.'

'Nothing much. I'm better now.'

There was uneasy silence as each tried to read some meaning in the other's courtesy.

'I suppose I should be off soon,' Julia said after a brief eternity. 'I'm back at work this afternoon.'

'They wouldn't let you have the whole day off?' Underwood asked.

'We're very busy,' Julia smiled softly. 'We always are.'

'I know that feeling. It must be difficult for you: building a career again.'

Julia was uncertain how best to answer. 'It's not easy, but then things that are worthwhile rarely are.'

'I'm pleased it's working out for you, though,' Underwood said.

'Why didn't you call me back, John?' Julia asked suddenly. 'I wasn't being difficult or playing a game, I just wanted to see if you were all right.'

'I'm fine,' Underwood lied.

'It would be nice if we could stay in contact,' Julia continued. 'Maybe catch up from time to time.'

Underwood saw a slight nervousness in her. She was the lonely girl at a disco asking a boy to dance. He wasn't sure how to respond: dance and disappoint her or stay hiding in the shadows.

'I'd like that,' he said eventually.

'Great,' she sounded relieved. 'Well, I'll call you then.'

'I'll look forward to it.'

So this was the way forward, he told himself. We have established a framework: constructed a paradigm of polite friendship. We will treat each other with respect and acknowledge our shared past without allowing it to crush us or divide us totally. If we have to be imprisoned by the past, then let's at least make the prison cell comfortable. Loneliness drives us into strange corners. Underwood had to decide whether it would be better to sit in the dark or to dance the loveless dance of desperation.

Better to dance.

Julia stepped over and kissed him on the cheek.

Alison Dexter watched them quietly. She felt a sudden surge of pity but was uncertain at whom it was directed. A moment later, Underwood rejoined her as she finished her glass of wine.

'Everything okay?' she asked.

'Friendly,' he replied.

'That's good, isn't it?'

'I'm not sure.' Underwood looked uncertainly at her. 'What do you think, Dex? You try and break away, start again. And the past keeps overtaking you. Do you think it matters?'

'We're nothing without memories, are we? Just a consciousness trapped in a body. Like a fucking goldfish.'

'Sometimes I wish I could just wipe it all away. You know, leave stuff behind and pretend it didn't happen?'

Dexter shook her head. 'You have to pick what's important then dump the rest. If you break your television you take it to a rubbish heap and get shot of it.'

'You've lost me.'

'You don't have to sit and watch a dead screen every night.'

Dexter suddenly felt ashamed of her hypocrisy. She wondered whether she had the courage to act on the words herself; whether she truly possessed the courage to become someone new. She had always prided herself on dealing in realities and yet she had allowed herself to become ensnared by an imagined past. The false memory of a father who had deserted her: the false memory of a man who had used her; the false memory of a child who had never existed. Her desperation had painted pictures on the dead screen.

She thought for a second of a photograph: faded and dog-eared, fluttering away from her through a forest of scuffling feet. She remembered blindly reaching out for it. She remembered the agony of her hand being stamped on.

That memory contained a message.

Finally, she understood it.